THE KILLER'S GUIDE TO ICELAND

Zane Radcliffe

BLACK SWAN

THE KILLER'S GUIDE TO ICELAND
A BLACK SWAN BOOK: 0 552 77217 8

First publication in Great Britain

PRINTING HISTORY
Black Swan edition published 2005

1 3 5 7 9 10 8 6 4 2

Set in 11/13pt Melior by
Falcon Oast Graphic Art Ltd.

Black Swan Books are published by Transworld Publishers,
61–63 Uxbridge Road, London W5 5SA,
a division of The Random House Group Ltd,
in Australia by Random House Australia (Pty) Ltd,
20 Alfred Street, Milsons Point, Sydney, NSW 2061, Australia,
in New Zealand by Random House New Zealand Ltd,
18 Poland Road, Glenfield, Auckland 10, New Zealand
and in South Africa by Random House (Pty) Ltd,
Endulini, 5a Jubilee Road, Parktown 2193, South Africa.

Printed and bound in Great Britain by
Cox & Wyman Ltd, Reading, Berkshire.

Papers used by Transworld Publishers are natural, recyclable
products made from wood grown in sustainable forests. The
manufacturing processes conform to the environmental
regulations of the country of origin.

For Natalie

BESTU ÞAKKIR

Einar Sveinn Þórðarson: good friend, midnight golfer.
Friðrik Ásmundsson: proprietor of 'Bar Frikki', Jökulsárlón.
Elli Cassata: knows how to handle a dirt track.
Ásta Hrönn Stefánsdóttir: dishes up a mean puffin
carpaccio.
Helga Brá Árnadóttir: the craziest Greek in Reykjavík.
Snorri Þórisson & all at Pegasus/Panarctica
(www.pegasus.is)
Les 'I like whale but I couldn't eat a whole one' Watt.
Colonel Simon Mallinson & all at MTP, Glasgow.
Anna Margrét Björnsson: a judicious, critical eye
(and not a bad singing voice).
Kristin Zoega: gave me books and told me all about
Icelandic girls.
Iceland Review (www.icelandreview.com) kept me
reliably informed.
Huge gratitude to Simon Taylor, Jonny Geller and all the
nice people at Transworld, Curtis Brown, and Newhaven.

SKÁL!

'. . . around the Arctic rim
the days are strained and sieved through the nights,
and the nights arrive with the days stirred in.'

(*'From where we stand / the land'*)
Simon Armitage

1

In a matter of seconds Glasgow was wiped off the face of the earth.

Callum Pope felt little emotion as he watched his city evaporate, as he saw his family, his friends, his history become consumed by a dense and voluminous cloud.

Glasgoing-going-gone.

The 757 continued its ascent, elbowing its way through the vapour that cocooned it. *Grey candyfloss*, thought Callum. *Sky soup.* He was lost in the gloomy cumulus, his forehead pressing hard against the fat window by 7A. The thrumming glass was the only thing preventing him from being sucked into oblivion like meat through a straw.

The cloud got thicker and darker, dropping a black shutter over the window, but Callum remained glued to the view, a punter at a peepshow waiting for the reveal. And when it came, the show was dazzling. The plane levelled out over a stratospheric snowscape illuminated by interminable purples and unblinking pinks. It was a scene that might have fooled him into thinking he had already arrived in Iceland, the country where he had chosen, on a whim it seemed, to spend the rest of his life.

He was bursting for a piss. A backlit icon above his

head reminded him that he was not yet allowed to unfasten his seat belt. He considered his options. Pee in the sick bag? Its paper was wax-coated but he wasn't sure if this rendered it waterproof. Remove a shoe? Grab the handbag belonging to the woman next to him? She had been rifling through it prior to take-off in search of a boiled sweet for her ears. Callum had noticed that she was carrying a pregnancy-test kit. If he peed in her bag would it confirm, beyond all doubt, that he was about to become a father?

This wasn't supposed to happen.

Whenever Callum had thought about becoming a dad he had always pictured himself – like his father before him and his father before that – dragging his frazzled reflection across a polished hospital floor, an uncut cigar in his breast pocket pulsing expectantly with every heartbeat as he incanted the mantra: *please God let it be healthy.* He had never imagined it would be like this.

Sure, he had butterflies. He had dragonflies, if he was honest. His heart had lodged in his throat. And yes, he had a cigar. Difference being that Callum's cigar was 150ft long with wings and a tailfin and it was propelling him at improbable speed towards a new home with a new woman and a new life as a father to her eleven-year-old daughter.

This wasn't supposed to happen, repeated Björk.

Callum removed his earphones and killed the music on his new iPod. His staff had presented him with it at his leaving lunch earlier that afternoon. In the end only four people worked for him at Strawdonkey. He appreciated the fact that they'd all dug deep.

'Neil, Morag, Becca and myself had a whip-round,' said Young Kenny, handing Callum a small box wrapped in Eeyore paper. 'It's just a wee token to say thanks for six unbefuckinlievable years at The Donkey.'

'Jeez, Kenny,' said Morag. 'Thank Christ you're good wi' IT, cuz you're S-H-I-T wi' speeches.'

Trattoria Porchetta was packed. It was all-you-could-eat for £4.95 and the queue was two-thick onto Argyle Street. Tables were butted up to each other from the front door to the WC and diners sat tightly together doing their best to keep their elbows out of each other's linguini. Callum could have chosen any restaurant in Glasgow as the venue for his leaving do, but the Strawdonkey posse had become part of the furniture at 'Porky's', regulars on the last Friday of every month, and Callum saw no reason to make an exception for this, his last Friday ever.

All eyes were on him as he carefully unpicked the tape from his tightly wrapped gift.

'Hurry up, wull ye,' guldered a well-sozzled Morag. 'There's drink tae be drunk.'

Callum slid his present out of its wrapping. 'An iPod,' he said, stating the bloody obvious. He was good at that. He removed the gadget from its box.

'Two thousand songs in your pocket,' explained Young Kenny. 'Six and a half ounces of audio wizardry with super-fast FireWire auto updating. If you scroll down the menu bar, you'll see I've already started your iTunes library.'

'You shouldn't have.' Callum toyed with the buttons. Two dozen songs had already been uploaded into the smooth white brick the size of a chocolate bar and every damn one of them was Björk or Sugarcubes.

'I thought it was apt,' said Kenny.

'Really, you shouldn't have.'

'Speech!' cried Becca, clanging a knife against the rim of her wine glass.

'Where do I begin,' said Callum. Where *do* I begin,

he thought. He cursed himself for not having prepared something. 'I, em . . . that is . . . Young Kenny is right. These last six years have been unbebloodylievable.'

'Unbefuckinlievable!' corrected Morag.

'That too,' said Callum. 'But I . . . I don't feel it is me who should be making this speech. Sarah was much better at this sort of thing. I guess none of us would be sat round this table if it weren't for her.'

Neil bowed his head.

Morag reached for her napkin.

Callum fought with his throat. He could feel them looking at him in that way again, the way they always did whenever he mentioned Sarah's name. It was a look that managed to be both deferential and accusatory at the same time. Callum tried hard not to let it get to him.

'Back in '96, when I had the idea for strawdonkey.com, I didn't know the first thing about the Internet or setting up an e-business,' he said. 'Christ, I still can't program my video recorder.'

A murmur of laughter.

'All I had then was the beginnings of an idea, but it was Sarah who was prepared to not only back it, but to jack in her job and go into partnership with me, turning that idea into something that would revolutionize travel publishing. And that simple idea, as we all know, was a website that publishes travel diaries written by the public. Sarah was convinced that Strawdonkey could become a valuable resource for millions of travellers. And she knew how to get the right backing.'

Callum was aware that other diners were eavesdropping. His leaving speech had become a sales pitch. The irony wasn't lost on him.

'The real beauty of Strawdonkey is that our travelogs are written by real people with real stories to tell. In

1996, all the big-name travel guides were operating defensive web strategies, providing only top-line content to protect sales of their guide books. I identified a gap in the market but it took someone like Sarah, with her business nous, to get Strawdonkey off the ground. She was the one who had the venture capitalists falling over themselves to back our concept of an online travel community *written by you, for you.* These have become famous words. These were Sarah's words. It is a tragedy that she was never able to share in our success.'

Callum raised his glass. He made an unspoken toast and necked his Amaretto. He saw that Morag was dabbing her eyes with a napkin. He let her blow her nose before he continued.

'You are a talented, hard-working bunch of arseholes and Sarah would be proud of you.'

'To arseholes!' cried Neil, spilling red wine onto a shirt that already looked like the 'before' side of a split screen in a soap-powder advert.

The interruption threw Callum. He was sure that the 'arseholes' was directed at him. It took him a few seconds to find his thread.

'In the . . . em. Sorry. Over these last six years, the dotcom industry has experienced massive ups, but also massive downs. Nobody, not even Sarah, could have foreseen it. But you lot made sure our bubble never burst. By showing initiative and implementing some innovative revenue strategies, notably the selling of hyperlinks to restaurants, bars and hostels . . . no names, Becca . . . you guys have made Strawdonkey the eighth most visited site in the UK. I suppose it was inevitable that a big-money player like Backpackers would one day make an approach.'

A sarcastic grunt from Neil. He had never been good at hiding his feelings.

'My decision to sell Strawdonkey may seem like a sudden one but I can assure you it is something that I have agonized over for a long time,' explained Callum. 'I know there are those among you who think I am selling you all down the Clyde, and I don't blame you, but it was not a decision that I took lightly. I wish I had been able to discuss it with Sarah.'

'Sarah would never have sold out on us,' barked Neil.

'Don't listen to him,' urged Becca. 'He's pished.'

'Neil might be right,' said Callum. 'Sadly, we will never know. What I do know is that it was important to Sarah, in the event of a takeover, that the Strawdonkey name and ethos should remain intact. Fortunately, your new owners agree. They want you to carry on doing what you've always done best. The extra investment that Backpackers have promised will enable Strawdonkey to attract a larger global audience. So it's a case of business as usual. And even though the time is now right for me to pursue a new life and resurrect an old career, Strawdonkey – and by that I mean all you guys around this table – will always have a special place in my heart.'

Yeah, yeah, Callum, their eyes appeared to be saying. *Take your money and run.*

Whatever they were thinking, they gave him a clap.

The cappuccinos arrived and Callum swapped places with Becca to sit beside Neil. He needed a word.

Neil edited all the travelogs submitted to the Strawdonkey site. Now that Callum was leaving, Neil was to run the Glasgow office, but he had reacted badly to Callum's decision to sell up. He made no secret of the fact that he was considering other options. Callum recognized that Neil, more than anyone, was the creative juice at Strawdonkey. He was key

16

to the company's continued success and it was important to keep him on board.

'I guess I'm leaving you holding the baby.' Callum refilled Neil's glass.

'For now at least,' he conceded. 'But I'm a bit like you, Cal. I've got some important life decisions to make. I don't want to edit travel diaries for whatever I have left of my three score and ten.'

'What sort of thing are you thinking of?'

'I'm juggling a few irons on the back burner.' Neil pushed his glasses back up his nose.

Callum didn't think that Neil suited his new specs. They deadened his expression, like those novelty glasses that come with the eyes already printed onto them.

'I think I'd like to concentrate on writing, not editing,' continued Neil. 'In fact, I'm working on a screenplay at the minute. *The Inaudible Man*. I'm going to give it the big Hollywood sell: *He was a man with something to say, but no way of saying it*. Hell, I might turn it into a West End musical. Two hours of show-stopping instrumentals.'

'As movie tag lines go, that's right up there with the one you suggested for *The Usual Suspects*.'

Neil adopted his best straight-to-video VO: '*Kevin Spacey IS Keyser Soze, in* . . . The Usual Suspects.'

'Glad to see you haven't lost your sense of humour, despite everything.'

'That's what keeps me going, Cal. And that's what I've always loved about The Donkey. We're a bunch of mates. There's no hierarchy here. We've always been able to take the piss out of each other. But all that's going to change now that we're answerable to a load of suits down in London.'

'That won't happen,' said Callum. 'You'll still have a laugh. You're running the show now, nobody else.

And I've never known Neil Byrne to take the day job too seriously.'

'True. But is this still the day job I want?'

'Course it is,' Callum assured him, but Neil looked like he still needed to be convinced. 'You said it yourself. You love this job. It's a gag. Picture it, Neil . . . a rainy Monday morning, your train's late into Queens Street and you're still trying to recover from watching the Jags ship five goals to Motherwell on the Saturday afternoon . . . but you get into The Donkey and there's a new travelog in your inbox and within ten minutes you're creasing yourself. That's what you love about it. And it's not going to change. Hey, remember the diary we got from the guy who went bush-walking in Mozambique?'

Neil nodded and allowed himself a wry smile. He knew it word for word but he was still happy to let Callum retell it.

'*I would advise all people travelling into the bush,*' said Callum, '*to wear little noisy bells on your clothing. This will give advance warning to any lions close by, so you don't spook them. I would also advise that you carry pepper spray in case you encounter a lion. And stay vigilant for signs of fresh lion activity. It is important to be able to tell the difference between lion-cub shit and big-lion shit. Lion-cub shit is small and contains lots of berries.*'

'*Whereas big-lion shit has bells in it and smells like pepper,*' concluded Neil.

'Classic!' laughed Callum. 'You see . . . you live for that stuff. It's why you get up in the morning.'

Neil's face soured. 'I can see what you're trying to do, Cal, but it's not working. I'm not stupid. You don't give a shit about what I do or don't live for. You're just trying to make yourself feel better about fucking off on us. You've jumped ship and I'm

18

starting to get the feeling that the ship is about to sink.'

'That's not true.'

'Bollocks!' said Neil, his voice rising above Dean Martin who had been crooning brassily through the trattoria's speakers. 'Something smells, Callum. You don't just suddenly decide to sell a company you've been building for half a dozen years and then piss off to live with Eskimos. Not unless you know something that we don't.'

'I know there are no Eskimos in Iceland.'

'That's not the fucking point.' Neil wrapped his wine glass round his mouth and nose and drained the remaining liquid. His dead eyes fell on Callum again. 'It's the timing of it that I don't get. Why the big hurry to sell? If I were a conspiracy theorist, I might think it had something to do with the visit of the Strathclyde polis to our offices last month. And I wouldn't be alone in thinking it. The whispers have started, Cal.'

'I think we should take this conversation somewhere more discreet. I know a few hacks from the *Herald* who like to eat in here. I don't want the ins and outs of Strawdonkey splashed over the business pages.' Callum prised his legs out from the table. 'I'll see you in the Gents.'

He made his way down a set of cabin stairs and entered the cavernous bogs in the dark and unventilated bowels of the Italian. The tiles reeked warmly of garlic and piss.

Neil followed and stood beside him at the urinal. They didn't say anything for a while. One of the chefs was standing next to them, holding his cock in the same hand that held a lit fag. They waited for him to shake himself dry and zip up his blood-covered trousers before they spoke.

'Jesus, you'd think he'd wash his hands,' said

Callum, once he heard the chef clopping back up the wooden stairs. 'I won't be eating in here again.'

'Is that supposed to be funny?' asked Neil.

Callum shook his head. 'Look, we've been through this. You know my reasons for leaving The Donkey. These last few years I've done everything that I wanted to do with the business. It's been a hell of a journey but I've gone as far as I can with it and now it's time for a change. I'm starting up the film-production thing in Iceland because that was my first love. I gave up my job as a locations scout to launch Strawdonkey but I always promised myself that if I ever got bored with it, or if I had a bit stashed away in the bank, I'd start my own production company. This is something I've wanted to do for a long time.'

'That may be so, but I still don't understand your rush to sell. You took the first bid on the table, Callum. If you'd been serious about raising the dosh for your new venture, you would have held out for a better offer. The company is valued at nearly twice what you sold it for. Backpackers have got themselves a bargain.'

'Backpackers offered enough, that's all that matters.' Callum shook himself dry. 'I'm not a greedy man, Neil. They offered me enough money to do those things that I've always wanted to do. Sure, I knew they had more in their coffers than they were letting on, and if I'd held out they might have stumped up, but I figure it's better that they pour their surplus cash back into Strawdonkey and make it a stronger and more profitable company for all of you.'

'Ha!' laughed Neil, his voice sparking off the tiles. 'You make it sound like some great, philanthropic gesture. But it doesn't wash, Cal. The polis are onto something, aren't they. Why else would you suddenly decide to sell up at a fraction of the asking and then announce that you're leaving the country for good . . .

to pursue your first love of film production? Smells like bullshit to me.'

'Believe what you want to believe.' Callum made his way over to the sink and ran his hands under the tap. 'I don't know why you're so bitter. You've got a promotion out of this.' He was addressing the Neil reflected in the bathroom mirror. The glass had been decorated with enthusiastic graffiti: *AMORUSO IS A DEAD MAN*.

'It's hardly a promotion, is it,' said Neil.

'Course it is. You're running Glasgow.'

'Aye, I'm running an outpost. I'm not running the business,' Neil protested. 'Before you sold out on us, I reported to just one person: you. Now that you're gone and I'm "promoted", I'll be reporting to a board of fucking directors in Mornington Crescent. I'd hardly call that a step up.'

'Fuck sake, would you stop feeling so bloody sorry for yourself and deal with it.'

'Deal with it?' Neil got Callum by the throat and slammed him against the hand-drier, triggering a blast of hot air. 'This is how I'll fucking deal with it.'

'Easy now,' said Callum. The air was scalding his back. 'I know you don't mean this. You've made your point. Just put me down and we'll blame it on the booze.'

'*Volare!*' yelled Dean Martin as the door to the toilets was opened. Young Kenny bounced in. His face dropped when he saw the pair of them. 'What's gan on?' he asked.

'Nothing,' said Callum. 'Neil's just showing me his Vulcan death grip. Isn't that right?' He looked hard at his pal.

Neil said nothing. He removed his hand from Callum's neck and forced his way past Young Kenny. They heard him stumble twice on his way up the stairs.

'Fuck me,' said the youngster. 'He's guttered.'

Callum ignored Kenny and checked himself in the mirror. He bent his head to the sink and rinsed his face with a few handfuls of cold water. When he checked his reflection again, his forehead still read: *DEAD MAN.*

The Strawdonkey posse, minus Neil, had kept their departing boss generously topped up with JD and Coke for the remainder of the afternoon. Callum's inability to say no to a drink was now contributing to the urgency in his bladder. It had become a large inflatable castle with several small but excitable children bouncing on it. The turbulence didn't help.

He checked the time with the woman in the seat next to him: the woman with the pregnancy kit and the sweets for her ears.

'It iss a kortur aftur seffen,' she replied in that clipped singsong that the Icelanders have with the English language. It was this *delishoss* accent that had first attracted Callum to Birna Sveinsdóttir: her elongated esses, her curt kays, her softened vees.

Callum adjusted the nozzle above his head, forcing cold air onto his face. He needed a drink, something to suppress the anxiety, something to straighten him out.

He hated this feeling: this sick, pithy feeling. It had stayed in his gut too long, six years too long, like some parasitic worm eating him from the inside out. He knew that Iceland might not eradicate it, but he also knew that he had to make this move. Sure, he wanted to be with Birna. He loved Birna. At least, he thought he did. As much as you can love someone you've known barely a year. But he was kidding himself if he thought this move was motivated by anything other than fear: the fear that the past was about to come knocking on his door.

22

Callum thumbed his Icelandair magazine. *March 2003*. Two months out of date. No matter, he studied each page with the same determination that he'd studied the clouds; trying hard to take his mind off the things he was running away from.

He read the feature article, an exciting piece of investigative journalism detailing the huge export market for dried fish heads from Iceland to Japan. It contained an interview with Tokyo chef Ruichi Kim, an enthusiastic advocate of Icelandic seafood and a man famed for his 'Baby Mackerel Tofu'. Ruichi detailed his dish in the article. It involved placing a hunk of tofu into a pot of cold water in which an infant fish is happily swimming. The pot is then plonked on a hotplate and set to boil. As the temperature of the water becomes unbearable, the young mackerel seeks refuge by burrowing his way into the cool chunk of bean curd. Sadly, there can be no escape and the fish is cooked in his safe house.

Callum raced towards Reykjavík feeling for all the world like that mackerel.

2

Callum had fallen in love with Iceland the first time he saw her, which was barely, through a veil of rain and thick, flitting snowflakes. Being a west-coast Scot he was well acquainted with horizontal rain but never before had he experienced rain that fell upwards.

He sat on his suitcase and watched the shivering raindrops as they boogied their way up the glass doors that fronted the Keflavík terminal building. His modest case contained all his worldly possessions. At least, it contained those things he deemed worthy of salvage from the detritus of his recent past: as many articles of clothing as he could gather between two arms and a chin, the odd book, a wallet of CD-ROMs cataloguing Icelandic locations, the rental agreement on his leased-out Glasgow house, a laptop, a clutch of dried heathers wrapped in tinfoil, a fluffy Loch Ness monster and a couple of photographs zipped discreetly into a pocket hidden in the case's lining. It seemed a pathetic haul for his thirty-three years.

Callum allowed himself only a brief flicker of reflection, however, for he had spotted Birna making her way across the car park towards the terminal's entrance.

She didn't run. She didn't hunch her coat over her head in an attempt to stay dry. She wasn't even wearing a coat. She strolled nonchalantly through the downpour like she revelled in it. When she entered the building her eyes found Callum straight away: bright, cognizant, as blue as a lagoon. Only then did her feet quicken.

He caught her in mid-flight. They kissed. Her tongue was as sweet and cold as a popsicle. Callum's cheeks became wet with rainwater that smelt of her shampoo. Vanilla? Banoffee? His hands found the side of her head and steadied it so that their kissing became less eager and more purposeful. When they finally broke, Callum asked, 'Does it ever stop raining in this country of yours?'

'How should I know? I have only lived here for twenty-nine years.' Birna kissed his bottom lip.

'So,' he said, holding her out at arm's length where he could get a really good look at her. 'Here I am.'

'Here you are,' said Birna, like she couldn't quite believe it.

Callum felt a little nervous. He was giving up everything to be with this woman but it still felt like some teenage holiday romance. He was afraid to take his eyes off her in case she disappeared. She just didn't seem real.

Birna was tallish without being awkward. Slender, not skinny. Her hair had the deep russet colour and the thick silky feel of a just-popped chestnut. When it wasn't pulled back into a stubby ponytail it fell level with her jaw. A spoonful of cappuccino-coloured freckles had been deposited on each of her cheeks. She was not classically beautiful, but then Callum believed that the most beautiful women never are.

He hooked his thumbs into her belt loops. 'What's the plan?'

'My mother and Ásta are preparing a meal for us.'

'How are they both?'

25

'Mother, she is looking forward to finally meeting you. And Ásta ... well ... Ásta is Ásta. Eleven is a difficult age for a girl. But hey, we do not need to rush back to them. You must be tired after your flight.'

'A little,' said Callum. 'It's been a long day. Feels like a week ago I was saying goodbye to everyone.'

'Then I have the perfect pick-you-up.'

'Pick-me-up,' corrected Callum.

Birna tapped him on the nose. 'Until you can speak Icelandic, you have no right to make fun of my English.'

'Agreed.' Callum knew his place. Birna made sure of it. He loved that about her. She didn't suffer fools. She didn't take shit.

Birna grabbed his case.

'No, let me get that.' Callum tried to prise it out of her hand.

'Do not be the macho man,' she scolded. 'I have lifted heavier things than this. I have dragged my dead father across a field.'

Callum retracted his hand and followed her, wide-eyed, into the rain.

The sky was surprisingly bright given the weather and given the late hour. Callum adjusted his watch to the time on the dashboard of the 4x4: ten to ten.

They were speeding along the Reykjanes peninsula, on the single road that connects Keflavík to Reykjavík, a seemingly sterile route that cuts through desolate fields of lava. Moss and lichen had softened the rocks, turning them a muted oatmeal colour and giving the landscape the appearance of broken digestive biscuits as far as the eye could see. Callum had travelled this route half a dozen times and even though Birna was invariably at his side, he always experienced a deep sense of isolation (Birna had explained that this was perfectly normal, that isolation was a national pastime in Iceland).

To their left, the North Atlantic spat up its white-caps. Bright yellow signs cautioned drivers that the road was liable to flood. And there was a fair chance it could freeze over. Every half-mile a roadside gauge alerted Callum to the ground temperature but this did not seem to deter Birna. She aimed her chunky Suzuki at the central white line, bullying her way past the lumbering coaches and dopey hire cars that had beaten her out of the airport.

Callum knew better than to criticize her driving. He opted instead to have a pop at Iceland's highways.

'Are there not a lot of accidents on this stretch?'

'*Já.* Many accidents. Reykjanesbraut is in the top five most dangerous roads in Europe,' said Birna, with what Callum detected to be considerable pride. 'Of course we have many deaths on this road. But at least it is a proper road with asphalt over it. Most of the roads outside Reykjavík are gravel tracks. That is why a four-wheel vehicle is necessary, especially for my fieldwork. You will be needing such a vehicle when you go on your film shoots.'

'I know,' said Callum. 'That's what scares me. I once came off a dirt road on the Isle of Skye and ended up in a gentle, babbling burn. I have a feeling that if I veer off a dirt track in Iceland I'll be sent spiralling into an abyss of burning sulphur.'

'Our roads are not so bad. It could be worse. You could have chosen to live in Greenland.'

'And why would that have been worse?'

'It is like the joke,' said Birna. 'What is the quickest way to get a laugh in Greenland?'

'I don't know but I've a feeling you're going to tell me.'

'Ask for a road map.' She slammed her foot on the brake and broached a sharp right.

A sign told Callum that they were now headed for Grindavík.

'Why are we going to Grindavík?' he asked.

'Why does anyone go to Grindavík? I have always asked myself this question.' Birna was shaking her head. 'But tonight we will not find the answer because we are not going to Grindavík.'

'Where are we going?'

'The lagoon,' said Birna.

'The lagoon?'

'You know, I must take my car to be fixed. I think there is an echo inside it.' Birna tapped her side window and feigned quizzical looks at the roof.

'But you hate the Blue Lagoon. You made me go by myself the last time I was over.' Callum remembered that visit, how an elderly bather had loudly scolded him because he had neglected to shower before entering the water. The man was so irate that Callum thought he was being accused of something more heinous, like shitting in the guy's shoe. It wasn't until the cantankerous old sod pointed to a cartoon on the wall depicting a naked man showering himself that Callum realized the true nature of his crime.

'You are right. I hate the Blue Lagoon,' admitted Birna. 'I hate the Blue Lagoon with the nice logo and the coach park and the swimming costumes for hire and the changing rooms and the restaurant and the wooden decking and the chrome chairs. I hate the Blue Lagoon with the steam spas and the gift shops and the expensive beauty products and the malt and hot dogs and the women who massage fat Americans who look like hippos in the water. Luckily we are not going to that lagoon. Instead we are going to the lagoon beyond the ropes and the warning signs, the lagoon that was always there before the tourists. We are going to the many small lagoons that the Icelandic people used to bathe in before they carved out one big area and channelled the geothermal water into it and put a building beside it and an admission price on it. We do not need a ticket for our lagoon.'

Birna blasted the car's interior with hot air, redirecting the vents so the condensation peeled off the windscreen. Up ahead of them a dark, conical hill revealed itself as a charcoal smudge on the grey canvas of the evening. Glued to this hill was a pulled-at ball of cotton wool, a seemingly static plume of white smoke that hovered above a solitary, industrial-looking building. Small pools of colour were spattered low in the foreground. They constituted the only colour in this monochrome scene, as though they were driving into a hand-tinted photograph. It was a colour beyond classification, a colour without a Pantone reference or a CMYK breakdown. It was a colour Dulux couldn't match. Astral Azure? Fluorescent Lunar Blue?

Birna ignored a loudly signposted turning, a road with a wide mouth that gobbled up coaches and cars like it was popping pills. Instead, she drove another hundred yards and pulled up by a lava bank. She killed the engine and with it the air conditioning, leaving only the sound of rain rapping the roof like impatient fingers.

Without a word, Birna pulled her T-shirt over her head. She unhooked her bra. It slid down her arms and fell into the footwell. She pushed her bottom onto the front edge of the seat and raised her hips. She steadied herself by clamping her thighs either side of the steering wheel. She unbuttoned her jeans and tugged them over her knees. Her panties came off with them. She managed to wriggle her feet out of the ensemble without removing her trainers.

'If I'd known you were that hot, I'd have turned the thermostat down,' said Callum.

'That is so British.' Birna switched her accent to plum Pathé newsreel. 'Take your clothes off, old bean. We are going for a skinny dip.' She opened her door and stepped into the rain.

Callum watched her move left-to-right across the windscreen, the roll of her hips accentuated by the light of the headlamps. She was long-limbed and sure, her skin as milky as the calcified fringes of the lagoon, the brushstroke of hair between her legs as dark as the petrified lava. This ethereal vision was somewhat compromised by the puffy trainers stuck clumsily onto her feet. As Birna clambered over the rocks – a cover girl from Led Zeppelin's *Houses of the Holy* – the need for the shoes became apparent. She faltered, her knees buckled, her arms flailed like those of a drunk driver asked to walk a straight line and the rocks took skin from her ankle. By the time Callum was out of his clothes and out of the car, she was sporting a sock of blood.

'Are you OK?' he asked, marshalling her by the points of her elbows and guiding her between sharp islands of lava. The rocks revealed hidden purples and sulphurous yellows now that he was close to them.

'I will survive,' she said. 'I am from Iceland. We are good at surviving. We have survived the worst natural catastrophes. We have survived the largest volcanic eruption the world has ever seen. The ash blocked out the sun for many months, but still we survived. We just shrug off these things.'

Callum chuckled to himself. This was typical Sveinsdóttir. 'I keep forgetting that I'm dating a vulcanologist,' he said.

'Vulcanologist, glaciologist, geologist,' said Birna. 'And survivor.'

But she couldn't disguise her limp.

This is all too mad, thought Callum. That afternoon he had been rattling round in the back of a Glasgow cab listening to the driver spitting bile about the spiralling cost of the Scottish parliament building at Holyrood, how the Government had blown two million pounds of taxpayers' money on windows that were too small to fit the apertures in the exterior walls. Hours later and he's walking naked on Neptune and this beautiful, alien creature is taking him to her leader.

'Stop,' said Birna. 'Here is good.'

She propped one hand on Callum's shoulder and used the other to release her injured foot from its trainer. Her blood had marbled the inside of the shoe like the last sticky swirls of raspberry ripple melting into an empty cone. She lowered her bloody foot into the blue water. A purple thundercloud bloomed round her ankle. She kicked it free.

'They say this water can heal,' she said. 'They say it is good for psoriasis, eczema and many diseases of the skin.'

'And is it?'

'Well, I have never had psoriasis, eczema or many diseases of the skin.' Birna removed her other trainer and lowered her naked body into the steaming pool like a cookie being dunked into a mug of hot milk.

Callum slid in beside her. He had been reluctant to take off his shoes until Birna had assured him that he would not cut himself. She was right. When his soles met the lava bed it was soft as putty. Warm mud suckered his feet and licked between his toes. It felt like this rock pool had been carpeted in anemones.

'The lava is covered in silica,' explained Birna. She scooped some of the white mud from a rock at the water's edge. 'It makes a great face mask.' She rubbed the abrasive porridge over her forehead, cheeks and chin, leaving circles of hot pink flesh round her eyes and mouth.

'See, now you look like you've got a skin disease,' said Callum.

Birna grabbed another handful of white mud and threw it into his face.

'Cut it out!' Callum blinked and the warm paste exfoliated his eyeballs. 'Jesus, you're right about this water. It does perform miracles.' He raised his arms to the darkening sky. 'Praise the Lord! Once I could see and now I am blind!'

Birna splashed him.

Callum pushed a wave into her face but she turned her head in time.

When her face reappeared, her smile had flattened out. She threw her arms over Callum's shoulders and locked her hands behind his neck. She pulled herself onto him and allowed the water to take her weight. Her legs slipped easily round his waist like two water cobras constricting him.

She kissed him: a pumice kiss that left white grit on his lips.

She bit his neck. It hurt but it was a good hurt.

He was inside her now. Everything below the surface of the water was molten, yet the coldness above it stole their breath.

Birna fell backwards, a floating Ophelia, her nose, lips and breasts forming small, disconnected islands on the milky surface of the lagoon.

When she came, her entire body went under.

Her joy surfaced in a rush and pop of bubbles.

'This is all too mad,' said Callum.

These were the first words he had spoken – the first words that either of them had spoken – in what had seemed like an ice age. He had only uttered them in an attempt to rouse himself, the aural equivalent of a fork in the thigh. They had been in the water a long time and Callum had started to drift off in the post-coital haze. He sat squat in the geothermal pool with only his head exposed to the cold rain that clattered into the water. A thousand liquid craters danced all around them.

Callum's knees were bent at ninety degrees to form an underwater chair on which Birna was sitting. She was facing away from him, her back tight to his chest, her head heavy against his collarbone. He threaded his arms under hers and enjoyed the soft rub of her belly as she breathed, her lungs filling with steam, her shoulders rising out of the water and sinking back again, the powerful billow of steam from the nearby power plant begging a kettle click.

'Birna, are you sleeping?'

'*Já.*'

'So you didn't hear me say that this is all mad.'

'What is mad?'

'This. Us. I mean . . .' Callum stopped himself. What did he mean?

A swoosh of water. A flick-flack of limbs. Birna now faced him. 'Are you having second thoughts?'

'No. God, no. It's just . . .'

'What is the matter, Callum? You are making me worried.'

'It's just . . . there is still so much that we don't know about each other.' He let it hang.

'But do you not find that wonderful?' asked Birna. 'That we still have so many things to discover together? Is that not the very thing that keeps a relationship alive?' She took his arms and pulled him close again. 'It is not those things that we know that make a relationship exciting. It is those things that we do not yet know, the jokes we have yet to tell, the surprises we have yet to spring and all the beautiful revelations that we might some day share. A good relationship is like a good story. You must not know everything by only page four.'

'But this isn't just about the two of us, is it? There are three of us in our relationship.'

'You, me and Ásta?' asked Birna.

'That's right. You, me and Ásta.'

'But I thought that it did not bother you that I have a child. We have discussed this many times. Every time you come over we talk about Ásta. It is the same in our phone calls and emails, and you have never once said that it bothered you.'

'It doesn't bother me, it's just . . . I've never . . . I'm not sure I can . . .'

Birna took his hands. 'Callum, I would not have asked you to live with us if I did not think that you would be good for Ásta. I did not date men for ten years because I did not meet one man who was good enough for my daughter. But then I am doing my Christmas shopping in Glasgow and I meet this wonderful man in a bookshop café – a man who pays for my lunch when I realize that my bag has been stolen – and I think to myself, this man is different. This man has a good heart.' Birna kept hold of his hands and pushed herself away from him, allowing her legs to float out behind her.

'My heart ain't so good.' Callum looked into her blue eyes. 'And if I'm honest, I'm a wee bit scared.'

'Scared? What are you scared of?'

There were many things that scared Callum Pope but for now he could concede just the one. 'Ásta, I guess.'

'Ásta?' Birna reeled in her legs and sat up in the water. 'You are scared of my little girl?' She laughed, even though she did not feel like laughing.

'I'm scared of blowing it with her,' admitted Callum. 'And you just said it. She's *your* little girl. She's not *our* little girl. I barely know her. I've only met the kid once and she didn't say a word to me.'

'Ásta is not used to men being around.' Birna rubbed the tops of his arms. 'I told you, it has been a long time since I brought a man back to the house. But trust me, Ásta will soon get used to you. She will come round. Life has not been kind to my girl. She has never known her father.'

'There you go. Ásta doesn't know her father and neither do I. Don't you find it weird that I'm about to embark on a new life with you and your daughter and yet I know nothing about the last significant man in your lives? Or is this one of those *beautiful revelations* that you're holding back to liven things up when our relationship starts to go stale?'

Birna looked stung.

It hurt Callum to see her like that. 'I'm sorry,' he said. 'It's been a hell of a day.' He planted a kiss on her forehead and her frown lines dissolved on his lips.

They hugged, each looking over the other's shoulder.

When Birna found her voice again there was a crackle in it like an old 45. 'Arnar, Ásta's father, he died before she was born.' She cleared her throat. 'Eleven years ago there was an eruption in our hometown of Heimæy in the Westmann Islands. It was small compared to a lava flow that nearly destroyed our island in the Seventies, but as a precaution everyone was evacuated to the mainland. Everyone except Arnar. The last man to board our boat said that he had seen Arnar looting a pharmacy close to where the fissure had opened. The building became engulfed by lava. It is not clear what killed Arnar first. My guess is that he was poisoned by toxic gases before the lava consumed him. Ásta's father was turned to stone.'

Callum had his hands on Birna's back. Her shoulder blades had tightened into hard arcs as she spoke.

'I'm sorry,' he said.

'Do not be sorry. I had ended things with Arnar many months before his death. He was not the person I fell in love with. He had become a drug addict, the sort of man who would loot a pharmacy for pills while his town burned around him. I wanted nothing more to do with him and told him so on the day that I found out I was pregnant. I had come to a decision. I did not want my baby crawling over his needles.'

Birna removed herself from Callum. She climbed out of the pool and palmed the rainwater over her breasts, thighs and forearms, rinsing off the last milky residues of the lagoon. She jammed all eight fingers into her hair, pushing it tight to her scalp.

'You must be hungry,' she said. 'We should go.'

3

They avoided the centre of Reykjavík, taking a road south of the capital that drew a smile under it from west to east. They were heading for the suburbs. The rain had eased off and the clouds were relenting, but darkness had not yet enshrined the smoky bay from which Reykjavík took its name. The Stygian gloom of the long Icelandic winter was giving way to the endless light of summer. The night sky was dark blue, like an ink-sodden blotter, but it was still bright enough for Callum to discern vibrant clusters of houses painted in lurid shades of lilac, tangerine, lime and raspberry.

Reykjavík had been coloured in by a five-year-old.

Birna's house was similarly naive, a solitary box in duck-egg blue that sat stupidly on a knuckle of land that protruded from the most exposed stretch of the bay. The weather had destroyed any attempt to keep the outside of the building in order. Old paint curled off the walls as if someone had tried to remove it with a cheese-slice. Most of the corrugated sheeting designed to protect the wooden structure had been torn away by one storm or other and deposited in the forest of weeds that surrounded it. A wide fissure had opened up in the ground, three feet deep and five times as wide, forming a natural path from the house down to the sea. Three ponies were grazing on the clovers and sea pinks that had colonized this earthy scar.

'So this is it,' said Callum. 'This is Chez Sveinsdóttir.'

'You do not like it?' Birna lifted his suitcase out of the boot.

The house was far from perfect and not what he had expected but, as Callum stood with salt air filling his nostrils and a blonde pony feasting wetly from the grass in his flat palm, he could not think of anywhere in the world he would rather be.

'I love it,' he said. 'It's completely barmy, but I love it.'

Callum wiped his hand on his bottom. He took the suitcase and lugged it up the few steps that led to the house. Outside the front door he noticed a small pair of red wellington boots that stood to attention beside an identical adult pair. Like mother like daughter, he thought.

When Callum had heard people talk about Iceland's dark interior he had not realized they were referring to the inside of Birna's house. There was little light in the hallway, a hallway that was barely wide enough to allow two people to pass each other. He was sure the walls were closing in on him, as if by crossing the threshold he had fallen foul of some ancient curse.

A rectangle of light outlined a closed door at the far end of the passage. Callum guessed that the room behind this door was the kitchen. He could hear the clap and clatter of pans and the whir of an extractor fan. A smell of burnt tyres and aniseed had infused the whole house. Callum was already apprehensive about meeting Birna's mother and this smell made him all the more reluctant. He had read enough about Icelandic home cooking to speculate at the horrors she was preparing for him.

'Callum, this is Sigriður,' said Birna, nudging him through the door and into the cramped kitchen. 'And Mother, this is Callum Pope.'

Callum offered his hand to the woman. She was in her late fifties, smaller and broader than her daughter, but she retained a straight back and a steady head, an elegance that Birna had inherited. Her salt-and-pepper hair sat coiled on top of her head, secured by a hefty clip. Where her daughter had freckles, Sigriður's had merged into tea stains. She looked at Callum through narrow eyes as though he was an alien emerging from a bright light. She wiped her hands on a tea towel and threw it over her shoulder. She took Callum's hand between her palms and, rather than shaking it, she gave it a brisk rub like she was trying to warm it up.

'You have soft hands,' she complained. 'Are you sure you are ready for Iceland?'

Callum examined her tea towel. It was brown with blood. The same blood, he noticed, had dried under Sigriður's fingernails and lent her hands a fake tan. It appeared that whatever she was cooking, she had slaughtered it herself. This did nothing for Callum's appetite.

'I'm sure your daughter will toughen me up,' he said.

'*Já*,' said Sigriður. She pronounced it 'yow' and inhaled the word. 'You will need to be tough to handle my daughter. She is just like her father.'

Birna did not agree or disagree. She wasn't listening. She had been distracted by something outside the window.

'Is Ásta outside?' she asked.

'She is collecting weeds for the table,' said Sigriður, as if collecting weeds for tables was a perfectly normal thing to do. It was a trait that Callum had found particularly endearing in the Icelanders, their ability to say the most extraordinary things in the most matter-of-fact way. He loved it that Birna could describe a volcanic catastrophe as though it was no more consequential than a spot of rain.

'Is it normal for a child to be out at this time?' ventured Callum.

The women looked at him like he was mad.

'As long as it is light, we cannot stop her.' Birna fed her arms around his waist and kissed him.

'What's that for?'

'You were thinking about my daughter.'

Sigríður bristled, as though she wasn't yet ready to tolerate such a public display of affection. 'Birna, fetch this young man a beer and I will feed him some fish,' she barked, as though Callum was a performing seal. She offered him a bowl that appeared to contain several ripped-up tufts of bright yellow loft insulation. 'This is *harðfiskur*,' she explained. 'Dried fish. We hang the catch out on racks and when the gulls lose interest in it, we consider it ready to eat.'

Callum threw a look at Birna that she interpreted as a cry for help.

'Ignore my mother. She is always making fun.'

He reluctantly accepted some fish and bit into it. The two women watched him chew. Impish smiles formed on their faces like they'd given him a stick of joke gum and they were expecting his teeth to be dyed blue. Callum chewed the cud, or cod, a thick knot of salty rope that proved impossible to swallow.

'This will help you wash it down.' Birna handed him an uncapped bottle of Thule lager. 'You can entertain my mother while I take your suitcase up to our room.'

'No. You mustn't carry it,' said Callum. 'You've hurt your ankle.'

'What is wrong with your ankle?' asked Sigríður.

'It is nothing, Mother.'

'Let me see it,' said Sigríður. 'I will tell you if it is nothing.'

Birna shook her head. She raised her leg and set the injured foot on the worktop. She rolled up her trouser leg to reveal a bright red teardrop torn into the skin above her ankle. It was half a centimetre deep and wide enough to accommodate the tip of Callum's little finger, should he so desire. The skin around it was badly grazed and black grit had become embedded in the angry pink flesh, turning it into a gravadlax.

'Looks like it needs a stitch or two,' said Callum.

'*Nei*,' said Sigríður. 'It will heal if I make a wrap for it.'

Sigríður leant across the sink and tore leaves from a few of the many pot plants that lined the window sill. She removed a shoebox from a high cupboard and rooted around inside it. The box was stuffed with freezer bags that appeared to contain dried-out divots of grass, the kind that litter golf courses in summer. Each plastic bag had an Icelandic name written on it in green marker pen: *Rjúpnalauf, Ljónslappi, Vallhumall*. Sigríður tipped some mint-coloured fronds out of a bag marked *Blóðberg* and fingered them into a stone bowl. She tossed in the leaves from the window plants and opened another cupboard. It contained over a dozen jam jars filled with oils in varying colours that could otherwise have been mistaken for whisky, perfume and piss. The labels had been steamed off the jars and replaced by small, white stickers inscribed with yet more impenetrable Icelandic handwriting. She drizzled a little of this, a splash of that, into the stone bowl and mulched the lot with a pestle.

'My mother is one of the few people in Iceland who still practise *grasalækning*.' Birna had sensed Callum's confusion. 'It is grass medicine. It is passed down from mother to daughter but I have not learned the art.'

'Birna was a stubborn child,' rued Sigriður. 'It is a shame. The possibilities offered by nature are limitless. It is only sensible to turn to plants for cures. We all sprout from the same soil.'

Callum remembered he had a present for Sigriður. He had wanted to bring her a gift that she would really appreciate and had asked Birna's advice. As a consequence, he had spent a large part of his last weekend in Scotland stripping heathers from the grey crags that broke the sweet monotony of a Perthshire birch forest.

He rested his beer and unzipped his suitcase. He pulled out a fat cone of tinfoil and handed it to Sigriður. 'This is for you. It's a little piece of Scotland.'

Sigriður set the parcel on her breadboard and sliced the tinfoil open with her thumbnail, KitKat style. She separated out the individual plugs of heather, giving each a name. 'Ah . . . *Erica cinerea. Daboecia cantabrica.* And *Erica arborea.* These are good plants, Callum. Of course, they are not as powerful as Icelandic plants. Our sun shines all summer to give them a steady supply of energy. But I suppose I can use your Scottish plants to treat minor ailments, like constipation and flatulence.'

'We get a lot of that in Scotland,' said Callum. 'I blame it on a diet of deep-fried pizza.'

Sigriður laughed, though it was clear to Callum that she had no idea what he was talking about. She thanked him again and returned to her stone bowl. She used a teaspoon to apply a green pulp to her daughter's open wound. She sealed it with a sheet of gauze and bound the poultice to Birna's ankle with three twists of cloth. 'Can you stand on it?' she asked.

Birna slid her foot off the worktop and slowly transferred her weight onto it. She nodded.

'Good girl. Now, the two of you must go and freshen up. I have prepared a very special dinner for the man of the house. Callum, I hope you will like my *súrsaðir hrútspungar.*'

Birna laughed.

'What's so funny?' he asked.

'Mother said that she hopes you like her testicles.'

Callum filled the sink from both taps. The water smelt of eggs, a pungent reminder, as if he'd needed it, that he was in geothermal Iceland. A blue worm wriggled out of a canister and into his hand. He squashed it between both palms and moved his hands in slow circles, churning the gel into cream. He spread it on his cheeks, along his jawline and over his throat. He scraped his thumbnail across his lips, removing some foam and giving himself a clown's mouth.

He shaved.

He pulled out the plug and watched the water whirl and drain. The plughole gargled. It belched. Callum's stubble remained stuck to the sink. He ran a finger through it. The porcelain was rough as sandpaper. He examined the dark crescent of iron filings that had collected on his fingertip.

'The man of the house,' he said.

He found Birna at the bottom of the stairs. She welcomed him with a wide smile. 'You look so handsome.'

'You sound surprised.'

'And you smell good . . . like Christmas.'

'Must be that cheap aftershave you bought me.'

She showed him into a living room that had been art-directed by David Lynch. The ceiling had bowed in the middle and the bookshelves were all angles. Other shelves displayed not books but stones – melted stones – lava that had cooled into strange, anthropo-morphic shapes. A small table filled a bay window at one end of the room. Four glass plates sat on four slate table mats. They fought for space amid a riot of outsized dandelions and huge nettle-like plants with leaves in the shape of starbursts that more commonly contained the words 'THWACK' and 'KERPOW'.

A taxidermized puffin presided over the table from atop an upright piano. The bird was albino, almost entirely white with eyes of red glass, but Callum still recognized it as a puffin by its distinctive colour-by-numbers beak. A long wooden pole with a net attached at one end was fixed to the wall behind the bird.

Callum noticed that all the walls had been covered in a quaint New England wallpaper: vertical stripes of blue and cream fringed with gold. A dozen framed photographs had been hung at irregular intervals around the room. Each photograph depicted a heart: a solitary patch of moss formed a vivid green heart against a black sand plain; a block of bright blue glacial ice held a dark heart of volcanic ash, its beat frozen in time; a mussel shell had opened up to form a pearlescent purple heart; and a lopsided peak had become a heart when reflected on the glassy surface of a calm fjord.

'Did you take these?' asked Callum.

'*Já*,' said Birna. 'I do my field research in all kinds of environments and over the years I have noticed that hearts are everywhere in nature. They burst from shells, twist from roots and become fossilized in stones. If you watch an eider duck curving its neck under the water for food, it forms a momentary heart. I always carry a camera with me, so it is easy to capture these hearts whenever I see them.'

'But these are beautiful,' said Callum. 'Have you never thought of exhibiting them?'

'Oh no. Iceland already has too many exhibitionists.'

'Shame. I wouldn't mind using some of these pictures on my new website.'

'Use what you want,' said Birna. 'Did you get the other location shots I sent you?'

'Shit, I forgot to thank you for those.'

'That's OK.' Birna pulled out a chair. 'I will still let you sit at the head of the table.'

Callum took his seat. It afforded him an uninterrupted view of the bay and the brooding sweep of Mount Esja on the opposing shoreline. The mountain was a black seam caught between two thicker bands of sea and sky, the liquorice in an allsort.

'One o'clock in the morning and I'm sitting down to dinner. Is this normal?' he asked.

'Perfectly normal,' said Birna.

'And that gaping chasm in your garden, is that perfectly normal? Or the cracks in this ceiling, are they normal?'

'I guess not. All houses built in Iceland in the Sixties were made to withstand tremors of 6.5 on the Richter scale. This house was built long before that and so, when we had an earthquake recently, the place started to come apart.'

'Recently?' asked Callum, with some alarm. 'How recently?' He held onto the corners of the table like a drunk on a listing ship.

'You are funny,' giggled Birna. 'The last big quake was on our National Day in 2000, so we do not forget it easily. I was far away in the Snæfellsnes peninsula writing up a paper, a study of the Upper Pleistocene volcanics at Snjófjöll. I must read it to you sometime. It is very humorous. Anyway, the epicentre of the quake was at Þorlakshöfn, south of Reykjavík, but I experienced the reverberations from nearly 200 kilometres away.'

'Sounds like a biggie.'

'For sure. The tremor was even felt out at sea. My cousin and his crew thought that a whale was rubbing against the side of their boat.'

'Where were Ásta and your mother?'

'Ásta was in town, enjoying the festivities. Unfortunately my mother was in the house when the earth shook. She was thrown against the cooker and she broke three ribs.'

'Ouch.'

'Not so. The ribs belonged to the sheep she was cooking. She was lucky. The ground split in two. The earth could have gobbled up the house with my mother inside, as easy as eating a chocolate.' Birna smiled a wicked smile. 'A chocolate with a nut inside it.'

'I'm glad you see the funny side. Is that sort of thing likely to happen again?'

'*Já*. Because God has not yet finished making Iceland.'

To Callum, Birna seemed remarkably relaxed for someone who lived on top of such earthly tumult.

'In geological terms, Iceland is a baby,' she explained. 'We straddle the mid-Atlantic ridge, where the European and American plates are being pulled apart.' Birna demonstrated this by taking the butter dish and the saucer of pickled herring and dragging them away from each other. 'Our island is literally being torn in two. But do not worry. We are automatically covered by Icelandic Catastrophe Insurance.'

This didn't make Callum feel any better. 'We could always move out of here. Get a bigger place. Remember, I've just sold my business back home. There's money in the bank.'

'You need that money to set up your production company.'

'Not all of it. I've only used a fraction for the office

in town and I've already cabled it up. I'll need a bit more to furnish it and hire a couple of assistants. And I'll need to splash out on a ludicrous off-road vehicle with tyres the size of rubber dinghies, but there'll still be enough krónur left in the pot to get us any pad you want.'

'But I am happy here. The four of us can be happy here.' Birna curved her hand round the back of Callum's neck and pulled his lips onto hers. When they broke, she saw that there was still an anxiety in his eyes.

'Are you still nervous?' she asked.

'A little.'

'Why?'

'I don't think your mother approves of me. It's a gut thing.'

'Give her time, Callum. And do not be so wary of her. My mother does not bite. Not all the time, anyway.'

'And what about Ásta? What if she doesn't warm to me?'

'Relax. Everything will be fine. Tonight is the start of our new life together. And I mean all four of us. By sitting down at this table, you are already part of our family.'

Callum nodded. 'I am happy, you know. I may not look it, and I know I don't tell you often enough, but this is the happiest I have been in a long time. This is everything that I want, Birna. You're everything that I want.'

She kissed him again.

Callum brightened. 'I still think we should move out of here before the place falls on top of us.'

'Let us talk about it again one year from now. In a year the Immigration Office will review your situation and we will be in a better position to talk about houses and other things.'

'Other things?'

'*Já*,' said Birna. She inhaled the word, just as her mother had done. 'Other things. I am not getting any younger.' She took his hand and placed it on her belly. 'I think it will be good for Ásta to have a brother or sister.'

'*Nei!*'

Callum withdrew his hand. The shout had made him jump. It had come from the doorway. Rather, it had come from a young girl who had been hovering in the doorway, a girl who disappeared as abruptly as she had announced herself. Callum was sure he had seen a ghost, an unholy apparition in a white party dress with hair as black as a Labrador's and eyes that looked betrayed.

'I will go after her,' said Birna. 'She is just a little nervous about meeting you.'

She left Callum at the table, the only guest at his own party. It was hard not to feel a little unloved.

She will come round, he told himself. *She is at that difficult age. She is not used to strange men in the house.*

He turned his attention to the two balls of raw flesh that sat on his glass plate. They had been worrying him. One was very pink and sore-looking and the other was a gelatinous black marble. He prodded the darker one with his finger. He had never seen such black meat. It looked like it had been marinated in creosote.

'It is guillemot.' Sigríður had entered the room. She placed a violent red sauce on the table and sat opposite Callum. 'Smoked guillemot. The lighter one is smoked char. They are both very delicious.' She cut her meat the American way, using only the side of her fork. 'You know, guillemot eggs are wonderful things. They are so blue, bigger than a hen's egg and they taper at one end. Nature has designed them for the narrow

48

cliff-edge nesting places so that when the bird accidentally nudges her egg it spins round instead of plunging into the sea.'

'We used to have a similar thing in Britain,' said Callum. 'Weebles. They wobbled but they didn't fall down.'

'I have not heard of these Weebles. But I am sure they taste delicious.' Sigríður poured him a glass of wine.

Callum kept his arms below the table, leaving his food untouched more out of trepidation than etiquette. He used the pause in the conversation to examine the bookshelves. He spotted the three books written by Birna: two studies in vulcanology and one concerning glaciers. Callum had not read them, but only because they had yet to be translated into English.

'It seems that Birna may be some time,' said Sigríður. 'She is having words with young Ásta. You may go ahead and eat your balls.'

'I wish you wouldn't call them that,' said Callum. 'For a moment I actually believed that you had cooked testicles for our dinner.'

'I have. This is just the starter. The rams' balls are the main course.'

Callum stopped his fork before it got to his mouth.

Sigríður winked at him. She accompanied it with a chuckle.

'Very good,' said Callum. 'You got me again. Can you believe that I thought that Icelanders ate testicles? I do apologize. We foreigners can be so patronizing.'

'Apology accepted. Tonight's main course is lamb and sugar-browned potatoes. And you are right; we do not eat testicles. At least, not these last few months. Nordlenska, the meat-packing plant, they processed many tonnes of ram testicles during the fall before last, but this year they face a domestic shortage. This has disappointed many of our children. They like to eat the sheeps' balls as snacks.'

'And I'm supposed to believe that?'

Sigriður performed a nonchalant shrug.

'You are supposed to believe what?' asked Birna. She had returned to the table without her daughter.

'I was telling Callum that children like to eat the sheeps' balls as a treat,' said Sigriður. 'But he does not believe me.'

'I used to munch on them all the time,' said Birna.

Callum shifted uncomfortably in his seat and quickly reappraised some of Birna's more adventurous lovemaking.

'Is Ásta not joining us?' he asked.

'She is tired,' said Birna, but Callum could tell from her expression that it was more than that. 'You will see her tomorrow. Remember, I will be driving out to Eldsveitirnar to finish my fieldwork. I know the timing's lousy, but a deadline is a deadline, even in Iceland. Anyway, I thought that perhaps you and Ásta could do something together while I'm gone. You could take her out to the Kringlan mall. She needs new shoes. It would be a good chance for you to get to know her.'

'I can't,' said Callum. 'I'm doing interviews tomorrow.'

'Of course. I forgot. Some other time then.'

'Definitely.' Callum knew that his interviews were pencilled in for the Saturday afternoon and that if he was really keen to spend time with Ásta, he could take her to the mall in the morning. He suspected that Birna knew it too, but she didn't bring him up on it.

The three of them tucked into their raw meat, creating a soft percussion of cutlery on glass.

'So Callum,' said Sigriður, filling the void. 'Birna tells me you are going to make films in Iceland.'

'Films and commercials. I don't actually make them;

50

I just make them happen. My new company will facilitate their production, sourcing locations, hiring crew, that sort of thing. I used to do a bit of it in Scotland.'

'I have never been to a film theatre,' said Sigríður.

'Really?'

'You sound surprised.'

'I am,' said Callum. 'I've never met anyone who hasn't seen a film.'

'I did not say that I hadn't seen a film. I said that I had not been to a film theatre. Of course I have seen many films on the television.'

'But it's not the same. You need the big screen to really bring a story to life.'

'Mother believes that the only way to bring a story to life is to tell it,' said Birna.

'Or write it down,' said Sigríður. 'The pictures that I cast in my head when I read a book or hear a story told are bigger than those on any big screen. And anyway, I will bet that nobody has yet built a screen big enough to capture Iceland.'

'Maybe not,' said Callum. 'But my job is to give directors every chance of doing it justice.'

'Then I feel sorry for you. For you have set yourself an impossible task. More guillemot?' Sigríður offered Callum a plate of dark meat.

'No thanks,' he declined.

'You do not like it?' asked Birna.

'I love it,' said Callum. 'It is, without doubt, the finest guillemot I've ever eaten. And it sure makes a pleasant change from albatross.'

'I think Callum is joking with us,' said Sigríður. 'But that is no bad thing. It means we shall have a lot of fun.'

Callum nodded. 'Looks like it.' He raised his glass and called a toast: 'To fun.'

'Já,' said Sigriður. 'Because you are a man who could use some fun.' She rested her fork on her plate and folded her hands on the table. She looked at him as intently as when he had first walked through her kitchen door. 'A great darkness is overwhelming you, Callum. I can see it in your aura.'

'Mother!' Birna admonished her.

'My aura?'

'Ignore her, Callum.'

Sigriður refocused her eyes on him. 'Já. I can see dark spots on your aura. They fly around you like ravens.'

Callum set his glass on the table. He could feel a heat in his cheeks and it wasn't the wine.

'Pay no attention to my mother. This is just her little party trick.' Birna stared angrily at Sigriður.

Callum's temples were throbbing. He would have attributed it to jet lag had he crossed more time zones. He had the feeling, both bizarre and disconcerting, that Sigriður knew more about him than she was letting on. Had she been doing some homework on him?

'Relax, Callum,' said Sigriður. 'Birna is right. I am just having fun with you.'

'I don't know when to take you seriously,' he said, feigning a smile.

'That is OK. I can see that it will take me some time to work you out too.' Sigriður's eyes reached in to Callum's, but he looked away.

She stood up from the table and gathered the plates. 'Now,' she said, 'who's for lambs' cheeks?'

4

Rain. Relentless rain. Animals running everywhere: rhinos, elephants, a giraffe. They are terrified. A man scuds up the river in a dinghy. He has a rifle. He is taking pot shots at the mad animals. He shoots a deer in the neck. It stops running. It thrashes its head about but it cannot get at the dart that has taken root in its muscle. The deer no longer looks frightened. It looks baffled. It tries to run again but smashes straight into a tree trunk and collapses. It is still breathing. Its ribcage rises and falls. A girl at a newspaper kiosk explains to me that the army are sedating all the animals. She is speaking Czech but I can understand her. She tells me that the animals were released from the zoo when it became flooded. She warns me that the entire city will soon be under water too and even as she says this, the river bursts its banks. It takes a bridge with it. People are shouting. A woman rushes past us pushing a pram full of sand. A helicopter rattles over our heads. The girl takes my hand and we head up into the hills overlooking the flooded city. We are running on cobbles and she loses a shoe. We hear the sound of jazz coming from the basement of a blackened building and we follow it. The girl guides me down one hundred steps exactly, she counts them out, and we enter a cellar bar cut into the hillside. The

Strawdonkey lot are drinking at a corner table but they don't seem to know me. I call Neil's name and he looks up at me. He removes his glasses and rubs them with his sleeve. He has no eyes. Morag is eating a foetus. The Czech girl pulls me over to the bar. An albino puffin pours us a drink. He fills our glasses with green syrup. When I drink it, the Czech girl isn't a Czech girl any more. She is a green fairy. She starts to laugh at me. She won't stop laughing. So I put my hands round her neck and I throttle her. And she isn't a green fairy any more. She is Birna. And I have strangled her.

Callum woke in his own sweat.

Birna was gone.

He rolled over onto her empty half of the bed. It was cold. He guessed she had been gone some time. He buried his head in her pillow. It smelt musty but sweet like the air after heavy rain.

A fuzzy red glow from the clock radio came into focus as 08:12. Callum calculated that Birna must only have slept for a couple of hours. But even that was admirable, as her bedroom curtains had failed to black out the near-persistent light.

He remembered falling into bed at around four. Sigriður had insisted on playing the piano after dinner, a set that included a funereal psalm about the life of man being as transitory as a tiny arctic flower that gets chopped by a scythe. Honky-tonk, it wasn't.

Birna had warned him that she needed to get an early start. She was driving south-east for the week-end, to the fire districts of Eldsveitirnar, the most volcanically active area in Iceland. She had been working hard to complete a paper on jökulhlaups, the violent meltwater floods that occurred when glacial volcanoes erupted in this part of the world. She had shown Callum photographs of the place. The floods had destroyed everything in their path and created vast deserts of black ash streaked with silver rivers. It looked like some B-movie *Land of the Giant Snails*.

Callum was confident that he could pitch this area to British and American production companies as a ready-made moonscape for sci-fi flicks. And if they wanted Mars, he could point them north-east to Mývatn with its cratered plains and its canyon dug by ice bursts, a faithful replica of those found on the Red Planet. He had done his homework and was excited about getting back into the locations business. His early career had been confined to sourcing shortbread-tin villages, barren battlefields and gloomy lochs for dour Scottish dramas. But Iceland was an altogether different kettle of *fiskur*, a diverse and ever-changing organic landscape that continually threw up surprises. Callum believed there were countless netherworlds still waiting to be captured on this new island and no shortage of foreign film crews willing to pay top krónur to secure them.

He washed and dressed and made his way downstairs, conscious that Birna had left him at the mercy of her mother and daughter. In at the deep end, he thought. Thankfully it was just for the morning. That afternoon Callum would be conducting interviews at his new premises downtown. He had two positions to fill: an office-bound PA and a production assistant to accompany him out on recces and shoots.

He had asked Birna to place an advert in the national daily instructing interested applicants to show up at Fire and Ice Locations, Fríkirkjuvegur 5, 101 Reykjavík. Callum wasn't interested in people sending him their CVs. He intended to put personality before prowess. His previous experience as an employer had taught him to recruit on gut instinct. Callum believed that this was the reason Strawdonkey had been such a happy ship. He would never have hired Neil Byrne if he had heeded the reference from a previous employer that concluded: *Neil has delusions of adequacy. He sets low personal standards and constantly fails to achieve them. It is hard to believe he beat one million other sperm.*

Callum found Sigríður reading a newspaper in the kitchen.

'Morning,' he offered.

'*Góðan dag.*' Sigríður didn't look up. 'You may help yourself to breakfast. I have made some flatkökur and you will find *skyr* and cowberries in the refrigerator.'

'Where is Ásta? I've brought her a present.' Callum set a fluffy Loch Ness monster on the worktop. 'I didn't get the chance to give it to her last night.'

'Ásta is watching television in the dining room. She is in a better mood this morning. I am sure she will love the furry snake.'

Callum lifted a saucepan that simmered on the stove and decanted some tea into a mug. He positioned himself at Sigríður's side to steal a look at her paper.

'It is rude to read over shoulders,' she scolded.

'Ah, but technically I'm not reading it,' said Callum. 'I can't understand a word of it. What's the big news this morning?'

Sigríður returned to the front page and read out the main story that was positioned directly under the *Morgunblaðið* masthead.

'*MAYOR IN WHEELCHAIR* is the headline,' she said. '*Mayor Thórólfur Árnason spent yesterday in a wheelchair to support Sjálfsbjorg, an association for disabled people. Árnason said that the experience was an interesting one and that he had to face many hurdles.*'

'That seems unnecessarily cruel,' said Callum. 'I mean, why make things harder for the guy. He was only doing his bit.' Callum jabbed a finger onto the page, indicating a colourful picture of a toy duck. 'What's the story there?'

'*CALLING ALL RUBBER DUCKS,*' translated Sigriður. '*American scientist Curtis Ebbesmeyer has asked people in Iceland to contact him immediately if any rubber ducks appear on their beaches. Eleven years ago a cargo ship sank in the Pacific carrying 29,000 buoyant rubber animals.*'

'And that's the top national story?' Callum was incredulous. 'Nothing much happens in this country, does it. Can't wait for tomorrow's headline: Cat Stuck up Tree in Hafnarfjörður.'

'That is unlikely.'

'How come?'

'Because there are no trees in Hafnarfjörður,' she replied. 'There are no trees in Iceland. Well, there are a few, but not nearly as many as we once had. Our Viking ancestors chopped most of them down to make their longboats.'

'But if there are no trees, what do young Icelandic boys fall out of?'

'I do not know,' deadpanned Sigriður. 'But it is not trees. We have a saying that if you are lost in an Icelandic forest all you need to do is stand up.' She folded her paper and set it on the worktop.

Callum cracked the pages open again and skim-read the gobbledygook. He managed to glean that KR Reykjavík had beaten Akranes three–nil and that *The Benny Hill Show* was being televised at eight thirty, but he understood little else.

'I'll never get the hang of this language of yours. I'm supposed to take a course in Icelandic if I want to become resident. Birna says I have to complete 150 hours of study. I reckon that if I did twice that it still wouldn't make a difference. I'm just too old to learn.'

'Nonsense. You are never too old to learn.' Sigríður handed Callum a buttered pancake. 'The best time to plant an oak is twenty years ago. The second best time is right now. If you would like, I could teach you.'

'I might just take you up on that.'

There was another thing that he had considered taking her up on: this professed ability of hers to see auras. Whether Sigríður had some supernatural ability to peer into his soul or not, he found the woman unnerving. From the moment he had been introduced to Birna's mother she had made him feel naked, exposed, like she could see right into him. He had initially dismissed this as the natural scrutiny of a mother assessing the eligibility of her daughter's would-be mate. But now he wasn't so sure. Her reading of him had been too frank and too accurate. In truth, Callum found the whole aura thing a bit weird. He didn't understand it, nor was he sure that he wanted to. He decided that it was probably best not to interrogate Sigríður about it. He would not allow her a window into his head. If he did, she might see all sorts of horrible stuff.

'I do not mean to be rude but I will need to chase you out of here. My first patient arrives soon.' Sigríður tidied some pans away.

'You're a doctor?' asked Callum.

'Of sorts. Sometimes this place can resemble an outpatients' clinic.' Sigríður looked momentarily confused, like she couldn't make sense of her kitchen. 'They come to me for the grass medicine. But I do not perform tests on them like a regular doctor. I just ask for symptoms and then I create a combination of herbs to suit. Birna gets a lot of the plants for me when she travels around. I am hoping that tomorrow she will bring me back some Arctic thyme. It sharpens the brain and strengthens the tendons.'

'I'll remember to take it next time I'm on *The Krypton Factor*.'

'I am guessing that is a joke,' said Sigriður. 'But you are taking Arctic thyme right now. The tea you are drinking is Icelandic mountain tea. I brewed it this morning from Arctic thyme, common yarrow and alpine lady's mantle.'

'And what will that do to me?'

'It will induce menstruation.'

Callum's mug hit the Formica.

'I was brewing it for my first patient,' laughed Sigriður. 'Her cycle is disrupted.'

'Are you sure she isn't pregnant?' Callum emptied his menstrual tea into the sink and rinsed the mug.

'She is not pregnant,' said Sigriður. 'This girl is only fourteen.'

'In Glasgow, that's the average age of a mother of three.'

'Then I am glad that my granddaughter does not grow up in Glasgow.'

'Och, Glasgae isnae sae bad,' said Callum, thickening his accent. 'You should fly over with Birna on one of her shopping trips. You'd like Kelvingrove Gardens. You could steal some roses. I believe they're good for healing marital rifts.'

'I have never been tempted to leave Iceland.' Sigriður used a damp cloth to wipe big shiny circles onto the worktops.

'You've never left Iceland?'

'Never. I have no need to travel elsewhere.'

'Jeez. If everyone had that attitude my last business would have fallen flat on its face. Are you not even slightly curious to visit new places and experience different cultures? Isn't that what life is all about?'

Sigriður gave Callum a withering look. 'I am content with my life as it is. I keep myself busy. I get up in the morning and before I know it the day is done. I have no need to see the world because I am happy right here.' She clenched the cloth in her fist and held it tight against her chest. 'If you are happy in your heart, you are happy anywhere. You would do well to remember that.'

The back door opened. A teenage girl sauntered into the kitchen and removed her coat. She hadn't knocked but that didn't seem to bother Sigríður.

'Ah, Ingibjörg. *Hvað segirðu gott?*'

'*Allt fínt, en þú?*'

'*Ó, allt í lagi,*' said Sigríður. She turned to Callum. 'Ásta is in the dining room. Perhaps you should go and keep her company.'

Callum stole another pancake on his way out the door.

Ásta lay on her belly on a rug that resembled a flattened sheep. Her head was balanced on both hands. She was watching television and didn't seem to notice Callum enter the room and set a Loch Ness monster by her side.

He fell into the armchair behind her. He didn't say a word. In truth, he didn't know what to say. Perhaps he didn't need to talk to the girl at all. Just occupying the same airspace as her for more than five minutes, well, he could call that a breakthrough. He would sit quietly and watch whatever she was watching. It would be the first activity they'd done together, their first shared experience. It was a start. Pretty soon he'd be giving her lifts to ballet, teasing her about her first bra and scaring the living shit out of her boyfriends. All those things that normal dads do, he reckoned.

Ásta wasn't watching a children's programme. Nor was she watching an Icelandic programme. She was engrossed in an English documentary, a natural history special filmed in the early Eighties, or so Callum guessed from the grainy pictures. The images cut from razorbills to diving fulmars to a great skua to a small island dotted with puffins, their thick guano spilling down the rock face like custard over cake.

'The wind-scarred Westmann Islands,' announced the narrator, 'lying just off Iceland's southern coast. Thirteen green emeralds set into the deep blue Atlantic, each one ringed by sheer cliffs and crowded with seabirds, easy prey for ... THE PUFFIN CATCHERS.' The last three words appeared on screen as a title. This was accompanied by the squalling sound of a brass ensemble detuning their horns.

'For two months each year these seasoned puffin catchers risk life and limb scaling the steep North Atlantic cliffs in hazardous conditions,' continued the narrator. 'For them, modern technology is an after-thought. Nothing has changed since their grandfathers stood on the same peaks, poles in hand, reaching out for that most peculiar bird, the orange-footed parrot of the sea.'

Callum turned away from the screen to re-examine the living-room wall, the one that held a long wooden pole with a net attached to one end. He looked again at the piano, at the albino puffin perched on top, as if it was preparing to dive into the surf of white thrashing against black on the keyboard below. He suspected that Ásta knew the origin of the stuffed bird and the long net. He considered asking her but she was lost in the television, in a sky black with puffins in flight, their wings flapping comically like wind-up toys.

The TV picture switched to a young man with dark hair. He was clad head-to-foot in green waterproofs. He blended in well with the grassy clifftop on which he was sitting. Dotted around him were a dozen dead puffins that he had impaled on rods to act as decoys.

A long wooden pole was positioned between his legs with its net lying flat on the grass. With every dark flash above his head, the young man whipped his pole into the sky. On the third attempt he netted a puffin. The more the bird struggled, the more it became entangled in the net. The young man carefully separated the bird from the nylon thread that cocooned it. He snapped its neck. There was a sound like a kazoo – a puffin's last breath – and the bird fell limp.

Ásta didn't flinch. This surprised Callum. He wondered how a girl of that age was able to watch these cute birds being slaughtered while absently clicking her heels in the air like she was watching Kylie on *Top of the Pops*. He was also aware that she hadn't touched the gift he had set beside her. Perhaps she hadn't noticed it. It wouldn't be the first time that Nessie had gone unsighted.

More worryingly, Birna's girl hadn't uttered a word since Callum had entered the room. She had made no sound at all, save for the occasional muted rasp of her thickly ribbed tights when she crossed and uncrossed her calves. Not only was she ignoring him, she was making a show of ignoring him. Callum was convinced of it.

'The puffin catcher will not kill birds that have fish in their mouths,' explained the narrator. 'These are adults returning to their nests to feed their young. He only kills those birds not fortunate enough to have offspring. Once caught, the dead puffins are smoked for twenty-four hours in lamb manure.'

The young man with the dark hair emptied his heavy burlap sacks of dead puffins. He tied a dozen birds into a banana bunch and set them on a smokestack. He spoke to camera as he repeated this process. His words were Icelandic but subtitles translated them:

'It is best to let the birds sit overnight before breaking them down because fresh birds are still warm and their bones are too hard.' He took a bird in his hand and demonstrated to Callum and Ásta exactly what he meant by *breaking them down*. 'First you snap off a wing,' he explained. 'Secondly, you slide your finger into the cavity and break off the opposite wing. Then you pull back the stomach and take out the breast meat.' With a sharp tug, the young man removed the claret-coloured meat from the puffin's puffed-up chest. This was accompanied by a fibrous sound, like denim ripping, as the muscle tore away from the bone.

Ásta giggled.

Callum thought back to when he was Ásta's age, to the time he had watched his mother skin a hare that his dad had shot in Aberfoyle. He remembered having nightmares about that hairless hare for months afterwards. It chased him everywhere, like a living abortion. But Ásta? She appeared to find this sort of stuff entertaining.

Only then did Callum notice that she was watching this ornithological autopsy on video, not TV. And from the grain on the tape he guessed that this was a video that she had watched many times.

How can this be normal, he thought. How can an eleven-year-old girl derive so much pleasure from such viscera?

He didn't have to wait long for the answer. It came from the programme's narrator. 'Arnar Jónasson can net over one thousand birds a day,' he intoned. 'It brings him good money. But what does Arnar spend it on? There is little need for fast cars and sharp suits on an island like Heimæy.'

'I am saving up to buy my girlfriend a ring,' said the young man with the hair as black as Ásta's. He looked directly into camera. He blew a kiss.

The tape paused, freezing the kiss in mid-air.

Ásta turned to face Callum with the remote control in her hand. 'That is my father,' she said. 'He is a big hero. He was killed when he saved a little girl like me from a burning volcano.'

Ásta set the remote control on the carpet and got to her feet. She smoothed out the creases in her dress and fixed her fringe into a flat black line. She kicked the Loch Ness monster under the sofa and skipped out of the room.

5

Callum's taxi deposited him at the harbour. It was a bright afternoon but a cold one. The wind wound round his neck as he passed a fleet of four identical whaling boats, each bearing the name *Hvalur*. Their pointed black bows sat proudly on the water, neck and neck and in perfect alignment like the prongs on a set of hair clippers. But it had been many years since these boats had cut through the North Atlantic with their harpoons primed. The fleet had been kept on a permanent mooring ever since a ban on catching whales had been imposed. Despite this, a group of men in orange oilskins were hosing down the gleaming vessels.

Birna had told Callum that the boats were being maintained in the belief that Iceland was about to recommence whaling for 'scientific purposes'. She was dead against it. So, too, was Callum. *There is no scientific purpose that can justify a cull*, he had agreed. *Whales should only be killed to be eaten.* Birna had punched him for that. And she had refused to speak to him when he'd said that he thought it was OK to eat dolphin as long as it was 'tuna friendly'.

Callum cheered himself with the memory as he crossed Geirsgata and entered Reykjavík's Custom House. He had remembered that the weekly

Kolaportið flea market would be in full swing and was hoping to pick up some knick-knacks for his unfurnished office.

The indoor market pulled off the remarkable trick of being both drab and cheerful at the same time. Bygone gumball machines made playful reflections in the glossed concrete floor. Slip-ons, slingbacks and sandals were vertiginously displayed atop tall stacks of shoeboxes that formed a Road Runner landscape as Callum walked among them. In every dark corner, fat black bin bags were bent double, throwing up gutfuls of old clothes. The place was a mishmash of tat: hats, lamps, lighters, flammable lingerie and plastic flowers, Marilyn Manson T-shirts and portraits of Christ. If Callum had been after a 1960s Kenwood food mixer, a sideboard or a wireless, he had come to the right place.

He stopped to finger through some dog-eared vinyl that spilled out of a split Cape apple box. At another stall, he scanned the back-cover blurb on Ruth Rendell's *Dauða Dúkkan* and Alistair MacLean's *Forsetavélinni Rænt*, though the Icelandic reviews were lost on him. He toyed with some empty VHS boxes, wondering whether Ásta kept a large collection of videos or whether she only ever replayed the documentary that starred her father. After some deliberation he bought two cassettes for her: Eddie Murphy in *Klikkaði Prófessorinn* and Gwyneth Paltrow in *Ástfanginn Shakespeare*.

He was beginning to feel hungry. When he had left the house, Sigriður's rye pancakes were still sitting heavy in his gut like two sodden socks left in the drum of a washing machine. But now he craved sustenance.

He made his way over to the food stalls. Sadly, the choice seemed limited to candyfloss, raw vegetables or *pylsur*, the ubiquitous Icelandic hot dog. Callum believed that wherever you went in Iceland, even into the middle of its unpeopled vastness, you were never more than fifteen feet from one of these godawful hot dogs. It was not uncommon for *pylsur* to be sold in petrol stations, swimming pools and, for all Callum knew, public toilets. He baulked at the rack of raw-red sausages stacked in front of him. They reminded him of a previous visit to Reykjavík's Phallological Museum.

The fish stalls were similarly repugnant. It was all Callum could do to prevent himself gagging as he watched locals using cocktail sticks to stab and devour oily cubes of rotting shark meat from resealable take-away tubs. Birna had told him that the Icelanders liked to bury a shark in the ground for several months to allow it to putrefy. She said that some people liked to urinate on it to hasten the process. It was perfectly fine to leave a shark outside to rot, as no self-respecting animal would go near it.

Callum found a machine that dispensed a powdery soup into a flimsy paper cup that scalded his hand. He took a tentative sip and was unable to deduce whether it was mushroom, chicken or narwhal.

He was quickly losing his appetite for the market when something caught his eye. It was an old tin poster advertising Tunnock's Snowballs, complete with the legend: 'Made in Uddingston, Glasgow'. It featured a rosy-cheeked urchin tucking into one of the sickly sweet chocolate and mallow explosions. The wholesome image was spoilt by spots of rust that had infected the enamel, covering the boy in blemishes. To Callum they looked like cigarette burns, as though the kid was some abused child of the schemes. He'd seen plenty of those, growing up in Glasgow. Though Callum had decided that he was well shot of Scotland, the poster had a resonance that compelled him to part with five hundred krónur. He wedged the large metal sheet under his arm, not anticipating that it would act as a sail for a wind that did its determined best to waylay him as he navigated his way through town.

The new office for Fire and Ice Locations occupied the top floor of a brutal concrete block that sat next to a church on Fríkirkjuvegur. Callum had chosen the office because of its proximity to the centre of town, though he considered Reykjavík so small that pretty much everything of consequence was within a whale-blow of the town centre. What clinched the deal for him, however, was the view the office afforded over the Tjörn, an oval lake with colourful wooden houses arranged around it like an artist's palette.

When Callum arrived at the lake it was almost entirely obscured by a dense colony of swans, ducks, geese and gulls. He guessed that the Tjörn must be the Schipol airport of the ornithological world, a global hub where birds made migratory stopovers and met connecting flights to far-flung habitats. He stopped for a while on the pedestrian walkway and watched a flock of single mothers feeding their children to the birds. He felt more settled now that he had re-acquainted himself with Reykjavík.

Callum crossed the road and took the two-person lift to the top floor of his office block. He was running a little late and he expected the metal doors to slide apart and reveal a long queue of impatient hopefuls waiting outside the office. He was somewhat disconcerted, then, to step out of the lift and be greeted by a solitary blonde girl sitting shoeless and cross-legged on the corridor floor. She immediately jumped up, balancing alternately on each leg as she slid her painted toes into a pair of funky-looking flip-flops.

'*Afsakið,*' she said. Her face was flushed. She held out her hand. '*Ég heiti* Anna Björk.'

'I'm sorry,' said Callum. 'I don't speak Icelandic.'

The young woman brightened. 'Don't apologize. That is a good thing. Icelandic is for farmers and fishermen. I prefer English. Hugh Grant is so sexy.' She offered her hand again. 'Anna Björk Kristjánsdóttir. I am here for the PA job.'

'Callum Pope. You'd better come in.'

Callum ushered her into a large, bright room with windows filling two of its four walls. The place had just been refurbished and a dizzying smell of floor varnish thickened the air. He struggled to open a window. A recent slapdash paint job had threatened to seal the frame for good. There was a gummy crack as the paintwork finally yielded and the window opened, leaving a long rind of elasticated gloss attached to the frame. It whipped and recoiled in the breeze. Fresh air filled the room, agitating tiny cones of plaster dust that had formed directly beneath each of the new telephone and cabling points. Callum remembered to add a vacuum cleaner to his ever-increasing list of office requisites.

The only furniture that the room contained was a stack of four plastic chairs and the boxed components of a free-standing lamp that had yet to be assembled.

'I apologize for the minimalism. The furniture isn't due till Monday. Still, at least we can amuse ourselves with a game of musical chairs.' Callum freed two of the plastic seats and placed them in the middle of the open floor, one facing the other.

Anna Björk hadn't been listening. She had opened one of the two doors that led off the main room and was grimacing at whatever was behind it.

'That's the kitchen,' said Callum. 'If you're looking for the bathroom, try the other one.'

'I do not need to use the bathroom, she replied.' She deposited herself on one of the chairs and ran her hand over her bronzed calf. 'Though maybe I need to shave my legs.'

'Your legs look fine to me. Where did you get the tan?'

'In Reykjavík.'

'Of course. I keep forgetting that it can be sunny in Iceland too.'

'You misunderstand. I got the tan from a shop in Reykjavík. It is a cream that you rub in.'

'Ah.'

Anna Björk smiled. She repositioned her shades on top of her head and set her duffle bag between her feet. The bag fell open a fraction, revealing a rolled-up towel bound by a pair of swimming goggles.

'So . . .' Callum wasn't quite sure where to start. He knew Anna Björk's name but nothing else. He had decided to recruit on personality alone, but his reluctance to look at CVs left him a bit stymied when it came to initiating the sort of conversation that could tease out her credentials.

'So,' he repeated. 'You like swimming?'

'No. I have never learned to swim.'

'But . . . ?' Callum nodded towards her open bag.

'Ah, the swimming costume. I see. You are confused. It is like this: you English socialize in your pubs, the French mingle in cafés and we Icelanders go to the pools. We do not always go to swim. We go to gossip with our friends.'

'And you need goggles to gossip?' Callum ignored the fact that she had accused him of being English.

'I need the goggles to check out the men's butts.' Anna Björk allowed herself another benign smile before adding, 'And the women's butts. Sometimes.'

She was certainly frank, Callum had gleaned that

much. He rocked back in his chair. He had a feeling he was going to like this girl.

'Tell me a bit about yourself, Anna.'

'Anna Björk,' she corrected. 'I am from Ólafsvík originally, which is the most boring place in the world.' She crossed her hands over one knee and let out a sigh. 'Boring, boring, boring. I grew up dreaming that one day I could escape Ólafsvík by becoming Miss Iceland and touring the world. But when my big moment arrived and I entered the Miss West Iceland heat, I came only third. My prize was a bag of cosmetics and a life condemned to work in the fish factory. But a couple of years ago I came to Reykjavík to celebrate my eighteenth birthday and I never went home. Since then I have worked in many jobs, sometimes three at the same time. I am good at multitasking.'

'And what prompted you to apply for this position?'

'I need the money. I was fired from my job at Óðal.'

'Óðal?'

'The strip club.'

Callum was intrigued. 'If you don't mind me asking, how do you get sacked from a strip club?'

'I fucked one of the clientele.'

'Ah.'

'It is not as bad as it sounds. See, stripping is all about teasing the guy, getting him to fall for you so he'll buy more dances. Men are dumb like that. But there was this one guy and, well, I did more than just tease him. He was an Italian-American. He had beautiful dark eyebrows. He offered me two thousand dollars to fuck him. I refused the money but I took him home and fucked him anyway. I am not a whore. I just fancied him. He was a good talker. He was different to Icelandic men. I do not fuck Icelandic men any more. They are not good talkers. They are descended from the Vikings who knew only two phrases: *Take that*, to a man and *Take this*, to a woman.'

Callum laughed. Birna had said much the same thing after the first time they'd made love. She had described him as 'attentive' and even though he had hoped that his lovemaking merited a more thrusting adjective – fiery? unstoppable? wanton? – Birna had assured him that 'attentive' was the most wonderful thing he could be.

'I don't understand,' he said. 'If you took this guy out of the club, how could they sack you?'

Anna Björk leaned forward to effect at least a small degree of intimacy in the breezy emptiness of the room. 'My Italian stallion was an undercover worker for the Icelandic Commission. They had been sending their men to all the strip clubs to try to lure the girls into prostitution with large offers of money. If the Commission can show that the strip clubs are offering sexual services, they will be able to close them down. Ha!' She slapped her hands on the tops of her thighs. 'They should go out to the genetic research centre at deCODE and offer those educated girls that type of money. Then we will see how many takers they get. It is a trap and it fucking stinks.' Anna Björk was shaking her head. She removed her denim jacket. 'I got fired because I slept with a guy after he had offered me money, even though I was not interested in his cash. The girls in the clubs, they are doing nothing immoral but the Commission cannot see that. Believe me, stripping is much less degrading than working in a fucking fish factory.'

Callum guessed that Anna Björk had earned a decent living from the stripping and not just because she was, as his father would have said, 'well put together'. Every article of clothing on her taut frame bore a different designer label, though they had been immaculately co-ordinated into one coherent ensemble. It was a look that didn't come cheap.

'So how bad was the fish factory?' he asked.

'It was very bad. They made me wear a horrible plastic coat, rubber gloves and a shower cap.' Anna Björk bristled at the memory. 'I was forced to stand on a production line all day and remove the guts from . . . urgh . . . big slippery slabs of silvery fish on those horrible illuminated chopping boards. When I close my eyes I can still see their ugly silhouettes.'

The way she said it, with another shake of the head and her eyes so determinedly wide, Callum didn't doubt her.

'I tell you,' she continued, 'working in a fish factory is not for humans. Hours and hours of the same movement over and over . . . slice and gut, slice and gut, slice and gut . . . like a robot. Your mind just empties itself onto the floor and your spirit is hosed away with the guts. When I first started, they made me shell shrimps. I cried for three days.'

A repetitive bleeping drifted into the space between them, getting incrementally louder. Anna Björk lifted her bag onto her knees and fished out a hairbrush. She looked at it with undisguised irritation and tossed it back in the bag. On the second attempt, she retrieved her mobile phone. She stared at the screen and pressed a button. 'Shit!'

'Something wrong?'

'I forgot to take my pill. I get an SMS message at the same time each day to remind me.' Again she dived into the blind depths of her bag. 'I'm sorry. I seem to have left the packet at home. This does not give a good impression, does it? I really am a good organizer.' Her face fell into a sulk and she dropped the bag to the floor. 'I will have to go home. Shit. I really needed this job.'

'Relax,' said Callum. 'There are two reasons why I'm going to hire you. One, you're honest. And two, nobody else has shown for the interview. You're the only option I've got.'

'You won't regret it.' Anna Björk gathered her things.

'You can start Monday. If you want I can send you a text message to remind you.'

'No need,' she beamed as she shuffled backwards to the door. 'See you Monday.' She blew him a kiss as she left.

Callum was alone now, in an empty room, with only his thoughts for company. It was perhaps the first time he had been truly alone since arriving in Iceland. There was nothing to distract him from the terrible guilty feeling that he could be spending time with Ásta. But rather than returning to the house to take her out for new shoes, thus forging the first tentative bond with Birna's girl, he convinced himself that the most important thing he could do right now was to plug in his laptop and check out the Partick Thistle score. It was Saturday afternoon, after all. If he'd worked out the time difference correctly, the final whistle would have blown.

He logged onto the *Glasgow Herald* website, but rather than go straight to the live Sports pages, Callum found himself scrolling through their news archive. This had become a bad habit. He knew exactly what he was looking for – a story dated 12th October 1996 – and it didn't take long to find it. He read it again, even though he knew he shouldn't.

Scottish Businesswoman Murdered in Prague?

Strathclyde police are investigating the death of Sarah Glass, Scottish Businesswoman of the Year, whose body was found in the early hours of Sunday morning in Prague. As yet it is not clear how she died but a spokesperson from Strathclyde has said that they are not ruling out murder.

Detective Inspector John Wedderburn claimed that the circumstances in which the deceased was found were 'highly unusual' but he would not be drawn further. 'We must wait until all the forensic evidence is released to us from the Czech police before we can progress our investigation.' He added that Ms Glass's body would be flown back to the UK on Wednesday.

It is believed that Sarah Glass was in the Czech capital to celebrate the flotation of Strawdonkey, the e-business that she launched in January of this year in partnership with fellow Glaswegian, Callum Pope. Glass and Pope have become the darlings of the British business pages as Strawdonkey's profits have soared. Within six months of its launch, the online travel guide had received upwards of thirty million hits and its founders had secured lucrative advertising contracts with nine of the top ten UK travel providers including Thomson Holidays, BA and Virgin.

A successful year culminated in Ms Glass being awarded the 'Scottish Businesswoman of the Year' title at a gala event in September. When she announced that her company was launching on the stock market, shares in Strawdonkey were six times oversubscribed.

City analysts fear that the death of Ms Glass could send the share price into a downward spiral when markets reopen tomorrow.

'Hello?'

Callum looked up from his screen.

'Hi there,' said the young man filling the office door. He was six foot two with arms the size of legs. He had the beginnings of a beard and bleached Kurt Cobain locks that jutted out of the beanie hat suckered onto his head. He was wearing a red and white candy-striped football shirt and had a motorcycle helmet wedged under one arm. 'Is this the film company?' he asked. 'Are you the guy looking for a production assistant?'

'Yes . . . of course. Come in.' Callum snapped his laptop shut. 'Sorry, I was miles away. One of the perils of starting a business . . . lots of bloody spreadsheets to mull over. I'm still getting used to your currency. The name's Callum Pope.' He extended a hand.

'Fridrik Fridriksson. But people call me Frikki.'

'Freaky?'

'F, R, I, K, K, I,' said the big man, spelling it out.

'Frikki, do you mind if we do this over a beer?'

Callum needed to get drunk.

6

'A couple of years ago an Icelandic millionaire bought Stoke City. He employed our national coach as their manager and now many Icelanders play for Stoke. That is why I wear the football shirt.'

'For such a small nation, you lot certainly get around. I read that a consortium of Icelanders has just bought Hamleys in London.'

'Stoke City and Hamleys, they are Iceland's first steps to world domination.' Frikki raised a half-litre glass of Viking lager and clinked it against Callum's. '*Skál!*'

The two men had commandeered a dusty couch in Kaffíbarinn. They were on their third beers. The warm sunlight drew a gold window onto the wooden floorboards at their feet. The walls of the bar had also been panelled in wood but the slats were painted the colour of mushy peas. This was a new treat for Callum. He had never managed to get into Kaffíbarinn on any of his previous visits. Rumour had it that the bar was co-owned by Blur frontman Damon Albarn and consequently the place was usually crammed with teenagers. But this was a Saturday afternoon. The crowds didn't come out to play until midnight. Callum and Frikki had the upper floor to themselves.

'So, we've established that Iceland is home to the

world's strongest men and the world's most beautiful women and that one day your country shall govern the planet.'

'And we will start by invading Denmark,' said Frikki, a little loudly, though Callum supposed that there was nobody in the bar, let alone a Dane, to take offence.

'What have you got against Danes?'

'For years we were ruled by them. And trust me, Danes are only fit to rule Danes,' cautioned Frikki. 'But you British are OK. You lost the Cod War to us. We Icelanders like losers, so long as you lose to Iceland.' The big man laughed and slapped his glass on the table. 'You know that if you change around the letters in Cod War you get coward. How else do you explain the retreat of the mighty British Navy when confronted by a fleet of Icelandic fishing tugs?'

'True,' agreed Callum. 'Not that I think of myself as British. I'm a Scot first and foremost.'

'I like the Scottish. I am part Scottish.'

'And how do you work that out?'

'The Scottish and the Irish settled in Iceland a long time ago. OK, so our forefathers were mostly Vikings from Norway and Denmark, but there is some Celtic blood mixed in. Put it this way, if a Dane tries to claim ancestry over me I will tell him I am descended from the Scottish, just to piss him off.'

Just as it had been with Anna Björk, Callum had warmed to Frikki straight away. The guy made him laugh and right now a laugh was exactly what he needed. This wasn't an interview in the strictest sense. Sure, the pair of them hadn't stopped talking, but none of it had concerned the job. On that basis alone, Callum had decided to employ the guy. He would be spending a lot of time on the road with his assistant. An ability to make engaging conversation was a key requirement of the post. Nevertheless, Callum thought he ought to at least pretend to be interested in Frikki's other credentials.

'So, remind me, what experience do you have of film and TV production?'

'None at all. I work the fishing boats for five months of the year, which earns me enough money to get drunk for the rest of it.' Frikki offered his glass again. '*Skál!*'

'If you don't need the money, why apply for the job?'

Frikki replaced his smile with a frown. He thought about his answer. 'This is the end of winter. It is also the end of the shrimp season. The boats have swapped their nets for lines and now they will head further out into the ocean for cod. But this year I will not be joining them. I have decided that I need a change of career.'

'How come?'

A new sobriety had taken hold of the big Icelander. His irises contracted, retreating to some faraway place. 'It is not much fun on those trips. You are at sea for a long time. It is cold and wet for twenty-four hours a day, every day. The only warmth is from a single stove below deck. You must heat your rubber gloves on it at regular intervals. If you don't, the pain in your hands when you handle the lines is too much.' Frikki looked a little embarrassed. 'Even for a Viking like me.'

Callum could see beyond the bravado. 'But you don't mind the shrimp fishing?'

'No, I don't mind that at all. We harvest rækja, a red shrimp that stays close to the fjords. It can be really peaceful out there, chugging along with the green nets spreading out behind you. The only thing you need is patience. The boat will trawl slowly for an hour, maybe two, before it is time to bring the nets back up. The seagulls always crowd around when they hear the winch. My father says they are like schoolboys sensing a fight. They go berserk when the nets are opened and a tonne of fresh red shrimp spills onto the deck. It is like waterfall made of fire.' Frikki made a whoosh sound, feathering his fingers through a warm bar of sunlight to mimic the fiery flow. He settled back into the sofa with his beer tucked close to his chest. 'No, I don't mind that sort of fishing at all. If it is a nice evening I like to sit on the deck and play my guitar.'

'What do you play?' asked Callum.

'This and that. But mostly I play Bob Marley and the Whalers.' Frikki waited a beat before slapping Callum on the shoulder and laughing loudly. 'I joke with you!'

'Actually, you're probably a good man to ask,' said Callum, changing the subject before he incurred further bruising. 'What restaurant serves the best shellfish in Reykjavík?' He wanted to take Birna and 'the girls' somewhere special.

'I am not sure. I do not eat shellfish.'

'You don't eat shellfish?'

'No. I am allergic to them.'

Callum waited for another slap. It wasn't forthcoming. 'Are you serious? You catch shrimp for a living and you're allergic to them?'

'Only if I put them in my mouth. I am allergic to shellfish and kiwi fruit. Both can kill me. Of course, we had no kiwi fruit in Iceland until the Nineties. Life was less dangerous back then. These days, when I have a fruit salad it is like playing Russian roulette.' Frikki tipped the last of his glass into his mouth and got to his feet. 'Another Viking?'

'Let me get these. The beer's pretty pricey in here. I'll let you buy me a drink when I give you your first wage packet.'

'No, I insist,' said Frikki. 'Remember, I have just earned a lot of money on the boats. In five months I can earn double what a policeman or a university lecturer is paid in a year. I think I can treat my new boss to another beer.' He dropped his hand into the pocket of his jeans and pulled out a soft ball of banknotes. 'You know, it was only fifteen years ago that proper beer became legal in Iceland. Before that, we had to make our own brew from low-alcohol beer mixed with strong spirits. We called it *bjórlíki*, which means "like beer". But it was more like piss.' Frikki steadied himself on the back of an armchair. 'My father used to make money outside the fishing season by smuggling homebrew up the coast in his boat. He supplied it to people in the remote communities as far north as Bíldudalur, a place so isolated that if you run out of sugar in October you must wait until April to get more. The coastguards used to chase us. It was very exciting for a young boy from the fjords. I thought my father was James Bond.' Frikki chuckled beerily. 'Father always said that one day he would write down his adventures and call it *Fridrik's Saga*. But the stupid bastard couldn't write.'

'He never learned?' asked Callum.

'Sure, he learned to write. But he was not able to put this knowledge into practice after his right arm got ripped off by the boat winch.' Frikki returned to his money and scrutinized the denominations on his crumpled notes, looking more like a baffled tourist than a local. 'He still holds the national record for one-handed press-ups,' he added. With that, he turned away from his new boss and got swallowed up by the floor on his way down the stairs.

Callum could feel his back stiffening. He hauled himself out of the sofa and over to the window. He scanned the tidy streets, the colourful buildings that snuggled up to each other and the rooftops so sharp and precise against a bluescreen sky. Reykjavík's architects had seamlessly blended the old with the new, the flakily quaint with the cleanly modern, like chefs fingering disparate spices into a hearty chowder.

Callum noticed that a group of workmen were prising flagstones off the pavements on Laugavegur, the main shopping street. Further down the road their colleagues were uncoiling the underground heating cables that would keep the pavements free of ice for the long and irrepressible winter. They set the white piping into the black asphalt in such a configuration that Callum imagined he was looking at the emerging skeleton of some mammoth creature entombed since the ice age. He was suddenly filled with a great love for this daft place, this northernmost capital, this gale-blown toy town with whalebones under its flagstones. Where else in the world could he pay five pounds for a beer and be happy about it?

He returned to the sofa to finish his drink and consider his new hirings. Anna Björk and Frikki had moved to Reykjavík from outlying areas. Birna, too, had made her way to the city from the Westmann Islands. She had admitted to Callum that this was symptomatic of a big problem in Iceland. Many small communities were slowly dying, haemorrhaging their young people to the bright lights of the capital. The entire island boasted a population barely one fifth the size of Glasgow and ninety per cent of that number resided in Reykjavík. Apart from Akureyri in the north, there were few towns in Iceland that merited more than one page in the phone book (the same phone book that listed every resident of Iceland by their first name).

'Damn.' Callum cursed himself. He had meant to phone Birna. His mobile had been switched off for the interviews and he had forgotten all about it. He removed it from his jacket and watched it flicker into life, the word '*Síminn*' surfacing from the liquid crystal to be joined by the time: 15.34.

'Bollocks.' He punched in a number and put the phone to his ear.

His call was answered, but the only sounds that Callum could hear were the thrum of an engine and the bark of a cranky gear stick.

'Birna?'

'Hi Ca-m. -ow is my lov-boy? -ope -y mother made -ou a -ice bre-fast,' she said.

'You're breaking up. Where are you?'

'-out -n hour from Rey-ví-. -ve deci- to dri- back.'

'You're coming back?'

'*Já.*'

'How come? Aren't the glacial volcanoes unleashing their great, ark-bearing floods?'

'Not -day. But mayb- -morr-,' joked Birna. 'You nev-know wi- this place. W- a minu-.' The engine noise died. Callum heard a click followed by a silky rasp: the sound of a seat belt being released? This was followed by the unmistakable clunk and thud of a car door being opened and closed. 'Hello,' said Birna. 'Is the signal better now?'

'Clear as a bell. I thought you weren't coming back till tomorrow evening.'

'That was my plan. But I miss you.'

'Aw shucks. She misses me.'

'I do,' said Birna. 'The university wanted me to spend the weekend out here in the flood plains, analysing the glacial rivers. It is important research. If the rivers are unseasonably high it could indicate volcanic activity beneath the glacier. But this morning I was up to my knees in water, plotting changes in the flow pattern, when a strange thing happened. I suddenly felt very alone.'

'That's because you *were* very alone.'

'True. But I am used to working in isolated places. Sometimes the only living thing I will see all day is lichen. But today it was a different feeling. You know when you lie back on the bed at night and the world suddenly drops from beneath you. It was like that. I was standing in this stream and I panicked. I thought to myself, I miss Callum. He has only just arrived and already we are apart again. We have been apart too long. So I packed my instruments into the car and turned around.'

'You needn't worry about me,' said Callum. 'You should do your work.'

'No,' came the defiant reply. 'Work can wait. For a week or two at least, until we get close to each other again. I should never have left you this morning. Not after Ásta's outburst last night.'

'Uch, that was nothing. You said it yourself, she was nervous. She's not used to having men around.'

'I am afraid it is something more than that.'

There was an audible silence. Callum thought he could hear Birna biting her lip. 'Are you still there?' he asked.

'Já. Sorry. It is Ásta. She saw you with your hand on my belly. She thinks I am pregnant. She is afraid that I will love your baby more than her.'

'But that's ridiculous.' Callum was unsure whether he was referring to Ásta's anxiety or to the very idea of Birna and he having a child.

'That is what I told her but she would not believe me.'

'Well that might explain why she kicked the Loch Ness monster.'

'She did what?' asked Birna.

'Oh, it was nothing. Listen, can we talk about this when you get back? I should go.' Callum had spotted Frikki coming up the stairs, two beers disgorging

84

themselves over his outstretched hands. 'I'm in the middle of an interview.'

'Have you seen many people?'

'I've seen enough.'

'Great,' said Birna. 'I knew the advertisement would work. I will call you when I arrive in town. We should make a big night of it. Mother is looking after Ásta and they do not expect me back. We have the night to ourselves. I thought we could get a room and pretend it is the old days.'

'Can't wait.'

7

'What's this?' asked Callum, pointing to an item on his menu.

'You do not need to know what that is,' said Birna.

'It is whale steaks in pepper sauce.' Frikki ripped a bread roll in two and wrapped one half of it round a cube of frozen butter, popping the lot into his mouth without spreading it.

The three of them had managed to secure a window table in þrír Frakkar, a salmon-coloured fish restaurant tucked away from the main drag as though consciously hiding from tourists. Callum could not hear a single word of English coming from any of the surrounding tables.

'I don't understand,' he said. 'If whaling is banned, how come you have whale steak on the menu?'

Birna was about to answer but Frikki beat her to it. 'Sometimes a whale will get beached. The law says it can then become a source of food. The Icelandic word for a whale beaching is *hvalreki*, which is also our word for a windfall. It is an appropriate word.' Frikki skewered another butter patty with his knife. He ignored the remaining half of his bread roll and ate the patty neat. 'Also, there are times at sea when a whale will be killed accidentally. It will become tangled in our nets and dragged backwards. This can drown it.

One time our boat hit a fin whale full on the nose and killed it instantly.' Frikki shrugged. 'I guess accidents happen.'

Callum looked at Birna. Her elbows were on the table and her hands were locked firmly under her chin. It was a determined posture and one with which Callum was well acquainted. Her expression was primed like a harpoon. He knew what was coming. He folded his menu and settled back into his chair like a marlin fisherman strapping himself in for the long fight.

'Accidents do not happen.' Birna had accepted Frikki's bait. 'Whales are the aristocrats of the sea. And fishermen like you are the murderers.'

Frikki smiled. He turned to an elderly man sitting at the adjacent table and tugged at his sleeve. 'Did you hear that, my friend? She called me a murderer.' He stabbed his butter knife in the air, *Psycho*-style.

The old man looked suitably alarmed.

Frikki returned to Birna. 'Fishermen are not murderers. We are the lifeblood of Iceland.' The Stoke City badge appeared to swell on his chest. 'Look,' he motioned his hand round the cramped dining room. 'There are fish on all our tables.' He selected a one-hundred krónur piece from the loose change stacked against his cigarette packet and turned the coin over on the tablecloth. 'There are fish on our coins,' he indicated. 'Think about it. Fish factories surround our harbours . . . harbours that are full of fishing boats. Thousands of fish are hung out on racks to rattle in the winds that sweep through our coastal villages. The life in Iceland, said Halldór Laxness, is salt fish.'

Callum was surprised and encouraged by Frikki's reference to Iceland's Nobel Prize-winning author. It was a relief to know that he hadn't hired an illiterate.

'Fishermen are our saviours,' continued Frikki. 'We

are not murderers. It is the whales that are killing us. They are reproducing too quickly and swallowing millions of tonnes of krill. This is starving our codfish. We have to control the whale population or our fish stocks will be devastated. Iceland will be devastated.'

'Have you finished,' said Birna. It wasn't a question. It was an order.

Callum concealed a smile.

'Iceland will only be devastated if we return to whaling,' she said. 'If we whale again we will have a repeat of what happened in the Eighties. The environmental organizations will encourage big companies all over the world to protest by refusing to buy any more Icelandic fish products. And do you want a repeat of what happened in the Eighties? Do you want the Green extremists sabotaging and sinking more boats in our harbour? Do you want us to—'

'You see, this is what makes me angry,' interrupted Frikki. He was a braver man than Callum. 'Why do people think that if animals are in danger in one part of the world, then they must be so everywhere? The whales in our waters are in no danger of extinction. There are plenty and we must manage them as a resource. The Arabs have their oil and Iceland has the fish in its sea. We survive by using the resources in the ocean around us.'

'What about tourism?' asked Birna. 'Tourism is a resource, too. Iceland gets only a tiny trickle of the tourists who travel between Europe and North America. An issue like this could stop them coming altogether. And what about the whale-watching industry that has grown since the ban on whaling? Most visitors to Iceland take one of these trips. Watching whales has become more profitable than killing them.'

'She's right, Frikki,' said Callum, trying to diffuse

things. 'I went whale watching on my first visit. I was hoping to get a photograph of a breaching humpback, the sort you see on the cover of *National Geographic*, but I only managed a blurred snapshot of a distant minke fin. Or was it dust on the lens?'

Birna kicked him under the table. She transferred the accompanying glare to Frikki. 'I am from the Westmann Islands which became home to Keiko, the star of *Free Willy*. Look at all the positive publicity we received as a consequence. As long as we take people on whale-watching trips and harbour Keiko, we are the good guys. As soon as we begin whaling again, we will be the bad guys. And whales have long memories. Today the calves are friendly and pose for the cameras. But if we start harpooning them, they will remember to stay clear of all boats. Think of the many jobs that will be lost in Reykjavík, Husavík, Klettsvík, Hafnarfjörður, if whale-watching trips are stopped.'

'You are wrong,' said Frikki, just when Callum was willing him to throw in the napkin. 'Whaling will create jobs. The meat will bring in money. A fin whale can weigh seventy thousand kilos. That is a lot of meat and it requires a lot of people to process it.'

'This is bullshit. Whaling was never an important industry in Iceland,' asserted Birna.

'Personally, I think it's more worrying that you eat puffin,' said Callum.

Birna glared at him.

'Well . . .' he continued, '. . . you have to question the attitude of a nation that eats one of its national symbols.'

'Do not interrupt me,' said Birna. 'I am trying to tell your ignorant friend that whaling has never been big business. Whale products were barely two per cent of our total export in the years before the ban on killing them.'

Frikki remained defiant. 'I still think we should kill them,' he said.

'Why ... because you are a proud man of the seas?'

'No,' said Frikki. 'Because they taste nice.'

A silence descended on the table. It was filled by a foghorn of a voice that came from an indomitable waitress who had positioned herself between the table and the window, eclipsing all light. She had shoulders that Callum could only describe as 'childbearing'. She honked something in insistent Icelandic.

Birna translated for Callum. 'She would like us to order our food.'

'Right,' he said, grateful for the intervention. He reopened his menu and consulted it, even though he already knew what dish he wanted. 'I'd like the duck, please.'

'Ah, you are a man with expensive tastes,' said the waitress.

Callum was worried now. 'Expensive' in an Icelandic restaurant meant certain bankruptcy. 'How much is the duck?' he asked.

'About fifty British pounds,' said Birna, converting the price on the menu.

'Fifty quid!' Callum was mortified. 'Jesus, if I'm going to pay fifty quid for a duck I expect it to sing show tunes and perform street magic.' He revisited his selection.

'This is a fish restaurant,' said Birna. 'The seafood will be more reasonable.'

'I'll have the sea bream,' he decided.

'Wolf fish,' said Birna, smiling at the waitress.

All eyes were on Frikki.

He looked at Callum, then Birna. He returned his gaze to the handwritten menu and hovered a finger over the whale steak.

The waitress buzzed her pencil across the spiral binding on her notepad.

Frikki snapped his menu shut, inspiring his blonde fringe to dance. He looked at Birna again, more directly this time.

'I will have the lamb,' he capitulated.

'Come on Birna, he's not that bad,' said Callum.

'Puffinshit! He is an arrogant asshole and you should never have hired him. Was there not a more suitable candidate?'

'No.'

'I do not believe you. How can that pig be the best you have seen?'

'Because he was the only pig to reply to your advert. It seems that there aren't many people in Reykjavík who are actively seeking employment. Everyone's already got a job. Some of them have two or three on the go.'

Birna thought about it. 'True . . . this used to be a big problem,' she conceded. 'It used to be that in Reykjavík if you wanted a job, you did not have to attend dozens of interviews like elsewhere. You could just call up a friend or a relative, or go to the harbour and jump on a boat. There have always been too many jobs and not enough people to do them. And even though unemployment is starting to rise, we still get this crazy situation where our postmen build houses, our dentists drive taxis and our waitresses cut hair.'

'And your strippers become PAs,' said Callum. 'Today I hired a girl who got fired from one of the strip clubs.'

Birna tugged his arm back, halting their walk up Laugavegur.

'You've hired a stripper?'

Callum shrugged. 'She's a nice girl. No organizational skills but hey, fantastic legs.' He smiled and braced himself for a shot to the ribs. But Birna refused to play that game, the one that usually started with a play fight before inevitably escalating into a full-blown carnal tussle in the nearest available doorway.

'The strip bars are bad for this place,' said Birna. She turned her head to look down the steep street that swept into the centre of town, scooping it up like a shovelful of snow. Reykjavík was all lit up, as if a surplus of stars had fallen from the too-crowded sky. Birna hooked her arm under Callum's and led him away from the lure of the lights, walking him back up the hill. 'What you do not understand is that these clubs are just a front for prostitution. I have seen some of the girls. They are desperate. They are lured here from all over Europe, America, Asia, into an industry that is degrading for all involved. Ten years ago we did not have this problem in our country.'

'Anna Björk isn't a prostitute.'

'Anna Björk?' asked Birna, as though this was someone she knew. 'This stripper is an Icelander?'

'She's from Ólafsvík.'

'This surprises me.'

'Watch!' Callum pulled Birna off the pavement, allowing three skateboarders to rattle past them. The teenagers clattered over the flags, each one carrying two cans of beer that acted as counterbalances to their erratic, alcohol-fuelled descent.

'Anna Björk says that there's nothing unsavoury going on at the clubs.'

'Maybe not,' said Birna. 'But they are still degrading to women.'

'Not according to Anna. She told me that the girls have all the power. Apparently it's all about getting the guy to fall for you, teasing him so he'll buy more private dances. She said that men are dumb when they are in that situation.'

'Do you fancy her?'

They had stopped again. Callum felt Birna's eyes searching him.

'No,' he said. 'I don't fancy her.'

'You looked away from me when you said that. This means you are not telling the truth.' Birna did her best to look hurt but a smile struggled free to spoil her pretence.

Callum slipped his arm over her shoulder and brought her tight into his side. 'There is only one woman in my life.' He planted a kiss on top of her head.

'And what about my mother and Ásta? I think Callum Pope has three women in his life.' Birna was teasing him now.

'Then Callum Pope is a lucky man.'

They ducked into a dingy corridor that ran along the side of the Mál og Menning bookstore. Its scrawled-on walls were bathed in a greenish-yellow fluorescence from the strip lighting above their heads. A thin stream of urine crept across the tiles where someone had recently peed, its progress slowing as it became absorbed into the grout. A broken beer bottle was ground to a fine brown powder by Callum's boot as he walked up to a metal door. Birna buzzed it open and they were admitted into the *Room with a View* apartment block. She knew the owner – Gudni – and had collected a key from him on her way to dinner.

An elevator carried them up to the fifth floor and into another corridor, this time devoid of light. They felt their way along the wall until they found apartment 512. Birna fed the key into a slit and opened the door. She flicked on the lights.

'Welcome to your old home,' she said.

Callum had stayed in this studio apartment on his previous visits to Iceland. It was laid out in open plan with a set of wardrobes separating the bedroom from a main living area that was dominated by a gluttonous leather sofa. How many times had they made love on that sofa, reflected Callum. Just looking at it, he could feel the fetishistic tug of the cold hide against his bare ass.

The bathroom was visible through a wall of blue glass bricks. A triumph of ergonomics, it contained possibly the smallest sink in Europe. After taking a shower, Birna liked to rest her foot on this sink while she towelled her leg dry and to Callum, who would be lying on the bed watching her through the coloured glass, she looked like one of Degas's blue ballerinas performing a stretch.

A kitchenette had been built into one wall and was concealed behind two heavy wooden panels. Callum opened one of them and collapsed it back on itself. He set his carrier bag on the worktop. The bag sagged a little to reveal the neck of a bottle of Pölstar vodka.

Callum opened the fridge and leaned in to check its contents.

'Gudni's all out of Coke. Will orange juice do?'

'Sure.' Birna had pulled the quilt off the double bed and was trailing it across the room. She opened a glass door that led onto a balcony built for two.

'What are you up to?' asked Callum.

'I thought we could enjoy the night. We are getting only a few hours of darkness these days. We must make the most of them before they disappear entirely.' Birna lowered her bottom onto the floor of the balcony and rested her back against the exterior wall of the apartment. 'You must switch off the lights before you come out here,' she shouted. 'That way we can see the stars.' She pulled the quilt over her knees and up to her chin.

Callum threw the apartment into darkness and joined her. He slipped under the quilt and handed Birna a large vodka and orange. 'I apologize for the mugs. Gudni still hasn't replaced the glasses we broke on your birthday.'

'*Skál!*' Birna's nostrils tightened as she sipped the sour citrus mix. 'This is so beautiful.'

'Do you reckon? I think it could do with a little more orange.'

'No, I am talking about the view. Hallgrímskirkja looks very beautiful.' Birna was indicating the church that presided over Reykjavík from the top of the hill. 'Some people think it is very ugly but I do not agree.'

The church shot up from the rooftops like a space shuttle at launch. A simple, elongated pyramid, it was lit in a way that sharply delineated it from the mole-skin night. Its concrete columns curved up into an apex, giving the impression of organ pipes, as if the whole building was one vast instrument that could be operated by keys, pedals and stops.

'The design was based on the basalt columns at Seljalandsfoss,' said Birna, sensing that Callum was similarly entranced. 'The clock at the top never tells the correct time. It is the highest point in the town and the wind is so strong that it regularly blows the hands off course. You know, it is rare for any two public clocks in Reykjavík to be telling the same time because the wind conditions are always changing.'

Callum chuckled through his nose. 'So what time is it?'

'About three.'

Even at this hour the streets below them fizzed with life. Car horns complained, youths screamed at each other in rat-a-tat Icelandic and from the many bars, live guitars battled break-beat DJs for air supremacy. Reykjavík sounded like a radio caught between stations.

'The night is so beautiful here,' said Birna. 'Have you ever seen the Northern Lights?'

'Aye. We get a good display up in the far north of Scotland. I once did a location shoot on the island of Lewis and saw the whole ghostly show.'

'*Já*, it is the same in Iceland. The borealis is much clearer in the north. Reykjavík compensates by having big firework displays on our Cultural night and at New Year but compared to the Northern Lights these fireworks are always second best. You know, I think that when I die I want to be cremated and have my ashes packed into a firework.'

'Is that what they mean by going out with a bang?'

'Could be,' said Birna. 'I want to explode into colour and light. I want to illuminate the faces of my loved ones. I want to dance in their eyes. Or perhaps I shall have my body carbonized and turned into a diamond.'

Callum shifted his bottom until it sat tight against Birna's. 'It is pretty special out here. In Glasgow, there's so much artificial light that you can't see the stars. Not properly anyway. And we get a lot of pollution back home. But here, the air's so clear that it makes your head spin. Or maybe it's the vodka.'

'Do not worry,' said Birna. 'This happens a lot with foreigners who come to Iceland. They OD on oxygen.'

The temperature had dropped, so they conjoined their bodies to feed off each other's heat. Callum slipped his free hand between Birna's legs and curved his palm under the back of her thigh. She fed her arm round his waist and slotted her cheek into the curve of his neck, the last piece in their jigsaw. Alcohol and eiderdown helped stave off the cold.

'We're going to make this work, aren't we?' asked Callum.

'Of course we will.' Birna stroked his cheek. 'You and I, we are unstoppable.'

The moment would have been perfect had something not been nibbling away at Callum. He didn't want to mention it. He didn't want to put a bolster between them. They had never been closer. But the masochist in him needed to know.

'Why did you tell Ásta that her father was a hero?' Even as he asked the question, he regretted it.

Birna lifted her head and Callum felt his neck go cold. She looked right at him but said nothing.

'You told her that he was killed when saving a little girl from a volcanic eruption,' he continued. 'But you told me that he was looting a pharmacy for drugs when he died.'

'Arnar was no hero,' spat Birna.

'Then why make your daughter believe that he was?'

'What was the alternative?' Birna's voice had risen to a level that drew an echo from the opposing block. 'Sorry, I should not be angry with you.' Her face softened. She nodded in answer to some unspoken question. '*Já*. I should tell you what I could not tell Ásta.'

Birna gripped her mug with both hands, as though the vodka was coffee and she could draw heat from it. There was a look on her face that Callum had not seen before, like she was wary of him.

He held the quilt open, inviting her to fall back in beside him.

She accepted.

Callum said nothing as she spoke to the stars.

'Arnar started on weed when he was sixteen and by nineteen he was a heroin addict. He said it was an escape, which really hurt me. We had been sweethearts since childhood and I thought it was me that he wanted to escape from. Of course, Arnar insisted that it was the island that was suffocating him.' Birna laughed an ironic laugh. She guzzled more vodka. 'We talked about getting a boat to the mainland but I could not go through with it. My father's health was getting worse and I was needed on the farm. Arnar was no help. The drugs put his head in the clouds. Appropriate, really. He liked to sit in the clouds, high up on the cliffs, waiting for puffin, even when it was not the season for catching them. That way he did not have to deal with reality.'

Birna closed her eyes. When she opened them again, they were liquid. 'It was a sad time. Arnar became an outcast, forced to sleep in his little hut up on the clifftop. His parents had found out about his drug-taking and they refused to have him in their house. He stayed with us for one night but my mother caught him stealing money from her bedside. He used to steal from me and think that I would not notice. All the money he earned from the puffins and the egg-collecting, it all went straight into his veins.'

Birna's pupils had become flat black circles in heavy eyes. She stole another glug from her mug. 'I once gave him money to get a coat. I followed him down to the harbour and watched him buy heroin off one of the Danish boats. That is the scary thing, that drugs are available everywhere, even somewhere as isolated as Heimæy. I once heard a doctor say that to get a heroin addict to stop, you have to put them on an island. That is such bullshit.'

There was a pause and Callum wasn't sure whether he was supposed to fill it. He was glad he didn't, for Birna's eyes narrowed in anger.

'Addiction is grim, it is shitty, it is paranoid,' she said. 'I used to be amazed at what Arnar's body could tolerate. I had to sit and watch him use. It has haunted me ever since.' She brought her arm out from under the quilt and set it on her knee. She rolled her sleeve up to her elbow. 'He would tie his arm like this and wait for a vein.' Birna ran her finger along the whiter side of her forearm. She turned to face Callum. 'Have you ever seen heroin?'

He shook his head.

'It is like mud, like rusty water left in an old bath.' Birna fell back against him and faced the night.

Callum adjusted the quilt so that it covered her feet.

'I have been through some low points in my life,' she said. 'My father's death hit me hard but Arnar shooting up was the shittiest thing I have ever witnessed. He was someone I loved, someone I grew up with, someone I thought I would grow old with. We used to play together as kids, make snow angels, fly kites. We used to creep up behind sleeping sheep and tip them over. Hard to believe the person he became. And hard to believe I stayed so loyal. I even joined him on the boats when he saw his dealers . . . those sacks of shit with spyholes in their cabin doors. I had to sit there and smile when all I wanted to do was beat them with both fists.'

Callum felt foolish. He had been jealous of Arnar, jealous of an all-action hero who had saved the life of a young girl. How could he compete with that? How could he hope to win Ásta's affection? Compared to her real father, Callum would only ever be a lousy second. The only act of heroism that he could boast involved the resuscitation of a friend's gerbil using a hairdryer and a fingertip dipped in whisky.

But there was a bad part of him, a bitter residual dreg that wanted Ásta to know the truth about her dad. It was selfish and Callum hated himself for wishing it. Why tell her that Arnar was a junkie? Why upset the girl? And would it change things? Would she suddenly seek to adopt this alien Scotsman, this bearer of awful truths, as her paternal role model?

Would she heck. She would despise him for robbing her of a father for the second time in her short life; for killing the father that she believed in. And then what? Would he follow up by telling her that Father Christmas wasn't real? Icelandic children had thirteen Santa Clauses to believe in, the 'Yule Lads' who take it in turns to visit the town on each of the thirteen days before Christmas to deposit little presents in the shoes that the kids have left by their open bedroom windows. Would Callum discredit them one by one – Skyrgámur the Curd Glutton, Gluggagægir the Window Peeper, Grýla the Ogre – until Ásta was left with no magic in her life, until she had nothing left to believe in?

Ásta had reacted badly to the notion that her mother might have a child by Callum. She seemed threatened by it, that a second child would somehow dilute her mother's love. But perhaps this was the only way that Callum could become an integral part of this impregnable family, by weaving himself into their genetic fabric. If he had a child by Birna, surely Ásta would see it as a sign of his commitment to her mother, a promise that he was not about to desert them, that he was here to stay.

And Ásta needed to know that Callum was staying. The only man in her life had, rightly or wrongly, removed himself from it. And she had never known her grandfather. How could Callum expect this poor girl to invest anything of herself in him when she only knew men as these elusive, ungraspable beings who might at any moment disappear?

Callum set his mug down and threaded his arms round Birna's waist. Her T-shirt had ridden up a little and her belly felt warm.

'Birna, I don't think we should wait a year,' he said. 'I want us to try for a baby now.'

The mug fell from Birna's hand and hit the decking. The handle broke off and came to rest in a downturned smile. She remained silent, her head pressing heavily against him like it had taken the full weight of his words. He waited for her to reply, a laugh or a sob, a yes or a no. But all he got was a grunt.

She was out for the count.

8

She woke up in a room with a view, with a mother of a hangover and an impatient boyfriend cajoling her into consciousness. She hadn't yet opened her eyes and Callum was mumbling something about children, insisting that they try for a baby. But Birna was having none of it. She explained that she wasn't ready. There were a couple of things she needed to do before she could consider having his child.

She went to the bathroom, brushed her teeth and threw her pills in the bin. Now she was ready.

The sex was tentative and unsure. It was highly unlikely that they would hit the bullseye at the first attempt – there were books to be read, cycles to be diaried, vices to be abstained from and folic acid to be consumed – but it was a possibility all the same. Suddenly sex wasn't sex any more. It was reproduction. Callum and Birna could no longer simply abandon themselves to lust. Lust seemed inappropriate when trying for a child; it seemed wrong.

And so, without recourse to animal passion, their lovemaking assumed an uneasy reverence. When Callum found himself on the threshold of orgasm, he battled manfully to delay it, aware of the seismology of the act. If the earth moved, the aftershock could be felt over the next nine months and for the ongoing duration of a human life. It was a hell of a thing.

It took a coughing fit from Birna to tip him over the edge, her involuntary spasms inducing those of his own. Callum gritted his eyes – something that he had only thought possible with teeth – and a succession of images fast-cut in his head like an MTV promo: a newly painted room . . . a mobile suspended over a cot . . . a bottle of milk bobbing in hot water . . . a soiled bib . . . a sandpit . . . white dog shit . . . chewed felt tips . . . a tricycle upended in nettles . . . a knee graze . . . a sack race . . . a pencil case . . . a birthday cake . . . hundreds and thousands . . . hundreds of measles . . . a broken window . . . a burst ball . . . a racer in the hall . . . posters on walls . . . a newly painted room.

When they had recovered their breath, Callum reached a pillow from the floor and stuffed it under the small of Birna's back.

'What are you doing?' she asked.

'You need to keep your bottom raised. I read that you should stay in this position for ten or fifteen minutes, to let gravity work its magic.'

This made Birna laugh so hard that it had the opposite effect to the one Callum desired. He scrambled for the box of tissues, urging her to clamp her thighs together.

They lay naked on top of the mattress, their duvet long consigned to the floor.

'Are you sure this is what you really want?' Birna's eyes stayed fixed on the roof fan that whirled directly above them, cooling their wet skin.

'Of course I'm sure. But shouldn't you have asked me that before we had unprotected sex?' Callum rolled over on his side and propped himself up on one elbow, to get a better look at her.

'I guess so,' she conceded.

'You're not having second thoughts, are you?'

Callum traced his finger round the soft curve of her navel.

'Not second thoughts. But . . . well . . . you said you were anxious about becoming a father to Ásta. Do you think it will be any easier to rear a child of your own?'

'I know it's not going to be easy. But I really want us to have a kid,' he said. 'I'm good with children. Some of my best friends used to be kids.'

Birna removed the pillow and thwacked him with it. 'You are not taking this seriously.' She was laughing now.

'I've never been more serious about anything in my life. I want us to be a family. I've made such a hash of my own life that I reckon it's about time I started living vicariously through the achievements of my offspring. With your sharp brain and my devastating good looks, I reckon our child is destined for big things. Who knows, one day he or she might even run their very own fish factory.'

Birna laughed again. 'And what is Ásta's destiny?'

'I'm tempted to say that as the child of a geologist and a drug addict, she'll spend her life getting stoned. But Arnar isn't around any more. Hopefully I can be a more positive influence on her. It'll be a good test of nature versus nurture. If she develops an addiction to haggis and shortbread, we'll know that nurture has won.'

'We must talk to her,' said Birna. 'We must let her know that we are trying for a child.'

'She's not going to be happy about it.'

'She will be OK, as long as we reassure her that we will not love her any less when a new baby arrives. We should speak to her today.'

'Should we not wait a while, at least until you get pregnant? It would give me time to get to know her.

How can I be of any reassurance to her while I'm still a stranger?'

'The sooner we tell her, the sooner she gets used to the idea of you being a permanent fixture in our lives,' said Birna. 'You said that you wanted us to be a family, so we should start behaving like one. The three of us should go somewhere for the day. We can collect Ásta and take the ponies out to the countryside.'

'Ponies?'

'Já. We will go riding together.'

'When I said I wanted us to be a family, I wasn't envisaging a pony trek. I was imagining something more sedate, like Monopoly.'

'Icelandic Monopoly is called Matador.'

'Great,' said Callum. 'What piece do you want to be: the puffin, the harpoon or the sheep's testicle?'

The late-morning sun broke through the clouds to rouse the mountains from their slumber. They stretched their rocky limbs into view, some still tucked under crisp snowy sheets. Below them, three people and three ponies were as insignificant as ants as they stood by a vast lake. This impressive body of water had partially retreated into the earth following some cataclysm or other, leaving a substantial part of the lake bed exposed. The residual mudflat was covered in cracks, craters and gaping wounds that refused to heal: steaming vents that hissed and booed and threw out rotten eggs.

The sun turned up the brightness and the shadow of Callum's pony unfurled across the grass, swelling into life like a foal standing up on all fours for the first time.

He was struggling to mount the beast.

'You have never ridden before, have you,' laughed Birna.

'How did you guess.' Callum was hopping on one

foot while his other remained trapped in a stirrup. He knew that he looked ridiculous but continued to toe-poke his pony in the ribs while fanning flies with his hands.

Ásta was not amused. She turned her horse away from them and steered it down the grassy bank that led onto the fuming lake bed. She normally enjoyed bringing the ponies out here and taking them for a run, but today she had not wanted to come and had said so, loudly, in front of Callum.

'It is easy,' said Birna. She had not noticed her daughter sidling off. 'Grip the saddle with both hands and throw your standing leg over him like you are vaulting over a fence.'

The last time that Callum vaulted over a fence he was twelve years old and his zipped-up Harrington jacket failed to conceal a knobbly belly, pregnant with half a dozen cans of IRN-BRU that he'd liberated from the corner shop.

'I'm trying to throw my leg over but he keeps moving away from me,' Callum protested. He thought he would steady the horse by placing a hand on its nose but the animal had other ideas. It flicked its head back and gobbled his fingers in its hot, velvety mouth. Callum cleaned the slabber off his hand, wiping it in the pony's long blonde mane. The horse complained with a snort, filling the morning air with a yeasty breath that further maddened the flies.

'Do you want me to help you up?' asked Birna.

'No,' said Callum, a little abruptly. He wasn't going to be beaten. He thought about taking a run-up but he was worried that his pony might step out of the way at the last second, leaving him to fly pointlessly through the air like a footballer diving for an invisible header in a Spot-the-Ball photograph. He considered approaching the animal from the rear but realized that this would put him within striking distance of its hind legs. He had lost too many games of Buckaroo in his youth to suddenly be so foolhardy.

After several aborted attempts he managed to scramble onto the pony in a rather undignified manner, like a drunk trying to haul himself out of a swimming pool while fully clothed. His confidence was restored once he got into the saddle but it quickly evaporated when Birna informed him that his pony was blind.

'You've given me a blind pony?'

'*Já*. Our ponies are rejects from a stable in Dalland. Both your pony and my pony are blind. They are brothers: Hálfdán and Fróði. They were born with a genetic disorder so the stable could not even use them for breeding.'

'Afghan and Frothy?'

'Hálfdán and Fróði. Ásta named them after two characters in one of the sagas that I used to read to her. Hálfdán and Fróði were brothers. One was genial and gentle, while the other was a savage.'

'Let me guess. I'm riding the savage.'

'True,' laughed Birna. 'When we first got the ponies Fróði was the unco-operative one and Hálfdán was good-natured. But now they are both well behaved, though Fróði will still have a bite at people if he does not like their smell. Blind horses have sensitive noses.'

'What are you trying to say?' Callum made a show of sniffing his armpits.

Birna shook her head. She kicked her pony forward. 'Hurry now. Ásta is getting ahead of us.'

Callum flapped his reins. Nothing. He bounced in the saddle and said 'giddyup' but the pony refused to budge. He tried digging his heels into its ribs. Fróði responded by dipping his head and using his teeth to pluck a tuft of moss out of the ground. 'How do you start these things?' Callum ran his hand over the animal's neck like he was searching for the ignition.

'You ask him nicely.' Birna's breath came alive in front of her face as she spoke. There was still a chill in the air, despite the sunshine. 'Icelandic horses are very intelligent,' she explained. 'They are born of pure bloodstock. The Vikings brought them here in their boats and because they had limited room, they only brought the best of the best. Because of this, the Icelandic pony is now famous for its strength, endurance, strong will and intelligence.'

Callum smiled. He could not have found a better set of words to describe Birna herself.

'So how do I ask him to move?'

'*Komdu!*' she shouted.

Callum's pony brought him towards her.

'Ah,' he said. 'The magic word. *Komdu.*'

'It means come.'

'And what if I want him to stop?'

'You say: *stansaðu hérna, takk.*'

'You what?'

'I am joking,' said Birna. 'We have not taught him the word for stop.'

'Jesus, why not?' The ponies were now walking alongside each other but Callum had no confidence that he was in control of his beast.

'Do not panic. If you tug sharply on the reins he will stop.' Birna could see the unease in his face. 'Try to relax. Riding an Icelandic pony is much easier than riding normal horses. They are more sure-footed because of their unusual gait. Most horses have four gaits: walk, trot, canter and gallop. These ponies have a fifth.'

'Like a fifth gear?'

'I suppose so. We call it the *Tólt.* It is like a running walk and it makes for a very smooth ride. When you ride them over ice you can hear the beat of it so clearly. It is very special.'

'How long has Ásta been riding?' Callum was aware that Birna's daughter was becoming a dot on the horizon and he was worried for her safety, not least because he found it impossible to gauge the distance between his own horse and hers. Iceland's open countryside was such that Callum could never decide whether the horizon was two miles or twenty miles away.

'Do not worry about Ásta.' Birna had detected his concern for her daughter and seemed pleased by it. 'She has been riding since she was six. That is when her hands became strong enough. I used to sit her between my legs and she would grip onto the front of the saddle.'

'Is her horse blind too?'

'*Nei*. Ásta's pony was rejected because he is too small. Snær suffers from stunted growth, so they let him go. The stables judge all the young foals to determine their future prowess. They check for bearing and pace, they examine the position of their heads and the way they carry themselves. Snær failed in all areas.'

'From the look of him, I'm guessing that Snær is named after another character in the Sagas . . . a dwarf or a cripple?'

Birna laughed. 'You will have to start your Icelandic lessons very soon. Snær means snow. Ásta named him Snær because of his white coat. In winter, when he is standing outside our house, it is difficult to tell where the snow ends and the pony begins.'

'I'm finding it hard to get used to all these weird names,' said Callum.

'You will have to get used to Icelandic names if we have a child.'

'No chance. If we have a kid it will get a good

old-fashioned Scottish name, a name with very few letters in it and none of those funny runic symbols. A good Glaswegian name like Tam, Rab or Ally . . . short, to the point, no fucking about.'

'Those names may not be possible. You may have no choice but to give our son or daughter an Icelandic name. It will be up to Mannanafnanefnd.'

'Bless you!' said Callum, like she had sneezed.

Birna moved her pony to within kicking distance of him. 'Mannanafnanefnd is the Committee for Icelandic Names,' she explained.

'Why do you need a committee for names? And why do you listen to them, when they named themselves after an involuntary nasal reflex?'

Birna ignored the jibe. 'It is all part of preserving our language. The committee has authority over which names are legal first names in Iceland. If you and I have a child we must choose a name of Icelandic origin or one that conforms to Icelandic grammar. The committee validates a certain number of new names each year. For example, this year they approved Engilbjört, Marela, Ástvar and Dísella.'

'They approved Engilbjört? Jesus. Poor kid. Makes you wonder what names they rejected.'

'Damon,' said Birna.

'Damon?'

'After Damon Albarn. It is a joke we have in Reykjavík that ever since the Blur singer made a home in the city and discovered Icelandic women, there are now lots of little Damons running around. But the committee have not approved the name, so this is not possible. I guess that if he did misbehave himself, the women that he loved and left could console themselves that in Iceland, the father's Christian name forms their child's surname. But as yet there are no Damonssons or Damonsdóttirs at Ásta's school.'

Callum's attention returned to Birna's daughter. They were gaining on her but she was still small enough to fit between his finger and thumb when he pinched them in front of his eye.

'Where did you get the name Ásta?' he asked.

'It means love.'

'Ásta Birnasdóttir . . . it has a nice rhythm to it.'

'Ásta Arnarsdóttir,' corrected Birna. She could feel Callum glaring at her but she did not return his gaze.

'You named her after Arnar? But he died before she was born.'

'I know he died.' Birna seemed irritated. 'We have already been through this. Arnar may have died, he may have been a loser when he was alive, but he was still Ásta's father. I thought it was important that she took his name.'

Callum felt foolish for questioning her, but if ever there was something to stop him becoming a father to Ásta it was her name. He could work on their relationship, he might one day win her confidence, but she would always carry that name: Arnarsdóttir. It was a name that said: *This girl belongs to Arnar.*

'Sorry,' he apologized. 'You're right. It's none of my business. It was just a surprise, that's all.'

Birna mellowed. 'It is OK. You feel excluded. I understand.' She reached across and rubbed his shoulder. 'Hey, think about it, if you and I have a child it will take your name. He will be a Callumsson.'

'You think we're going to have a boy?'

Birna smiled and nodded with surprising conviction. 'My mother saw it in my aura.'

Here we go again, thought Callum. 'She can really see auras?'

'My mother can see lots of things that other people cannot see.'

'Like those Magic Eye pictures?'

111

'You may laugh but you are not so far from the truth. Reading auras is a similar process to reading those pictures. You just have to change the way you look at things. If that thing happens to be a person, you must focus on the energy around them.'

'Can you do it?'

'No. I was not blessed with my mother's gifts. But I think they may have skipped a generation. Ásta is showing signs.'

'Christ, you make her sound like she's some child of Satan.'

Birna laughed. 'Her father was never *that* bad.'

Callum forced a smile but he was uncomfortable with the way the conversation was going, not least because Birna's mother had already tuned into the energy around him and she hadn't liked what she had seen. 'Promise me one thing if we do have a boy,' he said.

'What?'

'Promise me that we won't call him Snær.'

'Snær Callumsson,' giggled Birna. 'The Abominable Snowman.'

Callum noticed that the snow was still clinging to the uppermost reaches of the mountains. This was hard to comprehend with the sun so hot in his face. The strong light had brought out the many colours and textures in the earth and rocks around them. It was as if a giant box of coloured pastels had been trodden on to create the landscape.

The two of them eventually drew level with Ásta. She slowed her horse to a canter but Birna and Callum slowed too, positioning themselves on either side of her like mounted escorts.

'How is my star?' asked Birna.

Ásta shrugged. At least, Callum interpreted it as a shrug. Perhaps it was just a roll of her shoulders as she shortened her reins in an attempt to pull away from them again.

'Ásta, shall we tell Callum about your collection?' Birna said this like they had rehearsed the question and she was willing her daughter to remember the next line.

But Ásta had forgotten the script. And she didn't respond to her mother's nods of encouragement. She remained tight-lipped and bowed her head so that her sharp black bob hid her face.

'What do you collect?' asked Callum. He guessed that this was what you had to do with kids; you had to pretend to be interested in everything they were interested in. Why else was he riding a blind pony across a stretch of land so scarred and blighted by open chasms that it had already swallowed half a lake? One hoof out of place and Callum and his mount would be starring in their own re-enactment of *Journey to the Centre of the Earth*.

Birna did not allow her daughter to ignore his question. She answered it for her. 'Ásta collects weather.'

'Weather?' asked Callum. He had intended his voice to be filled with childlike wonder but it came out like he thought Ásta was nuts. Callum had never heard of anyone collecting weather before. He did not need to feign an interest in Ásta's hobby. He was genuinely intrigued. 'How do you collect weather?'

'Ásta collects weather in her grandmother's jam jars,' answered Birna. 'Rain, snow, hail, all kinds of weather. When she collects wind, she catches a leaf as it is blown through the air and she seals it in the jar. One time, she trapped a tuft of wool that the wind had freed from a barbed-wire fence. And she has even collected thunder. Ásta, tell Callum how you collect thunder.'

113

Silence.

'She records it on a tape and puts the cassette in a jar,' said Birna. 'I am sure that Ásta will show you her collection when we get home. It is well organized. Each jar is labelled with the date, the type of weather it contains and the name of the person whose birthday it is. Ásta only collects the weather on family birthdays. Don't you?'

The girl responded with a nod. Callum was sure it was a nod. It was definitely a more pronounced movement of the head than the repetitive loll induced by her pony's lazy gait.

Birna saw this as a breakthrough. 'Tell Callum the type of weather you collected on your last birthday.'

'Sunshine,' said Ásta, in a tone that robbed the word of its light.

'Sunshine?' asked Callum, restoring its luminescence. 'Wow, that's amazing!' He pointed to the blazing orb in the blue sky above them. 'How did a little girl like you cram that big sun up there into a wee jam jar?'

'I took a photograph of it ... stupid,' she tersely replied. 'And stop talking to me like I am a kid.'

Birna's face hardened. 'Apologize to Callum,' she barked.

'No need,' he said. 'Really.' He held up a placating hand.

Ásta chased her pony forward, putting a little distance between them again.

'Ásta!' yelled Birna.

But her daughter had quickened her pace. She lifted her bottom out of the saddle and forced her white pony to the edge of the receding lake, sloshing him through the water. They followed the wide curve of the lake bed and disappeared behind a rockfall that intruded upon it.

'I should go after her,' said Birna.

'Uch . . . leave her,' said Callum. 'If she's not in the mood to talk, then we can't force her.'

'She never used to be so moody. She was always such an easy-going child.' Birna scrunched her eyes as she faced up to the sun. 'Sometimes I think that having an eleven-year-old daughter is like holding a hand grenade with the pin half out. At any moment she might explode.'

'She's just sulking. She didn't want to come out with us and she's letting us know about it. God knows I used to be a terrible sulk when I was her age. Am I right in saying that it's normally just the two of you who go riding?'

'*Já.*'

'Well, that's it then. I'm spoiling the experience for her. She normally has you all to herself and now she has to share you with me. So she's sulking . . . seeking your attention.'

'I still think I should go after her.'

'You can't,' urged Callum. 'That's what she expects. If you go chasing after, she's won. You just have to let her get on with it.'

Birna gazed anxiously at the empty horizon. 'I am not so sure. This is a difficult time for her, Callum. By moving you into our home I am asking her to make a big adjustment. I should have prepared her better for your arrival. I did not give her a say in the matter. I really think I should go and talk to her, mother to daughter.'

'No, Birna. She's got to learn that running off is not the answer. My parents never gave in to emotional blackmail, not even when I threatened to hold my breath for ever unless they let me stay up to watch *Match of the Day*.'

Birna stopped her pony. 'That is so cute.'

'I was far from cute.' Callum tugged his reins and, to his amazement, Fróði came to a halt.

'You were a difficult child?'

'Not difficult,' said Callum. 'Stubborn.'

'My mother says I was the same.'

'Impossible. Nobody was as stubborn as me. When I was a kid, you couldn't make me do anything that I didn't want to do. At mealtimes in our house, if you didn't finish everything on your dinner plate, you weren't allowed to leave the table. I would do as I was told and clear my plate but days later my mother would find Brussels sprouts in my pockets or bits of chewed-up meat in the turn-ups of my trousers.'

Birna's smile broadened. She looked at Callum like she'd found a secret compartment hidden inside him, a compartment that contained something old and precious and rarely seen. 'You see, this is what I was telling you. It is good that we do not know everything about each other. Our relationship will always be full of surprises, just like your trouser pockets.'

'I can assure you that there are no vegetables in my pockets, though if you stick your hand in deep enough you may find some of your mother's smoked guillemot.'

'You are cruel to my mother. I am sure you will get used to her cooki—' Birna's voice faltered. Something beyond Callum had got her attention. She thrust out an arm and pointed. 'It is Snær!'

The white pony was galloping towards them with the unstoppable confidence of a Grand National racehorse that has unseated its rider.

'Ásta?' shouted Birna. 'Something's happened to her. *Komdu!*' Birna's pony obeyed the command and shot off from a standing start.

'Wait,' shouted Callum, but Birna was already out of earshot. 'Right, Fróði . . . it's just you and me now. Don't let me down. *Komdu!*'

The pony stayed rooted to the spot.

'Jesus, are you deaf as well as blind?' Callum tried again – 'Komdu!' – but the animal wouldn't budge. Perhaps he hadn't got the accent right. Perhaps his pronunciation of 'komdu' meant something completely different to 'come'. He could have been saying 'coat' or 'spanner' and been none the wiser. Desperate times called for desperate measures. He removed a pen from his jacket pocket and jabbed the nib into Fróði's behind. The pony bolted forward like its trap had been flung open.

Callum chased Birna into the lake. It was the only way around the rockfall that blocked their way. He hung on for dear life as Fróði thrashed through the water before emerging again onto dry land. The area behind the rockfall revealed itself as another sweeping stretch of cracked mudflat dappled black by volcanic ash and strewn with untidy boulders.

Lying in the middle of this wasteland was a little girl, all balled up and motionless like the stones around her. A set of deep tyre tracks had made their recent impression in the mud, swerving like sidewinders round Ásta's body before ribboning off into the distance. The tracks led Callum's eyes to a green Jeep that was ascending a grassy bank on the far side of the lake. Before he could locate his pony's supposed fifth gear and chase after it, the Jeep had found the dirt road. The sunlight bounced off its windows as it disappeared between the surrounding mountains.

'Off-roaders,' shouted Birna. 'They must have spooked Snær.' In one fluid movement she pulled up her horse and dismounted. She ran to her daughter and fell to her knees. 'Ásta, it is me. Speak to your mother.' Birna stroked her daughter's hair and immediately recoiled. She held her hand to the sun. It glistened with blood.

'Jesus,' said Callum. He knelt down beside Ásta and used his fingers to create small partings in her sticky black hair.

'What are you doing?' Birna sounded angry.

'I'm trying to locate the wound. Before we attempt to move her, we need to establish how badly she's hurt.'

'Get your hands off my daughter,' shouted Birna. She pushed Callum, not too hard, but with enough force to upset his equilibrium and tip him onto his back. 'This is your fault,' she screamed. 'You should have let me go after her. This is all your fault.'

9

Darkness was descending as surely as the rain by the time I surfaced into the square at Malostranská. The tube train had transported me under the Vltava, a river that now sounded like the sea. Above me, torrents of water spewed from the mouths of gargoyles that tried vainly to jump clear of the brimming gutters on a cathedral roof. Traders removed their racks and rails from the streets while their customers fought over raincoats. In a restaurant set low on the water by the foot of Charles Bridge, carpets were being pulled up, furniture lifted and electrical fittings removed. The flagstones simmered and spat.

A knot of locals had gathered round a newspaper kiosk, everyone craning their necks and arching up on their toes to gain a better view of the vendor's miniature television set. The broadcast featured a man wrestling a deer. Was this prime-time entertainment in Prague? A girl standing beside me sensed my confusion and explained in student English that her city was bracing itself for a flood. They had already begun sedating the most agitated animals in the zoo. I watched some more of the newscast. Sure enough, the zookeepers moved among the distressed creatures with the determination of Noah.

A woman rushed past me pushing a pram full of sandbags.

A helicopter patrolled overhead, presumably monitoring the river level. I thought it prudent to head for the hills. I would not be sipping my Pilsner on a weir-side terrace tonight.

A little panic, a touch of mayhem; events were conspiring very nicely. Not that I could have orchestrated a flood. I'm not God. The only thing I have in common with The Big Puppet Master in the Sky is the power to take life. And that is what I was in Prague to do.

'Writing your memoirs?' asked Frikki. He was standing at Callum's shoulder, gazing at the document on his boss's laptop.

Callum diminished the window. 'Oh . . . no. I'm . . . eh . . . just reading over a brief that's come in from a production company in London.' Callum swivelled in his chair, putting himself between Frikki and the screen. 'They're enquiring about locations for a car ad. They've got a script for the Renault Scenic that calls for waterfalls, geysers and a grand finale where two of the vehicles dance on a glacier. I've invited their director over for a recce.'

'Cool. Our first shoot.' Frikki handed Callum a take-away coffee.

'It's not in the bag yet,' cautioned Callum. 'We need to do a real number on this guy, leave him in no doubt that Iceland's the place to film.'

'If it helps, I could give him a private dance,' said Anna Björk. She was sitting on the other side of the office with an open paper on her lap. Her feet would have been on the desk had the desks been delivered. A mix-up in dates meant that the majority of the furniture would not arrive until the following week. As a consequence, the office retained a spartan air. Fire and Ice Locations wasn't the dynamic, cre-ative environment that Callum had envisaged. Spit and Sawdust Locations would have been more appropriate.

Anna Björk had at least made an attempt to spruce the place up by re-homing half a dozen pot plants that had previously lived a life starved of light in her basement apartment. And Frikki had donated a sofa bed to flesh out the general scheme, though his philanthropic gesture was somewhat undermined by his asking Callum if he could spend a few nights kipping at the office until he found himself an affordable flat.

'And when do I get my private dance?' Frikki handed Anna Björk her herbal tea. 'I have been saving up a pocketful of coins to drop into your G-string.'

'I don't dance for loose change,' said Anna Björk. 'This body's top dollar. You couldn't afford it.'

'I could always swipe my credit card down the crack of your ass,' offered Frikki.

Anna Björk wasn't amused. She returned to her paper.

'What's news, AB?' asked Callum. He was enjoying this, being in a working office again, engaging in the banter. It provided welcome relief from the strained atmosphere at home. Twenty-four hours had passed since Ásta's accident and in that time, Birna had said barely twenty-four words to him. That was if he excluded her unstoppable rant in Icelandic on their drive back from the lake. Sigríður might have been able to treat Ásta's head wound, but she had no grass medicine to relieve Birna's anger.

'Let me see.' Anna Björk set her tea at her feet to let it stew. She scanned back through the newspaper. 'What is going on in this oh-so-exciting country of ours?' She sounded bored. '*MILK IN BOTTLES*,' she announced, translating a headline. '*Reykjavík dairy, Mjólkursamsala, plans to sell bottled milk at the end of May. It has been 36 years since milk was last available in bottles. Marketing manager Baldur Sigurjónsson commented: "This is great news for people who like their milk in bottles."* ' Whoa, tell it like it is, Baldur. What else ...' Her eyes darted around the page before coming to rest on another headline. *'COW AHOY. Fisherman Sturla Jónasson was surprised to see a dead cow float by his boat as he sailed off the coast of Patreksfjördur. The cow had all fours in the air and rocked gently in the waves as if it was sunning itself.'* Anna Björk smashed the pages together and reopened them. *'SOLAR COLA. Coffin-maker Kristinn Kristmundsson of Egilsstadir has constructed a solar-powered soda dispenser in the middle of open countryside. According to Kristinn, hikers think it is a toilet and are surprised to be able to buy a Coke.'* She threw the paper to the ground. 'God this place sucks. I should move to England where all the thrilling stuff happens, like royal weddings and sex scandals and great train robberies.'

'And great train crashes and road-rage killings and child abductions and institutionalized racism and self-aggrandizing politicians ignoring the will of their people and starting wars. Yes, all the thrilling stuff happens in England,' said Callum. 'Morris dancing, cheese rolling, I could go on.'

'You do not like England?' asked Anna Björk.

'I'm a Scot,' asserted Callum. 'Haven't you seen *Braveheart?*'

'No. But England has got to be better than this place. It is so boring here. I spend my life waiting for roses to sprout from the lava.'

'Then go and live in England if you are so unhappy,' said Frikki. He picked up the ruffled newspaper and smoothed it out on his knees. 'Iceland is a great country. There is always excitement. You just have to look for it.' He thumbed through the inky pages, determined to prove his point. 'You see, listen to this. '*GATOR AID. A fish-processing company in Husavík is hoping to import alligators. The giant reptiles will serve as the town's waste disposal, eating up the fish remnants and meat offal ejected by the factory.*' He threw Anna Björk an I-told-you-so look. 'I bet that they do not have such alligators in England.'

Anna Björk was busy prodding her tea bag with her middle finger. She raised the wet digit and held it in Frikki's face (a piscine face, still flushed from his coffee run).

The big man paid little heed. He had found another story. 'Here is news that an Icelandic tour company have purchased llamas from South America to be used as pack animals on excursions. *Llamas*,' he stressed, like they were unicorns. 'You see, Iceland is not just exciting, it is exotic.'

'You will not be saying that when the alligators eat the llamas,' said Anna Björk.

'Children, please.' Callum raised a moderating hand. 'This is only week one of our wonderful new adventure. Let's try and get along.' He motioned them over to his laptop. 'Come, I want you to see something.'

Callum typed the company name into a Google search engine and a link to his new website, created by the guys at Strawdonkey, was proudly displayed as the top result. His delight was short-lived, however, and he immediately regretted asking Young Kenny to choose the URL for Fire and Ice Locations. Either Kenny had little confidence in Callum's new venture or he was having a laugh at his old boss's expense, for he had boiled the company name down to its initials to create the unfortunate web address *www.fail.is*.

'Here we go,' said Callum, hurriedly activating the link and calling up the home page. '*Welcome to Fire* and Ice Locations in Iceland, a world of green, blue, water, fire, ice, snow and light,' he said, reading the introductory paragraph that had been laid out over a dramatic shot of Eldhraun, one of the world's largest lava flows: bright green moss clinging to dark volcanic rock to create a landscape of chewed-up chocolate limes. Birna had taken this photograph with the digital Nikon that accompanied her on research trips. She had contributed all the location shots on the site and Callum brought them up in turn, guiding Anna Björk and Frikki past endless horizons, surging glaciers, rhyolite mountains, daunting fjords, conical volcanoes and heaving seas that dealt their white waves onto black and scarlet beaches. His favourite picture was one that Birna had taken of a frozen waterfall that stood petrified for all time like some long-burned church candle.

Callum turned to Anna Björk. 'Look at these shots and tell me you still want to live in England.'

She did her best to look unimpressed.

'This is my point,' he continued. 'Iceland can be England. Your country can be Greenland, Africa, Mars. It can be whatever you want it to be. That's why foreign film crews are falling over themselves to come here.' He felt a rush of excitement like helium bubbles in his blood. Haemogoblins, thought Callum. It was a pure feeling, one that he had not experienced in some time. With every new scene that filled the screen, he was opening up a world of possibilities.

'And they won't just come for the locations, they'll come for the subarctic light,' he continued. 'Even in winter when the sun hangs low on the horizon, it casts long shadows that can transform the most mundane shot for a fridge commercial into high drama.'

'But the light is only good in fine weather,' said Frikki. 'And we can never rely on fine weather.

Iceland does not get real weather, just samples.'

'You're right,' said Callum. 'We can't rely on the weather but we can be prepared for it. This will be a big part of the Fire and Ice offering. I asked my colleagues in Glasgow to embed a link to the Icelandic Meteorological Office on our site.' With a couple of clicks, Callum opened up the Met Office home page. 'In any given day, at any one location, we may experience up to five different weather systems. We've got to be able to check the weather all the time, to stay at least two hours ahead of any incoming front.'

'I would not rely on the Icelandic Meteorological Office,' said Anna Björk. 'They are always getting it wrong. If they say it will be a fine weekend to go camping, you would do better to lock yourself in your storm shelter with a week's supply of tinned food.'

'For once I agree with the stripper,' admitted Frikki, asking for and receiving a thump on the back. He smiled, glad that he'd rattled her. 'I remember when I was six and they warned us about a hurricane coming towards us from the North American coast. They said it would rip our wooden houses apart and people were told to write their name, age and next of kin on their arms with a waterproof marker, so they could identify the dead. Of course, the storm never arrived. If I remember, the wind was not even strong enough to support my kite.'

'Unfortunately the Met Office reports are all we have to go on,' said Callum. 'We shall just have to advise our clients to take out weather insurance. And when we're on location, we must encourage them to be patient. Imagine that we're filming on an isolated stretch of the east coast where the weather is more volatile, and imagine that we're shooting a storyboard in sequence. We could be picking up a scene that has been filmed with no snow in it and then a blizzard could take hold. In Reykjavík we'd be able to clear the snow off houses in a matter of hours but out on the coast it would be impossible. How could we clear it off the mountains? Answer: we couldn't. We would have to wait for a thaw. In really remote locations an entire crew and cast can become stranded for weeks by the weather. So patience is paramount.' Callum patted Frikki's shoulder. 'But I'm sure this won't be a problem for you, big man. You'll discover that filming is a lot like fishing . . . long periods of time just waiting around. If we are patient, we will get the right shots for our clients.'

'And how are we going to get the right shots for this Renault commercial?' asked Frikki.

'What do you mean?'

'Well, you said that the script called for glaciers. How are we going to recce glaciers when we do not have a vehicle capable of driving over them?'

Callum smiled. 'I thought you'd never ask.'

'This, my friends, is our pride and joy: the Toyota Tundra V8 Double Cab. She can handle any terrain in any weather. What is more, you are looking at the only one of her kind in Europe. The manufacturer will not be launching this model until the fall and it will only be available in the US. Helgason Automotive is lucky to have her. Toyota road-test all their new ATVs in Iceland and then they sell the vehicles to us as it is more cost-effective than shipping them back.'

Callum and Frikki were standing on the forecourt of one of the many auto retailers that lined a busy highway. A cadaverous salesman with baby teeth was giving them a guided tour of an immaculate 4x4 in 'pearlescent salsa red', though Callum was paying more attention to the giant beer bottles that fronted the Egils brewery on the other side of the busy road.

It wasn't that he was uninterested in the sales patter; he was terrified of it. Callum had never been big into cars let alone all-terrain vehicles, and he was scared that the salesman would find him out. He was about to spend a serious amount of money on one of these gleaming monstrosities, yet he was sure that his inability to get excited by chrome-bumper inserts and 60/40 split/fold/tumble rear seats would mark him out as something less than a man. His apathy towards all things automotive, a legendary ineptitude at DIY and a long history of being 'last one picked' at team sports meant that Callum wasn't your typical man's man. He didn't buy into all that yard-of-ale-downed-in-one-through-a-dirty-jock-strap male posturing. Not that he was a Moscow-Mule-sipped-through-a-curly-straw sort of guy, either.

But even to Callum's uneducated eye, the Toyota Tundra looked impressive. The double cab at the front of the vehicle could seat five people. This appealed to him as it would more than accommodate Birna, Ásta and himself should they ever get round to doing all that 'family stuff' that he and Birna had talked about (should she ever start speaking to him again). And like a traditional pickup, the 4x4 had an exposed flatbed at the rear that was large enough to carry lighting gear, camera equipment or Birna's mother, depending on whether the drive was business or pleasure.

Callum was happy to take a back seat and let his production assistant check the rest of the spec.

'How good is the traction?' asked Frikki. 'We may need to take her up onto the glaciers.'

A smile opened up on the salesman's sallow face like a crack in an ice floe. 'The Toyota Tundra eats glaciers for breakfast. Let me explain. The problem with driving on compacted ice is the excess ground pressure. And how do we measure this? We take the all-up weight of the vehicle divided by the area of the tyre's contact patch, times the number of tyres. Are you with me?'

'Já,' said Frikki.

Callum nodded, not looking at the salesman but marvelling instead at the branded flags above his head – Land Rover, Suzuki, Toyota, Jeep – as they pole-danced in the sleazy breeze. He realized that the Jeep that had charged at Ásta could well have been bought at this garage. Maybe that was how vehicles were test-driven in Iceland. No pleasant tootle around town to acquaint yourself with the pedals, knobs and gears; in Iceland it's straight out to the country to carve up lake beds, perform handbrake turns on glaciers and ram little girls off their horses.

The salesman coughed, a transparent attempt to regain Callum's attention. 'The easiest way to improve traction is to increase the size of the tyre's contact patch with the ice,' he explained. 'The most obvious way to do this is to fit wider and larger tyres, and this is where you guys are blessed.' He stroked one of the Toyota's front tyres like a man with a rubber fetish. 'The Tundra has a modified suspension and customized frame to accommodate four nineteen-inch Goodrich tyres. They have a less aggressive tread pattern that gives increased contact area, so the vehicle sticks like glue to ice, snow and sand.'

Callum couldn't imagine glue sticking to ice or snow but he didn't query it.

'What about pack ice?' asked Frikki. 'We need to be able to move in extreme conditions.'

'In such conditions, you can deflate the tyres halfway,' said the salesman. 'By releasing the air pressure you are again increasing the contact area between tyre and ice. Be careful not to let too much air out or the tyre will be pulled off the rim and you may be stranded on a glacier with no garage for miles and the only food available to you will be the meat on each other's bones.' The salesman waited for the look of alarm to register on their faces before hitting them with his sucker punch. 'But relax, for you will not be found dead in the Toyota Tundra . . . its tyres are tubeless!'

He crouched down beside the front wheel on the passenger side and talked them through the physics of the tubeless tyre. 'You see, you can refit a tubeless tyre in seconds, even if you are stuck in the middle of nowhere or, worse still, if you are stuck in the middle of Iceland.' He forced a laugh but neither Frikki nor Callum joined him.

Sensing that he was losing his audience, the salesman became more animated. 'But wait . . . you must watch this. It is time for my big finale. I will show you how easy it is to refit the tyre.' He released air from the tyre and the black rubber started to melt, slowly flattening out until the Toyota lurched forward to perform a polite curtsey. The salesman disappeared into the showroom.

'What do you think?' asked Callum.

Frikki scratched his beanie hat. 'I am thinking that I could buy a fleet of fishing boats for the same price as this vehicle.'

The salesman returned, armed with a yellow canister.

'What have you got there?' asked Callum.

'Lighter fluid.' The salesman crouched down, peeled back the tyre and squirted the flammable liquid round the inside of the hub. He stood up again and, as the blood drained from his already anaemic face, he removed a box of matches from his pocket.

'Jesus, he's going to torch it.' Callum had seen this scenario played out many times before, by the joy-riding youths who ruled the wastelands behind his first flat in Glasgow.

'Stand back,' said the salesman, but Callum and Frikki had already retreated. He threw the match against the wheel rim and, with a comical *whumph*, the tyre instantly inflated itself, becoming fat and taut. 'And that's magic!' The salesman patted the bonnet, leaving dull, skeletal handprints in the red lacquer. 'The Tundra comes with traction control, an adaptor mount for your snow plough, interior heating vents and a moonroof as standard.'

'A moonroof?' queried Callum. 'Don't you mean a sunroof?'

'This is Iceland. In the summer it is a sunroof, in the winter, a moonroof.' The salesman handed Callum his card and confidently concluded the showroom spiel. 'The Tundra also comes with a satellite navigation system, which is especially handy if your vehicle happens to disappear into a glacial crevasse. The system is accurate to just a few metres so it will be able to tell you precisely where you died. Any questions?'

'Yes,' said Callum. 'Does it have one of those wee hooks for hanging up your blazer?'

They hadn't driven a mile from the garage when the traffic slowed to a near standstill. They were caught in a snarl-up where four lanes converged into two on the way into town.

'The Tundra may be able to handle snow, rocks and ice, but can she handle a traffic jam,' said Callum. He put his foot to the floor – on the brake rather than the accelerator – and brought the vehicle to a halt.

'We could cut across the park,' suggested Frikki. He indicated an area of greenery to the right of the highway. Children were playing on the lawn while their mothers lay on the grass.

'It's full of people,' said Callum.

'No problem for the Tundra,' said Frikki, mimicking the salesman's patter. 'She's all-terrain: snow, ice, flesh and bone.'

Callum didn't laugh.

'I was joking.'

'I hope so,' said Callum.

'Of course I'm joking. What do you think I am?'

'Frikki, there are guys out there who wouldn't think twice about driving over a kid.'

'What makes you say this?'

'Uch, we had a bit of an incident yesterday,' said Callum. 'Birna and I took Ásta out to the country and a joyrider knocked her off her pony.'

'Is she OK?'

'Who . . . Ásta or Birna?'

'The pony,' said Frikki. 'Joking,' he added. 'I mean Ásta.'

'She's fine. Her wrists are bruised and she's got a lump the size of a golf ball just above her left ear, but she'll pull through. It's Birna I'm worried about. She's gone off the Richter scale. She blames me because I let Ásta ride out of sight. Like I was driving the Jeep that spooked her bloody pony! So now I'm getting no end of grief about it.'

Frikki shook his head and sucked air through his teeth. 'Hell has no fury like an Icelandic woman scorned.'

'Any advice?' asked Callum.

'You want advice on women from me: the man who has just been kicked out on the street by his girlfriend because he used her Dido CD as a beer coaster?'

'Ah, so that's why you're kipping at the office.'

'It's just for a few days. You could say that I'm between apartments.'

'And are you "between relationships" too?' Callum made the quotation marks with his fingers.

'I am in no hurry to jump into bed with another woman, if that's what you mean. It would only lead to a whole world of pain.'

'You think Icelandic women are difficult?'

'I think all women are difficult,' said Frikki. 'But I can understand why Birna is angry. It sounds like some asshole could have killed her kid. I may have traditional views on women, but I have traditional views on family too. If a guy ran his Jeep over my kid, I would kill the bastard. No hesitation. It is the one situation where I know I could kill someone.' Frikki blew his blonde fringe out of his eyes and stared at the solid red glow of the brake lights on the cars in front. He turned to Callum. 'Do you think you could kill someone?'

'Yes,' said Callum. Defiant. Unswerving. Unerring.

'You seem pretty sure.'

'Oh I'm sure,' said Callum, and rain started to spot on the windscreen, just as it had done on the windows of his police cell one wet night in Prague.

10

'Let us start with the basics,' said Sigriður. 'The Icelandic alphabet has thirty-two letters. It is the only language that still uses runic symbols. For example there is *eth*, which is written as a *d* in Roman script but has a stroke placed through the stem.' Sigriður pulled Callum's unmarked A5 notepad over to her side of the kitchen table. She drew the symbol *ð* onto the blank page in soft, dark pencil. 'This is pronounced as a hard *th* sound, as in *that*. It is not to be confused with the symbol *thorn* which is written like an extended *p* and is also pronounced with a *th* sound, only it is a softer, more elongated *th*, as in the word *thing*.' Sigriður drew the symbol *Þ* onto the pad. 'Callum, you look at me like I am a madwoman.'

'I'm sorry, it's just I now realize that there are three things that are impossible to do in Iceland.'

'And what are these things?'

'It's impossible to climb a tree, be a vegetarian or learn Icelandic.'

'Hmm. I see. What is it that you find most difficult about our language?'

Callum thought about it for a moment. His gaze fell into the deep-throated glass of red wine in his hand and the answer came to him. 'Asking someone to speak Icelandic is like asking them to mimic this

133

sound . . .' He flicked the rim of the glass with his finger and let the *ping* resonate. 'It's like asking them to pronounce this . . .' He removed a match from a box on the table and struck it, making it rasp and flare. 'Icelandic weaves braids in my vocal cords. Each sentence reads like a long line of high-scoring Scrabble racks.'

'*Já,*' said Sigriður, sucking the word into her lungs. 'I agree that it is a difficult language. There is even a poem which tells us how difficult it is.' Sigriður raised her chair off the floor, just a fraction, before slamming it back on the tiles. '*You must sit down to speak this language,*' she said, her voice loaded with portent. She was staring hard at Callum. '*It is so heavy you cannot be polite or chatter in it / For once you have begun a sentence the whole course of your life is laid out before you / Every foolish mistake is clear, every failure, every grief.*' Sigriður held his gaze before relaxing back into her chair. 'You are not alone in finding our language difficult.'

Callum was a bit spooked by his wild-eyed tutor. Before they had begun, Sigriður had switched all the kitchen lights off and filled the room with lit candles to set the scene for her lesson. How this was supposed to help him assimilate Icelandic, Callum would never know. As it was, he felt like he was attending a séance and Sigriður was putting him in touch with a dead language.

'Do you read a lot of poetry?' asked Callum. He was employing the same tactic that he had used on her granddaughter the previous afternoon, feigning an interest in her interests in order to ingratiate himself.

'Poetry, novels, plays, sagas,' said Sigriður. 'I read them all. Snorri Sturluson is my favourite poet. He was an amazing man. He maintained a herd of 120 cattle in order to produce the calves on whose skin he wrote *Egil's Saga*. The sagas have given us Icelanders a great appetite for literature. We have a saying: it is better to go barefoot than to go without books.'

'You must be proud of your daughter, then.'

'Yes, because it is not only scholars who enjoy Birna's books. She writes about our landscape in a way that brings it alive for everyone. It is a talent that she gets from her father. Svein was a great storyteller. It was a shame that he never wrote anything down.' A wistful look came over Sigriður. The candle flame retreated in her dark irises before disappearing entirely, like a burning match that is dropped into a deep well. She caught hold of herself. 'But Iceland is full of storytellers. We have more writers per head than in any country on earth.'

'God,' said Callum. 'I think I can only name two Icelandic writers and one of them is Magnús Magnússon. Actually, I'll take Magnús back. I want to claim him as a Scot.'

'*Rófur!*' said Sigriður.

'Sorry?'

'*Rófur!* It means turnips. You Scottish eat lots of turnips. You call them neeps.'

'Haggis, neeps and tatties,' said Callum. 'I'm impressed.'

'You see, you do not need to travel to other countries to learn about their cultures. I have lived all my life in a place so isolated that it is regularly left off the maps of Europe but I still know an awful lot about an awful lot. You can get all the knowledge you need from books.'

'Not true. Take it from me: Iceland has to be visited to be understood.' Callum clinked his glass against hers.

'Haggis,' said Sigriður. 'Now that is an interesting dish. And to think you criticized my cooking.'

'When did I criticize your cooking?'

'You ate none of the *slátur* that I made for you tonight.'

'Only when you told me it was guts, blood and fat sewn into a lamb's stomach.'

'And what is haggis if it is not guts, blood and fat?'

'I don't eat haggis.'

'Ah,' said Sigriður, like it all made sense.

'Besides,' said Callum. 'Even if I did eat haggis, I wouldn't eat *slátur*. That's one Icelandic word I do know the meaning of. Back in the UK, families sit down to cosy dishes with pretty little names like "cottage pie" and "Angel Delight". Not in Iceland. In Iceland you tuck into a dish called "slaughter". That, in a nutshell, or on a dinner table, is the difference between your country and mine.'

'This is good, Callum. You do know some Icelandic. This is definitely a good start.'

Callum couldn't share in her enthusiasm. He wasn't going to get very far in Reykjavík if the only two words he knew were 'turnips' and 'slaughter'. And 'Snær'. He knew that *snær* meant snow. 'Turnips', 'slaughter' and 'snow'. It was nearly enough to form his first Icelandic sentence, though he could not begin to imagine what that sentence would be or what sort of occasion would beg its use.

'Birna said that you have a committee to decide Icelandic names.' Nice one, Callum, he thought. Sound interested. Teacher will give you a big gold star. And teacher's daughter might want to sleep with you again.

'*Já*, Birna is right. We have a committee to protect not only our names, but also our language. We do not permit words from other languages to enter our vocabulary, so when a new innovation comes along, like the computer, the committee will hold a national

136

competition to create a new Icelandic word for it.'

'So what's the word for a computer?'

'*Tölva*. It is a combination of *tala*, meaning number, and *völva*, which is our word for a prophetess. So a computer is literally a number prophetess.'

'We have one of those in the UK. She's called Carol Vorderman.'

The joke was lost on Sigríður. She might have read a lot of books but she did not watch a lot of British daytime television.

'What's the word for television?' asked Callum, filling the void.

'*Sjónvarp*, which literally means throwing out pictures. Here, give me your notepad and I shall write down some words for you to learn. You will find that Icelandic words are easier to remember when you know how they are made.' Sigríður lifted the pencil and scrawled as she spoke. 'Compact disc is *geisladiskar* which combines our words for ray and disc. A satellite is a *gervitungl*, an amalgam of artificial and moon. A helicopter is a *þyrla* which means whirler. And my favourite is our word for a pager, which is *friðþjófur*. It literally means thief of the peace.'

'Wait, I've remembered one,' said Callum with an enthusiasm that surprised not just Sigríður but himself. 'At least, I can't remember the exact Icelandic, but I know that your word for a whale-beaching is the same as your word for a windfall.'

'*Hvalreki!* You see. You are already picking it up. There is no need to be afraid of our language. Not when you have the best teacher in Iceland.' Sigríður winked at Callum and refilled his glass. 'Tell me. Do you speak any other languages?'

'No. Just English.'

'That is unfortunate. We say that a person who

speaks two languages is bilingual, but a person who speaks only one is English. No offence.'

'None taken. I'm Scottish,' said Callum. 'But I'm impressed that everyone in Reykjavík speaks fluent English. You put Glaswegians to shame.'

'Do not be ashamed,' said Sigriður. 'Icelanders like to impress by speaking English at home, but as soon as they go abroad they will revert to their native tongue.'

'How come?'

'Because they can be as insulting as they wish without giving offence.'

Callum might have found this funny had Birna not only yesterday subjected him to a torrent of ill-tempered Icelandic on their urgent drive back from the riding expedition. He hadn't understood a word of it, but he had guessed that she was threatening to prosecute him for manslaughter should her daughter's injury have proved fatal.

'It is a shame that you do not know any Norwegian or Danish words,' said Sigriður. 'It would make it much easier if you did. Many of their pronunciations are similar to Icelandic. Birna has an uncle in Copenhagen who is always confusing his languages and mixing his *danska* with his *íslenska*. Birna calls him an *ísdanski*.'

'He's an ice-dancer?'

'Helgi? An ice-dancer?' Sigriður clapped her hands together and laughed like Callum had never seen her laugh before. 'Now I have heard it all. Helgi the Ice-dancer! Please! I have seen sheep with better feet!'

The door opened. 'You two seem to be getting along,' said Birna. She wafted past Callum without looking at him and made her way to the fridge. Her words were as curt as her expression.

'Would you like to join us for a glass of wine?' asked Callum.

'*Nei.*' Birna opened the fridge door, throwing cold light onto a face so sour that it appeared to have curdled. 'I am getting Ásta some milk and I will read her a story. Then I shall go to bed, too.'

Callum wasn't sure what to say. He cast an imploring glance towards Sigriður but she had abdicated herself from the situation by doodling on the open notepad, sketching a small box with a pointed roof and a cross on top: a church. It seemed that not even God could save Callum from Birna's obvious wrath.

'How is she?' he ventured.

'Like you care.'

'Of course I care.'

'Too late, Callum. If you had shown the same concern for my daughter yesterday afternoon, she would not be lying in bed with a split head.'

'Let us just be thankful that her injuries were not too severe,' said Sigriður. 'She is not concussed and she has not broken a bone. The preparation that I applied to her wound should heal it in no time.'

'She's right, Birna,' said Callum. 'It was a nasty accident. The damage could have been much worse.'

'It was no accident,' said Birna. She tipped the milk carton onto the lip of her glass.

'What do you mean?' asked Sigriður.

'Ásta says they drove at her deliberately.'

'Why would they do that?' asked Callum.

'For kicks,' said Birna. 'Who knows?'

'Do you want me to call the police?' asked Callum. 'I didn't get their registration number but I could give a pretty good description of the Jeep.'

'No point,' said Birna. 'Our police are useless. They are always turning a blind eye to the drunk drivers and joyriders who carve up our roads. Outside the city things are pretty lawless. And anyway . . .' she returned the milk carton to the fridge, slamming it hard, 'you've done enough harm already.'

'Birna . . .' pleaded Callum. 'Please don't be like that. I said I was sor—'

She brushed his hand off her dressing gown and carried the milk through to her daughter.

Callum made to get up and go after her but Sigriður motioned him back into his seat. 'Let her go,' she said. 'She just needs to simmer for a while. If you go to her now it will be like throwing water onto a pan fire.'

'I knew she could be stubborn,' said Callum. 'But Christ, she's making me suffer.'

'She is strong-willed, that is all. I told you that Birna gets creativity from her father but she also gets her strength of character from me. You must not take it personally. Icelandic women are renowned for being strong-willed and self-sufficient. These qualities go back many generations to the days when our women organized the home and managed the farm while waiting for their men to return from sea. Often our men did not return. This is the reason why you will see so many single mothers in Reykjavík.'

'Because all their men are dying at sea?'

'No! Thankfully that does not happen so much these days.'

Callum was mortified that it still happened at all.

'The reason you see so many single mothers is because there has never been a social stigma attached to it. Icelandic women have always brought up their children alone. We are used to it.'

Sigriður wasn't making Callum feel any better. She was merely confirming what he increasingly feared, that Birna and Ásta could manage perfectly well without him.

She must have seen it in his face for she placed her hand on his wrist. 'Do not look so worried. She will be fine in the morning. Birna can be difficult even at the best of times.'

Callum nodded in agreement, inspiring Sigriður to smile. She withdrew her hand and returned it to her wine glass. 'I always said that my daughter would make a great politician because she is no pushover. And Birna would not be the first female politician in this country. It is no accident that Iceland was the first nation to elect a woman as Head of State and we were the first country to put a women-only party into parliament. You see, Callum, women have always played a forceful role in our society.'

'So you're a nation of Vikings and feminists? That's a pretty potent combination. No wonder the sparks fly.'

Sigriður seemed tickled by this. 'True, the young men today retain something of the Viking. That is why so many of them are still walking away from their girl-friends and leaving them to bring up their children alone. Our parliament recently passed legislation to grant Icelandic fathers at least three months paternity leave but it was a futile exercise. A lot of our men already take a lifetime's paternity leave. So I guess that half of what you say is true. Our men may be Vikings but our women are not feminists. We have maintained our strength and independence for hundreds of years. Feminism would be a backward step for us. Why fight for equality when you already have superiority?' She winked at Callum.

'Fair point. But if women are so superior and if they often bring up the family alone, how come you still have this system of naming children after their fathers?'

'Aha,' said Sigriður, narrowing her smile. 'Birna told me that you had a problem with that. She said you reacted badly to Ásta's name. Perhaps this was the reason you were so brittle with her yesterday.'

Callum couldn't believe what he was hearing. 'I did not have a problem with Ásta's name. I was a little surprised, that's all. But I wasn't brittle.'

'Are you sure? You seem a little irritable right now.'

'That's because you're winding me up.'

'Callum, tell me, are you finding it hard to fit in?' asked Sigríður. She was talking to him like he was one of her patients.

He didn't appreciate it.

'I'm fitting in fine.'

'Are you sure? Are you sure that nothing is troubling you?'

'What is this . . . the Icelandic inquisition?'

Sigríður raised her hand and moved it in a broad arc as though she was tracing his outline. 'I can still see those dark spots in your aura. Something is sitting heavy with you.'

'Could you please take your hand off my aura,' said Callum. What else could he say? She was freaking him out. 'Is it any wonder you're seeing dark spots, there's no bloody light in here.' The skin on his back had started to prickle. He had the sweats.

Sigríður had both hands in the air now. She was mumbling something.

'This is nuts,' said Callum. 'I'm turning the lights on.'

'Sit!' barked Sigríður. 'You must not move. There is a man at your shoulder.'

'What the—?'

'Quiet, Callum.' Sigríður was looking more intently now, towards a point some distance behind him. 'No, it is not a man. It is a young woman. She was wearing a mask but now she has taken it off.'

'FUCK YOU!' yelled Callum. He made a lunge for the light switch and, in doing so, knocked his wine glass off the table.

Everything went very quiet.

Callum thought he could hear someone shovelling gravel outside the window. Then he remembered that the house sat beside the sea. Guilt washed over him like surf over shingle. Sigriður seemed smaller and older under the harsh kitchen light. She sat with a glass smashed at her feet and red wine drip, drip, dripping from the tablecloth onto the floor tiles like an unstoppable nosebleed.

Callum bent to pick up the stem of the broken wine glass.

'Leave it,' said Sigriður. 'I will clear up this mess.'

Callum straightened. 'I'm sorry. I shouldn't have—'

'Hush, now! It is not a problem,' she said. 'Nobody has died.' She was no longer focusing on the energy around him. She was looking right into his soul. 'Have they, Callum?'

11

'OK, the plan is to drive Route One, right along the south coast of the country.' Callum spread out a large waterproof map on the bonnet of the Toyota and used a finger to indicate the route to Rudi Jackson, the young director who had that morning flown in from London. 'It should take us about six or seven hours to drive the whole way from west to east. Now Rudi, if you decide you want to use any of the locations in the extreme east, say the ice lagoon, we can fly our cast and crew out to Höfn on the day of the shoot. But today we're going to drive it. That way you get to see the variety of landscapes and the proximity of locations along the coast.'

'Sounds good to me, man,' said Rudi.

'Is this your first time in Iceland?' asked Anna Björk. Callum had let his PA tag along on the recce just this once, to give her a taster of the production business.

'First time,' confirmed Rudi. 'I've shot all over the world but never this far north. I guess you could say I'm an Iceland virgin.'

'We can change that,' said Anna Björk and even though Rudi's face was as black as his bituminous coffee, the director appeared to blanch.

'How do you like Iceland?' asked Frikki.

'Give me a chance, man! I've only just stepped off

the plane.' Rudi turned to Anna Björk. 'So far I like what I see.'

'We do not have many black people in Iceland,' said Frikki. 'Or dogs.'

Alarm bells sounded in Callum's head. He dived straight in. 'I apologize, Rudi. I don't think Frikki means to equate dogs and black people.'

'We banned them because they shit on our pavements,' added Frikki.

'That's a bit harsh,' said Rudi. 'Some of us brothers are house-trained.'

Callum could already see this job slipping through his fingers. 'I'm sure Frikki means no offence. Icelanders can sometimes sound a little blunt. It's just their way.'

'Relax,' said Rudi. 'Frikki's cool by the pool.'

The four of them climbed into the Tundra. Callum had instructed Frikki to do the driving. He invited Rudi to sit up front while he and Anna Björk shared the back seat, much to her evident disappointment. Callum took her aside. 'Don't panic. I'll swap with the guy when we get to Skógafoss. Then you'll have him all to yourself until Jökulsárlón.'

'You think I want to sit with him?' asked Anna Björk.

'Oh please. You're like a love-struck schoolgirl. You've gone all hormonal since he arrived. When I first brought him into the office I thought you were going to throw your panties at him.'

'You misjudge me,' said Anna Björk, in a way that made Callum feel bad. 'I am not wearing any panties.' She held her skirt tight to her knees and brought her legs into the truck.

Callum slid in beside her. He was too tired to drive. The coffee was helping but his head was still sore from an excess of red wine and a lack of sleep. Despite this, he was grateful for the early start. It meant that he had an excuse to sneak out of the house without having to face Sigriður. Or Birna.

The two of them would be up by now, he reckoned. They'd be eating their breakfast and having a good old bitch about him. Birna would be complaining to Sigriður that Callum had more time for his work than he did for her daughter. And Sigriður would be telling Birna about his temper and his language and the broken wine glass. Would she also mention the young woman that she had seen by his shoulder? Callum hoped not. He prayed that the two women were debating nothing more sinister than the best way to cook his testicles: *shall we have them sugar-browned or doused in remoulade?*

'Tired?' asked Frikki as he pulled the Tundra onto the highway. He addressed the question to Callum in his rear-view mirror.

'A little,' Callum replied.

'You are not yet used to our bright nights. You will find it much easier to sleep in winter. That is when the Icelanders hibernate. Whatever sleep we miss in summer, we make up for it in winter during twenty hours of darkness. It all evens out.'

'Well I don't know about you guys but I feel great,' said Rudi. 'I got the head down early last night coz I knew I had to be up for the red-eye. Slept like a log.'

'In Britain you sleep like logs,' said Frikki. 'But when it is winter in Iceland, we sleep like stones.'

'Last night I slept like a baby,' said Callum. 'I woke up screaming at four in the morning and realised I'd shit myself.'

Rudi slapped the dashboard and unleashed a booming laugh.

'You think I'm joking,' said Callum, remembering

the nightmare that had shaken him from his sleep: Prague and puppets and murder.

The Tundra thundered out of Reykjavík, following the signs for Hveragerði and Selfoss.

The weather couldn't make up its mind. Sun and rain played tag across the mossy fields of stratified lava. After some time these inhospitable plains gave way to a fertile patch of green velvet studded here and there with turf-roofed houses, symbols of an older Iceland, their dusty net curtains lying still against darkened windows. They passed a Toblerone of small white farm dwellings that sat perilously close to the base of a sheer cliff, so close that if a farmer slammed his door too hard he risked his home being flattened by a coyote-crushing boulder. They sped through more farmsteads and fields full of hay bales covered in white plastic sacks. Creamy sheep watched them pass, unconcerned about anything except the taste of grass. Frikki pointed to a field in which a family was attending a lambing. It was the first human life they had seen in over an hour of driving.

They slowed as they approached a hump in the road and a sign that read: *blindhæð*. Though it had seemed likely that they could drive all day without passing another vehicle, the hump concealed the one car that was coming in the opposite direction. Frikki swerved, inspiring Callum's head to smack against the window.

'Shiiiit!' screamed Rudi. 'Man, that was close!'

'*Helvítis útlendingar!*' shouted Frikki as he fought to keep the Tundra on the road. 'Bloody foreigners! They do not know how to drive on our gravel tracks. They brake too suddenly instead of letting the vehicle slide. No wonder they are always toppling off our roads and killing themselves.'

'It is not their fault that our roads are so shitty,' said Anna Björk.

'There is nothing wrong with Iceland's roads.'

'Hah! Our Minister for Transport is also the president of the National Drag Racing Club. I think that says it all.' Anna Björk leaned forward, positioning herself between driver and passenger. 'Frikki, why must you always defend this place?'

'Because I am proud to be an Icelander. We sit on top of the world. Literally.'

'You are full of crap,' she replied. 'Literally.'

'Please . . . we have a guest.' Callum was beginning to regret bringing the pair of them along.

'Don't mind me, man.' Rudi's smile suggested that he had recovered from his near-death experience.

'But Frikki is talking crap,' protested Anna Björk. 'Iceland is dull. People only live here because they are born here.'

'Not true,' said Callum. 'I wasn't born here. I moved here by choice.'

'You did not choose to live here,' contested Anna Björk. 'You fell in love with an Icelandic woman. That is different. You had no choice in the matter. And now love has blinded you to the fact that you are living in the most boring place in the world, a small rock of 280,000 people that dares to call itself a country.'

Frikki turned up the music in an attempt to drown her out. It didn't work.

'There is so much nothing to do here,' she continued. 'If Rudi was filming a commercial for Iceland, how would he sell it? *Come to Iceland and salt some herring!*'

'Could I remind you that we are currently trying to sell Iceland to our esteemed director,' said Callum. 'He is looking for waterfalls, geysers and ice fields for a Renault commercial and, luckily for us, this "dull" little country has all those things in abundance.'

'Man, I hope so,' said Rudi. 'But after we've seen them, can I salt Anna Björk's herring?'

It was another hour before they reached their first location; an hour of Sigur Rós, Trabant, Apparat Organ Quartet, Múm, Ské and whatever else was on Frikki's *Iceland Airwaves* compilation tape. He slowed the Tundra and broached a left, turning off the main highway.

They trundled down a long gravel track towards an insubstantial cluster of buildings that comprised Skógar. Callum had brought Rudi here to show him Skógafoss, a wall of water over sixty metres in height. They parked up some distance from the waterfall but the second they opened their doors, a fine spray atomized on their faces. Callum removed a bunch of waterproofs from the back of the truck and handed them out. 'You're going to need these, Rudi. Skógafoss looks impressive from a distance but it's even better close up.'

The water fell from a high plateau and clattered into a raucous cauldron below. As they walked along the black gravel riverbank, the roar got louder and the front of their legs got wetter. High above them, hundreds of fulmars were diving from impossible nest sites. The birds wheeled through the white spray and ducked under the two rainbows that had been cast across the falls.

'You lot stay here,' directed Callum. 'I'll go right up to it to give you an idea of the scale. Imagine how great the car will look when set against such a dramatic backdrop.'

Callum ran past a group of schoolchildren: a dozen wet, woolly bobbles bobbing on a dozen wet, woolly hats. The roar of the falls filled his ears. Skógafoss fell straight and true, like wet hair run through with a comb. The spray drenched his waterproofs, running in streams across his cheeks as he got closer to the loud wall of white. To his colleagues further downstream, Callum had become little more than a dark asterisk at the foot of a blank page.

'It's almost perfect,' said Rudi, when he had dried himself off.

They were sitting at a picnic table drinking what little coffee remained in Callum's flask. Frikki had opened an icebox and he now offered out cartons of *skýr*. Rudi and Anna Björk tucked in, but Callum declined the curd-like concoction, having learnt from very bitter experience that it tasted like tile grout.

'What do you mean *almost* perfect?' asked Callum, ignoring Rudi's sour face and protruding, *skýr*-smeared tongue. 'Waterfalls don't come much bigger or better than that.'

'Don't get me wrong, man.' Rudi wiped his mouth on a napkin. 'I asked for a waterfall and you've got me one fuck-off waterfall. But this is a script for the Renault Scenic. The campaign is about encouraging people to change their scenery. It's about firing people's imaginations, getting them to drive to places they can only dream about. So your waterfall comes pretty close. But it's got to work harder for me, man. I want to create a parallel universe, a world that only exists in my film.'

'Film?' asked Anna Björk. 'I thought you were shooting a commercial.'

Callum drilled his eyes into hers.

'I don't like to think of it as a commercial,' said Rudi. 'I want to approach it as a mini-feature, to give it an epic quality. And that's why I think we can make this location work harder for us. As I said, I want to create a surreal world, a world that is slightly off the reality that we know.' Rudi removed a biro from his pocket and used it to draw a single storyboard frame onto the wooden picnic table.

'I don't think you are allowed to write on that,' said Frikki.

'Let the director work out his shot,' insisted Callum. 'I'll OK it with the owners. If we have to replace the table it can come out of the production budget.'

Rudi applied the finishing touches to his graffiti. 'This is how I want to frame the falls.' He indicated a flurry of lines within his square box. 'I want the Renault to drive in a figure of eight in front of the waterfall and, on my command, I want three geysers to blow in the foreground. Woosh! Woosh! Woosh!'

'Geysers?' asked Callum.

'I know!' beamed Rudi. 'Surreal, innit!'

'But there aren't any geysers at this site. And even if there were, they're not the most reliable things. I can't guarantee that a geyser will blow on the word *action*.' Callum could tell that this was not what Rudi wanted to hear. He stared at the sketch, trying to fathom a solution. That was his job, after all. He solved problems. Pity he never took his work home, he thought. If he could procure three geysers and stop them exploding whenever they felt like it, then surely he could find a way to manage the three women in his life. Right now they seemed just as volatile.

'Here's an idea,' he said. 'We could go north and shoot the scene up at Geysir. The great Geysir itself has been inactive for about forty years but there's a smaller one beside it called Strokkur and it fires off a big spout every few minutes. It's pretty reliable. You could say it disproves the adage about a watched pot never boiling.'

Rudi wasn't impressed. 'But I want three geysers, not one. And I want this waterfall in the background.'

'What if we shoot the geyser three times against a large blue-screen? Each eruption would look different. Then we can film the car against the waterfall as a separate plate and marry up all the elements in post-production.'

'No way, man.' The director was having none of it. 'I don't believe in post. No matter how good your studio operator, you always see the joins. I've made my name by capturing everything in camera. Post isn't an option.' Rudi removed his sunglasses and rubbed his eyes. 'Hang on a momo. I've got it. Why don't we dig up some geysers and drive them down here?'

Callum resisted an overwhelming urge to punch the guy. 'I have a better idea,' he said, aware that he had to indulge this idiot if he was going to secure the job. 'We can make some geysers.'

'How do we do that?' asked Anna Björk.

'Fire and Ice Locations can do anything,' said Callum. He hadn't a clue. 'We make the impossible, possible,' he brazenly added.

'So you're cool?' asked Rudi. 'You can make me three geysers that will explode on my command?'

'I'm cool.' Callum could worry about the logistics later.

'Well if you're cool, I'm cool.' Rudi flicked his sunglasses onto his nose. 'Now ... let's see this ice lagoon.'

They stopped in Vík to refuel and to give Rudi a look at its black beach. At one end of the ghostly coastline, twisted fingers of black rock reached out of the foaming Atlantic like they belonged to a drowning, burning sea monster in the closing scene of a Godzilla flick. Well, thought Callum, Rudi had said that he wanted 'surreal'. As it was, the Londoner spent the next few miles of their journey complaining that the coarse volcanic sand had ruined his Nikes.

By the time they reached the barren, glacial flood plains of Skeiðarásandur the clouds had closed in on them, chopping off the tops of mountains and eclipsing the sun.

They belted along the single ribbon of road with their lights set to full beam, rain shearing into the windscreen. The Toyota's wheels protested loudly each time they crossed one of the many metal bridges that spanned the churning meltwater streams. Everything was wet, black and broken. It felt like they were driving along the bottom of a coal scuttle.

The road curved inland, giving them their first eerie glimpse of the snout of a glacier. They were heading straight towards Skaftafellsjökull, a giant river of ice flowing at an indiscernible pace and terminating in a fractured white wall that melted as slowly as it advanced. A small, blue-roofed hotel barred its way. The flimsy building reminded Callum of the student who had stood in front of a tank in Tiananmen Square: vulnerable but defiant. He would have panicked had he known that this hotel was where he would be forced to spend the night.

The encroaching glacier bullied the road back out towards the sea. The Toyota boomeranged round a concave headland that dipped its feet into the grey Atlantic. Almost immediately, the cloud thinned out and the sun dissolved into a lilac sky.

'It sure is changeable here,' commented Rudi.

'The sky is always changing in Iceland,' explained Frikki. 'One minute it is heavy with rain clouds and then they clear to reveal a mountain right next to you that you never knew existed.'

They buzzed over another Meccano bridge, a flimsy construction with no sense of permanence, as if the engineers had already conceded that it would one day be swept away by an irresistible torrent of floodwater and ice. The bridge spanned the mouth of a lagoon, right at the point where the fresh water flowed out into the sea and the gulls gathered to argue over the price of trout.

'Here we are,' said Callum. 'Jökulsárlón ice lagoon . . . Iceland's very own iceberg factory.'

They turned off the main road and crunched down a cinder track. It deposited them in a makeshift car park with a drive-in view of the lagoon. Bright blue chunks of ice clacked on the surface of the green water like a tacky cocktail. The icy monoliths performed a perpetual ballet of water and light as they drifted imperceptibly towards the sea. The bergs had calved themselves from the Breiðamerkurjökull glacier, a formidable field of ice that spread out beyond the lagoon before getting swept up into the clouds.

'*Where the glacier reaches up to the sky, the land ceases to be of this world and becomes part of heaven,*' said Frikki. He killed the engine. '*Heimsljós* by Halldór Laxness.'

'Yet again Frikki, I'm impressed,' said Callum. 'I'm beginning to suspect you have hidden depths.'

'Like an iceberg,' said Frikki. 'Only one tenth of me shows above the surface.'

'If Frikki is an iceberg, it is an iceberg that sits in a shallow puddle,' said Anna Börk.

'I am not shallow,' protested the big Icelander. 'You are the one who pretends she is something by wearing all those designer labels.'

'Nothing wrong with designer labels.' Rudi removed his sunglasses and held them in the air. 'Take these sunnies. Three hundred notes, they cost me. But if they're good enough for David Beckham, they're good enough for me.'

'Beckham does not impress me,' said Frikki. 'I'm a Stoke City fan.'

'Don't listen to him, Rudi. I think your glasses make you look sexy,' said Anna Björk. 'Frikki will never look sexy. The only designer labels he wears are Gore-Tex and 66° North.'

'At least my clothes are practical, unlike yours,' said Frikki. 'We are about to walk around an ice lagoon and you are wearing open-toe sandals made from *sjávarledur.*'

'Made from what?' asked Rudi.

'Fish leather,' translated Anna Björk. 'It is the only good by-product of our fish factories. Prada are starting to use fish leather and Dior are making bags from it.' She lifted her foot onto Rudi's knee and twisted her ankle to show off the shoe. 'This is a David Meyer original.'

Rudi's hand hovered above her leg.

'Go on,' she urged. 'You can touch it. It is very smooth.'

'Your leg or the fish leather?'

'Both.'

Rudi stroked her shoe, letting his hand err from the tiny buckles and delicate straps to dwell on the exposed arch of her foot.

'Enough of the chiropody,' interrupted Callum. 'We've got a lagoon to recce.'

They hauled themselves out of the warm vehicle and their bones immediately froze.

'Man, it's cold.' Rudi zipped himself into a fleece.

'Jökulsárlón has its own microclimate,' said Callum. 'With all these icebergs about, the place is a natural refrigerator.'

They made their way past the small wooden café-cum-gift shop and ascended a shale hill that offered them a more lofty view of the lagoon. A low mist clung to the dominant glacier, creating a backdrop that disappeared into infinity. A small Fokker 50 flew low to the ice, looking no more substantial than a toy plane made from balsa wood and propelled by a rubber band. Below it, an amphibious boat-on-wheels ferried fluorescent-jacketed tourists over a gravel track and into the water, taking them on a cruise around the ever-changing conurbation of icebergs.

'Can you swim in there?' asked Rudi.

'I would not try it,' said Frikki. 'You would be dead in less than one minute.'

'It may look tranquil and inviting but don't be fooled,' said Callum. 'It can be a very dangerous place. You'll notice that the boat keeps its distance from the icebergs. At any moment one of them could flip right over. And, as Frikki pointed out, each berg is nine times bigger under the water. If you were within twenty feet of one when it rolled over, you'd become a Slush Puppy.'

'So this is the place where they filmed the car chase in *Die Another Day*?' asked Rudi.

'The very same.'

Rudi scanned the horizon but looked confused. 'It doesn't look like it. I remember that in the film, they drove their Jaguars over ice sheets. I can't see any ice sheets, just a lot of icebergs floating in water.'

'That's because they froze the lagoon for the Bond film,' said Callum.

'How the fuck do you do that?'

'You dam the mouth of it, so the salt water from the sea can't mingle with the fresh water in the lagoon. Once it's dammed and free of salt, the water will freeze to a thickness that will support the weight of a car.'

'And that's what we're going to do for the commercial?' asked Rudi. 'That's totally wicked, man!'

'Don't get too excited. The Bond film was a big

number with big bucks. We've got to be a bit more realistic with our budget.' Callum pointed to a large flat area on the lagoon bank. 'I'm proposing that we get our art department to cover that area in snow. We'll use a boat to drag a couple of the smaller icebergs to the shore and a JCB can drop them onto the white carpet. We'll leave a clear area of snow large enough for the Renaults to perform their ice dance.'

Rudi was shaking his head. 'But it's not an ice field. The script clearly says that the cars dance on a dramatic ice field.'

'Trust me,' said Callum. 'If you keep the camera at a low angle you won't even see the water, it will look exactly like an ice field. We'll have the cars dancing over snow in the foreground and the backdrop will be filled with icebergs and the huge expanse of the glacier behind it. It'll knock people's socks off.'

'You should not take your socks off,' said Frikki. 'Your toes will get frostbite in less than one minute.'

Anna Björk tutted.

Rudi still bore the same look of confusion that he had carried for much of the day. 'Can we not take the Renaults up onto the glacier?'

'Two problems with that,' said Callum. 'You'll find that when you go up there, you don't get much of a horizon. The glacier is just a flat white void. It'll look like nothing on film. And secondly, the Renaults may be Scenic, but they're not All-Terrain. They just aren't built to be driven on ice.'

'I'm not sure about this, man. I'll need to think about it.'

'You don't need to make a decision now. When we get back to the office tonight we can go through some other location shots and see what else we can offer up. Now, I don't know about you, but I think we could all do with something hot inside us.'

'You read my mind,' said Anna Björk. She zipped Rudi's fleece the whole way up to his neck and patted his shoulders. She took him by the hand and led the way to the small café.

They ordered seafood chowder and took their bowls to one of the small plastic tables scattered about the wooden cabin. Frikki opted for the hot-dog alternative, explaining in great detail to Rudi the potentially fatal consequences of his shellfish allergy. The chowder-eaters remained undeterred. Their soup was hot and orange and teeming with so much sea life that Callum had to check to see that there wasn't a gull hovering over his bowl. He took his first welcome taste of the thin, saffron-tinged infusion and his mobile buzzed. It was Birna. Callum made his apologies and stepped outside to take the call.

'Hi,' he said.

'Hi,' she said.

Then silence. A deafening silence: the sound of icebergs on a lagoon.

'Callum,' she said, her voice rough and worn. 'I am not sure that I want you to come home tonight.'

12

She said she had been thinking.

He said *dangerous*.

She said that she thought they were rushing things. She believed that this was making things difficult, not just for the pair of them but for her mother and daughter too. She felt that they needed to slow down. She said that if he could not develop a meaningful relationship with her daughter then she could not consider adding to her family.

He replied that this was a bit of a U-turn and informed her that she could already be pregnant.

She explained that, as of this morning, it was no longer a possibility.

He said *ah*. He momentarily wondered whether her period might have contributed to her recent foul mood but he knew better than to suggest such a thing to a woman, let alone Birna.

She said that perhaps she had been a bit premature in moving him into her home.

He admitted that he had been finding the house a little claustrophobic.

She believed that things might improve if he stayed in Gudni's apartment for a while.

He didn't disagree.

She described their relationship as a rollercoaster

that had set off on a long ride before all the nuts and bolts were in place.

He realized that this was truer than she could ever know.

She said that she had packed his suitcase for him.

He was surprised at this but he guessed that his moving out was just a temporary arrangement and it was probably for the best.

She said she had found two photographs of a pretty-looking woman in the lining of his case.

He said nothing.

She put it to him that the suitcase probably belonged to an old friend of his and that he had no idea that the photographs were hidden in it.

He said *that's right*, but he said it a little too eagerly. He recovered by explaining that the suitcase was given to him by an old workmate, Neil Byrne.

She imagined that Callum did not even know the woman in the pictures.

He agreed that this was probably true, as Neil was notoriously private about his love life. He never talked about his girlfriends or brought them to work functions.

She asked why, in that case, was the pretty-looking woman wearing Callum's denim jacket in one of the pictures.

What made her think it was his jacket, he asked.

She said she recognized it by the red and yellow Partick Thistle badge that was pinned to the button flap on the left breast pocket.

He said nothing.

She said he could use their time apart to dream up the story behind the pretty-looking woman.

He said *Birna* . . .

But she wasn't listening. She had ended the call.

* * *

Callum and Anna Björk checked into Hotel Freysnes, the lonely blue-roofed building that they had passed earlier that afternoon. The prosaic hotel lacked a swimming pool, a gym and a business centre but all the rooms came with an en suite glacier. Skaftafellsjökull pressed its icy snout right up against Callum's bedroom window.

Frikki and Rudi were well on their way to Reykjavík, having boarded a small charter plane at Höfn airport. That's if you could call it an airport. 'Höfn International', as Callum had sarcastically christened it, amounted to little more than a square of tarmacadam, a Nissen hut and a windsock. It had been Callum's intention to join Rudi on the return flight and let Frikki drive the Toyota back along the south coast. But after taking the phone call from Birna, he realized that he had little to hurry back for. She wanted him to keep his distance. She had made that abundantly clear.

Callum thought he could use the long drive to help him get his head together. He had dragged Anna Björk along for company. Right now he needed some company. His girlfriend had kicked him out. And she had waited until he was about as far away from her as the island of Iceland would permit before she had packed his suitcase.

Anna Björk and Callum had disappeared into their respective rooms to freshen up and get themselves ready for dinner. As Callum had not expected the recce to involve an overnight stay, it was not going to take him long to deliberate over his evening wear. 'Come as you are' was his preferred theme.

He decided to use the half-hour before dinner to phone Neil Byrne. He needed to talk to somebody and Neil was about the best friend he had. He was still concerned that they had not parted on the best of terms.

The fact that they had so recently come to blows was testament to the depth of feeling between them, or so Callum had convinced himself.

He toyed with asking Neil to contact Birna and vouch that the suitcase, the photographs in it, and the woman in the photographs, belonged to himself and not Callum. But he couldn't ask Neil to lie for him. And anyway, Birna would never swallow it. As she had already demonstrated, she was way too clever for that. Nevertheless, he needed to think of a credible explanation for the snaps by the time he got back to Reykjavík.

Callum's bed wobbled as he sat down on it to make the call. He supposed that the sort of people who passed through such an isolated hotel were walkers, cyclists and hikers who were used to spending cold nights in remote huts or in cramped tents that had been hastily pitched on top of cheek-piercing lava. These flimsy beds would seem opulent by comparison.

It was outside office hours in the UK so he dialled Neil's mobile. The call was answered by a posh woman with an automaton voice. She informed Callum that the Vodafone he had called was not responding. She asked him to please hold while she diverted him to an answering service. After another couple of rings the same woman invited him to leave a message. But he didn't. Where would he start? There was just too much to say.

Callum found the bathroom and splashed water on his face. Hot water. His cheeks smarted. That's the trouble with living in a geothermal country, he figured. The water runs hot before it goes cold. He remembered the joke about the Icelandic boy who was making his way upstairs to the bathroom when his mother shouted after him, 'And don't use all the cold water.'

He used to find that funny.

He patted his face with a brittle towel. His mind was racing. *Hot water . . . fire water . . . fire and ice . . . Scotch on the rocks . . . good idea, Callum.*

He exited his room in search of a single malt.

He found Anna Björk in the brightly lit bar. She had her trademark Long Vodka in one hand and was using her other to give the finger to an Englishman standing next to her. At least, Callum guessed that the man was English as he sported a white rugby shirt with a red rose sewn onto the breast. He was doing his boisterous best to chat up Callum's PA.

'Do I not get a kiss?' he asked her. Loudly. 'Or is my little ice maiden a tad frigid?' He was putting on a performance for three equally sozzled mates who were egging him on from a nearby table. 'Go on, you know you want to,' he said, offering his cheek to Anna Björk. His face was as flushed as the rose on his shirt. His accent was plum-pudding posh.

'Ah, Callum!' said Anna Björk. She had never been so glad to see him.

'Is this guy bothering you?' he asked.

'Not at all,' said Anna Björk, nodding in the affirmative. 'This asshole was just leaving.'

The rugger bugger knew when he was beaten. He rejoined his pack.

'So, are you still in love with England?' asked Callum.

'I imagine that not all Englishmen are assholes.'

'But can you be sure?' he asked, with more than a touch of mischief.

'Rudi isn't an asshole.'

'See, I was right. You do fancy him.'

'Maybe.' Anna Björk ran a painted finger round the rim of her glass. It was only then that Callum appreciated the effort she had gone to in dressing for dinner. Her nails were glossy and long. Her cheeks were dusted with a fine glitter that announced itself with every turn of her head. She wore a simple black number that had been sprayed onto her body and her heels were as long and thin as the swizzle stick in her glass. Little wonder she had drawn some unwanted attention.

'Well I'm sure that if Rudi saw you in that dress, he'd melt.'

'Thank you.' Anna Björk adjusted her hem. 'It's a Westwood copy.'

It could have been a Wedgwood original for all Callum knew about fashion. 'So tell me,' he said, 'what has Rudi got that, say, Frikki hasn't got?'

'Frikki? Hah! He is a pig. He is just like the Vikings who stuffed their bellies with meat and beer and who molested girls late into the night before getting up early to fight. Except Frikki doesn't like to get up early.' Anna Björk's face softened. 'But Rudi . . . well . . . he is different to Icelandic men. For sure, a lot of it is to do with the colour of his skin. I have always fancied having a baby by a black man. How cute would that be, me having a black kid.'

'So not only do you wear designer clothes, you want a designer baby.'

Anna Björk laughed. 'You make me sound bad. It is not like that at all. It's just . . . well . . . when you have lived here all your life, you start to crave anything that is exotic. And you don't get much more exotic than black guys. Not to an Icelandic woman. I have seen only two black men in Reykjavík. They came into the strip club. They worked at the US air base in Keflavík, so nothing could ever come of it. The girls at the club are discouraged from forming relationships with the Americans. Still, nobody can stop me fantasizing about those lovely black guys smuggling me back to their base.' Anna Björk had a faraway look in her eyes but they quickly refocused to the here and now. 'The trouble with Reykjavík is that it is so small and incestuous. Everyone has fucked everyone else. And there is no romance. Guys here don't need to waste time getting to know a girl because everyone already knows each other. Dating is not a word in our vocabulary. In Iceland we just get straight down to business. That is why so many foreign guys come here. They think Icelandic women are easy.'

'Why are you so down about your country all the time? I mean, to the outsider, Iceland is exotic in its own way. Just look at that landscape.' Callum indicated the wide sweep of the Skaftafell National Park that was framed in the lounge window. The cobbled fields of mossy lava glowed vivid pink in the evening light. This was the Magic Hour.

'I am tired of hearing about our wonderful nature and landscape,' said Anna Björk. 'Do you not find it ironic that our biggest tourist attraction is not natural at all; it is a man-made lagoon. Only in Iceland do we take the water expelled from a geothermal power plant and dress it up with a name like the Blue Lagoon. It is no better than a sewer. And the sea is so cold up here that we had to build a thermal beach at Nauthólsvík. Give me Greece or Spain or Mexico or anywhere over Iceland.'

'OK,' conceded Callum. 'But you'll admit that the quality of life in Iceland is second to none. You have a great national health service, you enjoy a diet rich in fish and your country is almost entirely free of pollution. You have the longest life expectancy of any people on earth. I even read that your scientists up at deCODE have isolated the "Methuselah" gene, responsible for sustaining longevity in humans. I have a theory that they used Birna's mother as a guinea pig.

I suspect she's immortal. Whatever, this research means that the life expectancy of Icelanders will only increase.'

'Typical,' grunted Anna Björk. 'You mean I have to endure this place until I am two hundred years old?'

'Come on, if Iceland was that bad you would have left it by now.'

'Sure. Like every young girl in Ólafsvík I had dreams of travelling the world. I used to fantasize about becoming a stewardess for Icelandair. It is like I said before, I have always craved the exotic, even from an early age.' Her mouth flattened into a grimace. 'Sadly, I never grew tall enough to become an air stewardess. Hence the heels.' She cocked her foot in the air to give Callum a good look at her footwear.

'Is that still the dream of every little girl in Iceland, to become a trolley dolly for the national airline? I only ask because I'm having problems getting to know Birna's young daughter.' Callum straightened. He was uncomfortable talking about his home life. Not that he had a home to go to. But he realized that Anna Björk might be able to help him out. 'It would be great to get a steer on what it's like to be a young girl growing up in this country.'

Anna Björk looked puzzled. 'What age is Birna's girl?'

'Eleven, going on forty-five. She makes me feel like I'm the kid. The other day she called me stupid.'

'I am not sure that I know what she is going through. It has been ten years since I was her age. These days, things are a lot different for the kids. You see it is not just the precious landscape that changes quickly in Iceland. A decade ago there was no national television on a Thursday and large parts of the island still communicated by carrier puffin. But today the children are reared on MTV and every one of them owns a mobile phone. This was unthinkable when I was a girl.'

'Ásta doesn't have a mobile phone.'

'Then she must be the only girl in Reykjavík without one.'

'Well that's her Christmas present sorted,' said Callum. 'On second thoughts, she probably doesn't have a phone because her mother doesn't permit it. Best not go there.'

'Does Ásta have many friends?'

'Not that I have seen.'

'She is not a member of any sports clubs?'

'She rides horses.'

'Hmm. When I grew up it was only the wealthier girls who had horses,' said Anna Björk.

'Oh, Birna isn't wealthy. The horses are rejects from a nearby stable.'

'I see.'

'Is Ásta part of a sewing group?'

'I don't think so. I've never seen her with a needle and thread.'

'You take it too literally,' sighed Anna Björk. 'A sewing group is just a term for a bunch of girlfriends who stick together. They hang out together, look after each other. It is like a clique but not in a snobby way. I guess Ásta is still a little young to be part of such a group.'

'Like I said, I'm not sure that Ásta has any friends.'

'You don't know her at all, do you?'

Callum shook his head. He felt bad.

'Does Ásta hang out in town? Does she go to the mall? Is she into shopping? Does she annoy her mother by demanding make-up and thongs?'

'She's only eleven,' said Callum.

'And . . . ?'

'Well, did you wear a thong when you were eleven?'

'I could never persuade my grandmother to knit me one.' Anna Björk waited for Callum to stop grinning. 'I am serious. Young girls want different things these days, especially those girls who grow up in our capital. My hometown is barely one thousand people. We have no access to big stores in Ólafsvík, so shopping for clothes was never an issue. Maybe that is why I am such a fashion junkie now. But young girls today, they see Christina and Britney on MTV and suddenly they are wearing thongs. There is no innocence any more. Not even in Iceland, which for centuries has been the most innocent country in the world . . . though I would describe it as backward.'

'I don't think Ásta watches MTV,' said Callum. 'That's another thing her mother refuses to have in the house. Though she does watch videos of old British nature documentaries. And she collects weather.'

Anna Björk looked at Callum in much the same way as he had looked at Ásta when Birna had first mentioned her daughter's peculiar hobby.

'I know,' he said. 'Weird, isn't it? But then, this place is full of weird shit. It would not surprise me if collecting weather was a perfectly normal pastime for a young Icelandic girl.'

'It was not normal for me, but maybe this is a new thing that the kids are into.'

'So how did you entertain yourself when you were a girl?' asked Callum. 'I still feel stupid asking you that, like it was fifty years ago.'

'Sometimes it feels like it,' Anna Björk shrugged. 'But I know that I did not watch much TV when I was young. My friends and I would go down to the harbour and watch out for whales instead. If we were lucky we were allowed onto our fathers' boats. And if we were really lucky we would see a blue whale lazing near the top of the water and gazing up at us with his ancient eye.' A child's smile had surfaced on Anna Björk's face.

'I think you like Iceland more than you let on,' said Callum.

'Bullshit!' She drained her vodka. 'Whales stink. Their blowholes are full of krill and bacteria. They smell of dead people. Ólafsvík is full of the walking dead.'

The barman collected her empty glass. 'Same again?' he asked.

Callum nodded. 'And a Scotch on the rocks.'

He watched in silence as Anna Björk checked her lashes in a compact mirror. He found it hard to believe that she had worked as a stripper. She was only a girl.

'If I could do one thing to get young Ásta to start accepting me, what would it be?' he asked.

'That is easy,' said Anna Björk. She snapped her compact shut like a powdery castanet. 'You must stop thinking of her as *young* Ásta. You must stop treating her like she is a kid.'

'Funny, Ásta said exactly the same thing.' Callum accepted his whisky from the barman.

'I am closing up now,' said the barman. 'Can I get you lovebirds anything else?'

Anna Björk snorted into her vodka.

Callum reddened. 'No thanks,' he replied, and the barman turned on his heels. 'He thinks we're an item. How ridiculous.'

'Why would that be so ridiculous?' Anna Björk threw him a playful pout.

'Well, look at us. You're over a decade younger than me. And look at the way we're dressed. You look like a million dollars. I, on the other hand, look like fifty krónur. He must wonder what you see in me.'

'I see a lovely guy. A lovely guy with troubled eyes.' She leaned back in her seat. 'You remember how

Frikki claimed to be like an iceberg with only a small part showing above the surface. That is how I see you, Callum. There is so much more that you have yet to reveal and maybe when you do, young Ásta will see you for the man you are. A good man.'

'I don't know about good. Appearances can be deceptive.'

Anna Björk leaned forward again and set her drink on the table. 'I have a confession,' she said, bowing her head slightly, her wide eyes gazing up at Callum with a teenage deference.

'Don't tell me . . . you were born a man.'

'*Nei, nei, nei.* You are being silly now. My confession is not of such magnitude. I only wanted to tell you that I know about your novel. And, for what it's worth, I think you have the beginning of a brilliant story.'

Callum's face fell blank. 'I'm sorry AB, maybe it's the whisky but I haven't a scooby what you're talking about.'

Her face fell into a sulk. 'I thought you might react like this. It was bad of me, I know. But I couldn't resist reading it.'

'You'll have to throw me some rope,' said Callum. 'What novel?'

'It's OK, Callum. You don't need to deny it. Look . . .' Anna Björk recomposed herself in her chair. 'The other afternoon, when you and Frikki went to buy the 4x4, I . . . well . . . I was alone in the office and I got bored. There was nothing in the paper, there never is, so I thought I'd play Solitaire on your laptop. I saw that you had left an open document on the screen. I couldn't help myself. I read the start of *The Killer's Guide to Prague*. It's really good, Callum. It's so . . . brutal,' she added, with an almost sadistic glee. But her face became plaintive again. 'Please don't hate me.'

'Don't be silly. I don't hate you. But that thing you read, it's not what you think. At least . . .' Callum polished off his whisky, waiting for the burn to seize his chest before he could continue. 'It's work in progress,' he explained. 'It's all very hush-hush. Nobody knows I'm writing it, not even Birna. I guess I'm a bit protective of my writing.'

'Has Birna read any of your stuff?'

'No,' said Callum, a little too emphatically. 'Birna doesn't know that I'm writing at all. Nobody does. I don't like to talk about it. I've met too many bar-room bores in Glasgow's media land who are always spouting on about the novel or screenplay they've been writing. Of course, nothing ever sees the light of day. I don't want to turn into one of them. I've vowed that I won't tell anyone about the book until the draft is completed and I get buy-in from a publisher.'

'Then I won't mention it again. But I do feel very privileged that I have read it,' said Anna Björk. 'Especially the bit when the guy strangles the girl and he knows that she is dead when she stops coughing the green sugar onto his wrists.' Anna Björk placed her hand on Callum's knee. 'You see, beneath that lovely exterior, you have a truly fucked-up mind.'

'Yeah . . . well . . .' conceded Callum. 'You're not wrong there.'

13

Callum raced into town from his apartment. He was on his way to meet Birna and couldn't afford to be late. He hadn't seen her in three days; three days that had felt like as many months.

On his return from the ice lagoon, Callum had called at Birna's house to collect his belongings, but it was Ásta who had answered the door. She informed him that her mother had gone to the Westmann Islands for a few days. He wanted to know why, in that case, the curtains were drawn in Birna's bedroom. Ásta shrugged. Callum asked her if he could come in. She asked Callum if he had another girlfriend. When he said *no*, Ásta called him a liar and slammed the door in his face.

Callum sidestepped the drunks at the bus station and ran along Posthússtræti. As he turned into Austurvöllur Square, he was upended by a woman who had been kneeling on the pavement. He picked himself off the ground and examined the grazes on the balls of his thumbs. His nose was stinging, his heart was thumping and he felt nauseous. Shoppers glared at him.

'*Fyrirgefðu!*' The woman looked apologetic.

'What the fuck are you doing down there?' yelled Callum. He felt something warm covering his lips and noticed that spots of blood were erupting on the flag-stones. 'Jesus, my nose.'

The woman fussed in her pockets and handed him a tissue. 'Here,' she said. 'I am very sorry.'

'This is typical,' said Callum, conscious that Birna would be sitting in Kaffibrennslan, looking at her watch.

'You were running too fast,' the woman protested. 'I could not get out of the way.'

This was a timely reminder to Callum that he needed to slow down. Birna had told him not to rush things. Easier said than done, he thought. Callum had always been impatient.

The shoppers started to disperse, clearly dis-appointed that there was no ensuing argument, nor any broken bones to ogle. Nothing to see here, they were thinking, as they diffused across the square.

Callum noticed that the woman on the pavement was clutching a slim paintbrush and that several pots of brightly coloured paint were arranged around her knees. 'You didn't answer my question,' he said. 'What are you doing down there?'

'I'm painting *tyggigúmmí*,' she replied.

'You're what?'

'*Tyggigúmmí* . . . chewing gum . . . all these ugly grey spots on the pavement . . .' She stabbed at them with her sable brush. 'I am painting them cheery colours.'

'Why would you do that?'

'Because I am an artist. It is what I do. I paint chew-ing gum. I also tattoo bodily organs and make fetish masks for animals, but those exhibitions got me into a lot of trouble. With this work I am rediscovering my innocence.' The woman stood up, scratched her chin and surveyed the fluorescent constellation at her feet. 'It is pretty, don't you think?'

'I suppose so,' said Callum, though his head was tipped backwards and he was gazing at the sky. He leaned forward again to better examine her work and a circle of blood burst out of the concrete like a bullet hole.

'That's brilliant! You are really adding to it!' The woman retrieved a camera from her bag and took a digital shot of the pavement. She handed Callum her card. 'This has got my website on it. You can download the picture and put it on your desktop.'

He thanked her but he didn't know why.

It was lunchtime and Kaffibrennslan was crammed, which pleased Callum. He had chosen a popular, centrally located café in which to meet Birna because he knew it would be crowded. He had yet to explain to her about the woman in his suitcase and he thought it prudent to do so in a public place as there was less chance of her blowing up and creating a scene (though with Birna he could never be sure). Another reason he had suggested Kaffibrennslan was because he knew that Birna was addicted to their *Adalskaffi*, an ice-cold coffee concoction with double espresso, butter rum syrup, a dollop of whipped cream and a shot of Kahlua to slacken the pulse. He was hoping it might subdue her.

He saw Birna before she saw him. She was sucking a coffee bean onto the end of a black straw and depositing it into her empty, cream-lined coffee glass.

'Can I get you another one?' he asked.

'Oh . . . *já*,' said Birna, like she was surprised to see him. 'What happened to your nose?'

'A big boy did it and ran away.'

'Are you OK?'

Callum knew that Birna was angry with him, so he drew some comfort from her concern.

'I'm fine.' He dabbed at his nose and examined the

174

tissue. 'I think the bleeding's stopped. It gave me a bit of a shock, though. I need a sugary tea.' Callum collared a waitress and ordered their drinks. He joined Birna at her window table. 'So . . . here we are again.'

'And I see you have not lost your ability to state the obvious,' said Birna.

'It comes easy to me. Wait, I'll do it again . . . you look fantastic.'

'And you look like shit.'

'It's all those sleepless nights without you.'

'Bullshit, Callum. The last few nights when we were together you did not sleep at all. Something was distressing you.'

'It's too bright to sleep,' he protested.

'My bedroom has curtains.'

'I know, and they've stayed drawn since I moved out. By the way, how *were* the Westmanns?' He didn't disguise the sarcasm.

'You know that I did not go back to Vestmannaeyjar,' said Birna. 'I got Ásta to tell you I was away because I did not feel like speaking to you. I needed to be by myself.'

'Your daughter is a lousy liar.'

'Then I am glad. Because I do not like liars. Heroin turned Ásta's father into a perpetual liar. I ended our relationship because I was tired of his lies.' Either the caffeine had taken hold or the Kahlua had been replaced by a shot of adrenalin, but Birna was definitely on edge. 'I will not be lied to, Callum. I will not be messed around.'

'I have never lied to you.' OK, so perhaps he hadn't been entirely honest with her, especially concerning the photographs. He figured that sometimes it is better to protect people from the truth. What you don't know can't hurt you, or so he had believed. But he now realized that he was hurting Birna by withholding the truth. He could see it in her face. He wasn't even sure that it was Birna he was trying to protect by being so guarded about his past. Could it be that Callum was protecting himself?

'You are sure you have never lied to me?' she asked.

'Sure,' said Callum, keeping his eyes trained on hers. He had remembered how Birna believed in eye contact as a barometer of honesty and sincerity. But he could not have prepared himself for her next question.

'So you are not married?' It sounded like this was the one thing she had always wanted to ask him but had never dared.

The waitress set their drinks on the table, not that Birna noticed. She had zoned in on Callum, willing him to respond.

'Married? Christ, no!' Callum was surprised and confused. 'What made you think I was married? A couple of old photos in a suitcase?'

'You are telling me that there is not another woman back in Scotland?' Birna looked like she was preparing herself to go one of two ways – anger or despair – she had yet to decide.

Callum felt an overwhelming urge to just grab her and hold her but he knew he'd be crossing a line. It was a line that would stay drawn between them until he sorted this.

'The girl in the photos is Sarah, an old flame of mine from way back in the Dark Ages,' he explained. 'She was also my business partner at Strawdonkey.'

'She must still mean a lot to you,' said Birna. 'You do not carry someone's photograph around if they mean nothing to you.'

'I didn't know that the photos were in the suitcase,' Callum lied. 'They were put in there a long time ago and I must have forgotten about them. Which shows you how little Sarah means to me. It's been six years since we split.' Was he telling Birna lies or was he still protecting her from the truth? Callum didn't know any more. He only knew that he felt awful doing it, like he was being unfaithful to both women.

'How did your relationship end?'

'Oh, you know,' said Callum. 'The usual. We just drifted apart. I guess the rot set in when we started the business together. It's hard enough living with someone but when you work with her too, well . . . you start to crave your own space again.'

Birna did not need to know that Sarah was dead. Callum was not about to play that card, not yet, and certainly not here in the bright window of a busy downtown café. Not after Birna had so recently asked him to move out of her house. Right now, she might interpret news of Sarah's death as his pathetic attempt to win his way back into her heart and her home by begging her pity. Alternatively, she would feel genuinely sorry for him. And Callum couldn't have that. If Birna and he were to make their relationship work, they had to start by having an equal respect for each other. How could Birna respect Callum if she felt sorry for him? And how could Callum ever believe that Birna truly loved him if he suspected that her love was born out of pity?

'But there was a time when you carried her photograph around,' said Birna. 'She must have meant something to you when you were together.'

'I suppose so.' Callum tried hard to look blasé, like Sarah hadn't meant the world to him. 'But technically I never carried Sarah's photo around, not consciously anyway. I used to do location scouting all over Scotland, which meant that I was away from home a lot of the time. Sarah liked to surprise me by hiding things in my suitcase . . . hence the photos. Sometimes I would find a cuddly toy in my washbag or a pair of

177

her panties balled into one of my shoes. I guess it was her way of saying, "don't forget me" when we were apart.'

'She sounds nice.' Birna spooned the three espresso beans off her *Adalskaffi* and ladled them onto her saucer.

'I only date nice girls,' he replied, trying to cajole a smile out of her. He hoped that she was loosening up. He needed her to re-engage with him.

'I am not a nice girl,' said Birna. 'I have been unfair to you, Callum. I should not have jumped to these mad conclusions.'

'It's OK. I understand.'

'No. No, you do not understand. It is difficult for me.' Birna turned to look out the window and the light caught the moisture in her eyes. 'I find it hard to trust men. I have been hurt before and I do not want to be hurt again. I guess that is the real reason why I chose not to date men for such a long time. I was not thinking about my daughter, I was thinking about myself.'

Callum slid his hand across the table and placed a finger on her wrist. He wasn't yet confident enough to take her whole hand in his.

'I want us to be together, Callum. But I need you to be patient.'

'I'll try.'

'Look at you,' she said, sniffing sharply and smiling through her tears. 'You are like a wounded dog.' Callum offered her his bloodstained tissue but Birna declined it in favour of a paper napkin. 'Please, Callum, I do not want you to be worried. We are not about to split up. I just want us to rewind a bit. We need to have some fun again. And you need to settle into the way of life over here before we can settle down.'

'Are you annoyed that I am working so much?'

'No, I am not annoyed, but work is not everything. Over here we like to work all the hours that God sends, and in Iceland he sends more hours than elsewhere, but this can be an unhealthy situation when it starts to erode families. On our first night as a family, when you said you were conducting interviews and you couldn't take Ásta to get shoes, I knew that you had the Saturday morning free. And even though I didn't say anything at the dinner table, I was worried that you were using work as an excuse to avoid facing up to my daughter. I know the situation at home has been difficult for you. But it has been difficult for me too, bringing a child up on my own. And you are not the only one who has important work to do. I work as hard as anybody, but I will always put my loved ones first. That is why I quit my research on the flood plains and turned the car back to Reykjavík. It was your first full day living in Iceland and I knew I should be with you.' Birna smiled that smile that always got him. 'I may have kicked you out of my home and I may accuse you of having another woman but I do love you and I will always put you before my work.'

Callum grabbed her hand and buried it in his fist like it was a root ball that needed to take hold.

They didn't say anything, they just watched the world outside as it ebbed and flowed to a soundtrack of wet gurgles and gassy rasps from the cappuccino machine. A little doll of a girl with blonde hair and a huge stare pressed her mouth to the window and blew her cheeks out at them. Callum acted horrified, sending the girl into a fit of giggles. Birna laughed too and tightened her grip on his hand.

'So, how's work?' asked Callum, thrilled by the mundanity of his question. It had been a while since they had talked about the everyday, the humdrum. They had done nothing but argue since Ásta came off her pony, and their last conversation on the phone had seemed so loaded.

'I am working on some theoretical stuff,' said Birna. 'But I will not bore you with it.'

'No, go on. I like it when you bore me,' he said. And he meant it.

'OK, but you will regret saying that.' Birna fixed herself in her seat. 'Basically, I think there may be a huge misconception in geological theory concerning "hot spots" on the earth's surface. Try and stay awake while I explain.'

Callum held his eyelids open.

'For over thirty years the theory has been that the magma, deep underground in volcanically active areas like Iceland and Hawaii, travels from a depth of about 3,000 kilometres up to the surface where it cools to form landmass. But my research suggests that we may have to revise this.'

'Fascinating,' interrupted Callum.

Birna folded her arms. 'I told you it was not interesting.'

Callum smiled. 'I'm only messing. Carry on.'

'Well anyway, the hot-spot theorists believe that these magma tubes are thousands of kilometres deep. But from my studies of volcanic glaciers I believe that they may only extend to 400 kilometres below the earth's crust. If I am correct, we will have to rethink our whole concept of Iceland's formation and all the textbooks and university courses in the world will have to be changed.'

'You're right,' said Callum. 'That's not interesting at all.' He was being sarcastic.

Birna threw a sachet of sugar at him. 'Your turn, then. Tell me something interesting about this big sexy film company of yours.'

'Nothing much to report,' said Callum. 'Anna Björk

180

thinks I'll give her a pay rise if she dyes her hair red.'

'How so?'

'She read a survey that suggested that blondes in Reykjavík earn, on average, 20,000 krónur less than brunettes, and that redheads can expect the top wage. So she's threatening to dye her hair. I think she might be doing it to impress a director who's been over from London.'

'You've got the production job?' asked Birna. 'That is great news.'

'Nothing confirmed,' said Callum. 'I won't know for a few weeks.'

'In that case, if you're not too busy you could take Ásta out, go to the swimming pool or something. Just the two of you. The schools are on holiday tomorrow.'

'Tomorrow?' Callum's heart sank. 'I can't. I'm busy.'

'You are unbelievable!' Birna stitched her eyebrows into a frown. 'After all I said about putting family before work.'

'I know. I know. But I can't get out of this. As ridiculous as it sounds, I have an appointment with your Minister for the Environment.'

'*Já.* That does sound ridiculous.'

'I'm not making this up. It seems that there is a big problem with the shoot that I'm trying to organize. I need to build three geysers out at Skógafoss and a group of locals have objected to it.'

'How did they find out about it?' asked Birna.

'They read an article in *Morgunblaðið*. I foolishly let Frikki chaperone my London director back to Reykjavík on Saturday night. The pair of them got bladdered in Sirkus and blabbed everything to an off-duty journalist. But that isn't the best part. The loonies that are objecting say we can't disturb the land at Skógafoss because it is inhabited by elves! And now we have to meet with the Environment Minister and get him to sort it out. Have you ever heard anything so ridiculous?'

'*Huldufólk*,' said Birna, her face as flat and expressionless as a skimming stone. 'The Hidden People.'

'Hidden People?'

'According to our stories, they are the children that Eve hadn't finished washing when God came to visit, so they had to be hidden.'

'And you believe that crap?' Callum had caught the ears of fellow diners.

Birna lowered her voice to a near whisper. 'Like most Icelanders, I do not believe in these things, but I will not deny their existence.'

'Isn't that the same as believing in them?'

'No,' said Birna. 'If you ask an Icelander, "Do you believe in elves or ghosts?" he will more than likely say "*nei*". But if you ask, "Do you know anyone who has seen a ghost or been in contact with the hidden people?" and "Do you accept this person's experience as true?" nine out of ten people will say "*já*". So even though most people do not actively believe in these supernatural beings, they do accept their existence.'

'And do you know anyone who has seen a ghost or been in contact with these hidden people?' asked Callum.

'My mother sees them.'

'Why does that not surprise me.' Callum tried hard to sound flippant, but talk of ghosts had dredged up the horrible memory of the woman that Sigriður had seen standing at his shoulder; the woman who had worn the mask of a man, just as Sarah had done in death. The only way that Callum had been able to deal with Sigriður's vision was to dismiss it.

'Admit it, Birna, your mother's away with the fairies.'

'Sure, my mother has strong beliefs. Sitting here, drinking coffee, it is easy to laugh at her, just as it is easy to mock the idea of supernatural beings governing our land. But if this was winter and we were lying awake at midnight in a turf hut in the remote highlands, it would be a different situation. Your mind would interpret every sound and movement outside in devilish ways. The landscape here is such that we Icelanders cannot help but feel insignificant in relation to it. And because our land is unpredictable – what is grassy farmland today could be lava and ash tomorrow – we have learned not to rely so heavily on the evidence of our senses.' Birna supped her coffee and licked the cream from the corners of her mouth. 'Sometimes when I am doing my fieldwork I will see a shape or a movement in the corner of my eye. I will look around expecting to see a piece of lava jutting up or a bird taking flight, but the shape will disappear into the ground. Who is to say that I have not seen an elf? This land can play tricks on you, Callum. The silence and closeness to nature gives Icelanders a sixth sense.'

'I see dead people,' said Callum, in a distressed whisper. He was mocking Birna by seizing on her inadvertent reference to the Bruce Willis horror film.

'You should not joke about these things.' Birna chewed her lip, as if deciding on something. 'My mother was visited by my father after his death,' she said.

Callum felt foolish. He rinsed the smile off his face with a glug of cold tea. He had been quick to dismiss Sigriður because he didn't want to understand the things she believed in. But he now realized that if he wanted a future with Birna, he would have to start taking her mother seriously.

'Sigriður sees ghosts?'

Birna nodded. 'My mother sees many things. She sees colours and rays of light surrounding everything: people, animals, objects. She even sees colours when music is played. And she has seen the *huldufólk*. She told me many stories about them when I was a girl. She used to say that the world belonged to elves and that humans are only their guests. To her, the *huldufólk* are a personification of nature and its beauty . . . the fact that nature has rights. And that is why she campaigns to protect the areas where the *huldufólk* may reside.' Birna gave Callum a long, knowing look.

'Are you suggesting what I think you're suggesting?' he asked. 'You think your mother may be one of the people objecting to my film shoot?'

'It would not be the first time she has raised an objection with our authorities.' Birna moved her coffee to the side and cleared an area of table onto which she placed two pointed fingers. 'Imagine this is Reykjavík . . . and this is the town of Kópavogur over here. The main road that runs between the two is called Álfhólsvegur, or Elf's Hill Road. The road bears sharply left for no apparent reason.' Birna traced her finger across the table to indicate the sharp bend in the road. 'My mother was part of the group who success-fully lobbied for this road to be rerouted round an elf hill.'

'So there is actually a good chance that the Environment Minister will listen to these people?'

'Sure. It happens all the time. On the main street of Grundarfjördur, a rock stands between the houses numbered 82 and 86. It seems that elves live at number 84.'

'And you don't find that ridiculous?' asked Callum.

'No, I think it is charming. If someone in Grundarfjördur wants to preserve a large rock and declare that there are hidden people living under it, then that is just their Icelandic way of saying that they are on nature's side. And anyway, the *huldufólk* are not unique to Iceland. All over Scandinavia, Ireland and Europe you hear stories of hidden beings. The original settlers in Iceland were Irish monks. If we are in part descended from the Irish it should follow that we believe in the little people.'

Callum was sure he caught a twinkle in Birna's eye. 'So what is the likelihood that your Environment Minister will approve my shoot?'

'I would say you have no chance, especially as you are an outlander. And you will have less than no chance if you come up against my mother. And even if you are granted permission to dig up land for your shoot, past experience tells us that to attempt to disturb a *huldufólk* site is as futile as trying to lick your elbow. Your bulldozers will fail to start, your tools will break, your crew will fall ill and your lights will pop.'

Callum remained undaunted by Birna's pessimism. In truth, he wasn't paying much attention to her. He was too busy trying to lick his elbow.

'If you would stop doing that and listen me,' said Birna, 'then maybe I can help you.'

'How can you help?'

'I can go home tonight and work on my mother. I could try to persuade her that your film shoot will not damage the environment.'

'It won't,' insisted Callum. 'I'll put all the elves back where I found them. I'll even give them their own Winnebago when we're filming.'

Birna rolled her eyes.

'Anyway,' he continued. 'You don't need to do this for me. I can ask her myself when we get home.'

Birna grimaced. She held his hand. 'Callum, you

won't be coming home with me. I said we should take things slowly and I still mean it. Sure, I want you to try harder with my mother and my daughter. But the day Ásta begs me to let you come and stay with us, is the day you shall move back in.'

14

'Did you kiss and make up?' asked Anna Björk.

'I think so,' shouted Callum.

'Then why isn't Birna joining us?'

'She's doing a job for me,' he yelled. 'She's offered to have a word with her mother, to see if we can avoid this damn hearing tomorrow.'

They were sitting at one end of the long bar in Thorvaldssen, the end nearest the dance floor. Callum found it hard to make himself heard.

Frikki was chatting to the DJ, a good friend of his. 'Disc jockey' was a bit of a misnomer as the guy refused to spin discs on any wheels of steel, preferring instead to stream songs live from the Net using only his laptop and a mouse. Callum watched as he highlighted song titles from some website or other, dragging and dropping them into his set list. There was no mixing, scratching or cueing up of intros; his machine automatically cross-faded each song into the next.

Frikki had an excited look on his face when he returned to the bar. 'Daddi has offered me a chance to play guitar in his band,' he said.

'Daddy?' asked Callum.

'Daddi,' repeated Frikki.

'Freaky and Daddy. Jeez, what are the rest of your band called: Dozy, Beaky, Dick and Bampot?'

'Birgir and Sigtryggur,' said Frikki. 'Together we are The 101 Dalmatians.'

'As in the film?'

'*Nei*. As in 101, the postal district of central Reykjavík. The 101 Dalmatians are the dog's bollocks.'

'There are no dogs in Reykjavík,' said Callum. 'And there's a shortage of bollocks, if Birna's mother is to be believed. The kids have nothing to munch on.'

'Screw the kids. The important thing is that I'm in a band! And we're going to be touring!'

'You're hitting the road?' Anna Björk sounded hopeful.

'Not exactly,' said Frikki. 'Daddi has access to a helicopter. By day he is a pilot for a local tour company. He says he will fly us round the country to play the Sveitaball circuit.'

Anna Björk winced.

'Sveitaball?' asked Callum. 'Is that anything like volleyball?'

'The Sveitaballs are mad gigs in the remote villages around Iceland,' explained Anna Björk. 'The kids in these places have been starved of live music, so when a Sveitaball is held they all get drunk and act like berserkers. They are shit.'

'They are not shit,' insisted Frikki. 'I used to go to the Sveitaballs in the West Fjords when I was growing up. I remember that all the girls in our village wanted to fuck the band. They would just walk up to them and push their tits in the guys' faces.'

'And that's what you're looking forward to?' asked Anna Björk.

'No, I am looking forward to playing dumb covers of Bruce Springsteen and Bryan Adams to a bunch of bottle-throwing teenagers. What do you think?'

Callum guessed that a little of himself was rubbing off on Frikki. The big man had definitely picked up some Caledonian sarcasm. 'You only do covers?' he asked. 'You never play your own songs?'

'Nobody would pay to hear our songs. There are too many bands in Reykjavík who are playing their own songs and most of them spend their days in the fucking fish factories just to earn some money to eat. Fuck that. I will go where the money is. And the Sveitaballs pay good money.'

'So it's nothing to do with young girls pushing their tits into your face?' asked Anna Björk.

'I don't know why you are so smug,' said Frikki. 'Isn't that what you used to do for a living?'

'Sure. But I earned more money in one night than you'll earn on your entire tour.'

'At least I won't be degrading myself.' The big man returned to his pint.

'I'm not so sure,' said Anna Björk. 'Bruce Springsteen and Bryan Adams covers? It's kinda hard to claw any dignity back when you've been playing that shit night after night.'

'Enough.' Callum slapped his beer bottle on the bar top. 'We were supposed to be having a night out together, a bit of bonding before we embark on our first shoot, but if all you're going to do is argue then I'm heading back to the office. Besides, I need to get the head down. Big day tomorrow.'

Callum had replaced Frikki as the live-in lodger at Fire and Ice. There had been demand for the *Room with a View* apartments and Callum had been forced to kip on the office sofa bed until a German couple vacated Room 512. According to Gudni, the Germans had booked the apartment for two weeks. They were part of a New Age convention that had descended on Iceland in the hope of witnessing an expected alien landing at the Snæfellsjökull ice cap. Gudni had reassured Callum that the apartment would be vacated within the fortnight. 'If the Martians don't show up next Tuesday,' he'd said, 'the fruit-loops from Frankfurt will be out of here before you can say "take me to your leader".'

Callum retrieved his jacket from his stool.

'Stay,' pleaded Anna Björk. 'I promise we shall behave ourselves.'

'*Já*,' said Frikki. 'If it means that you'll come out and club with us, the stripper and I can pretend that we like each other.'

'I'll give the club a miss,' said Callum. 'To be honest, I'm shattered. I've had a day of it, what with Birna and all. And there's tomorrow's hearing at the parliament building. I need to be on top form if I'm to publicly discredit the elves.' He shook Frikki's hand and gave Anna Björk a peck on the cheek. 'You two have a mad one. I'll make sure the coffee's brewed and the paracetamol's on your desks by the time you struggle in.'

It was unsettling to walk out of a busy bar at midnight and be confronted by sunlight. As Callum staggered up Laugavegur, he felt that everyone was making a determined effort to avoid him, like they owed him money. It reminded him of his boozy Friday lunches with the Strawdonkey team, when he would exit Porky's and walk down Buchanan Street through the rush-hour throngs, drunk as a skunk and pinging like a pinball off pissed-off passers-by. It was only when he was in this state that he succumbed to the lure of the Glasgow street vendors and their trestle tables full of tat. Sarah would give him an earful when he eventually fell in through their front door and Callum would respond by proffering a conciliatory present of three pairs of socks or three lighters, all purchased for the princely sum of a pound.

Callum chuckled at the memory and then cursed

himself. He shouldn't be thinking about Sarah. He should be getting on with his new life. Sarah was history. He had Birna to think about now: Birna and her ready-made family.

But his thoughts immediately returned to his ex. Sarah and he had talked about starting a family too. Talking was about as far as they ever got. Somehow they had always found a reason to put off trying.

In the first heady rush of their relationship they had been too caught up in each other to consider children. And when the notion eventually occurred to them, they decided that they didn't have the money to support a child. When Sarah got a well-paid job at the Royal Bank of Scotland, a family seemed a real possibility. Unfortunately her contract stipulated that she needed to work twelve months before becoming entitled to decent maternity leave. The time flew quickly enough but the pair of them were still frittering money away in rent, in an area outside the catchments of the good primary schools. They resolved to buy a house with a more desirable post-code before trying for a kid. When the carpets had been tacked down and the paint had finally dried on the walls of their new three-bed terrace in Kelvinside, Sarah came off the pill.

It was a memory that again drew a smile from Callum. He recalled the day that Sarah told him she had forsaken all contraception and he remembered demanding that they have unprotected sex right there and then, in their new Shaker kitchen. But Sarah spurned his advances. Instead, she secured a calendar to the fridge on which she had marked out her 'fertile days'. She said they should hold fire for a few weeks until she was ovulating.

But a lot can happen in a few weeks. And a lot did happen. In that time Sarah resigned from her position at the bank, she registered an e-business in both their names and she asked her GP to write out a fresh prescription for a six-month supply of Marvelon. The pair of them had given birth to a different kind of animal and they decided to wait until Strawdonkey got on its feet before committing to a family.

Over those first two years they threw everything they had into their new venture – money, energy, time – and it paid off big style. Exactly one week after the successful flotation of Strawdonkey, Sarah was being flown home from Prague in a metal coffin.

Callum punched a code into a panel on the door of the office block, hitting the keys a lot harder than was necessary. He was admitted inside. He didn't feel too good. There was a nervousness about him, a quickening of the blood. He had felt this way since that afternoon, when he had first discussed Sarah with Birna. Luckily, Birna hadn't probed him too hard about his former lover, but it was only a matter of time. And how much would he be compelled to tell her then?

Callum waited for the elevator to descend to ground, but the number 3 remained illuminated, indicating that it was stuck on the same floor as his office. He took the stairs. He passed a tall man with a thick clod of black hair who was skipping down the concrete steps.

'*Gott kvöld*,' he said and Callum took it as a pleasantry, even though the guy's face stayed stony stern.

Callum returned a nod.

He had his keys out of his pocket by the time he reached the third floor. Before he went to the office, he walked to the opposite end of the landing to check on the elevator. Some prankster had jammed a fire extinguisher in the door. Callum removed it and the elevator responded to his earlier command to pick him up on the ground floor.

He returned the fire extinguisher to its wall-mounted casing and made his way back across the landing. He selected his door key and tried to guide it into the lock. He missed. He cursed himself for drinking too much. Again, he aimed the key at the dark slit in the door and again he missed. He kicked the door in frustration and it swung open. It was then that Callum noticed the thin slivers of split wood at his feet and the indentation to the door frame where entry had been forced.

'Hello?' he called out, scanning the office before he dared to set foot in it.

No response.

'Honey, I'm home!' he offered.

Again, nothing.

Callum stepped inside, checking first the kitchen, then the bathroom. It appeared that the burglar, or burglars, had gone. He presumed that the elevator had been rigged to stop anyone interrupting the break-in by gliding up to Floor 3 unannounced. The stone stairs, on the other hand, drew an echo that was loud enough to alert an intruder to anyone coming up them. Clever, he thought.

Callum noticed that his new iMacs still sat in their boxes on the office desks. This was odd. Why hadn't the thief, or thieves, swiped them? He checked the room to see what was missing. His suitcase lay open beside the sofa bed and his clothes had been tossed across the floor, but, as far as he could tell, nothing had been taken. Even his laptop remained on his desk, its screen sitting upright and proudly aglow.

Wait a minute, he thought, why hasn't it gone to sleep? After five minutes of inactivity its screen was programmed to go black.

He walked over to the machine. A number of documents sat open on his desktop and he diminished their windows one by one: the Fire and Ice P&L spreadsheet; his proposal to shoot a car ad at Skógafoss; a breakdown of the production costs for the commercial; and the story of a murder in Prague.

Fuck.

He had no idea who had broken into the office. But he did know that they had left it within the last five minutes and that they were now in possession of the truth: the truth about Sarah and the truth about her murder. His only hope was that they would interpret *The Killer's Guide* as fiction, just as Anna Björk had done. But Callum doubted it. He didn't get that lucky twice. Whoever it was who had broken in, they weren't interested in making off with anything of material value. They had forced their way into the place with the sole intention of getting information on him. And now that they were in possession of that information, they were unlikely to dismiss it as whimsy. That much was clear.

But who would do this? And what did they want?

Callum briefly speculated that the intruder might be one of the people objecting to his film shoot. Were the elf-lovers digging for information that might help them scupper his production? Somehow, it just didn't sound like their style. And as much as Birna had warned him about not messing with the *huldufólk*, he doubted whether elves were big into espionage.

The sound of an engine misfiring drew Callum to the window. The sky was frantic with flick-flacking flocks of birds, all evidently spooked by the loud bang. Callum watched as they resettled on the Tjörn. Only then did he notice a 4x4 pulling away from the waterside: a green Jeep. Callum was pretty sure it was the same green Jeep that had charged at Ásta's pony. And he now had the horrible conviction that Birna's girl had been telling the truth when she claimed that her fall was no accident. The Jeep had driven at her deliberately. Its driver had tried to harm Ásta and now he had infiltrated Callum's office.

But why? Callum struggled to make sense of it. He hadn't lived in Iceland long enough for someone to have a vendetta against him. But then, there was no guarantee that the intruder was Icelandic.

Callum's guts turned. Only close friends and family knew that he was in Reykjavík. Surely not, he thought. Neil . . . ?

He remembered how Neil had threatened him at his leaving do. He had resented Callum selling Strawdonkey and he had strongly suggested that the reason for such a quick sale might be less than savoury. Callum had put it down to the drink, but then, well, Neil had always been a bit of an odd fish, despite their friendship. When he wasn't spending more time than was strictly healthy playing shoot-em-ups on his X-box, Neil liked to scour auction houses for military ephemera. He had a bit of a fetish for Nazi memorabilia, and Callum remembered that he was particularly fond of the weaponry. And though Neil expressed no solidarity with Nazi doctrine, he liked to refer to his old home in the Gorbals as 'the Goebbels'.

'And what the fuck has that got to do with the price of fish?' spat Callum. He had caught his reflection in the office window and was scolding himself. 'You think one of your good friends is intent on fucking you over? You're paranoid, Pope. You're fucking paranoid.'

There was a quick way of resolving this. He decided to phone Neil at his home number in Glasgow. That would eliminate him from the enquiry.

Callum counted twenty rings before he gave up. He tried Neil's mobile but even if he had answered it, which he didn't, there was no guarantee that Neil wasn't taking the call from behind the steering wheel of a green Jeep.

'For fuck's sake, Callum, don't be ridiculous. Get a grip, man.' He was still giving his reflection a hard time.

He scrolled through the names on his handset and selected 'BeccaHome'. Becca was the only Strawdonkey employee who had kids and was therefore the most likely to be home at this hour. She would be able to explain why Callum hadn't been able to get hold of Neil.

'Hello, McCleod resi— I said stop it you two! . . . I mean it! . . . Darren, if I catch you sticking Lego up your sister's nose again I'll throttle you . . . Sorry, McCleod residence, Rebecca speaking.'

'You sound like you've got your hands full.'

'Callum! How the hell are you?'

'Oh, you know . . .'

'Is everything OK? You sound a bit down . . . Darren would you leave the dog alone! . . . I said *no scissors*! . . . Sorry Callum, the kids are a bit hyper. They were at their nan's this afternoon and she's been filling their faces with Coke. I think she does it to spite me.'

'I won't keep you long, Becks. Actually, I've been trying to get hold of Neil. He's not returning my calls.'

'Bloody hell,' said Becca. 'You mean you don't know about Neil?'

'No . . . why . . . what's happened to him?'

'Relax, it's nothing bad. Neil's off on his world tour. I can't believe he didn't tell you.'

'His world tour?'

'The new owners called him down to London on the Monday after you left. They're sending him round the globe to carry out an audit on cool travel destinations with a view to opening up a string of Strawdonkey cybercafés.'

'What do they want to do that for?'

'They say they're making the most of the brand name. Strawdonkey is synonymous with unique holiday experiences, usually the experience of lone travellers, and so Backpackers want to set up Strawdonkey outposts where the very people who write our diaries can come in, log on and stay in touch with folks around the globe. And hey, if they buy a milkshake, a slice of banana cake and a Strawdonkey mousemat while they're in there, then profits can only soar.'

'And is Neil getting behind this?'

'Of course not,' said Becca. 'But the lucky bastard gets to go all over the shop: South Africa, India, Thailand, Australia, Canada. He finishes up in the States. They want him to open the flagship caff in New York. Between you and me, I think he'll stay there.'

'Jeez, no wonder he hasn't been in touch. He's having the life of Riley.'

'That's just it. You'd think he'd be pleased about it but he had a face on him like a bag of spanners the day he jetted off. I think he's still bitter about the sale of the company. He reckons that Backpackers will bleed Strawdonkey to death. He's disillusioned, Cal. He doesn't believe in all this corporate wank that we're getting from London. I've got to say I'm with him.'

'But if he no longer believes in the company, why is he touring the world to promote it?'

'He reckons the tour will double as research for his writing. Travel book meets thriller, or so he said. He took his laptop with him. There's a bet running in the office that we have definitely seen the last of Neil Byrne. He'll end up penning plays on Broadway or joining a huge pool of writers on some US sitcom. Good luck to him, I sa— Kirsty! ... It's a bowl of spaghetti, not a hat!'

'Listen Becca, I should let you get back to the grue-some twosome. If you hear from Neil, tell him to give me a shout.'

'No problem, Cal. But you're as likely to see him first. He said he might pop over to Reykjavík when he's done Canada. Kirsty! ... Give me the remote control ... NOW! ... I'll have to go Callum, the wee girl's only gone and discovered the Adult Channel. I told my Davie to cancel his subscription but he never takes a blind bit of notice of anything I say. You take care, now.'

'I will,' said Callum.

He ended the call.

He gathered up his loose clothes and tossed them back into his open suitcase. He shut down his laptop and slid it into a drawer. He pushed one of the desks against the broken office door to hold it closed. He filled the kettle and emptied the last of a milk carton into a mug. He tried hard not to think the unthinkable.

15

Callum had expected the Icelandic Minister for the Environment to be some pot-bellied, sober-suited businessman, fat on the backhanders he enjoyed from the unscrupulous aluminium conglomerates that had bought up vast tracts of the country. He had not prepared himself for the stunning, cherry-haired Valkyrie in pencil skirt and black tights who met him in the hallway of the Alþing parliament house.

'Erna Snorradóttir,' was how she introduced herself, like it was a particularly seductive brand of perfume. 'And you must be Mr Pope of Fire and Ice Locations.'

'Thanks for seeing me,' said Callum. 'This is my colleague, Friðrik Friðriksson,' he added, the cue for Frikki to take the minister's hand.

'The others are already in the boardroom,' said Erna.

'The others?'

'You know, the representatives from the Spiritual Society . . . the people who are challenging your right to film at Skógafoss.'

'Are there many of them?' asked Callum, fearing a New Age lynch mob.

'Oh, about a half-dozen,' said Erna. 'Three elves, two trolls and a dwarf.' She smiled wickedly, with her eyes as much as her mouth.

Erna guided them through the dark corridor of

power (the Alþing was comparatively small) and showed them into a room dominated by an elliptical wooden table, around which sat Birna, Sigriður, Ásta and two elderly gentlemen. Callum felt he was here to resolve a domestic dispute rather than an environmental one. He took a seat beside Birna while Erna humbly served out cups of coffee that she accompanied with small glasses of sparkling mineral water.

'I wasn't expecting to see you here,' Callum whispered to Birna.

'I came to give moral support.'

'Who to . . . me or your mother?'

'Both of you. It is the least I could do. I was not able to persuade her to backtrack.'

'I'll warn you, this could get dirty,' said Callum. 'I've been delving into your mother's past to put together a savage character assassination. I figured that my only hope of winning this is to try and publicly humiliate her. You never told me she ran a chain of Scandinavian brothels. And as for the gunrunning . . .'

'I think Mother is up for the fight.' Birna was smiling.

'Well if it's going to be a bloody one, shouldn't Ásta be spared it?' Callum was conscious that Ásta's presence now put him in a catch-22. He didn't want to lose the hearing and so be seen as a failure by the girl who regarded her real father as a life-saving hero. However, should Callum win the day over Ásta's grandmother, he would only make bigger enemies of both of them.

'Ásta has to be here. I told you yesterday, this is the first day of her holidays and there is nobody at home to look after her.' Birna spoke it like an accusation.

'OK, OK,' said Callum. 'Tomorrow, I'll take her to the swimming pool. I promi—'

'Let us begin,' announced Erna Snorradóttir. She was sitting at the head of the table with a pristine set of untouched documents positioned in front of her. She held a pair of half-moon glasses under her chin, and, rather than putting them on, she scanned them over her papers like a magnifying glass. She talked while she skim-read.

'I want to make this snappy. I have a group coming to see me at three who are still moaning about the Kárahnjúkar dam project in the East fjords. They do not seem to realize that I am powerless to stop it now. The dynamite has already blown a hole through Dimmugljúfur canyon. What good is a petition to save sixty waterfalls and the breeding ground for pink-footed geese, when the area has already been flooded? Can they not see that the horse has bolted?' Erna shook her head like the world had gone mad. 'Nothing is ever enough for these damn environmentalists. I've just secured a ban on shooting ptarmigan for the next three years. They should be glad that their Christmas dinners will no longer contain pellets.

'Now,' she said, recomposing her papers and taking in the room. 'I have read through Mr Pope's case for shooting his commercial at Skógafoss – the creation of jobs for local crew, the attractive budgets paid by for-eign clients, the short-term benefits for a two-bar village like Skógar from an influx of film people with money to spend – all very good news. I have also read through the formal written objection from the Spiritual Society – some nonsense about elves – and it seems to me that this is pretty straightforward. I can see no reason why this filming should not go ahead.'

Frikki let out a cheer but Callum silenced him with a kick to the shin.

'How can you say this?' yelled Sigriður. She stood out of her seat and smacked her palms on the table.

'This is madness. You are supposed to be our Minister *for* the Environment, not our Minister *against* it.' Her head trembled as she spoke.

Birna's hands were over her mouth.

The minister bristled. 'Can I remind you that I have the power to eject you from this hearing. So please, sit down and let us try to remain calm. Now, you clearly feel passionately about the *huldufólk*, but we do not have any proof of their existence, other than these silly maps that you dispense to tourists.' Erna was referring to the maps that the Spiritual Society had submitted, their childlike cartography detailing the supposed habitats of the *huldufólk*. She held one of them up like it was a soiled nappy. 'Previous ministers may have been charmed by folklore and fables but, until you can prove the existence of these so-called "land spirits", I will only concern myself with the modern realities. Mr Pope has proven to me that his car commercial will create jobs, together with a valuable injection to the local economy. His proposal also assures me that the land at Skógafoss will be returned to the state in which he found it.'

'But it will be too late,' said Sigriður. 'The elves will have been disturbed.'

Erna seemed irritated. 'Has anyone in this room actually seen an *álfur*?'

Callum nudged Birna and whispered, 'What's an *álfur*?'

'An elf,' she replied.

'Well?' asked the minister, in a tone that simply defied anyone to challenge her.

A timid hand was raised by possibly the least likely contender in the room: a watery-eyed octogenarian with bluish-grey veins fanning across his cheeks like fossilized ferns. He was sporting the World's First Hearing Aid, a bulky sort more commonly powered by a car battery slung over the shoulder.

'I have seen many *kálfur*,' he said. 'As a young man, I made love with a *kálfur*.'

A silence seized the room, stripping away all sound to leave only the persistent hissing of nine glasses of sparkling mineral water. Callum could tell by the looks on the assembled faces that something was seriously wrong. Only Ásta was smiling. He nudged Birna again and whispered, 'What's a *kálfur*?'

'A *kálfur*,' she said, 'is a young cow.'

'You mean your mother's pal had sex with a—'

'It appears so.'

'I have seen elves,' said Sigriður, deflecting attention away from her confused gentleman friend. 'I was born with the ability to see them.' Callum saw no hint of madness or embarrassment in her demeanour. She spoke with utter conviction. 'They are social creatures that live in close groups and when we disturb their land, we are no better than home-wreckers.'

'So what do these elves look like?' asked Erna, with the smile of a sceptic. 'Do they have pointed ears?' She could not disguise her disdain. 'And why did you not bring some elves along with you? I would love to secure the support of the hidden people and double my vote in the next electoral campaign.'

'It is always the same with you politicians,' said Sigriður. 'You do not listen to the concerns of the people. You are always belittling us. You are only concerned about money and protecting your own positions, when you should be protecting the riches that are abundant in our land. But instead you blow up our unspoilt wildernesses to make room for dams and aluminium smelters that nobody wants. And today you have shown that you will allow anyone to dig up our sacred places so long as the money is right.' Sigriður was spitting as she spoke. 'It is another

203

example of the "blue hand" of the ruling elite crushing the will of the good people of Iceland.'

'Stop! I will not tolerate any more of this,' said Erna, with a severity that forced Ásta to hide behind a fold in her grandmother's cardigan, like an elf behind a rock.

But Sigríður was unstoppable. 'This government pollutes our rivers, spoils our countryside, bloodies our oceans and poisons our nature. And all the time you are doing this, you are destroying those communities of beings who have inhabited our land for centuries. But when you mess with nature, there is always a payback, and that is why she visits us with many more earthquakes and floods.'

'Enough!' said Erna. 'I have listened to both sides of the argument, I have made my decision and you must live with it. Mr Pope has submitted a reasoned and rational case for filming at Skógafoss, but you . . . you . . .' The minister looked at Sigríður like the older woman was a cruel relative who was attempting to disinherit her (though Sigríður would have argued that it was Erna who was trying to rob future generations of a landscape that was rightfully due to them). 'You bring nothing to this table,' she said. 'You only bring outdated concepts and romantic notions. It is all hearsay and nonsense. The filming will go ahead.'

'No, it won't.'

All heads turned to the source of the objection. It did not come from Sigríður, Eirik the Cowfucker or any of the other lobbyists. It came from Callum.

Frikki was as surprised as anyone. He lifted Callum's glass and sniffed the water to check it hadn't been spiked. He shrugged and let his boss continue.

'I'm sorry, Minister, but I have to disagree with you,' said Callum.

Erna glared at him. As her eyes widened, her lips

thinned into a bitter grimace. If she was affronted, the others were simply baffled. They looked at Callum like he was an *álfur*. Or a *kálfur*. He couldn't be sure.

'Sigríður talks sense,' he continued. 'I have only recently settled in Iceland and I'm not yet conversant with your history, your culture or the current political landscape. What I do know is that my locations business can only thrive as long as the countryside remains unspoilt. And although I had every intention of repairing any disturbance to the land at Skógafoss, I do not want to disturb those other things that make this country so compelling, and by that I mean its people and its *huldufólk*. I am not saying that the latter exist, but who can be sure that they don't? I have no intention of incensing the locals be they seen or unseen.' He directed this last statement towards Sigríður and, as he did so, Ásta reappeared from her cardigan. 'I will find an alternative to Skógafoss,' he concluded.

This roused a smile on Sigríður's face. It was an uncertain smile, but a smile nonetheless.

'You may not be conversant with Iceland's culture, Mr Pope, but you are starting to act like one of her citizens,' said Erna. She curled up Callum's proposal document and slotted it into her wastebasket. 'Since I took up this post I have come to realize that this country is full of time-wasters. You can be satisfied that you are fitting in well.'

'We could have made a lot of money on that shoot,' said Frikki. 'Why did you make such a U-turn? I don't understand.'

'I do,' said Birna, arriving at the table with three pints of Thule.

They were sitting outdoors in the beer garden at Sirkus, a paved area that was larger than the bar itself.

Callum was surrounded on all sides by bright blue skies and fat green palm trees that had been painted onto the enclosing walls, lending a Caribbean flavour to this most un-Caribbean setting (though the candied fug of burning cannabis sweetened the Reykjavík air).

Scores of pretty young things lounged around sucking on beer bottles, squinting in the sunlight and doing their best to look tragically hip, while two undernourished guys struggled through the thickening crowd with amplifiers and drumstacks to set up stage under an awning in one corner of the yard. Callum had thought that he recognized the music scuzzing out of the bar as the Jesus and Mary Chain but Frikki insisted it was the Slingers.

'Callum changed his mind about the shoot because he is finally putting his family first.' Birna placed a hand on Callum's back and rubbed it in slow, sincere circles.

'I did not know that Callum came from a family of elves,' said Frikki.

'I take it that you don't believe in the little critters either,' said Callum.

'No, I only believe in three things: rock music, beer and women. Actually, make that two things: rock music and beer. *Skál!*' Frikki necked half his lager in one go, leaving a white slug on his upper lip. He wheeked it in with his bottom teeth and burped loudly before continuing. 'I am too clever for elves. It is only uneducated fools who believe in such things.'

'You may think you are clever but you are just prejudiced,' said Birna. 'The more education people have, the more prejudiced they can become about the things they do not understand. Some of my mother's patients are educated people like teachers and lawyers and many of them have confided to her about the *huldufólk* they have seen. But they will always deny

206

their existence in public. They are scared that people like you will brand them insane.'

'They *are* insane,' said Frikki.

'If they are insane, then there are over 10,000 insane people walking our streets, serving our food, pulling our teeth and sailing our boats. The Spiritual Society counts that many members and they come from all areas of life.'

'And what do you get when you join this society?' asked Frikki. 'A pair of pixie boots and a bag of magic dust?'

'Cut it out, Frikki.' Callum didn't want this to degenerate into another slanging match between the pair of them, a repeat of their barney about whaling.

'I was only making fun,' protested Frikki, but he guessed that his boss was in no mood. He turned to Birna and made a show of apologizing. 'I am sorry, Birna, that I made light of your beliefs.'

'No problem, Friðrik. But I never said that I believed in *huldufólk*. If you want my view, I will give it. I do not believe in hidden people, I *accept* them. In the same way, I do not *believe* in the wind, the rain, the sun and the stars. I just accept that they are there.'

'And do you *believe* your mother when she says that floods and earthquakes are started by elves?' asked Callum.

'I am a scientist,' said Birna. 'Of course I do not believe that. I am not sure that my mother believes it either. I think she just liked the sound of it and that is why she used it to threaten our Environment Minister. My mother has always been good at telling ominous tales. I will bet that Erna Snorradóttir thinks about the elves the next time the earth shakes.'

A loud whistle pierced the air, syringing Callum's ears. One of the two guys under the awning had stood too close to an amplifier while tuning his guitar. He mumbled an apology into the microphone and dodged a blizzard of fag butts and bottle tops thrown by a group of lads in the front row. It was friendly fire, though, for all the young men appeared to know each other.

'That is the Slingers,' said Frikki. 'Though some of them also play in the Funerals. We are fortunate that they are playing here tonight.'

Callum didn't disagree. From what Frikki had told him about Singapore Sling's place in the Icelandic music scene, this performance was akin to Primal Scream playing the Docker's Fist in Clyde. But he wasn't about to hang around for the show. Despite the fact that he was sitting in the least claustrophobic drinking hole in Reykjavík, he could feel the blue skies and the palm trees closing in on him.

The events of the afternoon had only reminded Callum that he was an alien in this country. The Environment Minister had said that he was fitting in well, but she had intended it not as a compliment. Callum realized that he would have to work a lot harder than he had initially thought to master Iceland and her quirks. It was as if someone had stolen his familiar bagpipes and replaced them with a ball of wool, asking him to knit a *lopi* sweater with its distinctive snowflake pattern spreading out from the neck. Whatever had made him think that settling here was going to be easy?

'Birna, I think I might have to go,' he said.

'Is something wrong?'

'No, I just need some fresh air.'

'But we are outside, where the air is lovely,' interjected Frikki. He rocked back in his seat and inhaled deeply.

'You're only saying that because you're getting high on other people's smoke,' said Callum.

'True, but I still don't think you should go. I heard a rumour that Björk might be DJ-ing in Sirkus later tonight.'

'Then perhaps I'll pop back.' Callum stood up and buttoned his jacket. 'I'm going to head over to the office. I should email London and tell them we're looking at a new location for the Renault job. Rudi won't be happy, but at least I've finally managed to get someone working on his artificial geysers, so that should soften the blow.'

'I will join you,' said Birna.

'Don't leave me alone,' said Frikki.

'You are not alone.' Birna wound her scarf around her neck and pointed to something behind the big man. 'There is a beautiful elf girl behind you and she is giving you the eye.'

'I told you, I am too clever for elves,' shouted Frikki as Callum and Birna made their way towards the main bar. When he thought they were out of sight, he fixed his fringe and glanced over his shoulder.

Callum and Birna hit the main drag.

'It was nice of your mother to take Ásta off your hands and let us have some time together,' he said.

'She appreciates what you did. And so do I. Keep it up.'

'I'll try.'

'Wait.' Birna tugged his arm back. 'We should not go to your office. If we have this time to ourselves, we should do something wild.'

'Something wild?'

'Já. Hey, seeing as we are slowing things down, we could pretend that we are going on a first date.'

'Interesting,' said Callum, though he looked sceptical. 'Well in that case, I suppose we should find some-where to shag.'

'Shag?'

'Isn't that the form with first dates in Iceland?' asked Callum. 'Frikki told me that you lot like to dispense with formalities like flirting and chatting people up. He said you get straight down to the nitty-gritty.'

'Frikki is an oaf. That is why he is sitting in a bar by himself with no girlfriend to go home to.'

'Good point,' conceded Callum.

'What do British couples do on the first date?' asked Birna.

'They argue. Usually about who pays for what.'

'Is that it? They argue?'

'Mostly.'

'But where do they go?'

Callum thought about it. 'Us Brits are pretty unadventurous. The cinema is a popular first date. It's hardly "wild", though.'

'It is perfect. We shall go to the cinema. It will be just like the old days.' Birna threaded her arm through his and pulled him along the streets.

Callum was happy to be dragged along, newly buoyed by her words. They made him realize that his feelings for Birna were very real. This was no holiday romance, no carefree whim, no knee-jerk against the horror of his past. Callum was certain he had a future with this woman because, as she had just pointed out, they had already forged a history together. *The old days*, Birna had called it. If they had *the old days*, then they had something of substance. Until Birna uttered those words, Callum believed that *the old days* referred to that part of his life that had preceded Sarah's death. Everything after her funeral was a hiatus, a life put on hold, like he'd hit the pause button. He had come to accept that this was the way it would always be.

But he hadn't counted on this wonderful Icelandic woman gatecrashing his world. She was newness itself. She was tenacious, engaging, loving, and, importantly, her love was not born out of pity. Callum did not want to be pitied. After he'd buried Sarah, he had quickly tired of people he barely knew telling him how sorry they were for his loss and asking if there was anything they could do. Why did everybody and anybody suddenly think they could sort out the mess of his life for him? It was as if they only rallied around him to derive some vicarious pleasure out of his misery, like rubberneckers who slow down to examine a car crash.

At least Birna could never feel sorry for Callum because she didn't know that she had anything to be sorry about. As far as she knew, Sarah Glass was just an old flame and they had merely drifted apart. As far as she knew, Callum had a clean slate. And he needed it to stay that way so Birna could take him at face value.

Why should he tell Birna that Sarah had been murdered? Why should he spend his life being pitied, just because some nutcase decided to throttle the woman he loved? Was Callum's life always to be defined by one terrible night in Prague? Not if he could help it. And if that meant protecting Birna from the truth, then so be it.

'Here we are,' said Birna as they entered the quiet backstreet of Hellusund, not far from Callum's office. They were standing outside a small building that looked like a garage extension adjoined to the rear of an ordinary suburban house. A sign above its door read: Volcano Show.

'It doesn't look like a cinema,' said Callum.

'I said we should do something wild, and the films they show in here are the wildest thing imaginable.' Birna's eyes widened. 'Prepare yourself for a pyroclastic spectacle, a series of films featuring recent

211

volcanic eruptions, including Hekla, Surtsey and the big one that almost devastated my home island of Heimæy.'

'Who's starring?' asked Callum, for which he received a thump.

Birna hauled him into the theatre.

The two of them comprised the entire audience for the one-hour show. Birna held Callum's hand a little more tightly when the footage from Heimæy was screened. They watched as the lava flow consumed large parts of the island. It seemed destined to seal the entrance to the small harbour, the lifeline of her remote community. Were it not for the ingenuity of a local physicist and the Herculean efforts of two commercial dredging crews who used water cannons to pump over eleven million gallons of water a day onto the encroaching lava, Birna's parents would have been forced to settle on the mainland and Heimæy would remain a lifeless, redundant rock.

'Look on the bright side,' whispered Callum. 'If that had happened, you may never have met Arnar.'

Birna looked at him like he should know better. 'And my beautiful daughter might never have been born.'

'Sorry,' he said. 'I suppose if the island had been lost in the '73 eruption then Arnar would not have perished in the sequel.'

'1993 was not a sequel!' said Birna. 'You make it sound like some Hollywood production.'

'You mean this cinema isn't screening it? I was looking forward to coming back for *Heimæy 2: Return of the Lava*.'

Birna folded her arms.

'Sorry, I shouldn't trivialize it. It's just weird being in a cinema and watching this stuff. It's not the romantic comedy with bucketloads of popcorn that I had anticipated. And we don't even get to snog in the back row.'

'No?' asked Birna. She stood up and pulled him to his feet.

'What are you doing?'

'We are going to sit in the back row. And we are going to snog.'

And they did. And Callum felt that all his emotions were about to spill out at once like hot magma from cold rock. And crazy as it seemed, he felt sad, for he knew just how much he loved Birna and how much he now stood to lose. And Callum wasn't good with loss.

When Callum had first met Birna, he would have said that she was everything he had ever wanted, if he hadn't wanted only one thing: Sarah. But he knew he couldn't bring her back. And to have asked Birna to fill the void left by Sarah would have been like asking her to illuminate a blacked-out Albert Hall by holding aloft a single cigarette lighter. It was a futile task and Callum did not want to burden her with it. So before he moved to Iceland, he had taken the decision to never tell Birna about Sarah. Not only did he not want her pity, he thought it unfair to saddle her with such a precedent.

But Callum also knew that the longer he kept Sarah's murder a secret, the more he was doing Birna a disservice and the more he put their relationship at risk. For no matter what Birna did, no matter how much love she showed him, she could never repair his heart because she would never know that it needed repairing.

As they recomposed themselves for the final documentary, Callum felt sad but hopeful. He reminded himself that she had referred to 'the old days'. Birna was convinced that they had already created something tangible together – a relationship, a history – and Callum knew that they had forged such a relationship from a point of abject hopelessness. It was a sign that a new life had gained a foothold on dead ground.

The Volcano Show ended with a film documenting the creation of Surtsey, a volcanic island that appeared off Iceland's coast in the Sixties following an eruption beneath the sea. Even Callum had to concede that it was spectacular. Lava and rock bubbled up from a boiling ocean to create the world's newest landmass. The infant island hissed in the waves for three and a half years and, when it had cooled, it was placed under immediate protection as a natural laboratory. Access to it was restricted to a handful of scientists who could monitor the ways in which life colonized this new and seemingly infertile rock.

'A couple of years after its formation, a tomato plant was found to be growing on Surtsey,' whispered Birna. 'Nobody could explain how the seed got there, though there were a couple of theories. Was the seed trapped in the feathers of a migrating seabird? Was it carried by some intercontinental mistral?'

'Or did it fall out of a scientist's BLT?'

It wasn't such a daft hypothesis and Callum congratulated himself on his lateral thinking. However, as the closing credits rolled and the lights went up, he found it hard to formulate a theory that might explain how love had managed to flower again on the dead rock of his heart.

16

As they exited the cinema, they saw that the sun had disappeared and the sky over Reykjavík had turned a pissy grey like an unwashed net curtain. Petulant flecks of rain harangued the couple as they scurried through town to beat the impending shower. They stomped through puddles of wet bread and goose shit on the path by the Tjörn, the birds having given up on the sodden crusts that had been turned to bread sauce by an earlier downpour.

By the time Callum and Birna got into the office, the rain was battering the windows like buckshot.

'What happened to the door?' Birna ran her hand down the broken edge of the frame.

'Careful,' said Callum. 'You'll get a splinter.'

'Did someone break in?'

'Yes,' said Callum. 'I did.'

'You broke into your own office?'

'Last night I was out with Frikki and Anna Björk. I'd had a wee bit to drink and well . . . I lost my keys.'

'You should cut down on your drinking.'

'You're right. As always.' Callum held out his hands. 'Here, let me take your coat. I'll stick it on a radiator.'

'I'm soaked through. My jeans are stuck to my legs.' Birna indicated the wet patches running down the front of her thighs and shins like dark blue bones: a denim X-ray.

'Then whip them off and I'll hang them over the heat too.'

Birna threw him a dubious look.

'Come on Birna, this is no time to be coy.'

'OK, but I am going to need some help.' Birna fell back onto the sofa and held her legs in the air. She unzipped herself and tugged her jeans under her bottom. 'You will have to do my legs. I am scared that I might pull a muscle.' She kept her eyes fixed on Callum as he concentrated first on her right leg. 'You know, I am proud of what you did today,' she said.

'Really?' Callum placed one hand between Birna's legs, feeling the soft cotton of her panties rubbing against the tops of his knuckles. He slipped the same hand down the inside of her jeans, creating a break between the wet denim and her icy thigh. He used his other hand to slowly guide the trouser leg down to her knee.

'Já,' she said. 'And I think Ásta was proud of you too.'

'What makes you think that?' He unpeeled the sock from her right foot and rubbed her cold toes.

Birna's body bucked, throwing her hips into the air. 'That tickles,' she protested. When she relaxed again, her T-shirt had ridden up just enough to expose a slim band of purple silk underpinning her breasts. Her underwear didn't match – purple bra, white panties – something that Callum found particularly sexy because he believed it was more honest, more confident (the same reason that he was more attracted to women who wore little or no make-up).

'You haven't answered my question,' he said, turning his attention to her other leg. 'What makes you think Ásta is proud of me?'

'Because you did the right thing.'

'Simple as that?' Callum was finding Birna's left leg more problematic than her right. He cupped one hand under her bottom, just to steady her, while his other hand tugged the jeans sharply towards him.

'Simple as that,' Birna concurred. 'Ásta knows the difference between right and wrong. I have raised her this way. And this afternoon you did right. You stood up for her grandmother when the nasty woman in the Alþing tried to make out she was mad. At least, that is how Ásta saw it.'

Callum motioned Birna to roll over onto her front. Her jeans were clinging more obstinately to the back of her leg than they had to the front of her thigh. He reckoned it would be easier to remove them if she lay on her belly.

'You are just saying that to make me feel better about risking my first film job,' he said. He yanked Birna's trouser leg, inspiring her bottom to jut up towards him. Her panties had fallen askew to expose a pale and rounded buttock covered in angry pink fingermarks, as though Callum had spanked her.

'I am telling you, that is how Ásta saw it.' Birna's voice had become muffled as her face was pushed into the sofa cushion. 'She told me so, just before my mother drove her back to the house. Aha!' she screamed, finally free of her jeans. She rolled onto her back and presented her left foot to Callum.

He removed her remaining sock. He returned her foot to the floor and watched as she slid her bottom onto the front edge of the sofa and leaned back on her elbows.

Birna's fringe was still wet, the wind having freed it from the hood of her coat on their way to the office (the same wind was now scattering rain over the Reykjavík streets like salt from a gritter). Tiny beads of

217

rainwater rolled off the dark points of her hair, slaloming down her cheeks and neck and disappearing into the V of her T-shirt. She pulled the damp garment over her head and threw it onto the coat and jeans already balled up in Callum's arms. Birna lay flat on the sofa and pulled her panties back into position. 'What?' she asked, smiling at Callum. 'What are you looking at?'

'You,' he said. 'You're so beautiful.'

'Shut up!' Birna hurled a cushion at him. 'Go and dry my clothes and I will make us some hot chocolate.' Her bare feet slapped across the wooden floorboards as she made her way towards the office kitchen. 'But first, I need to do girls' stuff,' she added, grabbing her bag from the table and choosing instead the door to the bathroom.

Callum fed the jeans and T-shirt into the gap between the radiator and the wall. Birna's coat was too thick to slot in, so he let it hang by the hood from the back of his chair. As he was at his workstation, he remembered that he needed to send London an email. He scrubbed his mouse across the desk and his laptop glowed into life. He clicked the Netscape icon and hit 'Connect' in the next window. He shouted towards the bathroom, 'Birna, I've been thinking. I know you are nowhere near ready for me to move back in with you, but would you like to stay here tonight?'

Dialing . . .

'In the office? Where would we sleep?'

Dialing . . .

'The sofa folds out into a bed. It's quite comfy. This has been my home these last few days. Gudni's apartment is taken.'

Connection established. Verifying user . . .

'Oh. OK. I guess Mother can cook for Ásta. What will we do for food?'

Connecting to http://www.fail.is . . .
'We could send out for pizza,' he offered.
Done.
'Já. Ég ætla að fá silungur, sveppir en gulrætur.'
Checking password. Connecting to mailserver@fail.is
'In English?'
Inbox (1 message). Click.
'If you are going to improve your Icelandic, you must get used to hearing it spoken,' yelled Birna. The tiled bathroom lent an echo to her voice. 'I said I would like a pizza with trout, mushrooms and carrot.'

From: j.wedderburn@strathclydepolice.org.uk
Subject: Iago Kohl

'Trout, mushrooms and carrot on a pizza?' asked Callum. He said it quickly, determined to get to the end of the sentence before his voice cracked. His neck was hot and his heart was racing. 'Anyone would think you were pregnant.' Callum clicked on the detective inspector's name and opened the message.

It was brief. Terse, even. A lot like the man himself.

Callum.
Developments concerning Kohl. Call me.
JW.

The toilet flushed, a passable impersonation of the rain on the rooftiles. Birna re-entered the office, her semi-naked body barely illuminated by the slowly ebonizing sky outside the windows. She walked towards Callum and he saw that she'd tied her hair back, exposing a sweet and sanguine face.

'No Callum, I am not pregnant.' She rounded his shoulder to look at the message on his computer screen.

But before she could read a word, Callum hit 'delete'.

Birna brought her mouth to his ear. 'I am not pregnant . . . yet.' She pulled Callum's shirt over his head, forcing his arms into the air in an expression of surrender.

He couldn't sleep. A storm was throttling the office. It felt as if the whole building was passing between two speeding juggernauts on a rain-lashed motorway. Birna too had been tossing and turning. Some time around three she sat up, complaining that the sofa bed was hurting her back. Once roused, she found it difficult to settle down again. She was worried that the windows would implode.

Callum's insomnia was not prompted by a rogue weather system or an obdurate sofa bed. His mind had been too active to permit sleep. He had lain awake speculating on John Wedderburn's email. There had been 'developments', he had said. Developments regarding Sarah's killer: Iago Kohl.

Callum could only pray that the fucker had finally hanged himself from one of the radiator pipes in his Glasgow cell, or that a fellow prisoner had stabbed him in the showers, spilling his guts with a potato peeler.

The anxiety finally got the better of him.

He needed to know.

He waited until he was sure that Birna was asleep before he retrieved his mobile phone from his jacket and crept into the bathroom.

He called Wedderburn.

'John?'

'Mr Pope,' said the detective inspector. 'You do realize it's gone two in the UK.'

'Your message sounded urgent.' Callum was sitting

220

astride the toilet with a towel draped over his head. He thought the heavy material might deaden his voice. He didn't want to rouse Birna.

'Well, seeing as you've woken the wife up and condemned me to a night in the spare room, we might as well stay up and chat. How's life in the Land of Ice?'

'Permanently sunny,' said Callum.

'Glad to hear it,' said Wedderburn, not realizing that Callum was being literal. 'You deserve to be happy again. But isn't it expensive out there? What sort of mortgage do you get on an igloo?'

'There aren't any igloos in Iceland.'

'No igloos in Iceland?'

'There isn't much ice.'

'You mean all this hoo-ha I hear about global warming isn't such bollocks after all? Next you'll be telling me there's no ice hotel.'

'There isn't. The ice hotel is in Sweden.'

'So what's in Iceland, then?'

'Fish. And beautiful women,' said Callum. 'But mostly fish.'

'We've drawn Iceland in the Euro qualifiers. Should be an easy six points for Berti's boys but you never know, we were two–nil down to the Faroes after half an hour. How come these crappy little islands are suddenly producing decent football teams? Sometimes I think Scotland would do better if we fielded eleven sheepshaggers from the Shetlands.'

'John, I'd love to waste a policeman's phone bill reminiscing about Archie Gemmill's wizardry, David Narey's toe-poke, the crossbar coming down at Wembley and Scotland winning the "loveliest fans" award at every World Cup ever, but there's the small matter of my girlfriend's killer and these so-called "developments".' Callum was surprised at his own sarcasm.

'Yes. Sure.'

'Tell me he's a dead man, John. Tell me Kohl is dead and I might finally be able to get a good night's sleep. It'd be the first in six years.'

'It's not good news.'

'I had a funny feeling it wouldn't be.'

'He's out, Cal. They've granted him early parole.'

Callum placed one corner of the towel in his mouth and bit down hard.

'Callum? Are you there?'

He pressed another corner of the rough material into his eyes, soaking it all up. 'Tell me this is a joke, John. Tell me this is a fucking nightmare that I'm about to wake up from.'

'I don't make the rules, Cal. Listen, if it had been up to me Iago Kohl would still be behind bars but that's the way the law is today. Life doesn't mean life any more. Not when it's mitigated by good behaviour.' There was genuine anger in the DI's voice. 'Keep your cell tidy, puff up your pillows and eat all your greens, put the toilet seat down after you've slopped out, use a bookmark instead of folding down the corners in books from the prison library, do all this, keep your head down while you're doing it and no matter who you've murdered, you can be out in a five stretch.'

'How can you let him out? The guy's fucking dangerous! He threatened my girlfriend. He stalked her for months. He followed us to Prague where he abducted her and strangled her. He planned the whole show. Then he wrote it all down, every fucking detail, and submitted it to Strawdonkey as a fucking travel diary. And you're letting him out for good behaviour?' Callum's eardrums had filled with a hot noise. He realized he was listening to the movement of his own blood.

'I know it sucks, Cal, but you—'

'*It sucks?* Is that the best you can do, John? *It sucks?* You have no idea, do you?'

'Callum, I . . . you knew this was a possibility. That's why we called in at your offices just before you left.'

'Aye, and all that did was set the tongues wagging. The Strawdonkey lot think I sold the company because you were investigating financial irregularities.'

'That wasn't the intention, Cal. We just wanted to warn you that Kohl's situation was being reviewed.'

'You told me the review was just a formality. *Part of the penal process*, you said. You told me he'd be in for life and I took you at your word.'

'What can I say, I'm—'

'Don't tell me you're sorry, John, coz I won't fucking believe you.'

Callum killed the call.

He thought about Sarah and he thought about Kohl.

He thought about Birna, about how much he had to lose, and a column of bile raced up his throat like hot mercury.

He emptied his guts into the sink.

He re-entered the office and sat at his desk. His chair squeaked on the floorboards but the sound of the rain drowned it out. As far as he could tell, Birna was still sleeping. Her shoulders swelled with every long, lazy breath. Raindrops ran down her exposed back, projected onto it by the light that filtered through the storm-lashed windows.

As he often did in his blackest moments, Callum revisited Prague.

He switched on his laptop and called up Kohl's diary. He read it through for the umpteenth time, imagining that all he had to do was delete a paragraph, tone down a word or change a name, and somehow he'd be able to undo this whole bloody mess.

From: puppeteer@hotmail.com
To: travelogs@strawdonkey.com
Date: Mon, 12 Oct 1997, 02:39:45 +0000
Subject: THE KILLER'S GUIDE TO PRAGUE

A Gothic footbridge made of stone spans the broad Vltava River, linking five ancient towns together into Prague. West of it lies the pastel-coloured baroque of the Old Town. To the east sits Malá Strana (the Little Quarter), its cathedrals, cemeteries, cafés and parks tumbling down the hill that descends from Prague Castle to form irregular vistas over the city below. Renowned as the traditional craftsman's corner and the home of poets, drunks and mystics since the seventeenth century, Malá Strana seemed an appropriate base for me to enjoy Prague's annual International Festival of Puppetry. Moreover, its winding cobbled streets concealing graves, cellars and labyrinthine chambers make it appealing for those of us planning a killing.

Murder is already in the air.

This is Kafka's city, after all. It is a place of brooding surrealism where nothing is quite as it appears. It is a place steeped in alchemy and underpinned by tragedy, where the past is tangible, crowding the present-day streets with its ghosts. It is a place that turns men into cockroaches.

I had booked a room with a view at Na Kampé 15, a newish venture tucked up in Kampa Island between crumbling build-ings, quiet parks and the bubbling Devil's Stream (named, I was variously told, after a demon in the water or a washer-woman's temper). 4,300Kč bought me one night in a well-appointed room with exposed beams and a wonderful garret window overlooking the full and swollen river.

Booking into the hotel I commented on the sandbagging that

I had seen along the left bank of the Vltava. 'So the water is high,' the concierge shrugged. 'You want me to sell you my swimming shorts?'

The gloomy October weather – wet and unrelenting, the last of autumn bedding into winter – did not deter me from heading into the Old Town. Nor had it put off the many puppeteers who had gathered in the city. In every dark nook and crooked doorway marionettes played out their dramas.

I saw green sprites and water nymphs with silver hair. I saw white angels, red devils, kings, queens, princes and princesses in all their finery. I stopped to watch rod puppets enacting *Don Giovanni*, lip-synching to a too-slow cassette. I was charmed by a wooden peasant girl, her stained cheeks lending her slight smile a sense of unutterable joy. She was such a pretty thing. And along with several stoned teenagers I enjoyed the remarkable *Symphonie Fantastique*, a puppet show performed underwater in a 1,000-gallon tank.

'Don't fuck with a puppet. You'll only get splinters,' shouted a policeman on strings, while a real cop led away the student protester operating it. Berobed monks, nuns in their habits, jesters, foresters and numerous St Peters danced around my feet, helping me to forget the inclemency. At one point I was even cheering Death.

A blind man with a bootleather face was selling skeleton marionettes that he had carved by hand. I wondered how a blind man was able to make something so intricate. 'It is simple,' he dryly informed me. 'I just get a block of wood and chop away everything that isn't a skeleton.'

I love puppets and I love fantasy. The Czech capital is a fantasist's dream. Stories surrounded me everywhere I looked. Imps and nymphs straddled doorways, while demons cavorted on turret towers and held up the red tile roofs. Prague is the Brothers Grimm in stone.

I left the unseemly hordes in the Old Town and made my way back to the less cluttered streets of Malá Strana, to the casual and unmarked beer halls, to the hidden jazz dives where the locals exercise their hard-won right to gather, to argue and to create.

I had an appointment to keep.

Although the city's main attractions are walkable in a day, Prague is well served by bus, tram and metro. It was via the latter that I sought temporary respite from the foul weather. Unlike the fare-dodging locals, I paid the modest 8Kč to wait for an eastbound train at Můstek underground station. The platform walls were covered in large bubbled tiles in lurid metallic shades that resembled flattened Daleks (one wonders how they got down the steps, or if this was the very folly that flattened them).

Darkness was descending as surely as the rain by the time I surfaced into the square at Malostranská. The train had ferried me under the Vltava, a river that now sounded like the sea. Torrents of water spewed from the mouths of gargoyles that tried vainly to jump clear of the brimming gutters on a cathedral roof. Traders removed their racks and rails from the streets while their customers fought over raincoats. In a restaurant set low on the water by the foot of Charles Bridge, carpets were being pulled up, furniture lifted and electrical fittings removed. The flagstones simmered and spat.

A knot of locals had gathered round a newspaper kiosk, everyone craning their necks and arching up on their toes to gain a better view of the vendor's miniature television set. The broadcast featured a man wrestling a deer. Was this primetime entertainment in Prague? A girl standing beside me sensed my confusion and explained in student English that her city was bracing itself for a flood. They had already begun sedating the most agitated animals in the zoo. I watched some more of the newscast. Sure enough, the zookeepers moved among the distressed creatures with the determination of Noah.

A woman rushed past me pushing a pram full of sandbags. A helicopter patrolled overhead, presumably monitoring the river level. I thought it prudent to head for the hills. I would not be sipping my Pilsner on a weir-side terrace tonight.

A little panic, a touch of mayhem; events were conspiring very nicely. Not that I could have orchestrated a flood. I'm not God. The only thing I have in common with the Big Puppet Master in the Sky is the power to take life. And that is what I was in Prague to do. The biblical weather was merely a bonus. The threat of flood kept everyone occupied. Eyes were off balls. The long arm of the law would be grappling a sandbag.

I followed the steep drag of Letenská past the Church of St Nicholas and came out into Tržiště, my route marked out by ornate streetlamps, their watery light spilling down the hill and turning black cobbles gold. Alchemy indeed.

Cut into this street is the beer hall U Schody Vola. I descended the slate steps that gave it its _____ was here that I had arranged to meet Callum a_____ couple I had sat beside on the flight _____ promised them an induction into the B_____ drinking on this, their first night in the _____

In truth, my striking up a conversa_____ entirely coincidental. I had been f_____ engineered the seat next to them on the plane. It's a free-for-all on these no-frills airlines. Seats aren't pre-allocated. I've heard people complain about the undignified scramble at departure gates as you jockey for position, but this system has obvious advantages for anyone stalking a potential victim.

Killer Travel Tip: stick to your quarry like glue (I had made sure I was first up the steps behind her when boarding the plane).

In Prague, the real drinking is done in smoky holes with stained tablecloths run by surly servers with suspect maths. U Schody Vola refuses to buck this trend. It is comprised of a vaulted brick cellar decked out with steamer-trunk tables and is barely illuminated by 20-watt fluorescence. It is certainly smoky, unsurprising in a country that seems entirely populated by chain-smokers and which boasts a brand of cigarettes called Start.

Happily, U Schody Vola is one of the few central pubs that hasn't forced out local drinkers with inflated prices. It remains a barebones hideout for students, buskers and workers in overalls slaking their thirst with a well-earned *pivo* or two. In short, it attracts the penniless with a taste for good beer and bad Moravian wine.

I had arrived early to build up some Czech courage. My plan was a simple one. I knew exactly how I was going to prise this woman away from her partner. I knew pretty much how I would kill her. I was in two minds about how I would dispose of her body. I needed to dump it somewhere where it could remain undiscovered for at least twenty-four hours. I figured that when her boyfriend reported her missing, the police would allow that time to elapse before they treated her dis-appearance as anything more sinister than a lover's tiff. This would afford me ample opportunity to get out of the city unchecked. Wait any longer and the airport would be crawling. I had one chance to get out of Prague and I had to take it.

I had given this couple a false name, spinning them a yarn that I lived in Croatia, not Glasgow (this was partly true as I spent the first eight years of my life in Zagreb, so the pretence and the accent came easy to me). But I knew that, after the event, the boyfriend would be able to ID me on sight. He would give a statement detailing the last time he had seen his girlfriend alive and what he knew of the man she was with. The police would consult the passenger list on the flight we had shared. Thankfully, the name on my passport was not the name that I resided under in Scotland. Such duplicity became necessary many years previously when my family was refused asylum in the UK.

Killer Travel Tip: don't exist.

I was soaked through. I shunned the ubiquitous Staropramen and settled into a corner seat with a half-litre glass of Herold Tmavý Lezák 13°, a dark lager more akin to a stout with a chicory malt aroma and liquorice finish. It retained a good, thick head that left a succession of rings down the inside of my glass as I polished it off. A woman wearing an improbable wig replenished my beer without my having to ask, such is the custom. At 12Kč a glass, I couldn't complain. The problem would be remembering how many I'd drunk at the end of the night.

Not that I had any intention of hanging round to pay the bill. I would leave that privilege to a drunk Scotsman while I disappeared with his barely conscious girlfriend.

The hirsute waitress also deposited a jar in the middle of my table. It appeared to contain a badly preserved foetus. She quickly explained it was *utoponec*, meaning 'drowned man'. Apparently it is a favourite dish among Czech pub denizens who seem to enjoy the taste that only vinegar can impart to a sausage. By the time my guests arrived, I was burping pickled baby and toasting them with the unmissable, ruby-tinged Červený drak or 'Red Dragon', a steal at 10Kč.

Callum and Sarah were in Prague to celebrate the flotation of their new company. They asked me what line of work I was in. I told them my business was to ensure that, by the time our night was done, they would know the full versatility of Bohemia's legendary Žatec hop. And so it was that a procession of dark beers, light beers, perfumed lagers, crisp Pilsners and tarry stouts slid under our noses with an almost metronomic zeal. Sarah started to dither over a bitter Kozel, a situation I could not tolerate, but I got her back up to speed again with a couple of U Schody's famous fruit beers, Vinové and Banánové.

Our conversation soon became as boisterous as the weather. To anyone within a hundred yards of the pub we were advertising the joys available inside better than any neon sign on the door. In fact, it was a shame I had to kill Sarah. In other circumstances we might have become good friends. Prague has this uncanny habit of getting the unlikeliest people together. Or is that just the beer?

I upped the ante with some Becherovka chasers (14Kč a shot, but watch out for city-centre sharks who'll charge you for doubles you didn't order). Mixing this yellow herb liqueur with beer is risky alchemy, as effective as Rohypnol at inducing semi-coma (a necessary part in my endgame). But worryingly, my guests seemed immune to its limb-deadening charms. Hey, they were Scots.

The bar was all out of horse tranquillizer, so I ordered the next best thing – absinthe – the ruin of many a romantic poet. 'Tonight we're going to party like it's 1899,' I sang, as our waitress brought the green bottle to our table.

The intention was to ply Sarah with enough wood alcohol that she assumed the characteristics and mobility of an oak. But she was having none of it. She turned her nose up at the lethal green shampoo-in-a-shot-glass and demanded that her boyfriend take her back to their hotel.

Working on the Poppins Principle that a spoonful of sugar helps the medicine go down, I enticed Sarah into drinking her poison by observing a local ritual. Our waitress, who bizarrely had grown less and not more attractive as the evening (and the beer) wore on, fetched me the requisites. I instructed Sarah to load her teaspoon with sugar and dunk it in her absinthe. It took her three attempts to get it in the glass, filling me with confidence that she'd soon be where I wanted her. She pulled her spoon out and held it high. I used my lighter to set fire to the wet sugar – 'Chasing the Drunkard' – and watched as it burbled and caramelized in the ever-widening blacks of her eyes. When the flame extinguished itself I told her to plop the spoon back in her glass and stir.

'Close your eyes, glug it back and try not to think about tomorrow,' I said. For there will be no tomorrow.

Thankfully her drinking arm hit the table before her forehead, cushioning the blow. Callum took his absinthe neat. He asked me to watch his girlfriend while he went to the toilet. 'Like she could go anywhere,' he joked.

It was a job getting Sarah up the steps but once I did, it was downhill all the way and her legs moved forward with a gravitational volition. Her boyfriend's bladder was full of beer, enough to buy us a good three or four minutes' start.

The rain had washed the streets clean of people but I was taking no chances and shunned Mostecká in favour of the backstreets on our way down to Kampa Island. We crossed the small bridge at Hroznová and continued down to the jetty at Kampa Wharf. As I rightly guessed it had been abandoned due to the danger imposed by the rapidly rising river.

I wasn't tired despite my carrying the best part of Sarah's ten-or-so stone. The alcohol and adrenalin were keeping me going, flowing through my veins with the same urgency as the river running rampant around us. The Vltava was livid. The stretch of water that bisected the capital had become an oxtail torrent, coiling into violent eddies, flattening off the weirs and punching at islands in midstream.

My plan had been to strangle Sarah and dump her in the river. This time tomorrow she'd be in Dresden. Unfortunately, with the river set to burst its banks, she was as likely to end up in a tree outside Prague's magnificent Fred & Ginger building. I couldn't take the risk.

Earlier that afternoon, something on the wharf had caught my eye that inspired a change of tack. It was a spectacular puppet show put on by the Spejbl and Hurvínek Theatre. The troupe had erected a small crane on the jetty. Suspended on hooks from its single arm were four life-sized marionettes representing Greed, Vanity, Death and the Turk (the same characters that act out a lurid lesson in morality on the hour, every hour, beneath Prague's Astronomical Clock). Each figure was made of wood and dressed in appropriate garb. The arm of the crane had been swung out over the river and its height adjusted so that the feet of each marionette became submerged. The large puppets entertained the crowds up on Charles Bridge by appearing to dance wildly on the water, each step choreographed by the river's moods and movements (and boy was the river in a foul mood).

The cold night air seemed to be having a resuscitative effect on Sarah, so I strangled her before she came round. I knew she was dead when she stopped coughing green sugar onto my wrists.

I wheeled the crane back in from the water. This gave me a better look at the marionettes. I noticed that each wooden man had rings screwed into his head, his wrists and his knees, through which five hooked cables secured him to the metal arm.

Despite being much heavier than he looked, I had little bother unhooking Vanity and laying him beside Sarah. And it was with surprising ease that I was able to swap their clothes. Undressing Sarah was only slightly tricky as the dead are notoriously unco-operative. Her jeans were sopping and her puckered thighs proved more reluctant to let go of damp clothing than the puppet's polished wood. What became more problematic, however, was a mechanism by which I could secure the hooks to Sarah's limbs. Digging them into her new costume would not be sufficient. The material would rip before it supported her weight.

There was only one way this was going to work. The hooks would have to go through her.

I left two lifeless bodies on the wharf while I searched for something heavy. I managed to prise a loose keystone out of a small arch in the river wall (over the years the water must have given it a good battering).

I lowered the crane arm as far as it would go, until the cables came to rest on the jetty slats. I took Sarah's legs and dragged her body to within easy reach of the apparatus. The hooks were large enough to be hammered straight through the softs of her wrists. However, the backs of her knees were impossible. The points of the hooks refused to sit still on the fattier flesh. They either fell askew or kicked back with every hit. The more I persevered, the more her legs started to swell and the harder it was to get purchase. In the end I gave up and tapped them into her kneecaps.

I rolled Sarah onto her front again and folded her jeans under her face. The remaining hook slammed into the back of her skull in one. I gave each cable a sharp tug to check she was good and secure.

She was.

I removed Vanity's hooded mask and fastened it over Sarah's head. As I winched her to her feet an army dinghy bounced up the river. It slowed as it passed. One of the crew aimed a torch at us.

I held Sarah's hand and waved it at them. The crew waved back. They were laughing. They fired their outboard and disappeared under the vacant Charles Bridge (the authorities had sealed it off).

I wheeled the crane 180 degrees over the river and lowered the arm. I locked it in position only when Sarah began tapping her feet.

From my garret window at Na Kampé 15, with a passable bowl of room-service goulash warming my lap, I was able to enjoy her mad St Vitus Dance.

17

'Wake up.'

Callum felt a hand rocking his back. He sat upright and his shoulders were immediately cut in two by a knifeblade. He had fallen asleep at his desk and had woken with a crick in his neck.

'Could you not sleep on the sofa bed?' asked Birna. She was wearing Callum's Partick Thistle football shirt and her hair was wet, suggesting she had showered.

'It wasn't the bed. It's the light. This office could do with curtains.' Callum rubbed the sleep from his eyes. 'I thought that as I was lying awake, I might as well do some work and source some alternative locations to Skógafoss.' He closed his laptop. 'Hopefully I'll find a few places that aren't inhabited by elves.'

Birna stood behind him and rubbed his shoulders.

'God that feels good,' he said.

'Who were you phoning last night?' she asked.

Callum's shoulders tightened again.

'I heard you in the bathroom. Those tiles really echo.'

'Oh, that. I called one of the guys at Strawdonkey. Neil. I left some location shots on his company hard drive and I need him to mail them over.'

'And you called him at four in the morning?'

'Neil's an insomniac. He spends most nights with a gamepad in his hands pretending he's a US Navy Seal. I knew I'd get hold of him.'

Birna got Callum to turn his chair round so she could sit on his lap. 'Your eyes look puffy. Anyone would think you had been crying.' She kissed him on both eyelids.

'This is what persistent daylight does to me,' he said. 'I'll have to buy myself a pair of those sleeping goggles.'

'You must not do that. You will be blind in your dreams.'

'Honestly Birna, with the dreams I've been having, that would be no bad thing.'

She stood up. 'I should let you get dressed. I need you to drive me home.' She ran her hand along the radiator, scooping up her dry clothes.

They parked up outside Birna's house. Their cheeks were flushed and their bellies were full. They had stopped off at the Grey Cat café on their way through town to pump livening black coffee through their veins and fight their hangovers with waffles and jam.

The wind was the first thing Callum noticed as he stepped out of the Toyota and onto the carpet of weeds that led up to the house steps. A strong gust hit him full in the face, blowing a penetrating, clear cold that shook him fully awake. It was an arrogant wind, so clean and sharp that when he breathed through his nose he felt a sharp pain between his eyes (the same thing happened when he took a glug of cold water after sucking an Extra Strong mint).

Across the bay, Mount Esja was showing her colours in gratitude as the sun stroked her flanks. Shadows raced over her like ruffled fur as the wind chased the clouds above.

'Every time I look across at that mountain, it looks different,' said Callum. 'I'm convinced that it changes in size. Some days it's bold and brazen, other days it seems distant and aloof. And look at it now. It's positively glowing.'

'I do not think Esja changes in size,' said Birna. 'But she changes colour constantly. I put it down to her mood swings. And often, her mood will influence my own frame of mind. Each morning when I gaze across the bay, Esja lets me know what sort of day I am about to have. Today looks pretty good.' She kissed Callum's nose.

'Good morning.' Sigriður exited the house carrying a washing basket piled high with freshly laundered clothes. 'Did you have a good time?'

'We went to the cinema,' said Birna. 'I took Callum to the Volcano Show.'

'I'll bet it was not as violent as last night's weather.' Sigriður pinned a line of clothes pegs to the front of her apron and began the tricky business of attaching the laundry to a clothes line that refused to sit still.

'What about you?' asked Callum. 'Did Ásta and you get up to any fun and games?'

'It was not Ásta and I who were having the fun and games. It was the *huldufólk*.'

'Mother,' scolded Birna. 'Callum has already agreed to take his shoot elsewhere. Do not tease him.'

'I am not teasing him. While you have been watching volcanoes, the elves have been playing tricks on us.' Sigriður removed another peg from her apron and tagged a pair of undies to the line.

Callum guessed that the pants belonged to Birna's mother, as they were large enough to accommodate the whole family should Birna's house finally succumb to an earthquake.

'What tricks?' asked Birna.

237

'All this washing that I am putting up now, it is all stuff that I gathered in last night just as the storm was taking hold. But a number of garments are missing. Ásta said she saw one of the *huldufólk* making off with the clothes.'

Callum kicked at the gravel. He didn't want to be part of this. He felt that Sigríður was pushing her luck.

'Mother, there is a simple explanation for the missing clothes.' Birna too was losing her patience. 'We live on the coast. We are always losing clothes to this wind. And last night it was three times as strong.'

'It was not the wind,' said Sigríður.

'How can you be so sure?'

'Because it was only Ásta's clothes that went missing.' Sigríður draped a cardigan over the line and pinned it in place. The garment protested, gesticulating wildly with its arms. 'How would the wind know to only steal Ásta's clothes?'

At this, Callum looked up. 'Are you sure? He only stole Ásta's clothes?'

'Ásta cannot be sure that the *álfur* was a "he", but the only clothes that are missing belonged to her.'

'Listen Birna,' said Callum. 'I've got to get back to work.' He opened the car door.

'Wait,' she said. 'Haven't you forgotten something?'

Callum looked confused.

Birna pursed her lips.

'Oh. Right.' Callum gave her a quick kiss.

'Why the sudden hurry?' asked Birna.

'Oh, nothing. I . . . I have to let the staff into the office.'

'But your office has no lock. The door is broken.'

'Good point,' said Callum, but it didn't stop him hopping behind the wheel of his 4x4 and starting the engine.

Callum sped into town. He wanted to get back to the

office before Anna Björk and Frikki showed for work. He needed some space to think. According to DI Wedderburn, Kohl was a free man again. And Callum had a horrible feeling that Sarah's killer was in Iceland. It explained the Jeep charging at Ásta. It explained the break-in and the clothes disappearing from the washing line. Kohl was stalking him. Callum was sure of it. The bastard was free again and now he was intent on punishing the guy who put him away. Callum had robbed Kohl of six years by testifying against him, and now Kohl was trying to exact some revenge by destroying his second shot at happiness.

'You're a prick, Pope,' shouted Callum. He thumped his hands on the steering wheel. 'P-R-I-C-K. You should have killed that bastard when you had the chance.'

Sarah's body was flown back to Glasgow four days after Callum had returned from Prague. A Czech pathologist had performed the autopsy. He had found nothing in her blood, and no invasion to her body, to distract him from the first and most obvious hypothesis that the cause of her death was directly related to the strangulation marks on her neck.

Callum had helped the Prague police to compose an e-fit of the Croatian who had disappeared from the pub with his girlfriend. He had also given them a statement, though he struggled to remember every detail. There were small chunks of the evening that eluded him, largely due to the amount he had drunk and the fact that he had been awake for all of the twenty hours since Sarah's disappearance. A part of him refused to believe she was gone. It was as if he'd merely misplaced her, like his car keys, and he would find her again if he could just retrace his last movements.

But his world fell apart when they called him to

the main Prague hospital to identify a female body.

He was driven across the Vltava by a policeman who explained the unusual circumstances in which the deceased had been found. He said that due to the manner of the woman's death, all the blood had settled into the lower half of her body. He cautioned Callum that her face might not be immediately recognizable and advised him to concentrate on identifying his girlfriend by any distinguishing marks like moles, tattoos and scars.

But when the pathologist pulled the crisp green sheet back, Callum was in no doubt it was Sarah. Her face was thinner, more brittle-looking, but it was Sarah. Her drained cheeks had turned an insipid colour like week-old chicken fillet, but it was definitely Sarah. Two large purple flowers appeared to have been inked round her neck and even though Callum knew that his girlfriend had no such tattoo, it was unmistakably, unshakably Sarah.

They sedated him there and then.

When he'd slept off the drug, he was brought back to the police station for further questioning. A representative of the British Embassy had been summoned to offer support and to arrange his transfer back to the UK. Fat lot of good he proved to be. He was unable to prevent Callum lashing out at a Czech officer who, pointing to the woolliness of Callum's original statement, suggested that he killed his girlfriend following a drunken row.

They locked Callum in a cell to let him cool off but by that stage he was too far gone. In truth, he wasn't so sure that he wanted to be released back into the world again, the same world that had robbed him of the only thing that mattered.

But they put him on a plane that evening.

The Killer's Guide to Prague was waiting for Callum

when he returned to the Strawdonkey offices. In it, Sarah's murderer presented himself as an elusive, illegal immigrant living in Glasgow under a variety of names, but this could have been a red herring and he offered no further leads. However, the information contained in the travelog was enough for the Czech police to close their investigation and hand the problem over to Strathclyde.

And that was when Callum had his first visit from DI John Wedderburn, a man whom Neil Byrne would later christen 'The Minging Detective'. He arrived at Callum's door at 9 a.m. on the day after Sarah's funeral, clutching a translucent bag of greasy pasties from Gregg's bakery. He kicked off his questioning by asking Callum if he was in possession of any brown sauce.

Wedderburn was concerned that there appeared to be no motive for Sarah's murder. He would have understood it if she had been kidnapped and held to ransom, as Callum and Sarah had been hot news on the UK money pages. Two days before they had left for Prague, the couple had been pictured on the front of the *Herald* toasting the successful flotation of their company. The deal had catapulted the pair of them into the *Telegraph*'s list of 'Top 40 Earners under 40'. The six o'clock news had screened a short feature on Strawdonkey, an item that included a bizarre graphic to illustrate how many donkeys it would take to transport Callum and Sarah's projected fortune from Majorca to Glasgow if each mule carried a pannier loaded with £100,000.

Kidnap, Wedderburn could understand. But murder? It just didn't figure. The detective polished off a steak bake and fingered fish-flakes of pastry onto Callum's circular glass table. He asked Callum to get in touch if he could think of anyone who might have held a grudge against Sarah.

But Sarah had only been buried a day and Callum was in no fit state to think about anything.

The breakthrough came some weeks later, when Sarah's parents finally persuaded him to clear their daughter's stuff out of the flat. Not everything, just the odds and sods that no longer served a purpose. Callum owed it to himself to have a clearout, they said. By leaving everything of Sarah's in its place he was kidding himself that her death was nothing more than an extended holiday from which she would one day return.

And Sarah was never going to return. Callum needed a good dose of reality and her parents were the only people who were in a position to administer it. They were the only people who could possibly appreciate his loss.

He spent a full day getting rid of her clothes, shoes, bags, make-up, creams, powders, clips, tampons, jars of Marmite (Callum hated Marmite), and half a dozen 'All Woman' compilation CDs that Sarah had purchased when he wasn't looking. *All the odds and sods that no longer served a purpose.* He did not erase her memory entirely. Every painting in the flat had been bought with her judicious eye and they all stayed on the walls. He kept one of her hairbrushes, still cocooned in her blonde hair. And he promised himself (as he had always promised Sarah) that he would finally get round to organizing all their holiday snaps into albums.

He cleared out a miniature filing cabinet that Sarah had bought from Ikea on the day that she chucked in her job. It was stuffed with bills, receipts, statements, company contracts and old papers relating to her employment at the Royal Bank.

It dawned on Callum that it was Sarah who handled all their paperwork: the mortgage, the insurance, the council tax, the joint bank account, the debits and invoices. It was Sarah who paid for everything and it was Sarah who got competitive quotes for building work and arranged dates and times for that work to be carried out. As Callum flicked through her papers he realized that he wasn't sorting through the bureaucracy of his girlfriend's death, he was arranging a separation. Their separation. And he panicked. For that was the moment – more frightening than stroking her cheek and finding it as cold as a mortuary slab; more difficult than bearing her weight into a church – when everything unravelled and he knew he was on his own.

What was he going to do? How would he cope?

Days passed before Callum could gather himself, never mind the papers that he'd tossed across the bedroom floor. But it was within these pages that he first spotted the name Iago Kohl. Mr Kohl was the addressee on countless photocopied pages that bore the Royal Bank of Scotland letterhead. As Callum filed the sheets into chronology it emerged that Sarah had been corresponding with this strange, Shakespearian-sounding character for the six months before she quit the bank.

In the earliest communication, dated March 1995, Iago Kohl had requested a meeting with the bank. In his accompanying CV he listed himself as a former languages lecturer turned founding editor of Chameleon Press, an independent publishing house based in Glasgow. Chameleon had recently gone bust, forcing Kohl close to bankruptcy, but he was determined to start up again. He was therefore applying to Sarah for a New Business loan. He wanted to meet up with her to run his big idea past the bank.

The 'big idea' was outlined in a thick, ring-bound proposal document that Callum found hidden among Sarah's files. Kohl wanted to write, publish and market his own travel guides under the conceptual banner Europe for Two. He believed that the guides would satisfy a need that he had identified in the travel market. With the advent of low-cost airlines, more and more people were availing themselves of short city breaks in Europe, particularly couples. And couples, he had decided, are actually two individuals who want different things from their city break. None of the current guidebooks reflected this, or so Kohl believed. He was proposing to co-author a series of guides that reviewed all the major European cities from the different perspectives of the male and the female traveller. He intended to collaborate on the books with a 'Kirsty McNabb', one of his editors at Chameleon. They had already mocked up two guidebooks: *Rome for Two* and *Barcelona for Two*. The books could be read from the front or the back, depending on whether you were male or female. In other words, a guy could look up the fixture list for the Nou Camp and read reviews of all the strip bars on Las Ramblas, then his girlfriend could snatch the guide-book off him and flip it over to seek out the best shopping in Barcelona or ascertain the price of a sunbed on its man-made beach.

Kohl was convinced he was onto a winner. The Europe for Two guides could quickly become the World for Two guides; that was his tantalizing proposition. But he did not want to present his idea to other publishers. He was worried they would demand too large a cut or they would make him forfeit creative control of the concept. The big publishing houses would only insist on getting their own writers in. And he didn't believe they would give Europe for Two the big push it deserved. They would quietly seed it into select stores, taking care not to cannibalize the other travel guides on their lists.

For his idea to succeed, Kohl had to do it alone. But he needed a backer and the Royal Bank was his last hope. Rather, Sarah Glass was his last hope. But Sarah rejected his loan application without meeting him. She didn't believe his idea was original enough and she claimed that, due to his business history, he represented 'an unacceptable risk' to her organization.

As Callum read the months of correspondence that followed her curt but professional rejection letter, it became evident that Kohl wasn't a guy who took rejection lightly. His tone became increasingly menacing to the point where he resorted to threatening Sarah. One particularly vile letter had even been sent to their home address. The message was clear: *I know where you live*.

Callum wondered why Sarah hadn't said anything to him about the letters. She would have been frightened but he could have done something about it. Perhaps that was the reason she kept it to herself. She didn't want Callum getting himself into trouble.

The final letter sent to Kohl by the Royal Bank had been written by one of Sarah's managers. He threatened to report Kohl to the police. It seemed to do the trick, as the correspondence immediately dried up.

The bank moved Sarah away from Business Loans and switched her over to Mortgages. At the time, she had made Callum believe it was a promotion. She had seemed thrilled about it, claiming that the extra money meant they could at last try for a baby. But Callum found another letter from her manager in which it was clear that the move had been precipitated by the bank's genuine concern for her safety.

A little under four weeks into her new role, Sarah quit. She had come up with a business proposition of her own, one that also concerned travel.

Armed with these letters, Callum had been in a

position to speculate. He guessed that Kohl had been keeping an eye on Sarah long after she had left the bank. He had seen her launch a business on the back of an idea that was different but not dissimilar to his own and he had grown to resent her for it. Perhaps Kohl had got angry, in the skewed belief that Sarah had stolen 'his baby'. Perhaps he believed that he was entitled to all the money and publicity it had brought her. He would have tormented himself with the injustice of it: what was hers was actually his. Would he then have sought to get even?

Certainly, revenge was a motive, something that until then had been frustratingly absent from the murder investigation. And if Kohl had threatened to harm Sarah back in 1995, to the extent that her employer had expressed legitimate fears for her safety, he might well be capable of attacking her a couple of years later.

Callum had convinced himself that Iago Kohl was Sarah's killer: the self-styled 'Puppeteer' in the anonymous *Killer's Guide to Prague*. All he needed to do was hand over Kohl's letters to DI Wedderburn. The police would haul him into the station and offer him up to Callum in an ID parade. And Callum never forgot a face, not this one anyway.

But why should Callum involve the police? Why wait for justice when he was in a position to mete it out himself? He was in possession of Kohl's home address. He could nip across town and ID him on his doorstep. And when he did, he would have all the just cause he needed to stave the fucker's head in.

Callum drove to the heart of Glasgow's West End and parked his car illegally in a space reserved solely for the residents of leafy Lynedoch Crescent. He intended to do some serious damage to a resident of leafy Lynedoch Crescent, so a parking ticket was the least of his concerns. He was feeling pretty lawless. What would they do, sentence him to seven years for murder with a £30 fine thrown on top for a minor traffic violation? If that happened he would plead insanity in regard to the parking offence. That'd confuse them. For as far as killing Kohl was concerned, Callum was in cool, clear-headed control of his actions.

The wind shook the tree above Callum's car and the rain pasted the falling leaves onto his windscreen. He flicked his wipers. They restored his clear view into the window of a ground-floor terrace on the opposite side of the darkening crescent. Behind this window, a man was sitting at a grand dining table. Callum had been watching him for a good hour, though it had taken only a few seconds to recognize him as the man who had drunk him under a less impressive table in a Prague drinking hole.

Iago Kohl was not sitting down to a meal, however. He was tapping the keys on his laptop with the same dainty fingers that had done such irreparable damage in the Czech capital. He got up from his seat every so often to retrieve fat books from his fat bookshelves. Callum sat in his car with the heating on full blast. He didn't step into the rain until the afternoon had turned from grey to blue to black to orange as the streetlamps flickered into life.

Callum could have confronted Kohl at any time during that hour. But he hadn't. Not that he was in any doubt that he wanted to kill him. It wasn't as if he had spent that time asking himself searching questions about his own morality. He had simply figured that bloodstains don't look like bloodstains under orange streetlight. So he had waited until it got dark. No point in alarming the neighbours as he returned to his car after dispensing his own rather messy brand of justice.

Callum opened up the boot of his car. He removed a Louisville Slugger CU31 Alloy softball bat with 12″ barrel and cushioned grip. Young Kenny had given it to him as a present from the Big Apple. Callum read the writing that ran the full length of its sleek, tapered handle and wondered what a 'power end load' was. He guessed that Kohl was about to find out.

Before going to Kohl's door, Callum took a practice swipe – an air shot – just to find his stroke.

But the bat was removed from his hands on the backswing.

'I hope you're not thinking of using this,' said DI Wedderburn.

The detective held the bat like a snooker cue and potted an imaginary ball across the bonnet of Callum's car.

I should have killed the fucker when I had the chance.

Callum drank his coffee and watched the birds dive-bombing the Tjörn. He returned to his desk and searched the Net for news of Kohl's release.

For six years Callum had kept a picture of Sarah's killer in his mind: the face of the Iago Kohl that had once grinned beerily at him across a sticky-ringed table in Prague. Every time he closed his eyes that face was there. It was like a persistent after-image that had been tattooed on his retinas after staring too long at the one thing. He couldn't get rid of it . . . until now. For Callum had finally found a new face to replace it: the face of the Iago Kohl that had been printed in every Scottish newspaper on the day of his release. The same face that now looked up at him from his laptop.

Callum maximized the photo on the *Scotsman* web-site. After nearly six years of confinement, Kohl had grown blanched and bloated like a vegetable forced under a flowerpot. His own mother would not have recognized him. Doubtless she had not recognized the expressionless killer who had gone into prison in the first place. She would have sat in court and wondered how the dishevelled beast being led out of the dock could be the same beautiful boy she had reared all those years ago – her Iago, the boy who would never hurt flies, melt butter in his mouth, or say 'Boo' in the presence of geese.

Like Callum's heart bled for her.

Kohl may have looked blanched and bloated but there remained a keenness in his eyes that suggested the guy had a purpose. And Callum feared he was about to exact it. Somehow, he had to be stopped.

He phoned Wedderburn.

'John?'

'Cal?'

'I trust you eventually got some sleep this morning.'

'Aye.' The inspector yawned. 'That spare bed and I are becoming well acquainted. Is your head any clearer in the cold light of day?'

'It's just as clear as it was five hours ago, in the cold light of night,' said Callum. 'In fact, it couldn't be clearer. Kohl is stalking me. He's in Iceland and he has broken into my office.'

'Kohl is not in Iceland, Cal.'

'Why should I believe you?'

'Well, for starters, he may be out of prison but he's not a free man. We're watching him twenty-four/seven. And even if we weren't, he has to sign in with his parole officer twice a week.'

'Twice a week? Jesus, John, you can fly anywhere in the world and be back again in seventy-two hours.'

'You're not listening, Cal. We're watching him round the clock. And anyway, his passport has been confiscated. He won't be flying anywhere.'

'I'm telling you, he's in Reykjavík. Christ, you

249

Strathclyde boys are more stupid than I thought. Cast your mind back a few years to a certain murder in Prague. Kohl travelled there under a false passport. Who's to say he hasn't got another one stashed away?'

'Cal, please, you're getting paranoid. Trust me on this one. Iago Kohl has not left the UK, he is not in Iceland and is not stalking anyone.'

'Where is he now?' asked Callum.

'What?'

'Where is Iago Kohl right now, right at this very minute?'

'I can't tell you that.'

'You see, you haven't a bloody clue. The bastard's given you the slip.'

'Calm down, will you. Jesus, Cal, you know I can't tell you where Kohl is. We've put him in a safe house. We've given him a new identity. It's for his own protection.'

'You're protecting *him*? You're protecting that sick piece of shit?' Callum was incensed. 'What about protecting his victims? What about protecting me?'

'We are, Cal. In a way we're doing this to protect you.' There was a loud click on the line, like the inspector had closed a door. 'Look,' he continued, his voice softening, 'we've been here before. We can't have you taking the law, or a baseball bat, into your own hands. That's why Kohl's address and his new identity will remain a secret. I know this must be upsetting for you but—'

'Too fucking right it's upsetting! You have no fucking idea how upsetting it is. I can't believe you're giving him a new identity. The guy fucking *thrives* on duplicity. He came into the UK under a false fucking identity. He carved out a life, a career and a murder by changing his identity whenever it suited him. His publishing house was called Chameleon. I'd laugh at the fucking irony of it, if it didn't make me feel sick to the fucking core.'

'I know. I'd be the same if I was in your shoes.' Wedderburn couldn't disguise another yawn.

'You don't give a shit, do you,' said Callum. 'I mean, how can I even be sure that Kohl's in a safe house?'

'Because I say he is. You've got to take my word for it.'

'Why should I take your word, John? Because you're a policeman? You gave me your word six years ago that Sarah's killer would be an old man when he got out of prison . . . *if* he got out of prison. How do I know that you're not bullshitting me again? If Kohl has absconded, Strathclyde police would want to hush it up. It wouldn't look good, would it: a killer giving you the slip like that? Bad PR.'

'You're right. It wouldn't look good,' said Wedderburn.

'Yeah, I reckon you'd want to keep something like that really fucking quiet. As long as Kohl is stalking people in other countries, the precious citizens of the UK are not under immediate threat and the police have no pressing need to publicize his escape. And that's why you're going to do fuck all about this, isn't it. I smell a cover-up.'

'I can assure you there's no cover-up,' said Wedderburn. 'Look, if it makes you feel better I'll send a couple of my boys out to Helsinki.'

'And what good would that do? I'm in Reykjavík.'

'Don't be pedantic, Cal. You know what I meant.'

'Seriously John, what good will it do, you sending a couple of your monkeys over here?'

'It might help you feel more secure, give you time to get used to the idea that Kohl is a free man. Listen Cal, I understand that this is a real shock to your system. You're feeling vulnerable. And when a person feels

251

vulnerable, his mind can play all sorts of games.'

'I am not losing my mind!' yelled Callum. 'Kohl is in Iceland. He tried to kill Birna's girl. He's stolen her clothes and he's broken into my office. The guy's going to do some real damage and you're doing fuck all about it.'

Callum threw his mobile at the sofa bed.

It bounced back and spilled its battery onto the wooden floor.

He took his coffee mug to the kitchen. He sucked on his knuckles and waited for the kettle to boil.

Callum stood in the cold shadow of a warehouse on
the Reykjavík dockside. He tried hard to ignore the
squadron of yapping terns that were dive-bombing
him but they seemed intent on plucking every hair
from his head. He removed a fax from his back pocket
and checked the address against a sign on the building. This was definitely the place.

He made his way through two open double doors
that were big enough to allow the free passage of an oil
tanker. His ears were assaulted by a loud metallic yelp.
A policeman was lying prostrate on a workbench and
Callum watched helplessly as a circular saw sliced the
cop's head clean off his body.

The man operating the blade looked up. He wore
spattered overalls and a tinted visor hid his face. He
moved towards Callum, the saw still squealing in his
hand, like he was the star of a straight-to-video horror
flick. He unplugged his murder weapon and lifted his
mask to reveal a gaunt face with sunken eyes that had
something of the avian and the reptilian about it. He
looked like a bird that wasn't quite ready, like his egg
had fallen out of the tree. He introduced himself as
Ólafur and extended a hand that would soon develop
into a talon.

'Hi. Callum Pope,' said Callum.

'Aha, you are the geyser geezer! My SFX boys have been working on your brief all weekend. I think we have a solution.' The birdman clawed at Callum's arm. 'Follow me. They are out the back.'

Ólafur led Callum through the vast hangar that constituted IcePics, a collective that billed itself as 'The No.1 Film and Television Special Effects Facility in Iceland', though they did not have much competition. As a boast, it was a bit like Callum claiming to be Lanarkshire's No.1 authority on baboons.

'If you don't mind me asking, what's with the decapitated policeman?' said Callum, as they passed the headless mannequin. The air was sweet with the smell of wood sap.

'Hafnafjörour police asked us to make twenty wooden dummies and dress them in full police uniform. They wanted them to be as lifelike as possible. The dummies were positioned along the Reykjanesbraut road to remind drivers to respect traffic rules, but the idea did not work. Four of the policemen were struck by cars in the first week and another two were stolen.' Ólafur grimaced. 'We have been asked to destroy the dummies that survived. The police say they are only good for firewood, which is kind of ironic as some people have said the same thing about our real police force.'

Ólafur moved to the back of the airy workshop with Callum in tow. They passed a model-maker who was busy carving out a lifesize polar bear from a giant block of polystyrene. Callum saw that dozens of hand-painted panels had been stacked against the walls, redundant backdrops salvaged from broken-up film sets. Some of the panels had been painted with bright blue skies and bulbous white clouds; a few were covered in thick impasto to mimic the undulating walls of a subterranean ice cavern; and others replicated the interior walls of a penthouse apartment, replete with windows that looked out onto a blurry, sponged-on cityscape.

'I believe that you need the geysers for a car commercial,' said Ólafur.

'That's right.'

'I once art-directed a commercial for Porsche. We filmed it at Akureyri in the north.'

'I know Akureyri,' said Callum. 'My girlfriend and I flew up there a couple of months back.'

'Then your plane will have descended into a dramatic fjörd and you will have landed on a runway that almost touches the water.'

'I do remember it being pretty hairy.'

'On the Porsche shoot I was tasked with building a jetty that could connect the airstrip to the fjörd. In the commercial, our hero drives his car at speed along the runway.' Ólafur stopped by a workbench and recreated the scene with a strip of sandpaper representing the runway and a large pink eraser impersonating the Porsche. 'He drives onto the jetty and performs a handbrake skid, bringing the car to a halt just inches from the water.' Ólafur turned the eraser sideways to indicate the manoeuvre. 'The hero then jumps out and lands on the deck of his luxury boat which is moored at the jetty.' A tube of glue stood in for the boat. 'At least, that was the theory. But the stuntman had been drinking Brennivin with us on the night before the shoot and I think it clouded his judgement. On the first take, he drove the Porsche straight off the jetty and it crashed onto a Sunseeker boat worth nearly two million dollars. One of the locals who had been watching the scene said to me, you are lucky that the boat was there to stop the car going into the water . . . those Porsches cost thousands.' Ólafur resumed his walk. 'Our neighbours in the north are not the sharpest.'

He guided Callum through a door that led outside into an empty car park. Empty, apart from two bearded men and an oil drum.

'This is Bragi and Elli,' said Ólafur, though he failed to indicate who was who.

'Hi,' said Callum.

'They have been making a geyser that will explode when you tell it to.' Ólafur turned to the two men. 'How is it going, boys?'

'We are just about to do a test,' said the man with the redder beard.

Callum noticed that the oil drum had been beaten with a hammer so that it was narrower at the top than at the bottom. This inverted funnel was full of boiling water. Steam spewed from its aperture, grey wisps that performed wild pirouettes on the restless liquid before being seized and devoured by the cold quayside air. Two rubber cables threaded out of the base of the drum and snaked across the car park. Callum guessed that one of the cables was some form of immersion heater. It was connected to a small generator that housed a thermostat whose needle jerked like a nervous tic between 110° and 115°. The other rubber cable was fixed to a hefty gas canister, which in turn was connected to a control box in Redbeard's hand. The last time Callum had seen such a handset, his father was using it to guide a model plane into a tree trunk.

'I'm going to press this button,' said Redbeard, 'and a shot of CO_2 will be fired into the water. This will change the pressure of the hottest water at the very bottom, forcing it to rise very quickly towards the only avenue of escape. With any luck it will shoot up into the air just like a geyser. If it works, we can bury three barrels in the ground at Skógafoss.'

'Ah,' said Callum. 'I'm afraid Skógafoss has been

blown out. I'm looking at a few waterfalls in the north-east.'

'No problem,' said Redbeard. 'We can bury the barrels in whatever positions you like. We will be able to keep refilling them if they are near a water source, so it should be no problem to perform many explosions in quick succession.'

'Sounds good,' said Callum.

Redbeard's colleague marshalled them backwards. 'Please, you must stand back. This water is very hot.'

'Extremely hot,' cautioned Redbeard. He licked his finger and held it to the wind to gauge its direction. He adjusted his position and raised his handset. 'OK. Here we go. *Fimm . . . fjórir . . . Þrír . . . tveir . . . einn . . .*'

He pressed the button, the barrel exploded and dagger-sized shards of twisted metal fizzed over Callum's head, embedding themselves in the hull of a fishing boat. A heavy column of water had been jettisoned skywards in the explosion. It achieved a height of perhaps thirty feet before collapsing like a chimney stack and ripping across the tarmac. Redbeard was flattened in its path.

'Jesus Christ,' said Callum. He had hit the deck alongside Ólafur. 'What the fuck happened there?'

Redbeard was screaming. Callum turned round and saw him struggling to pick himself off the ground. One of his feet was the wrong way round and the skin was hanging off his forearms like unbuttoned cuffs.

'Bragi,' said Ólafur, addressing the other beard. 'It would be a good idea to call an ambulance.'

'He will be fine,' said Sigrún Hrönn Vilhjálmsdóttir.

She had the longest name of any of the nurses in the casualty ward. Callum knew this because he had spent the last hour looking at their breasts. That is, he had spent the last hour looking at the name tags on their breasts. Sigrún Hrönn had just pipped Magnea Solla Finnbogadóttir by a letter. And a cup size.

'We have repaired the degloved skin tissue on both arms without the need for grafts and Elli is now in theatre having his foot reset,' said Sigrún Hrönn. 'It is a routine procedure. We will keep him in until his arms have healed sufficiently for him to apply his own dressings.'

'He was lucky,' said Ólafur, as the nurse went to the aid of a boy with a fish hook through his eyelid.

'Not as lucky as us,' said Callum. 'Our heads could have been cut in two by that metal. As it is, I've barely a scratch on me.'

'So you will not be suing us?' asked Ólafur.

'No, I will not be suing you.'

'Because it was not our fault.' There was panic in Ólafur's eyes. 'Bragi thinks the equipment may have been tampered with. He noticed a hole in the CO_2 pipe when we cleared up the mess. Of course, it may have been punctured in the explosion. But a hole in the pipe would mean that too much CO_2 was released into the barrel. It would explain the big bang.'

'Why would anyone tamper with your equipment?' asked Callum, though he was already formulating his own theories.

'A lot of kids hang out at the docks. Most of them just want to play on their skateboards. We have even built them a quarter-pipe. We figure that if we're nice to them, they'll be nice to us. But there are always a few who like to cause trouble.'

'Should we go to the police?'

'The *löggan* will be no help to us. Not after the trouble with their mannequins. When they see that it is IcePics who are making a complaint, they will make sure that they are even more useless than normal. If such a thing is possible.'

Callum extended a hand. 'Well, if you change your mind, you know where to find me.'

'Am I to take it that you still want us to work on these geysers?' asked Ólafur.

'Sure,' said Callum. 'But be careful. I'm beginning to think that this job is ill-starred. Perhaps the elves are up to their tricks.'

Callum drove into town in search of a sugar rush. His nerves were in shreds. He returned to the quayside and squeezed himself into a table at Kaffivagninn with a good view of the boats. A young waitress brought him a half-litre glass of Coke and a Danish pastry. He had an hour to straighten himself out.

He had promised Birna that he would pick up Ásta and take her to the pool. Right now he wanted to pick them both up, together with Sigriður, and take them to the moon. It didn't matter that he had given up everything to live somewhere as isolated as Iceland; it now seemed that there was nowhere on this planet that Callum could be free of Iago Kohl.

He had convinced himself that Kohl had sabotaged the geyser test. If Kohl had broken into Callum's office then he would have seen the shoot proposal and the production schedule. Both had been left open on his laptop. The schedule listed the IcePics address together with the date and time that Callum was due to attend the test. It was a gift for anyone hellbent on hurting him.

Callum could picture Kohl now, walking into a Reykjavík bar and ordering his first beer in six years. Kohl liked his beer. He would order a Viking or a Gull, but he wouldn't drink it straight away. Callum remembered how Kohl liked to dip his little finger into his pint, forcing the head to swell to the point where it threatened to spill over the rim of the glass. Next, he would remove his finger and examine the ring of white froth that the beer had placed on it. The further this tidemark sat from his fingernail, the better the quality of the pint, or so Kohl had told a young Scottish couple one wet night in Prague. Callum imagined him sucking this ring from his finger – one of many fingers that had left their mark on Sarah's neck – as he enjoyed a taste of freedom that should forever have been denied him.

He picked the currants off his Danish and smushed them under his thumb like bluebottles. Kohl had to be stopped. But how?

Callum knew he was on his own. This was a definite do-it-yourself job. And Callum was not a natural when it came to DIY. He and Sarah had owned the only flat in Glasgow with a bolt fixed to the outside of the bathroom door.

His thoughts had returned to Sarah, as they invariably did. She loved that bathroom. She had devoted an entire weekend to hand-painting sea horses onto every third tile on its walls. Callum remembered her taking a well-earned soak after her artwork was completed. He remembered bringing her a glass of red wine and he remembered the look on her face when she invited him to join her in the tub. The hot water had smelled of mandarins. He could see her now, her hands all mottled with paint, how she used them to pull apart the bubbles that hugged her body, slowly revealing her nakedness. *Look at me*, she had beamed, *I'm all fur coat and nae knickers*.

The waitress cleared Callum's table. She offered him a napkin for his eyes. He thanked her and blamed his tears on the bright sun bouncing in off the bay.

He nursed the flat dregs of his Coke, wondering

whether he should drive to the police station and tell them everything: the Jeep that tried to mow down Ásta; the break-in; the missing clothes; the exploding geyser. But where was his proof? These events could variously be explained by boy racers (the Jeep); the wind and/or elves (the missing clothes); and rogue SFX equipment (the oil drum was a test, an experiment that went wrong). The only crime that could be proved was the break-in at the office, but Callum had told Birna that he had forced the door himself when he lost his keys. And anyway, nothing had actually been stolen.

What could he do? Strathclyde were no help. Wedderburn was still denying that Kohl had jumped his parole. Callum couldn't even turn to an old friend like Neil Byrne for advice. He was uncontactable and anyway, Callum was probably the last person Neil would want to listen to right now.

Callum considered the possibility that Wedderburn was telling the truth. What if Kohl was tucked up in a safe house? What if the wind had taken Ásta's clothes? And what if it really was some joyriding kids who had spooked Ásta's horse for a bit of a laugh? OK, so Callum had seen the green Jeep driving away from his office following the break-in, but there were hundreds of Jeeps in Reykjavík and he supposed that many of them were green. Who was to say that this Jeep was in any way connected to the intruder? For all Callum knew, it might have been driven by some middle-aged twitcher who'd been checking out the birds on the Tjörn.

Callum resolved not to mention any of this to Birna. Maybe Wedderburn was right. Maybe Callum was just being paranoid. And if Kohl was being watched twenty-four/seven as the DI suggested, then there was no need to worry Birna unnecessarily. She needn't know about Sarah's murder and she needn't know about Kohl. The consequences were too horrible to contemplate. Callum decided that if he wanted to hang onto Birna, then things had to stay exactly as they were. When a butterfly lands on your arm you keep very still or it flies away.

19

'I'm sorry I'm late,' said Callum.

'I was beginning to think you had chickened out,' teased Birna.

Callum saw that Ásta was already standing on the wind-battered porch with a duffle bag slumped at her feet. Her black hair flapped wildly about her head as if a crow was trying to get its claws into her skull.

Sigríður was kneeling in front of her granddaughter, zipping her into a shocking pink puffa jacket that was complemented by wine-coloured tights and flashy purple trainers. She walked Ásta down the steps and nudged her towards Callum.

'Hi there,' he offered. 'Are you looking forward to your swim?'

'My belly is sore,' complained Ásta.

'Enough,' barked Sigríður. 'You were well enough to eat pancakes for breakfast. Now, remember what we agreed.' Sigríður turned to Callum. 'Ásta has something for you. Haven't you Ásta?'

Ásta looked to Sigríður for a further prompt. It arrived in the form of a nod. The young girl took a step towards Callum and handed him a gold coin. 'This is yours, if you can stay in the hottest hot pot for longer than me.' She looked again to Sigríður, who returned a beatific smile.

'*Fimmtíu krónur*,' said Callum, surprising Ásta with his Icelandic. She did not realize that he was reading it from the coin. Callum turned the metal in his fingers and examined the crab on the reverse side. 'And do I have to give you fifty krónur if I lose?'

Ásta nodded and smiled a little, just enough to reveal that she was missing a tooth.

'But if I give you fifty krónur all the boys in Reykjavík will want to marry you for your money,' said Callum.

Birna laughed. She lifted her daughter's hair out of her eyes.

'I don't like the boys in Reykjavík,' said Ásta. 'They are always getting drunk and they are sick on the road.'

'But wasn't it a boy who kissed out your tooth?' asked Callum.

Ásta shook her head violently from side to side.

'OK, I believe you. But I'll bet that a fairy gave you this coin in exchange for your tooth?'

'Why would a fairy do that?' asked Ásta.

'Well, when I was a boy and one of my teeth fell out, I would put it under my pillow and during the night, the tooth fairy would take it away and leave a coin in its place. The tooth fairy collects baby teeth from all the children in the world and uses them to build beautiful fairy palaces.'

'Do you believe in fairies?' asked Ásta.

Callum saw that Sigriður was looking right at him and that her eyebrow was raised.

'Well, Callum?' the older woman asked, clearly intrigued. 'Do you believe in fairies?'

'I . . .' Callum floundered. He could see that Sigriður was enjoying this. 'I mean . . . when you put it that way . . .' He detected a look of hope in Ásta's eyes. 'Of course,' he said, reasserting himself. 'Yes, Ásta. I do believe in fairies.'

'Then you really are stupid.' Ásta pushed past Callum and opened the rear door of the Toyota.

'You can sit up front with me,' he offered, but she had already shut herself into the vehicle.

Ásta had done it again. She had made Callum feel like her dumb younger brother. He was annoyed with himself. He had remembered Anna Björk's advice, that he should stop treating Ásta like a kid. So what does he do the next time he engages the girl in a conversation? He turns himself into the presenter of a TV programme for the under-fives. Callum figured that he might as well have been wearing an outsize pair of orange dungarees with a big purple 'C' stitched on the front.

'Make sure Ásta dries her hair when she leaves the pool,' said Birna.

'Perhaps the hair fairy will dry it for her.' Sigríður couldn't disguise her laughter. She used the corner of her apron to dab at the wetness in her eyes. 'I am sorry. I should not be making fun. I should be thanking you for what you did yesterday.'

'Don't mention it,' said Callum.

'Will you lose a lot of money by cancelling the location?' asked Sigríður.

'A few bob. Nothing I can't claw back. In fact, the recovery starts now. I'm off to the pool to take fifty krónur off your granddaughter.'

'I would not be so confident. The hot pot is forty-five degrees and my granddaughter is as stubborn as I am.'

'*Já*,' said Birna. 'If you are to win that money, you will first have to poach your internal organs.'

'Then donate them to Sigríður after my death. They can't taste any worse than the stuff she usually dishes up.' He winked at Birna's mother and climbed into the car.

Callum found Laugardalur waterpark without any

help from Ásta, which was just as well, as she remained determinedly silent on the drive across town. In those moments when she forgot to clutch her stomach and feign illness, she used her hands to trace words in the condensation that she had breathed onto the windows. Callum noticed that she was writing the words backwards, not that he could have understood them if he had been reading them from the other side of the glass, for everything she wrote was Icelandic. A woman had pulled up beside him at traffic lights and she had given him a curious look, making Callum suspicious that Ásta had scrawled something apposite like: I'm with stupid.

He had remembered that the outdoor pool complex sat beside the national football stadium, having visited the latter on a previous winter trip. It was during one spare, snowy afternoon when Birna was working on a research paper that Callum had gone to the stadium on his own to witness the legendary goalless thriller between Iceland and Latvia. Not until the teams had bounded onto the frozen pitch did he realize it was a Women's international. A 'B' international. And a friendly at that.

Callum put his keys in his teeth and rummaged in his pockets for the modest entrance fee to the Laugardalur pools. He found a little extra, enough for two large towels. He rolled his keys and his wallet into one of them.

Before Ásta could tear herself away from him and seek sanctuary in the female changing room, he knelt down beside her and made her promise that she would not get into any of the pools until he joined her. He knew he was babying her – Icelandic children are reared in water and Birna often claimed that her daughter had been born with gills – but he couldn't help feeling responsible for her. His eyes needed to be on her at all times and he was unhappy about handing her a towel and letting her disappear on her own through a changing-room door. It was a precarious feeling, as if Birna had entrusted him with a china doll, the only one of its kind, and he was sending it into a carwash.

The male changing room was patrolled by a tall and slightly ghoulish attendant. It seemed that his sole purpose in life was to enforce the rule that everyone must shower and wash before entering the pool. The eldritch young man leaned on his broom, waxwork-still, and eyed Callum darkly as he stripped off.

The communal showers had two temperatures: glacial and scalding. Callum opted for cold water, and fought for breath as the shock of it constricted his chest.

When he was a boy a visit to the pool was a fun day out, but as an adult Callum found the experience draining. This exhaustive preparatory ritual was not something he remembered from childhood. There was a time when he would arrive at the leisure centre wearing his trunks under his trousers so he could thunder straight into the pool, casting clothes behind him even as he hurdled the footbath and dive-bombed into the deep end.

The grown-up approach to doing something as simple as entering a swimming pool – a protracted preamble that included not only a full-body wash, but the neat folding of jeans and the revisiting of reception to obtain the correct denomination of coin for the locker – was sapping what little energy he had. It was not the rest and recuperation he so badly needed. He had heard much about the restorative properties of an Icelandic hot pot but it was likely that fatigue would scupper him before he dipped a toe in the water.

And Callum was tired. He had hoped that a visit to a thermal spa might unravel the snarls of his stress. It was also a chance to get to know Ásta better, a one-on-one opportunity to win her confidence.

He was disappointed, then, to see that she had ignored his advice to stay out of the water. He found her sitting glumly in the huge circular wading pool, the tiles spreading out beneath her in concentric black and white circles like a target. She wore a one-piece swimming costume, cream in colour with a black Nike swoosh under each arm.

He tiptoed towards her, making scatty progress across the cold, concreted area that was home to a main pool, a wading pool, a whirlpool, a children's pool, a steam bath, a water slide and five hot pots. The place was hiving with people, mostly old people, but very few of them were swimming. They sat in the volcanically heated water, arguing and laughing and gesturing with their arms. Their red shoulders sat prominent against blue water and white steam like the cross on the Icelandic flag. Callum remembered how Anna Björk had said that the pools were a way of life for Icelanders. He decided that if he wanted to tap into the cultural essence of Reykjavík or simply flick through an impressive collection of sagging arm flesh, then this was the place to be.

'Is it nice in there?' Callum asked Ásta.

She shrugged, like she hadn't made her mind up.

Callum plopped in beside her. Where the water lapped at Ásta's chest, it wasn't deep enough to touch Callum's ribs.

'I expected it to be hotter than this,' he offered. He noticed that Ásta's hands were cupped over her stomach. She was looking down at them as though she had trapped a fish against her belly. He knew that he shouldn't indulge such transparent play-acting, but he thought that she might open up if he showed her some concern.

'Is your belly still sore?'

Ásta nodded.

'I'll bet it was all those pancakes you ate. Your grandmother's cooking always gives me a bellyache.'

He thought he detected the beginnings of a smile.

'Do you like Mars bars?' he asked.

'*Já*,' said Ásta, though it was barely audible.

'Where I come from, in Scotland, they cover Mars bars in pancake batter and fry them like fish.'

A question mark appeared above Ásta's head.

'I know,' he conceded. 'People in Scotland are a bit weird. The men wear skirts and hurl tree trunks into the air. And the women like to slide stones across ice and do their housework while they wait for them to stop. Some of them are so good at it that they even get given gold medals.'

'Do you wear a skirt?' asked Ásta.

'Only when your mother isn't around. But that can be our little secret.' Callum tapped his nose and gave her a conspiratorial wink.

'My mother says she loves you.' Ásta removed her hands from the water and used them to twist one side of her hair into a slick ponytail: the tail of the blackest pit pony working the darkest coal mine on the shortest day of the year.

'And I love your mother,' replied Callum.

'Then why did you make her cry?'

'I made her cry?'

'*Já*. When she thought you had another girlfriend she stayed in bed for two days and when I took her some soup I could tell that she had been crying.'

Again Callum wasn't so sure that he had the right words.

'I didn't mean to make your mother cry,' he offered. 'But sometimes crying can be good. People cry when they care a lot about each other. If you don't care about

269

someone, you don't waste your time shedding tears over them.'

Ásta at least looked like she was listening to him. It gave him the confidence to continue.

'You want to know another secret?'

Ásta nodded.

'Your mother told me that she cried when you were born,' said Callum. 'And she cried on your first day at school. And I know that she had a wee cry whenever you fell off your horse but she didn't let you see it. She cries because she loves you so much.'

'If she loved me so much, she would not want to have another baby.' Ásta released her grip on her ponytail and let it unfurl. She separated the hair into three strands and began criss-crossing them into a plait.

'Your mother will still love you, even if she has another baby.' Callum struggled for a better way to explain it. 'Your ponies . . . the two brothers . . . what are their names again?'

'Hálfdán and Fróði.'

'That's right. Hálfdán and Fróði. I'll bet that their mother loved them both equally. And if your mother gives you a brother or a sister, she will love you both the same.'

'That is not true.' Ásta seemed very sure of herself. 'Hálfdán and Fróði were rejected by their mother. They were born blind and she could not get them to feed. She left them to starve.'

Great analogy, Callum. This parenting lark was harder than he thought. How did people do this all day every day? And how did they cope with more than one child? Callum only had Ásta for one afternoon and already she had challenged his received wisdom on the fundamental subjects of love, parenthood and cross-dressing.

'So Ásta, this bet we have,' he said, changing the subject. 'Shall we go and climb into the hot pots?' Callum had already tested the steaming pots with his foot. They varied from 'Really Hot' in the first pot to 'Molten Pop Tart' in the last one.

Ásta seemed reluctant to get out of the water. Her hands had retreated beneath the surface again and she had pulled her legs into her chest to sit in a foetal position. While other bathers looked flushed in the geothermal heat, the colour had drained from Ásta's face. She rested her chin on her knees, looking very sorry for herself.

'Belly still sore?' asked Callum.

Ásta nodded.

'Perhaps you should give it a wee rub.'

'Will that make the pain go away?'

'I can't promise,' said Callum. 'But it works for me when I've eaten too many of your grandmother's pancakes. And when I've drunk too much beer.'

Ásta unwrapped her limbs. She looked a little unsure as she rubbed her tummy, as if she had been asked to simultaneously pat her head with her other hand.

'Is that getting better?' asked Callum.

'*Nei*,' groaned Ásta. She shook her head. She looked like she was about to retch.

'Keep rubbing,' urged Callum.

'My arm is getting tired.'

'Then use the other one.'

Ásta shifted her weight onto her opposite buttock and swapped hands. She pulled the tired arm out of the water to give it a stretch and a thin trickle of blood sped over her fingers, marbling her palm.

'Ouch. How did you cut your finger?' asked Callum.

'I don't know,' said Ásta, but both of them had already spotted the stain on her swimming costume: a

271

tiny blemish between her legs that was clearly visible in the shallow pool. Several thin brown threads hung vertically in the water, kinking round the inside of her thighs and clinging to her skin when they came into contact.

Ásta started to cry.

Callum took her shoulders. 'Ásta . . . listen to me . . . has this happened to you before?'

She shook her head. Her sobs had caught the attention of bathers in the next pool. They looked disapprovingly at Callum like he was a bad parent.

'You're going to be fine. This is perfectly normal.' Callum leapt out of the pool and stole a towel that had been neatly placed on top of a pair of flip-flops. He ignored the loud protestations of its Germanic owner and climbed back in with Ásta. 'It's going to be OK. You're going to be fine. We'll sort this out.' He opened the towel. 'Can you stand up?'

'But they will see.' Ásta's sobs had graduated to heaves. A bubble popped in her nostril. She looked very frightened.

'Nobody will see. I'll put this towel around you. Come on Ásta . . . do it for me. You can put your hands on my shoulders.'

Ásta put her arms round his neck and pulled herself onto her feet.

'That's my girl.' Callum wrapped the towel around her and used one corner to wipe her nose. 'There now, you're all wrapped up like a sausage roll. Nobody can see you.' He lifted Ásta out of the water. She was light as a bag of sticks. She tucked her head under his chin and buried her face in his chest.

Callum carried her towards the changing rooms. She was shaking. He hoped it was just from the cold. Her teeth rattled against his collarbone. He sought the attention of a female lifeguard.

'I'm sorry, I need your help, she's not very well, she's bleeding, I think she may have started her period and I can't go into the ladies, I'll need to call her moth—'

The lifeguard patted the air with her hands, gesturing for Callum to calm down. 'One thing at a time,' she said. 'What is your daughter's name?'

'Ásta,' he said, without hesitation. He knelt down and stood his girl back on terra firma.

'Ásta, I am Sigga.' The lifeguard tickled Ásta's nose, securing her attention. 'We girls are going to have a nice shower and get changed into clean clothes.' She held out her hand and Ásta accepted it.

'*Takk*,' said Callum. It was the only Icelandic word he felt confident enough to unleash in public and he was aware that he used it too often. 'Thanks,' he added.

'That's OK. It is all part of the job. We will meet you in reception.'

Callum took his time getting changed. There was no point in rushing. He needed to slow down. Ásta was in safe hands now. That lifeguard looked like she knew what she was doing. If she had been in any way alarmed by Ásta's situation she would have called for a doctor.

This sort of thing probably happened all the time, he figured. Sure, didn't it happen to every girl? Callum supposed it would have been a bit of a shock for Ásta, her first time and everything. It was distressing to see just how fragile she could be. Birna's daughter suddenly seemed like the nascent eleven-year-old that she was. Callum found it ironic that he had this perception of her at the very moment she crossed into adulthood. In a way, he felt honoured. He may not have witnessed her birth or her first steps but he was present when Ásta became a woman. He guessed that there weren't many dads in the world who could say

273

that. He reckoned that most men remained oblivious to the single biggest change in their daughters' biology until the tampons made a tangible dent in the household expenses.

They should be given out free, Callum decided as he dried between his toes. He turned to the changing-room attendant. 'No woman should have to pay for sanitary protection.'

The attendant's broomstick skidded on the wet tiles and he momentarily impaled his ribs upon it.

Callum towelled himself down. He felt like he too had become an adult.

He made his way into the busy reception area and fed a few coins into a soda machine, enough for two Cokes, one for himself and one for Ásta. He figured that her blood sugar might need a boost. He considered calling Birna but decided against it. He should allow Ásta to break the good news herself. This was between mother and daughter. Callum had had his moment and now it was time to stand back.

He took a seat and observed the steady stream of people coming in and going out of the building: fathers, daughters, mothers, sons, grannies, granddads, husbands, wives, boyfriends, girlfriends and everyone in between.

After some time, the lifeguard came bounding towards him with a confused look on her face. 'Hi,' she said. 'Have you forgotten something?'

'I don't think so. Have you?' Callum made a show of looking at her legs. 'Or is my daughter hiding behind you?'

'How long have you been sitting here?'

'About ten . . .' Callum checked the large clock mounted on the wall above him, 'sorry . . . twenty minutes.'

'But I walked your daughter to your car half an hour

ago,' said the lifeguard. 'She said she wanted to listen to the CD player. The poor girl has been out there all this time. She is probably asleep by now. She was very tired.'

'How did she get into the car? I keep it locked.'

'She had your keys in her towel. She said you always let her keep hold of them because she takes less time to get dressed. She said that you allow her to sit in the car and play her CDs while she waits for you.'

'Of course,' said Callum. He must have given Ásta the wrong towel. 'My head's all over the place. It's been a hell of a day.'

'I understand,' said the lifeguard.

'Was she OK?'

'Your daughter's fine, but I would hurry home and let her get some rest.'

'Cheers.' Callum stood up. 'I mean . . . *takk.*'

'*Takk fyrir.*'

Callum walked out into the blustery car park, formulating his apology on his way to the car. He could see that the windows of the Toyota had steamed up, resurrecting Ásta's earlier scribblings. Half an hour, he thought. He was concerned that it might have been longer as he could hear no music emanating from the vehicle, meaning a whole album might have played and ended while he dithered in the building.

'You poor thing,' he said as he opened the rear door.

But Ásta hadn't hung around to hear it.

The Toyota was empty.

Callum was left standing in the shadow of a football stadium with no keys, no wallet and no daughter.

20

He waited by the Toyota for a handful of minutes in case she had popped back into the swimming-pool area to find him, then he went back inside and scoured the building. He sent an English woman into the female changing room with a description of Ásta: wet black hair, pink puffa jacket, flashy purple trainers, downturned mouth.

One of the receptionists put out a tannoy message in English and Icelandic and Callum waited in the atrium, reading and rereading a poster that detailed how people had bathed on the Laugardalslaugin site since 1772, when they swam among eels. He peeled himself away from it only when it was obvious that Ásta would not reappear. He slumped in a chair and saw that the girls on reception were glaring at him. He wasn't sure if they were anxious on his behalf or if they were appalled by his skills as a father.

He phoned Birna and asked her to drive over with his spare keys. She cursed him for losing them and he thought it best to wait until they were face to face before breaking it to her that he had also lost her daughter.

'You are an idiot,' said Birna as she bounced through reception, jangling the keys. She wore dark jeans, muddy boots and a tight, camouflage-pattern T-shirt.

Her hair was in pigtails. She looked nothing like a mum.

She smashed the ball of metal into Callum's open hand. 'Your spares. Mother was complaining that you are always late but I defended you. I said that it was a good thing that Ásta and you are finally spending some quality time together, but Mother said she knew that something had happened to delay you. She said she had one of her feelings. She had to sit down. I guess she was right. Oh, and she wants you to know that dinner is ruined. But I am sure that this will not disappoint you.' Birna looked about the place. 'I hope Ásta is not in the shop buying chocolate. I thought that as our dinner is cremated, the three of us could go to Galileo and get some pasta.'

'Birna . . . I . . .' Callum couldn't look at her.

'You do not like pasta?'

'Birna, listen. Ásta isn't in the shop. I don't know where she is. She got dressed before me and when I came out, she was gone. She has my keys and my wallet.'

'What do you mean she is gone? Did the two of you have another argument?'

'No. Not at all. She wasn't feeling good so we got out of the pool. Those stomach pains were for real. I think she has started her . . . her thing.' Callum pointed to his belly.

'Her thing? What thing? What has happened to my daughter?' Birna was confused more than worried, but only because Callum seemed unable to tell her what she should be worried about.

'I'm not an expert on these things. I've no previous experience. But there was a bit of blood . . . down there.' He gestured again. 'Girls' blood.'

'Girls' blood?'

'Yes,' said Callum. 'Do you call it a period in Iceland?'

'OK. We are finally getting somewhere. My daughter has started menstruation. Where is she now?'

Callum was surprised at her lack of anxiety. This was seismic news but Birna remained unflappably calm. A strange rationality had taken hold of her, a need to cut to the chase and be apprised of all the facts. Callum knew that he would be hysterical in Birna's shoes. He wasn't good in a crisis. Birna's instinctive desire to stay focused, to not panic, was a reflex that only a true parent could possess.

'I don't know, Birna. I don't know where she is. The lifeguard who washed and dressed Ásta left her sitting in the Toyota, listening to music. But by the time I came out, she had gone. And so had my keys and my wallet.'

While Birna should have exploded, she nodded. Her face relaxed into a smile.

'What is it?' asked Callum. 'Do you know something I don't?'

'Ásta can be a prankster.' Birna was still nodding to herself and smiling.

'A prankster? You think she has run off as a joke?'

'*Já*, I think so.'

'Jesus, Birna, she was tired. She wasn't feeling well. She was in no mood to be playing practical jokes.'

'You do not know my daughter,' insisted Birna. 'Ásta gets stubbornness from my mother but also her sense of mischief. She is always playing tricks on us. One time she swapped Sigriður's toothpaste with her haemorrhoid cream.' Birna giggled. 'Of course, Mother remains tight-lipped about it.'

'Your daughter is missing and you're cracking jokes?' Callum's voice drew more looks from reception but he didn't care. Birna wasn't taking this seriously. Was she in denial, using humour to block out the cold reality of the situation? He wanted to shake her. 'I don't think I understand *you*, never mind your daughter.'

'Ásta is just having fun with you, Callum. You should not be so worried. This is a good sign. She feels confident enough with you to make a fool of you. She thinks she has forced you to walk home with no car and no money. She will be sitting in the kitchen and telling her grandmother how she tricked you.'

'And how is she supposed to get home?' asked Callum.

'The buses stop outside. Ásta has travelled here many times by bus.'

'But never alone ... I assume she travels with friends?'

'Not always. A lot of times she is by herself.'

Callum couldn't comprehend it. 'But she's only a girl.'

'Reykjavík is not like Glasgow ... or London ... or New York,' said Birna. 'It is safe for children to play in our streets without supervision. We do not have kidnappers and perverts like you do in your country.'

'How can you be so sure?' Callum knew he had to choose his words carefully. He didn't want to unduly alarm her.

'It is a fact. No child has ever been abducted from Reykjavík's streets. We love our children. Why would we want to harm them?'

'That may be so, but I'd feel a whole lot better if you phoned home to check that she's OK.'

Birna looked at Callum like she felt a little sorry for him. She punched a couple of keys on her mobile and paced away from him with a finger in one ear. She seemed perfectly relaxed. When she reached the window, she spun on her heel and walked back towards him.

If Birna was relaxed, did this mean that Callum

could relax too? She wasn't overly concerned about her daughter, so why should he be? Ásta was only playing a joke on Callum. He should be encouraged by it. The girl was showing an interest in him. Until recently, Ásta wouldn't have spat on Callum if he'd been on fire. He should relax and just go with the flow. Ásta would probably tease him about it later, but that wasn't a problem. In fact, Callum would look forward to it. He reckoned he might enjoy a bit of her banter. It would show how far the two of them had come. Perhaps, after the events of the afternoon, he had finally won her round.

But how could he be so confident that this was all a prank? They had to find her first. Back in Glasgow, if an eleven-year-old girl disappeared from a car park following an afternoon dip at the pool, she'd be on the news at ten and on the side of a milk carton by early morning.

Callum had to remind himself that this wasn't Glasgow. He thought about what Birna had said, how in Iceland there were no such things as kidnappers and perverts (she had referred to them in the same sceptical way that he had referred to elves and trolls). According to Birna, Reykjavík was child-friendly and crime-free. And she was probably right. Callum couldn't recall hearing a police siren or seeing a uniformed officer in all his time in the Icelandic capital. Reykjavík was safe as houses: simple but colourful houses.

'Mother says Ásta has not arrived home yet.' Birna slid the phone tightly into her jeans. 'She also says that she has salvaged a knuckle of lamb from the refrigerator and she is cooking it for us.'

Callum got the jitters again, and not because he was sure that sheep lacked knuckles. 'What if Ásta has tried to walk home? What if she got lost? She might have fainted. She was very pale.'

'Ásta is always very pale. She will be fine. Girls of her age are tougher than you think.' Birna bit on her lip. 'However . . .' she said, leaving it open-ended as she lost herself in a thought.

'However . . . ?' prompted Callum.

'Oh, nothing,' said Birna. But she was still distracted. 'Hmm . . . I am starting to think that you could be right. How long ago did Ásta leave here?'

Callum checked the clock: nine minutes to five.

'I'd say she's been gone forty-five minutes.'

'That is a long time.' Birna fixed her eyes on the window and looked sternly through her reflection at the road beyond the glass. 'Ásta can get a bus from here every ten minutes. She should be home by now.'

'You see. I've fucked up, haven't I?' Callum was beginning to panic.

'Aha!' said Birna, brightening again. 'She has gone to Lilja's.'

'Lilja's?'

'Lilja is Ásta's friend. She lives in Hólsvegur, not too far from here. It is maybe only a ten-minute walk but in true Icelandic style, we will take the four-wheel drives. Come, you can follow me.'

Birna hurried Callum into the car park but stopped him before they got to their vehicles. She fed her arms round his waist and kissed him. As their lips coalesced, birdsong trilled in Callum's ears and fairy lights danced on the periphery of his vision: Birna had unlocked her car remotely, using the key fob that she held behind his back.

'What was the kiss for?' asked Callum, once she had broken away.

'Your concern.'

Callum had more reason to be concerned than she could ever know.

If he was right, and Kohl was in the country, it would not be the first time that the Croatian had seized someone from under Callum's nose. He could only pray to God that the same fate had not befallen Ásta as the one that had been visited on Sarah. But this was not the time to mention Kohl. It would be the last thing Birna needed to hear. And if they found Ásta at her friend's house, Callum's relationship with Birna and her family might not survive the revelation that a man like Kohl was free to hurt them.

The traffic had snarled up around the park. It would have been quicker to walk, thought Callum, but he wasn't complaining. He might have lost Ásta, his keys and his wallet, but there was little chance of him losing her mother. Birna sat in silhouette barely ten feet in front of him, her taillights unblinkingly red.

A gaggle of teenage girls wobbled through the gap in the two static cars. They were dressed in traditional Arctic garb: short skirts, knee-length boots, cropped tops and goose pimples. It could have been Glasgow in January. Callum hoped that the similarities between the cities ended there and that Ásta was safe and sound and singing into a hairbrush in her friend's bedroom. He'd be happy if she was just talking to Lilja about what had happened to her at the pool. He wondered whether their first period is something that girls boast about, in the same way that young boys like to brag when they discover they can ejaculate (and some will gladly prove it, even on public transport). He buoyed himself with the thought, confident that this was the reason that Ásta had decided to abandon his car. She had just needed someone to talk to, and who better than her best friend. It made sense. Nobody can understand an eleven-year-old girl better than another eleven-year-old girl.

Birna parked up outside a bungalow composed of reddish-brown corrugated iron. It looked like it had been constructed from those flimsy sheets of ribbed cardboard that protect trays of chocolates. The single-storey building was partly shaded by The Only Tree in Iceland.

Callum's habitual reaction when he approached a strange house was to speculate on how much the place had cost, and then to guess at what jobs the owners would be holding down in order to afford it. But he had discovered that as so many of Reykjavík's houses were of a similarly frugal disposition, they were rarely indicative of the persons who lived in them. And Lilja's humble abode was no exception. For all Callum could guess, her parents were financiers, fishermen or fruitcakes.

He stayed in his car and let Birna go to the door.

She gave it two raps with her fist.

She waited.

Nothing.

She raised her hand again but, before she could knock, a tall woman opened the door. She sported a shock of blonde hair that was secured by a light blue Alice band and she wore glasses with thick black frames. A smaller version of the woman appeared at her side, same headband, same glasses. Birna smiled at the little girl and mouthed something at her mother. The tall woman shook her head. She removed her glasses and blew on the lenses. She wiped them with her sleeve while Birna talked.

The young girl bounded across the lawn towards Callum's Toyota, stopping abruptly when she saw that there was someone inside it. She squinted at Callum, her blonde hair alternating between a vivid orange and a muted olive as the tree above her flitted in the breeze, strobing sunlight and shadow. The girl's mother called out to her and waved her back into the house. The woman then gave Birna a quick hug before closing the door.

Birna shook her head at Callum as she walked back to her car.

He followed her home.

'The police say we should give it the night and if she hasn't turned up by morning, they'll send someone over.' Callum returned the phone to a hook on the kitchen wall. 'They've put out Ásta's description to all their cars and they're contacting the local radio station.'

'Useless bastards,' spat Birna.

'Shush now,' said Sigriður. She decanted a translucent brew from the saucepan into a mug and presented it to her daughter. The kitchen smelt heavily of cloves. 'There is not much more they can do.'

'We both know that is rubbish,' said Birna. 'They are lazy. They have so little to do and when something like this comes along they cannot be bothered. Ask a *löggan* to do something he does not want to do and he puts up a barrier of glacial stubbornness.'

'I gave them a description of the green Jeep,' said Callum, 'the one that spooked Ásta's horse.'

'Why would you do that?' Birna looked alarmed.

'I . . . I thought I should . . . you know . . . just in case.'

'You think Ásta has been abducted, don't you?'

Callum felt wretched, like he'd betrayed her. 'I'm sure she's fine. I was just trying to give the cops anything that might help.'

'Ha! The *löggan* will need all the help they can get.'

'But what more can they do?' asked Sigriður. 'They will only revisit the places that you and Callum have already searched . . . Lilja's, the stables, the shore.'

'It's ridiculous,' said Callum. 'If this was Britain the entire community would be out beating the fields with sticks.'

There was a couple of seconds of silence, like someone had sat on the mute button. Birna set down her mug and buried her face in a tea towel.

'Think about what you are saying,' hissed Sigríður.

'I'm sorry. I didn't mean it to sound . . . I just . . .' But words could not undo the damage.

'I'm OK,' said Birna, resurfacing. She folded the tea towel over her finger and scooped the tears out of her eyelids. 'I should not be upset. This is not the first time that Ásta has wandered off. She will come back in her own time.'

'You mean she makes a habit of this?' asked Callum.

'No. But there was one day last year when she did not return from school until two in the morning.'

'Were you not worried?'

'Of course I was worried. I am her mother.' Birna looked at Callum like he'd just stepped off the boat. 'It was a summer evening, just like tonight. At this time of year it is not uncommon for children to stay out and enjoy the light. And who would deny them some light, they get so little of it in winter. Look . . .' Birna pointed to the plants on the kitchen window sill, still perky in their pots. 'It is eleven thirty and our plants are still enjoying the light. That is why we let our children make the most of summer evenings. And that is why the police will do nothing about this until the morning.'

'Drink your tea,' said Sigríður, in a voice as soothing as the brew itself.

Callum poured himself a cup. He needed it.

'That first time Ásta went missing, where had she gone?'

'When she got off the school bus, she decided to walk home along the shore. A pod of dolphins had chased a herring school into the bay and Ásta sat down to watch them play. She sheltered in the hull of a boat that is washed up just a few hundred metres down the coast from here. I remember taking the pony out to search for her, but the wreck hid her from view. She walked through our door at two in the morning with her face still creased from sleeping on her schoolbag.'

'Were you not angry with her?' asked Callum.

'Why would I be angry? I had my daughter back.'

'I know, but she could have phoned you to tell you where she was.'

'I will not let Ásta carry a phone. She has no need for one. Who would she call? Ásta does not keep many friends other than Lilja and they see each other most days at school. This is not a big city like Glasgow. Why call someone when you can tap them on the shoulder or walk to their house?'

'Anna Björk said that every girl in Reykjavík has a mobile phone.'

'Ásta is not every girl in Reykjavík,' said Sigriður, tartly.

'I know,' said Callum. 'But if she had a phone, then at least we'd be able to contact her.'

'She would need to answer it first,' said Birna.

'She wouldn't take your call?'

'Who knows. She might want to be by herself. This has been quite a day for her.'

'But doesn't she know that you can help? If she needs to talk to someone . . . well . . . wouldn't she talk to her mother? Surely she knows that you'll be worried about her.'

Birna stopped her mug just shy of her mouth and thought about his question. 'Ásta is an independent spirit. She likes to do her own thing. I was the same when I was her age.'

'You still are,' joked Sigríður.

Birna smiled her first smile in hours. 'Ásta enjoys her own company. That is why she is not like every girl in Reykjavík. I would not want her to be like every girl.'

'What if she has run away?' asked Callum. 'Like you say, she's an independent spirit. And she has my wallet.'

'Why would she run away?' asked Birna.

'She might be feeling a little confused, you know, after what happened at the pool.'

'I doubt it. Ásta and I have had all those female-to-female discussions. I have made sure that she knows how her body works.'

'Then why was she so upset about it?'

'How little the man knows,' said Sigríður. Callum noticed that she was cracking eggs into a bowl.

'The first sight of blood is upsetting for any girl,' said Birna. 'But it would not be like Ásta to run away from home because of a little blood. And anyway, where would she run to? She does not have any friends outside Reykjavík.'

'Isn't it weird that she has so few friends?' asked Callum.

'Ásta has all the friends she needs.' Sigríður attacked the eggs with her whisk. 'She has her mother and grandmother, Lilja, her ponies, the birds in the sky, the dolphins in the bay. I know you find that strange, Callum. To most people nature is a hobby, a pastime. To our family it is a way of life.'

Not for the first time, Callum felt like an alien. He felt like his rules did not apply, like he counted for nothing.

Birna saw the hopelessness in his face. 'I know you

ask these questions because you care about my girl. I hope that you never stop caring about her. But try and understand her first. Then you will not be so worried. Ásta is a good kid. We should all be glad that she is the girl she is. And when she comes through that door, we will all tell her so.'

21

Birna slept alone in Ásta's room.

Rather, she lay awake all night on her daughter's bed, listening out for the door latch and hearing only sea and wind, rattling iron and cackling birds, the Arctic terns screeching their Icelandic name: *kría, kría, kría!*

When Callum brought her a coffee at six a.m., he found her on top of the bedcovers, still dressed in yesterday's clothes. She hadn't even bothered to remove her muddy boots.

'Here, get this down you.' He handed her the steaming mug. 'And I hope you're hungry. There's a whole pile of pancakes in the kitchen. They're touching the roof. Sigríður must have been cooking all night.'

'I can smell them,' said Birna. 'I guess it is Mother's way of coping. When my father died, every house in the Westmanns got one of her whortleberry loaves.'

Callum joined her on the small bed. He looked around a room that was surprisingly lacking in posters. He had expected to see Kylie's bottom jutting out at him, Justin's six-pack putting him to shame or Britney's school uniform begging a detention. But the only image on the wall was a framed square of linen embroidered with two horses – one brown, one white – their disembodied heads cradled in a garland of purple lupins. Callum noticed that Ásta kept her shelves well stocked with books. Wedged in amongst them were the two videos that he had bought her from the harbour market. Neither cassette had been removed from its protective plastic sleeve. Another set of shelves displayed row upon row of jam jars. Some were filled with water. Some held bleached-out Polaroids of unutterably sunny skies. Others housed cassette tapes with lightning bolts drawn childishly onto their labels. Each jar had been stickered with a name and a date scrawled in purple felt-tip.

'What are you thinking?' asked Birna, sitting upright so she could get at her coffee without spilling it.

'You don't want to know what I am thinking.'

'No, go on.' She placed a hand on his back. 'It cannot be any more terrible than the thoughts that have dogged me all night.'

'Well . . . it's just . . .' Callum shifted himself round, so that he faced her. 'Are you sure you want to hear this?'

Birna nodded. 'I need you to be honest with me.'

'OK,' said Callum, though he was a little unsure just how honest he should be. 'Thing is, I look around this room and I realize that an interesting little person lives in it. I want to get to know this person. I think I could learn a lot from her. But I'm worried that I may not get the chance.' Callum stopped. His eyes were beginning to well up. He pinched his nose. 'What am I like?'

'If you want to cry, then cry,' said Birna.

'I don't want to cry,' he said, as though affronted. 'It's my hay fever.'

'Callum, nobody suffers from hay fever in Iceland. Where are the flowers?'

'I'm fine. It's you that I'm worried about. What are you thinking?'

'The worst,' said Birna, with guillotine precision.

Callum caught his head in his hands. All this was his fault. Even if Birna hadn't said so, she undoubtedly thought so. Why wasn't she blaming him? She had left him with her daughter for one afternoon. One measly afternoon and he had managed to fuck everything up for everyone. There was no getting away from it. Why didn't she just have it out with him, slap his face, beat his chest with both fists, do whatever she was supposed to do in this situation?

'No, that is not strictly true,' she continued. 'I would be lying if I said that my thoughts were all bad. Before you came in I was remembering my time in hospital, just after Ásta was born. I remembered how the nurses brought me this tiny white bundle with a tuft of black hair sticking out. Before they handed her over to me, they made my bed while I was still lying in it. They tucked the sheets in so tightly that I was unable to wiggle my toes.' Birna set her coffee down and grabbed Ásta's pillow. She pulled it into her chest and rested her nose in a fold.

'There is no sense of peace that can compare to that moment . . . the moment when I first held Ásta in my arms. This little person opened her eyes and looked up at me like she was waiting for me to do something. But all I could do was smile. She must have got bored very quickly because she turned her head to look at the sun streaming in through the hospital windows. Then she stretched out her arms and went back to sleep, all pink and yellow and downy as a peach.' Birna looked up at Callum, like she too was waiting for him to do something. 'Please, Callum . . .' Her face crumpled. 'Get my baby back.'

He grabbed her before she could fall. He held her tight with Ásta's pillow safely incubating between their warm bodies.

* * *

'Birna,' whispered Sigríður.

She was standing in the doorway.

'Birna,' she repeated, louder this time. 'A policeman is in the kitchen.'

Birna separated herself from Callum. She fanned her neck with her hand. Her throat was all mottled and red.

'Tell him I will be through in a minute,' she said. 'I will go to the bathroom. I need to put my face on.'

'These pancakes are something else,' coughed Hallgrímur Hoskuldsson, through a mouthful of masticated mush. The policeman handed Sigríður an empty plate. She wasn't sure if he wanted her to refill it or put it in the sink. She played safe and used her spatula to scoop up another pile of floppy golden discs, reloading the officer's plate.

'*Takk*,' he said. 'But these must be my last. I will grow very fat if I stay too long in this house.' He laughed and patted the large spacehopper that he was smuggling under his shirt.

'Hallgrímur, you remind me of someone I know,' said Callum. 'It's uncanny.' He was thinking of Wedderburn.

'Is he very handsome?' Hallgrímur tapped Sigríður's thigh and invited her to join him in a laugh. But her face remained fixed.

Birna had entered the kitchen.

The policeman gently set down his plate. He had the look of a mourner at a wake who's been caught with a cocktail sausage in his hand before a single prayer has been offered. 'You must be the girl's mother,' he said, licking the jam from the corners of his mouth.

'*Já*. I am Birna Sveinsdóttir.'

Callum saw that Birna was wearing more make-up than usual. And she had swapped her camouflage

T-shirt for a sedate black polo that hid her neck.

'Birna Sveinsdóttir,' said the policeman, reaching for the jacket that was draped over the stool on which he sat. He bent down as far as his stomach would permit and pulled a notebook from one of the pockets. 'Bir-na Sveins-dót-tir,' he repeated, jotting the name in his book.

Birna gave Callum an incredulous shake of the head. He concurred with a nod. Sigríður shushed the pair of them with an admonishing finger. The policeman remained oblivious to their charades.

'Is there any news?' asked Birna.

Callum knew that she meant good and bad.

Hallgrímur coughed into his hand, peppering it with yellow flecks of undigested pancake. Birna looked away while her mother handed the policeman a tissue. 'News,' he said as he wiped his hand dry. He cleared his throat. 'There is none to report. There has been no sighting of the girl so far. However, last night's radio appeal brought us some joy. A reporter from *Morgunblaðið* has contacted us. She wants to put a photo of Ásta in the paper.'

'You are useless!' screamed Birna, catching every-one off guard.

'Please, Birna,' urged Sigríður. 'This is not helping.'

'No, Mother, *he* is not helping.' She pointed an accusing finger at Hallgrímur. 'Our police are clueless. They are completely inept at dealing with anything serious.'

'I assure you Birna, we deal with serious crime every day,' said the policeman. His eyes returned to his abandoned stack of pancakes. They were getting cold.

'Bullshit!' yelled Birna. 'The most serious crime you deal with is when you are called to the docks to break up a fight between a drunk and a seagull.'

'Come now,' said Sigriður, offering her arms to her daughter.

'That is not true,' said Hallgrímur. 'Only last night I was patrolling the Breiðholt area. That place is rough. Sometimes I think there is a drug dealer in every house.'

'So you were in Breiðholt confiscating a few funny cigarettes when you should have been searching for a missing girl.' The redness had spread from Birna's neck into her face.

'I understand your frustration but I can only say that we are doing everything we can,' said Hallgrímur.

'Bollocks,' barked Callum. 'Have you tried getting up off your fat ass and actually looking for her daughter?'

The policeman's face suddenly darkened. His blue eyes sat flatly in his baggy lids. 'Are you the girl's father?' he asked.

'No,' interrupted Birna, as if Callum had needed reminding. 'Ásta's father is long dead.'

The policeman returned his attention to the Scotsman. 'So you are . . . ?'

'Callum Pope. I'm Birna's partner.'

'And an outlander,' said the policeman.

'What the fuck has that got to do with anything?'

'Please, Callum,' said Sigriður. 'Control your temper or you will have to leave.'

Callum took a breath before going back at the policeman. 'Listen pal, the only thing about me that should concern you is that I was with Ásta when she went missing. I'm one of the last people to see her alive.'

'Are you saying she is dead?' asked Hallgrímur.

'Callum? What are you saying?' Birna looked at him like she didn't know him.

'It was a slip of the tongue,' he protested.

'How do you know she is dead?' asked Hallgrímur.

'Why would you say such a thing?' asked Sigríður. 'Why, Callum?'

'I didn't mean it like that. I wasn't thinking.'

Hallgrímur was talking to himself now. 'Well I never said she was dead. And the women never said she was dead. So how can he know she is dead?'

'Birna,' pleaded Callum. 'You know I would never harm Ásta.'

'Harm her? *Harm* her?' asked Hallgrímur. 'Now he is saying he harmed her.'

Callum bent down to the policeman and shouted directly into his ear, 'Would you shut the fuck up for one minute and listen to what I am saying. Ásta is not dead and I did not lay a finger on her.'

Birna was crying now, wrapped up in her mother's arms.

'I'm sorry, Birna.' Callum felt sick and it wasn't for lack of breakfast. 'I should go. I'm getting in the way. This is a family matter and . . . well, I'm not family, am I. You'll want to sort this out yourselves.'

Callum reached his jacket off the chair next to the policeman's and a cold metal cuff clicked round his wrist.

'The only place you are going,' said Hallgrímur, 'is the police station.'

'You will appreciate that Reykjavík is not like the Bronx,' said Hallgrímur as he drove Callum through town. 'It was 1984 before we had our first armed robbery. But during these last twenty years Iceland has been making rapid progress in everything else, so why should crime be any different? I am proud to say that we now experience two murders every three years.'

'You wouldn't know a murderer if he stabbed you in the stomach,' said Callum.

'Shit,' said Hallgrímur. 'I forgot to frisk you. Tell me
. . . are you carrying a knife?'

'No, I don't have a knife.' The novelty of Callum's situation was quickly wearing off. 'You know, Hallgrímur,
this had better be good. This had better be fucking
good. Because while you're wasting your time with
me, there's a kid out there who could be in trouble.
Real trouble, believe me. I mean, what is this? Am I
under arrest? Are you going to caution me?'

'I have not decided yet.'

'Of course you haven't.' Callum mouthed some
silent obscenities.

It had rained while they were in Birna's house and
even though the shower had eased off completely, the
windows of the police car were still covered in big
shimmering raindrops. Callum was grateful. The
diamond-studded windows made it difficult for the
rubbernecking locals to discern his features, their
attention having already been drawn to the car by
Hallgrímur's unnecessary and rather melodramatic use
of his siren.

Callum's anonymity was eventually blown when he
stepped out of the car onto the forecourt of the police
station. But it wasn't a gang of seasoned paparazzi who
pounced on him, their frenetic flashguns frying him
like whitebait. It was a shaven-headed girl armed with
a disposable camera, who made Callum regret coming
out without a pillowcase over his head.

Hallgrímur put his hand over the girl's lens. He
bleated some Icelandic at her, a sentence that didn't
contain the words 'turnip' or 'snow', of that Callum
was certain. He guessed that the policeman was
advising her that her camera would be confiscated.

'*Morgunblaðið*,' the girl offered in reply. She
removed a card from her wallet and showed it to the
policeman.

'Aah, Katrin Rós,' said Hallgrímur, returning the girl's card and proffering a smile of recognition. 'Callum, this is Katrin Rós Thórleifsdóttir. She is the journalist I told you about, the one who requested Ásta's photograph. It looks like we could both be joining the girl in tomorrow's paper.'

'Are you the guy who murdered her?' asked Katrin. 'How did you kill her? Where did you dispose of her corpse?'

'No questions, Katrin,' said Hallgrímur. 'You take pictures only. Leave the questioning to the professionals.'

'If I must,' said the shaven-headed girl. 'But can I ask both of you to turn around so your faces are in the sun. The flash on my camera is very weak.'

'What the fuck is this?' asked Callum. 'Can we please go inside?'

'No problem, Katrin,' said Hallgrímur, ignoring Callum. He bullied his prisoner into the required position.

The photographer wasn't happy. 'Hallgrímur, can you put your hand on his hair as if you are pulling it?'

The policeman seemed more reluctant this time. 'I will hold his hair only if you promise me that the picture will not accompany a story about police brutality.'

Katrin laughed. 'Of course not. I am just thinking that the arrest will seem more dramatic if it looks like a struggle. I have more chance of getting you onto the front page if you are manhandling the murderer.'

'I am not a murderer,' said Callum.

'No problem, Katrin.' Hallgrímur lifted a lock of Callum's hair and made a fist around it. 'Mr Pope, please tell me if this hurts you.'

'This is ridiculous,' said Callum. 'Totally fucking ridiculous. I'd laugh if it wasn't so serious.'

'Do I look OK, Katrin?' asked Hallgrímur. 'I could pretend to gouge his eye with my finger if you think it will be a better picture.'

'You look fine. But before I ask you to say cheese, can I ask if the motive was sexual?'

'Katriiin,' cooed Hallgrímur. 'You are a very naughty girl. I said no questions.'

Katrin shrugged. What did she care? She had got her shot.

Once inside the station, Callum looked back through the glass door to see the shaven-headed journalist draped across the bonnet of the police car. She was taking photos of herself to finish off the film.

'What was that all about?' he asked. 'I am assuming that they can't print anything until you find me guilty.'

'So you admit that you are guilty,' said Hallgrímur.

'That's not what I said. Jesus, Birna was right. You *are* inept.'

'I will pretend I did not hear that.' Hallgrímur positioned his bulk behind Callum and undid the Scotsman's shackles.

'Was it really necessary to cuff me?'

'Yes,' insisted Hallgrímur. 'It is necessary to use the cuffs once in a while to stop them rusting up. Now follow me, I think we have an interview room at the end of this corridor.'

'You *think*?'

'It's only a hunch. But I'm a detective, I have a nose for these things.'

Callum was shown into a small boxroom with walls the colour of nicotine. It housed a table with four orange chairs positioned around it. He had expected that there would be a DAT machine on the table with which to record the interview but it seemed that someone had broken in during the night and stolen it, replacing it with a dozen sour-smelling bottles of Egils

Gull, a well-thumbed pack of pornographic playing cards and a bowl that had once been filled with pretzels, judging by the detritus of broken twigs and rock salt that sat in it. A light tephra of fag ash covered the floor.

'I am sorry about the mess,' said Hallgrímur. 'It is these useless Filipino cleaners that we are now employing. They are cheap labour, but I guess you get what you pay for. Immigration will be the ruin of this country.' Hallgrímur fussed around the table, gathering up the empty beer bottles and setting them on the floor. He unpicked the playing cards from the sticky rings on the table, ripping off tits and cocks in the process, before returning these freshly censored pictures to their box. 'We have the purest gene pool in the world and now it is getting muddied,' he complained. 'Our daughters are fucking the Polaks. They are sleeping with Skoti.' He looked at Callum and smiled a sarcastic smile. 'Can I get you a wee dram?'

'You can get me out of here.' He pulled out a seat. A cigarette had burned a neat circle through the plastic. Callum suspected it had been done deliberately. Confirmation arrived when he sat down and a shot of cold air announced that the hole had been positioned in perfect alignment with the one in the middle of his backside.

'Are you sure I can't get you a drink? I am getting a coffee for myself. It is just as easy to make two cups as one.'

Callum waved him away. He had lost the will to speak.

He was glad when Hallgrímur closed the door, glad that he had his own air space, even if that air was thick with a cumulus of alcohol and tobacco.

Not for the first time in his life, Callum had been

accused of murdering someone; yes, someone he loved. His memory of his arrest in Prague was sketchy at best. He hadn't been in a mood to appreciate it at the time. There had been bigger horrors to deal with. But this was different. He was as lucid as a potted alpine on a sun-kissed window sill and it was clear to him that, unlike the Policie Praha, these guys were amateurs. Throwing him in shackles, tearing through town like Starsky or Hutch, an interview room that doubled as a speakeasy: bloody amateurs. And the more ridiculous his situation had got, the more terrifying it had become. Somewhere out there a young girl was in trouble and these guys hadn't a hope of finding her.

And then there was Birna. And Sigríður. They had done nothing to stop the policeman carting him away. They had done nothing to defend him. Surely they didn't think that . . . that Callum would . . . that he was a . . . how could they?

The door reopened. The girly calendar that had been pinned to the back of it fell flapping to the floor. Hallgrímur entered, balancing three plastic cups in his hands.

'I didn't ask for coffee,' said Callum.

'You didn't,' agreed Hallgrímur. 'But we have visitors.'

A hand appeared over the policeman's shoulder: a female hand. It held the door open for him. Callum recognized the bronze ring on the little finger. The black sleeve was another giveaway.

'Birna?'

She followed the policeman into the room, turned, and invited someone else to enter.

'Sigríður?' asked Callum.

A young woman walked tentatively through the door: the receptionist from the Laugardalur pool.

'This could be your lucky day, Mr Pope,' said Hallgrímur. 'It seems your alibi has arrived.'

The rain unleashed its full force on the windscreen of the Suzuki. Reykjavík was effervescing. Rooftops popped, buildings burbled and bodies bled into the gutters. Birna's wiper blades couldn't keep up.

'Thanks,' said Callum.

'I am not the one you should be thanking,' said Birna. 'Send your flowers to the swimming pool. That receptionist got you off the hook. She was the one who saw you sitting inside during the time that Ásta disappeared from your car.'

'I know, but if you hadn't got hold of her . . . I mean . . . I could have been held for . . . who knows when they would have . . .'

'The *löggan*? Hah! It would have taken them days to visit the swimming pool and weeks to get a statement from that girl. And I do not have weeks. Or days. I must find Ásta now.' Birna's gears barked as she fought with the stick. 'If you want something done properly, then you must do it yourself. My father believed in this saying. That is why he ran his own businesses, exporting puffin in summer, harvesting angelica in spring, farming oysters in the dark months. He never relied on anyone to do his work for him and neither shall I. My father was his own man and I am my own woman. I must find my daughter myself, even if it means calling on every house and stopping every person I see.' Birna wasn't looking at Callum. She was staring resolutely into the rain.

He was worried about her. Behind that steely facade he could tell she was suffering. She was putting up a front, like a wall of lava that cools and hardens but remains unstable and volatile beneath.

'Let me help you,' he offered.

'That will be difficult,' said Birna.

'How is it difficult? I have my own vehicle. We can cover more ground that way. Two pairs of eyes are better than one.'

'I know. But it is not possible.'

'Why not? Birna, you've got to let me help. I'm responsible for all this.'

'That is just it. Personally, I do not think you are responsible. But my mother is starting to think differently. She thinks you might have something to do with Ásta's disappearance.'

Callum couldn't believe what he was hearing. It had been a day loaded with conjecture and simmering with insinuation, a day that had just boiled over. 'Sigriður thinks I've done something to Ásta?'

'She has told me not to let you near the house. Not until Ásta is found. She says that we should never have let you move in with us in the first place. She is worried that there is much about you that we do not know.'

'What does she think I am?'

Callum couldn't believe that Sigriður would think him capable of hurting her granddaughter. But then didn't he, more than once, think that Neil Byrne might be trying to get back at him by breaking into his office and ram-raiding Ásta's pony? Perhaps you can never truly know people, he thought. Even those people closest to you. It was only after Sarah's death that Callum discovered her protracted correspondence with Kohl. Until then, he had thought he knew everything about her. Callum remembered how Birna had said it was a good thing for their relationship that they did not know everything about each other. She had looked forward to all the 'beautiful revelations' that they would one day share. Did she now suspect that there were horrible revelations too?

302

Birna flicked her eyes at Callum, then back to the road. 'Mother ... she ... she says you have a temper.'

'She said that?'

Birna nodded.

'Birna, you know me. Am I a violent man? Have I ever so much as raised my voice to you?'

'You are raising your voice now.'

'It's called frustration. Your mother is basically accusing me of ... of ... God knows.'

'She says you have raised your voice to her before. She says you argued with her on the night of your language lesson. She says you threw a glass at her.'

'I did not throw a glass at her! I knocked it off the table. It was an accident.' Callum rolled his head back. He had been waiting for this to come out. He knew a time would arrive when Sigriður would hurl that glass right back in his face. 'And I apologized to her,' he went on. 'We had a disagreement and ... you know ... I'd had a bit to drink. It's no excuse, I know. I shouldn't have reacted the way I did. I may have a touch of the fiery Scot in me but I am not a violent man.' Even as he said it, Callum had a flashback to a dark night in Glasgow. He remembered the feel of a softball bat in his hands, the weight of it, so deceptively light, and the clinical symmetry of the shaft, an extension of his body, a conduit of power.

'That is not all she told me,' said Birna, flicking her eyes back at him and looking increasingly unsure. 'Mother says I should not trust you. She sees it in your aura. She says that you are hiding something from me.'

'And you believe her?'

'I no longer know what to believe.' Birna sounded tired. 'I used to believe that this was a safe town and now my daughter is missing. Last night I believed she would come walking through my door but now I think

303

she . . .' Birna was shaking her head. 'No . . . I have to believe she is OK.'

'And what about us?' ventured Callum. 'Do you still believe in us?'

Birna fixed her eyes on the road. 'I cannot think about us.' She rounded a bend and slammed her foot on the brake. She swore in her native tongue and sounded her horn at an errant cyclist. Before she pulled off again, she turned to Callum. 'Right now, the only "us" is Ásta and I.'

22

Callum directed Birna to drop him at the *Room with a View* apartments. Frikki had phoned him to say that Gudni had swung by the office and dropped off the keys to the newly vacated Room 512. He had offered to take Callum's stuff round.

Birna rolled the Suzuki onto the pavement outside the apartment block. She said she would call him as soon as she had anything to tell him. She kissed his cheek but it was a platonic kiss. A sisterly kiss.

Sisters are doing it for themselves, thought Callum as he watched her drive away from him to go looking for her daughter.

He felt utterly redundant.

He spent the night on the balcony, scanning the town, listening for this, pinpointing that, deconstructing every sound and reinterpreting it as Birna's car, Ásta's laugh, the scuff of purple trainers on the street below *. . . or was that an echo? Was she over by the church?* His mind was playing tricks. No, it was Ásta who played tricks. Birna had said so. Tomorrow they would have a good laugh about it, Ásta and he. That policeman, was he for real? Pancakes? Filipino cleaners? Bald girls with cameras? Callum couldn't remember the last time he had slept. Must have slept through it, he thought.

God he needed to sleep.

He woke up to the sound of airbrakes and a smell like you wouldn't believe. He peered through the slats in the balcony and saw two men pulling something out of a lorry: a tray tightly packed with iced fish. The men were delivering it to the restaurant below. The sky above them was loud with hungry gulls. When Callum went to the bathroom he saw that one had shit on his head. He peed before he showered.

When he was dressed, he ventured out for a bagel. He had a real craving for one. Madness, he thought. They sell bagels in Reykjavík! He walked the length of Laugavegur and tried to think of a joke with the punchline: 'The Whaling Wall'.

He found a café that sold coffee and waffles. The cafés on either side of it sold coffee and waffles too. As did the café immediately opposite. Callum took it as a sign. Why flirt with fate? He ordered a sugar waffle and a cappuccino to go. He was late for work.

The woman serving him backed away when he spoke.

Callum cupped his hands over his mouth and nose and blew into them. He checked his breath. Minty fresh. What was her problem? A mirror filled the wall behind the woman and Callum gave himself the once-over, checking for seagull shit. Nada. So why was she looking at him like he'd eaten her firstborn?

'Is there a problem?' he asked.

'Smári!' she shouted, calling to a man wiping tables. She pointed at Callum. 'Smári!'

The man joined her behind the counter. 'Can I help you?'

'Are you still doing cappuccinos and sugar waffles?' Callum set a banknote on the counter-top.

'I am sorry,' said the man. 'This is not possible.'

'Ah . . . I get you . . .' said Callum, like he finally knew what the problem was. He swapped his note for a credit card. Everyone in Iceland accepted credit cards. Icelanders didn't throw coins into fountains; they threw plastic. He had been stupid to try and pay with cash. This had obviously alarmed the woman. She probably thought he had bad credit and was therefore likely to steal from her.

The man read the name on the card. He nodded at his wife. Was she his wife? Callum assumed so. Whatever, she disappeared into the kitchen. Her husband returned the card.

'I cannot accept this,' he said.

'I assure you it's good,' insisted Callum. It had to be good. It was the only card he had. The others were in his wallet. And his wallet was with Ásta. And Ásta was with . . . ?

'It's my business Visa,' he protested. 'I can charter a helicopter with that.'

'I am sorry,' said the man. 'We will not be serving you.'

A queue was building up behind Callum. 'Have it your way.' He snatched his card back. 'Jeez, it's not like you've got the monopoly on waffles in this town.'

He crossed the road.

Frikki and Anna Björk were already in the office by the time Callum arrived.

'Sorry I'm late, guys. A seagull crapped on my head.'

They didn't respond. They just looked at him gravely. He guessed they were angry.

'I know what you're thinking,' said Callum. 'It's the old "a seagull crapped on my head" excuse. Heard it all before. It's right up there with "my dog ate my homework". Though I suppose you don't get that a lot round here, not having dogs and all. What sort of animal eats an Icelandic kid's homework? Now there's a question for Magnús Magnússon.' Callum rubbed his head at the spot where the gull had anointed him. 'You know, they say that it's lucky. Birdshit, that is. I can't imagine that a dog eating your homework would be very lucky. Probably land you in detention. *They* say? Who are these people who *say* things? If you see one of them, tell them *I* say they're talking out of their blowholes. This morning I got covered in bird muck and what happened: three cafés and none would serve me breakfast. Lucky, my arse. I was forced to buy this from the hot-dog guy at the bus station.' Callum held up a carton of chocolate milk. 'Nice man. Ukrainian.' He noticed that his employees looked a little crabby. 'Sorry . . . I haven't said good morning to you, have I?' He toasted them with his milk. 'Good morning. Or is it afternoon?'

'Are you feeling OK?' asked Anna Björk. 'You're not making sense.'

'We didn't expect you to come in today,' said Frikki.

'We read about Ásta,' added Anna Björk.

'You *read* about her?'

Anna Björk slotted the small brush back into her bottle of nail varnish and reached into her duffle bag. She pulled out the morning paper. She handed it to Callum and tapped a painted finger on the front page. 'You are famous.'

Callum digested the photograph. With the aid of a Rennie. That bald girl with the disposable camera, she hadn't got his best side. And her thumb had intruded on the shot. But it was unmistakably Callum. And he appeared to be on the wrong end of a buggering from a fat cop.

'Did they rough you up?' asked Frikki. 'Did they burn you with cigarettes and put ash in your coffee? How long did it take to break you?'

'Shut your mouth,' scolded Anna Björk. 'Let him read it.'

'He can't read it. He can only look at the pictures.'

'Then let him look at the pictures,' she argued.

'Can the two of you stop bickering for one beautiful, heavenly minute and let me read the paper?'

'You can't read the paper,' said Frikki.

'True,' said Callum. 'But I can pretend to read it.'

'Why would you do that?' asked Anna Björk.

'Because . . . it would make me feel like I belonged.'

'But you do belong,' she said. 'You are upset, that is all. You should go home to your family. Birna needs you.'

'Ah, see, that's where you're wrong, AB. Because I don't have a family to go home to. Come to think of it, I don't have a home to go home to.'

Frikki smiled. He relaxed his shoulders and sagely extended a paw. 'Think of me as your family.'

Callum could only stare at him.

Anna Björk flicked an elastic band in the big man's face.

'What was that for?' asked Frikki, protesting his innocence, something neither he nor Anna Björk had asked Callum to do.

It did not go unnoticed.

'Why are you two still talking to me?' asked Callum. The question threw them. Neither seemed able to answer.

'I mean, why are you even here?' he added. 'My face is all over the morning paper. And I assume they're not saying nice things about me, otherwise I might have had a better reception from Reykjavík's waffle vendors.'

Callum smoothed out the broadsheet on the table and let it enjoy the dribble of light that struggled through the new window blinds. He placed his hands either side of the front page and arched himself over it like he was about to perform a press-up or vomit on it, he hadn't quite decided.

'I can't believe they printed this,' he said. 'Do they not have real stories to cover?'

'It is because you are an outsider,' said Anna Björk. 'You aren't well known in Reykjavík, so the paper can print whatever they want about you and nobody will question it. This would not happen if you were local.'

'But I haven't done anything,' insisted Callum. 'They're suggesting I've done something awful. You don't even have to read the story; the picture says it all. How are they allowed to do that?'

'They can suggest whatever they like because you are a new face in town. This is a small place, Callum. Most people know each other and families stay very close. If you were local, the paper would be too scared to speculate about you. They would need proof that you did something wrong. Without it, they would risk pissing off all your friends and family and that could be two hundred people. If you piss Icelanders off, they will stick together and want to get even.'

'Remember the Cod War,' said Frikki.

'What I am saying,' said Anna Björk, 'is that over here, two hundred people can quickly become one thousand people and suddenly the paper has a problem. That would be a significant blow to their sales.'

'I can't believe they can get away with this.' Callum opened up the paper and saw that the story had spilled over onto page two.

'Try not to give yourself a hard time,' said Anna Björk. 'The story has no substance. It is just gossip. We Icelanders love to gossip. Our top-selling magazine is nothing but gossip.'

'It's the same back in the UK.'

310

'Yes, but in the UK you have many more people to gossip about. We have very few. Almost everyone in Iceland has had more than his fifteen minutes of fame. But this creates a problem. We get bored reading about the same people all the time. You could say that because everyone in Iceland is famous, then nobody is famous. So when a story like this comes along and a new face is at the centre of it, there is bound to be interest. That is why they put you on the front page. And because nobody knows you, the journalists can create a story around you even if there isn't one. Who will challenge it?'

'It will get worse before it gets better,' said Frikki. 'Now they will do some proper digging. By the week-end, the whole of Iceland will know everything about you.' An ominous look appeared between the curtains of his blonde fringe. 'I hope there are no skeletons in your wardrobe.'

'Jesus.' Callum hadn't prepared himself for this. The whole sorry episode – his detention by the police, the bald paparazzo with the disposable camera – was like some bachelor-party prank that had now gone badly wrong. With journalists on his case and every Icelander wanting to know more, this was a potentially fatal fucking situation. How long before they found out about Sarah's murder? They wouldn't have very far to dig.

'You'd better tell me what they're insinuating,' said Callum. Even his voice had blanched.

'You must not believe everything you read in the papers,' cautioned Anna Björk.

'She is right,' said Frikki. 'They are always making up lies. Last summer they put out a scare story about a plague of dust mites hitting Iceland. But it turned out that the scientists had found only two dust mites in the whole of Reykjavík. And one of them had no legs. The dust mite, that is. Not a scientist.'

'Frikki, sometimes I think they should sew up your mouth and feed you through a drip,' said Anna Björk.

'Is someone going to translate this story for me?' Callum was losing his patience. 'The headline at least?'

Anna Björk read it out: '*IS THIS THE FACE OF A CHILD KILLER?*'

'And is it?' asked Callum. He pointed to his face. 'Do I look like a child killer? And what, exactly, is a child killer supposed to look like?'

'You are not a child killer.' Anna Björk pulled his hand down again. 'You loved that girl. When we had our drink at Hotel Freysnes I could tell that you loved her. You did not say so but it was written on your face. And that was not the face of a child killer.'

'You could see that I *loved* her?' asked Callum.

'Yes.'

'That I *loved* her. You said *loved*. Past tense,' he said. 'You think she is dead, don't you.'

'No!' protested Anna Björk, suddenly alarmed. 'I did not mean that.'

'Then what did you mean by *loved* . . . that I no longer love her?' Callum's voice was barbed. He knew he was upsetting her but he couldn't stop himself.

'No! Please . . .' Anna Björk sat on the sofa and even though her nails had already dried, she flapped her hands by her sides. 'No, Callum . . . I used the wrong word. My English is not as good as I thought.' Her distress was obvious, her innocence palpable.

Callum felt lousy. Why was he behaving like this? Why was he giving her a hard time? She had stuck by him, despite all the shit in the paper.

'I'm sorry, AB,' he offered. 'I haven't slept much. I shouldn't be taking it out on you.'

He returned to the paper and unfolded the pages.

'Come on, let's cheer ourselves up,' he said. 'Let's see what I've been keeping off the front page on Monday 16th June 2003.'

Anna Björk blew her nose on a crinkly tissue that already had lipstick prints all over it, colour copies of her mouth. 'Should I not read you the lead story?' she asked. 'It is small-minded rubbish but you should at least know what they're saying about you.'

'No need,' said Callum. 'Today's news is tomorrow's chip paper.'

The two Icelanders looked at him quizzically.

'It's a British saying,' he explained. He flicked through the paper and picked a story at random. 'Frikki, you like reading. What's this one about?'

Frikki squinted at the headline on page four. He seemed a little unsure but read it regardless. *'PHALLOLOGICAL MUSEUM TO LEAVE ICELAND. The Icelandic Phallological Museum is up for sale. Owner Heidur Hjartarson says he can no longer afford to run the museum, the only penis museum in the world. It is home to a collection of phallic specimens from hundreds of land and sea mammals native to Iceland. Soon to retire from his teaching position, Hjartarson says he will not be in a position to contribute personally to the collection.'*

'I should hope not,' joked Callum. But his colleagues weren't laughing. 'Come on, cheer up. Jeez, you'd think someone had died.' Callum dropped his hand onto page five. 'Frikki. Translate.'

The big man reluctantly obliged. *'It is alleged that some Icelanders have not been very accommodating to the members of Greenpeace who are sailing round the country to try and put a stop to Iceland's programme of "scientific whaling". According to the Greenpeace website, a group of Icelanders held a whale-steak barbecue right beside where* Rainbow Warrior, *the*

313

group's flagship, was docked. The locals threw eggs at the boat, and when their eggs ran out, they hurled sardines.'

'Now *that* should be on the front page,' said Callum. He turned to Frikki. 'This is good fun, isn't it?'

'Stop it!' yelled Anna Björk. 'This is stupid. A child is missing and we are doing nothing to find her. We should be outside searching.'

Callum closed the pages. He took the space beside Anna Björk on the sofa and ran a hand through his hair. 'You're right. But where do we start? It's been forty-eight hours now. She could be anywhere.'

The rain tapped on the windows, begging to be let in.

The three of them sat for a while, saying nothing. Nobody wanted to admit defeat but then, nobody threw a coat on to lead the search.

Tap, tap, tap.

They all knew Callum was right. Ásta could be anywhere. It would be like looking for a needle in a haystack. Or looking for a tiny body dumped in a fissure in a lava field the size of Lanarkshire.

Tap, tap, tappity, tap.

Callum sat upright, his eyes scanning the office, as if he had just woken up in a stranger's room. 'There is something different about this place,' he said, but he wasn't sure what it was.

'It will be the poster,' said Frikki, pointing to an area of wall between the two windows. 'I bought it for you. I thought it might cheer you up.'

Callum walked over to inspect it more closely. It was a map of Iceland. Rather it was a woodcut of Islandia, an ancient rendering of a bygone island comprising fire and boiling lakes. The cartography was not strictly accurate. The West Fjörds occupied one third of the island and the sea surrounding it was a primordial soup seething with beasties of all connotations. A sea serpent with a horse's head and webbed feet was vaulting the Reykjanes peninsula. A whale-sized creature, covered in scales and bearing the snarl-toothed mouth of a hog, spouted plumes of water from two blowholes. A giant feathered turtle did battle with a four-legged marlin. A fish-headed grizzly with a mouth that could swallow Hekla screamed at an eel with a lion's mane. Bulls breached the ocean and polar bears with men's faces looked on in horror from dislocated islands of ice. Islandia was the least welcoming place on God's earth.

Callum was beginning to feel that little had changed.

'You don't like it, do you,' said Frikki. 'I can see you don't like it.'

'No really, it's great. It's very . . . topical. Thank you.'

'But you look anxious,' said Anna Björk.

'Sorry.' Callum turned to face them. 'Something's still bugging me. This place definitely looks different.' Callum searched the room. 'Hold on . . . where the fuck are the Macs?'

'Ah,' said Anna Björk. She turned to Frikki for support.

'We agreed that *you* would tell him,' argued Frikki.

'I told him about the newspaper,' she protested.

'Can one of you tell me what's happened to the Macs?' asked Callum. All the desks had been cleared and the discarded cables now spread like ivy across the floor.

'The police were here,' said Frikki. 'They wanted to know which machine was yours. We wouldn't tell them, so they took all three.'

'Why would they want my Mac?' asked Callum.

Frikki dropped his eyes. 'They said they are looking for evidence. They think there might be some child pornography on your hard drive.'

'What the—' Callum lashed out with a foot, kicking the mess of cables. 'Fuck!' He sat on the edge of his desk. 'Jesus! When is this going to end?'

Neither Frikki nor Anna Björk had an answer for him. Not that he expected one. He had aimed the question squarely at himself.

'OK, deep breaths Callum,' he said. 'Your problems are nothing . . . NOTHING . . . compared to Birna's. You've got to keep it together, pal. They'll see you've done nothing dodgy and you'll get your Mac back. Jesus, it's only a machine. You can survive without it. There are plenty of PCs in town.' He hopped off the desk. 'Right, kids. I'm off to find myself a cybercafé, see if I can drum up some business. Be good.' He made his way towards the door.

'Stop,' said Frikki.

'Frikki! Frikki, Frikki, Frikki. I appreciate your concern, I really do. You think I'm overdoing it. You think I should just go home, go to bed, get drunk, do anything but work. You don't understand, do you? If I don't keep myself busy I'll only start thinking about things. And if I start thinking about things, I'll get upset. And if I get upset I'll probably blub and then everyone in this room will feel really awkward. So don't try and stop me.'

'I am not trying to stop you from working. I just thought that if you are going back into town you might want to borrow this.' Frikki removed his Stoke City beanie hat, the first time Callum had seen him without it, and suckered it onto his boss's head. 'That is better,' said the big man. 'Now nobody will recognize you as the murderer in the paper.'

Iceland's return to whaling had done nothing to dissuade the tourists. The streets were awash with pristine GoreTex in every colour under the rainbow, literally, for a multicoloured arc had formed over

Reykjavík harbour, a welcome band of iridescence in a dark, umbral sky.

For once, Callum did not object to the tourist hordes. They provided good cover for him, allowing him to slip undetected along Lækjargata. He figured they outnumbered the readers of *Morgunblaðið* by a good eight to one, so there was less chance of some have-a-go-hero rugby-tackling him and executing a citizen's arrest. Not that Icelanders were renowned for their rugby.

His pulse thumped in his ears. He had the sweats. He knew he should call Birna and demand that they meet up. He reckoned he had about sixteen hours to tell her everything – Sarah's murder, Kohl, the Prague diary – before she read about it in tomorrow's paper. Any half-arsed hack could dredge it all up if they knew how to use a search engine. He had to come clean.

Sigriður would love that, wouldn't she, thought Callum. (*The full confessional. Callum's Saga. She'd be fucking ecstatic. She'd tell Birna how she was right about me all along. 'I saw it in his aura,' she'd say. 'I knew he couldn't be trusted. I knew he was hiding something.' She'd fucking love it.*)

But he had to tell Birna everything.

Unless . . .

Callum wondered if there was some way he could slap an injunction on the paper. He wasn't familiar with Icelandic law, not on matters of personal privacy, but he guessed that if Anna Björk was right and everyone knew everyone in Reykjavík, then 'invasion of privacy' was hardly a charge that could be levied in an Icelandic courtroom as nobody had any privacy to invade. And anyway, getting an injunction would take time. Tomorrow's paper would be out before he could even get himself a lawyer (his lack of legal

317

representation had recently been brought home to him in the back of a Reykjavík police car).

What could he do? Surely there *had* to be a way of stopping them going to print. Perhaps he could contact the journalist, try and make her see his side of the story. He could give her every detail of his life other than Sarah's death and hope that she would delve no further. And if she did, he could always threaten her. He had a hunch she would respond to his threats. If she thought he was capable of murdering a child, she'd know that he wouldn't think twice about cracking open her bald little head and sucking out the yolk.

Or should he stay schtum and hope that Iceland's journalists were as sloppy as their policemen? There was just a chance that they might not uncover his terrible past. Which meant there was just a chance that Birna and he might stay together.

Which would have been good enough for Callum. But exactly three minutes and fourteen seconds into his allotted time on Machine 3 in a cybercafé on Klapparstigur, that chance was stolen from him.

As was any chance of finding Ásta alive.

From: puppeteer@hotmail.com
To: callum@fail.is
Date: Mon, 16 June 2003, 15:21:16 +0000
Subject: THE KILLER'S GUIDE TO REYKJAVÍK

So you're fresh out of prison and you're standing in Glasgow airport with cash in your money belt and a false passport in your hand.

Where do you go?

I thought I might avoid indecision by taking the first flight to Anywhere. But a glance at the departures board told me that Anywhere was La Guardia, NY. Fuck that. Their security had been tightened up since 9/11. I needed somewhere less obtrusive, somewhere where I could disappear for a while. I needed the back end of nowhere and luckily there was a direct flight.

I was on my way to Iceland.

I knew little about the country, so I purchased a guidebook from the airport bookshop. It made happy reading on my flight.

It seems that Reykjavík is the safest capital in the world. The Icelanders have no army to speak of and their police don't carry guns. Crime is confined to drunken assaults, the occasional burglary and a minimal trade in recreational drugs. Murder is rare. In fact, it is so unusual that a murder in the north of the country in the early nineteenth century still attracts debate. When another took place in 1990 the local police called in a detective from Hamburg because they were so out of their depth. According to the guide, the criminally low crime rate means that the Reykjavík police are often at a loss as to how they should treat antisocial and violent elements. Most prefer to turn a blind eye. Well wasn't I the lucky one? I had fallen in pigshit and come up smelling of Chanel.

The guidebook also claimed that in a 2002 poll of actors and pop stars, Reykjavík had pipped Paris to the number one spot as the 'Coolest Destination in the World'. This was inspiration, indeed. I thought it only right that I should see how Reykjavík rated as a destination for the discerning killer. Could anything top Prague?

There was a bus to transfer passengers directly into Reykjavík from Keflavík airport but I opted for a hire car, despite it costing roughly the same as a two-bed semi in Fife. It was the only way I could extricate myself from Bob and Jennifer, an unstoppable couple from Wyoming who were seeking to adopt me for the rest of their trip. I couldn't go making friends. Not unless I intended to cut out their tongues. And boy, was I tempted.

Killer Travel Tip: a killer needs his independence.

I had hoped to stay at Hótel Borg, a beautifully renovated art deco building right in the old town centre. Sadly there was no room at the inn. Their concierge reliably informed me that Reykjavík was inundated with tourists who were intent on joining in with the Independence Day celebrations on 17th June. This was a big deal for Icelanders, she said, a commemoration of the day in 1944 when her country declared full independence from Denmark. Reykjavík was getting ready for twenty-four hours of celebrations, with fireworks, parades, street theatre, and live music in every available venue. She advised that all the central hotels and guest houses would be fully booked and my best bet, if I wanted to stay at the heart of things, was the Salvation Army guest house just across the square.

The guest house did indeed prove to be my salvation. It came without frills but it was neat and clean and it had a bed. It suited me fine, as I would only be using it as a base. I intended to get out and about. My limbs were stiff from the flight and I had read that Reykjavík was blessed with many thermal pools and hot pots that had magical curative properties. I was assured that the baths at Laugardalur, just by the football stadium, would sort me out.

Reykjavík is a rarity, a modern metropole, yet unusually safe. One of the first things that surprised me as I drove through the town was the number of children. Kids were everywhere: they ganged up on corners, skated through squares, or sat abandoned in prams outside shops. It seemed they were trusting of adults and played without threat. The opportunity was glaring.

The pool, too, was full of thrashing children. If you were in the mood to abduct one – and, as I boiled my bones in a hot pot, I was certainly getting there – you could take your pick.

See, I was working on the theory that when you crash a car, the best way to get over it is to immediately get back behind the wheel. I had been careless with my last victim and the police they came a-knocking. I needed to rediscover my touch and I needed to do it soon. And just as the apprehensive crash victim will rehabilitate himself with a sedate tootle around the block, so I needed something undemanding to get me back up to speed. Why make life hard for yourself? Or death, for that matter.

I imagined that killing children would be less problematic than adults. They don't have the strength to put up a struggle and their bodies are smaller and lighter, making it easy to dispose of the corpse. Sure, kids make a lot of noise, terrible screamers some of them, but not if you silence them quickly (a razor to the throat might help in this regard). But you needn't be so brutal. A child will quickly acquiesce if you win their trust. When they don't think you are a danger to them, what's there to scream about?

How fortunate for me, then, that Icelandic children are so trusting.

The majority of the children in the pool were accompanied by adults. Those that weren't stayed in close groups, splashing, bombing and diving under the ever-watchful eyes of the life-guards. My best chance was to wait outside and pick off a waif or a stray: a girl waiting for her mother, a boy waiting for the bus, I wasn't fussy. Anything in the eight-to-twelve age group was fine and their sex didn't matter. This wasn't a sex thing. I'm a murderer, not a paedophile. Those guys need their balls chopping off.

I eventually saw her sitting alone in the back of a red Toyota parked right opposite my hire car. Her wet black hair was smudged against the window. She looked very sorry for her-self, like a sweaty dog locked in a car on a hot day with none of the windows open. She was listening to music. I tapped on the glass and motioned her to put the window down.

'What's the music?' I asked.
'Emiliana,' she said.
'It's very good,' I said. 'Can I see the cover?'
She reached into the front seat and grabbed the CD. She handed it to me.
'Is this yours?' I asked.
She nodded.
'So it doesn't belong to your mummy or daddy?'
'My dad is dead.'
'I'm sorry,' I said.

322

'He was a hero,' she said.

'Wow! You must be very proud of him.'

She nodded.

'So, does that mean that your mummy brought you here?'

She shook her head.

'A friend's mummy?'

She shook her head again. 'My mum's boyfriend,' she explained.

'And where is he?'

'He will be looking for his keys. He gave them to me by mistake but he doesn't know it yet. I am going to surprise him by hiding in his car.'

'You like playing tricks?'

She nodded.

'Well, why don't we play an even bigger trick on him?'

'How?' she asked.

'Why don't I let you hide in *my* car. Then, when your mummy's boyfriend comes out and sees that you aren't inside his car, you can hoot my horn and give him a big fright. He will jump out of his skin.'

She laughed. 'That would be funny.'

'Shall we do it?'

She thought about it and nodded. She opened the door and jumped onto the tarmac. 'Shall I turn the music off?'

'It's OK. I'll do it,' I offered. 'Your hair is wet. You should get into my car.' I leaned into the Toyota and switched off the stereo. I removed the keys from the ignition. A wallet sat on the driver's seat. I took that too. Mummy's boyfriend was going nowhere.

Unfortunately, neither was mummy's girl. She was leaning against my car, holding her tummy. She looked a little groggy.

'Are you OK?'

'My belly is sore,' she complained.

I felt a sudden bloodrush. This was perfect. I couldn't get the words out quick enough. 'Aren't you the lucky girl. Because I'm a doctor. And I know how to make you better.

If you get into my car, I'll take you to the hospital.'

'What about my mum's boyfriend?' she asked as she climbed into the back seat.

'I will leave him a note.' I made a show of producing a piece of paper from my pocket. I turned my back to her and crumpled it into my fist.

'Now,' I said, once I had got myself behind the wheel. 'Are you comfy back there?'

But there was no response from my girl. Whatever was ailing her, she had finally succumbed. The warmth of the air-conditioned vehicle had induced sleep.

Iceland's petrol stations are wonderful places. You needn't get out of your car. You can simply drive up to the pumps marked Full Service and a nice man will fill your tank to the brim, take your money, pay for your petrol and buy your provisions, before returning the appropriate change. While my pump attendant filled me up, he looked in at the little girl in the back.

'You have a beautiful daughter,' he said.

'I do,' I conceded.

'She looks just like you.'

'Everyone says that.'

'I've got two girls myself,' he said. 'Teenagers.'

'Then you've got trouble.' I gave him a knowing nod.

'Just you wait . . . It will not be so long before you have trouble too.'

'Don't I know it,' I said.

'What age is she?'

'Ten,' I guessed.

'They're great when they're that age.' He stole another look at her. 'And they look so beautiful when they're sleeping.'

'They do,' I agreed.

I paid him my money and he brought me my change, along with a road map, four bottles of water and four slabs of chocolate.

I was heading into the dark heart of Iceland. I needed to go where there weren't so many eyes.

The scenery changed every fifteen minutes, as did the terrain. Outside the city, the hills had ruffled up like a rug caught in a door, their smooth contours rising into sharp glacial peaks that sparkled whitely against a flat blue sky. We turned inland and followed the course of a river, being watched all the while by a dark mountain that remained dominant on the horizon and sinister in my mirrors. It resembled a gigantic Brazil nut, sideways on, with a cummerbund of cloud round its waist. The land surrounding it was a black crust, like the skin on a burnt lasagne. Twisted spires of shiny black obsidian glinted in the sun and the occasional flash of purple hinted at flowers among the rock. We dropped into a deep valley and passed a lake whose waters fed a hydroelectric power station. From here, our route wound upwards again, levelling out into a wasteland of dark grey sand; mile after mile after monotonous mile of it.

The wind whipped up the sand and the colour was abraded from the sky. We were driving into nothingness; the glaciers and mountains that fringed this desolation seemed a long way off. There were no birds, no cows, no sheep, no horses, no trees, no houses, no cars, no people. This was just man and mountain. This was just man and girl.

Of course, I could have finished her off there and then and she would have been none the wiser. But where was the sport in that? And anyway, the longer I let her sleep, the more precious and untroubled hours I was buying to get her clear of Reykjavík.

I briefly considered waking her. I could have used the company. This was a lonely journey into a barren land and it would have been nice to have someone to talk to. But I needed some headspace, some time to think. Not like it was a real brainbleed or anything. This was the fun part, the bit that every killer lives for: the bit where he decides how best to dispatch his victim.

We jostled through the sand, jolted over rocks and splashed through icy streams that coursed down from a distant glacier that must have been thirty or forty miles away, yet still filled the whole of my windscreen.

I wondered if it was possible to stab someone with an icicle. Would the ice be strong enough to get through the ribs and penetrate heart muscle? I guessed that it might, if it had been compacted over millions of years. If so, it could be the perfect murder weapon, as, once it had been used, the evidence would simply melt away.

The sands eventually relented but they were replaced by something satanic and irredeemably dark: a field of lava that had no end. Suddenly, we were unwelcome guests on an alien planet with strange exploded rocks dotted about its surface, the aftermath of some hellish battle of fire. The track went steeply up then dipped sharply as the terrain grew more severe. Inclines fluctuated between about one in ten and one in four, and now and again a pair of tyre marks would leave the cinder track.

I thought that the bump and grind might rouse the girl from her sleep. We had been travelling for the best part of five hours and there hadn't been a peep out of her. I stopped the car and checked she was still breathing. She was. Not that it would matter now whether she was asleep or awake. If she tried to make a break for it, where would she go?

As an added bit of insurance I removed her trainers. If she tried to go anywhere, the lava would cut her feet to ribbons.

326

That's if it didn't swallow her whole. While the car was stopped I was able to get a better look at the area. Some terrible act of geoviolence had wrought the landscape with cracks and fissures that were only a couple of feet wide, but interminably deep. To try and step over them would be akin to a movie hero leaping from the roof of one tower block onto the roof of the next, while his pursuing hoodlum falls short. There really was nowhere to run to.

I considered dropping the girl into one of these crevasses. If death didn't come instantly, it would undoubtedly come. And when it did, there'd be no hope of anyone finding the body. I supposed that even a helicopter equipped with heat-seeking technology would struggle to locate an ice-cold corpse. And I doubted that any animal would venture into such an abyss, even if they managed to pick up her scent. The cracks were so narrow and deep that if a fox or a bird tried to get at her meat, they'd never get out with her bones.

But I decided on another plan: an idea inspired by something that I had read in an *Iceland Review* that had been sitting in the guest-house lobby. The magazine had contained a feature on extreme kayaking, a popular sport in Iceland. It seems that because of the large ice caps and the volume of meltwater that feeds the rivers in summer, Iceland offers some pretty daunting waters. The magazine had been full of pictures of these rivers: great swirling eddies of gunmetal grey that turned green as they cascaded over horseshoe falls.

What the kayakers feared most was being trapped in a 'Maytag', a mini maelstrom that is created at the base of a waterfall, or in the hole where a boulder breaks the river flow. Here, the water spins round with such force that, should you go under, it will endlessly recirculate your body in a lingering death roll. Your only hope of survival is to dive as deep as you can and swim under it. But you are unlikely to do this as all instinct tells you to swim to the surface. And when you do, you are battered back down again like a rag doll. You can't fight the hydraulics. Up and down you relentlessly go, the weight of the water cracking your ribs and crushing your lungs, your body forever buffeted by ceaseless torrents. You are trapped in a 'keeper' from which there is no escape.

The article spoke about Iceland's Waterfall of Thieves, into which pilferers and rustlers were once thrown to meet their certain deaths. But this waterfall did not appear on my map. In fact, I was over one hundred miles from the nearest marked waterfall – Gulfoss – and even that was no good to me, being one of the most popular tourist attractions in the country. Too many eyes.

I spread the map full out on the dark volcanic track and noticed that a thick blue vein wriggled across six squares, skirting the far side of the lava desert and connecting a large white landmass in the south to the sea in the north. This looked like one mother of a river and it seemed I was already heading towards it.

It proved to be a convenient and reliable place of execution. So powerful was this river that it had cut a canyon through rock and lava. Enormous boulders had fallen down from the canyon walls and they now stood in midstream as obstacles to the river's relentless continuum. The largest of these boulders looked the most likely candidate. The current raced around the rock, creating a whirlpool on the downstream side. I was sure this was a Maytag as the river constantly tried to fill it, thundering water in from all sides and creating a deep, foaming, spinning drain.

As I carried the girl to the edge of the canyon, the roar of the water began to resuscitate her. The cool spray clung to her skin, forming fevered droplets on her forehead. All I had to do was drop her in but I was worried about missing the spot. Survival would still be unlikely. She would be quickly ferried away by a freezing and furious current. But there was always a chance that her body would scout a clear line through the puzzle of rocks and cross-currents and be carried clear of the rapids. And it is well documented that children are resilient in cold water. It's something to do with having a metabolism that slows to a near standstill, preserving the faint hope of life. Kids have been known to fall through ice, be submerged for half an hour and survive with all their faculties intact. I needed to get this right.

I stood her upright on the edge of the rock. She wasn't fully awake and her legs buckled, pitching her body forward. I caught her before she fell in.

I had saved her life but now I had to end it.

I grabbed her waist and held her straight out, aiming her shoeless feet at a point downstream of the boulder. She was light enough to hold like this without her weight pulling me over, but she wasn't so light that the wind would waylay her on the way down.

I released my hands and watched her disappear without a splash. The river sucked her down into its dark green belly. Billows of churning current hoisted her back to the surface, giving me a teasing flash of her pink jacket, before a white-water blast hammered her down again.

Up she came and down she went, up and down for eternity, like a ping-pong ball under a tap.

23

'Hello?'

No response.

'Look, I can hear someone in the hallway so don't pretend that you aren't there.'

'Go away. We are not talking to the press. We need to be left alone. I said the same to your female colleague only one hour ago.'

'Sigriður, it's me. It's Callum.'

'Then you must leave too.'

'I have to speak to Birna. It's about Ásta. There's news.'

Sigriður opened the front door just a fraction. She made sure that the gap was not wide enough for Callum to wedge in a foot.

'What news?' she asked.

'Birna needs to hear it first.'

'Then it cannot be good news.'

'Just let me in,' said Callum. 'Apart from anything else, I'm getting soaked out here.'

He wasn't lying. His T-shirt was sopping. The rain had pasted it onto his skin so that Sigriður could have been forgiven for thinking he was wearing body paint. Callum had left his coat hanging over the back of the chair at Machine 3 in the Klapparstigur cybercafé. Frikki's Stoke City beanie remained there too, sitting on a mouse mat. He had dropped everything on reading *The Killer's Guide*, but he hadn't gone straight to Birna's. He had first called in at the Salvation Army guest house to see if Kohl had checked out.

It appeared that Iago Kohl had never checked in, at least not under that name.

The downpour had been as sudden and as gushing as Proms applause. It made a similar rapturous sound on the corrugated sheeting that covered Birna's house.

Sigriður relented. She opened the door and showed Callum into the living room. 'Birna is sleeping. She is exhausted. My poor girl has been out in the car all night. I will see if she wants to speak to you.'

Callum sat at the table in the bay window, in the same chair he had sat in on his first night in Birna's house; the night that Sigriður had served him raw guillemot and then been surprised that there was sadness in his aura. This chair had come to be known as 'Callum's Chair' in the days before Birna kicked him out of the house. Straight-backed and armless, Callum's Chair now felt like it didn't fit him. It was hard, cold and formal like the pew at the back of a church, the one nearest the gale-blown doors. Of course, he could have sat in one of the comfy chairs – the armchair or the sofa – but neither seemed to provide an appropriate repose for telling Birna that her daughter was dead.

Callum had no idea how he was going to do this. He had printed off *The Killer's Guide to Reykjavík*: a travelog that described the abduction and murder of a child that was undoubtedly Ásta. And Callum was certain that Kohl had written it. The freed murderer had made it sound like he was merely an opportunist killing the first child in Reykjavík that he could get his hands on. He had said he wasn't fussy. But Callum knew different. He knew there was nothing random in

331

Kohl's selection of Ásta. He had killed Ásta to get back at Callum for putting him away. It was clear as day. And night, for that matter. Everything pointed that way: the bastard was out of prison; he had jumped his parole and the Strathclyde police were covering it up; and Kohl knew Callum was in Iceland. He had sent this diary to his '.is' web extension. He had followed Callum to Iceland just as he had once followed him to Prague. And he had killed Birna's little girl to rob Callum of a second shot at a life.

Callum folded the printed email into his back pocket. He wasn't so sure he should let Birna read it. He knew from bitter experience the damage it would do. There had been many times over the years when Callum had regretted reading about Sarah's murder in that Prague diary. The pain had been in the details; not the gory stuff like her strangulation or the hooks through her limbs, but the personal stuff, the intimate stuff. Why had it bothered Callum so much that Kohl had undressed her? Why did it still upset him to know that when Sarah's body was found, she was dancing? Was it because they had first met at a ceilidh?

Callum used to believe that he would have coped better with Sarah's death had he not been forced to read about it. He used to believe that what you didn't know couldn't hurt you; that ignorance was bliss. That was one of the reasons he didn't tell Birna about Sarah and, therefore, Kohl. What she didn't know, couldn't hurt her. But Kohl could hurt Birna. And he had hurt her. And it was Callum who now had to deliver the icicle to her heart.

She entered the room, her dressing gown over her clothes. Her eyes were red and sore-looking but Callum could not be sure if it was tiredness or tears. 'Mother says you have news about Ásta,' she said.

Sigríður followed her into the room and threw a dry towel at him.

'Thanks,' said Callum. He gave his hair a brisk rub and set the towel on the floor. 'Birna, I should speak to you alone.'

'*Nei*. Anything that concerns Ásta, concerns Sigríður too.'

'I am the girl's grandmother,' Sigríður reminded him.

'Then you had better sit down.'

'Why should we sit down, Callum?' shouted Birna. 'Do you expect that our legs will give way when you tell us that Ásta is dead?'

'Please Birna, try and be strong.' Sigríður held her daughter's hand. 'You must let him say it.'

The two women stood side by side and looked down at Callum like they were staring into a grave.

'You're right,' he said. 'Ásta is dead.'

Birna nodded. 'You see. We are still standing. Nobody has fallen to their knees.' She freed her hand from her mother's and used her finger to wipe something from her cheek. 'Where did they find her?'

Callum closed his eyes. He had anticipated this question but it didn't make it any easier to answer it. 'They haven't found her,' he confessed. When he opened his eyes again, Birna had become a blur. The room was a watercolour.

'But the police must have found her. Otherwise, how would you know she is dead?' asked Birna.

'The police don't know she is dead yet.'

'Then how can you know?'

'This is most strange,' said Sigríður. She was beginning to flap, like an unsettled hen. 'Most strange,' she repeated.

'Answer me, Callum. How do you know my daughter is dead?'

'I have lied to you, Birna. Your mother was right. I am hiding something.'

'What have you done to my girl?' screamed Birna.

'I haven't done anything to Ásta,' shouted Callum. 'Why does everyone keep suggesting I've done something? I assume you've read that shit in the paper. For the last time, I wouldn't have done anything to hurt Ásta. OK, so we had a difficult relationship, Ásta and I, but why would I have wanted to hurt her? You think that I have no feelings for her because we aren't flesh and blood?'

'Possibly,' said Birna. 'Maybe. I am not sure what I think any more.' She was irritated now. 'But it does not matter what I think. What matters is how you know that my daughter is dead.'

'Well if you would let me tell you!' shouted Callum. The windows rattled and he wasn't sure whether it was in response to his raised voice or to the freshening gusts outside.

The women seemed shocked at his tone.

'I told you, Birna. I told you he had a temper,' said Sigríður.

'Oh fuck off,' said Callum.

'What right have you to tell my mother to fuck off?' shouted Birna.

'Every right. The woman has had it in for me from day one. She made a great pretence of accepting me into this house but we all know that she didn't want me living here and she eventually got her wish. She has never wanted our relationship to work and look at us now, we are arguing with each other at the very moment when we should be supporting each other. She must be fucking delighted.'

'You misjudge me,' said Sigríður.

'Stop this!' screamed Birna. 'Stop it now.' She tightened the cord on her dressing gown. She walked across the room and sat on the piano stool, turning it slightly so she faced Callum. 'Tell me how you know that my daughter is dead.'

'Her murderer told me.'

'She has been murdered,' said Birna. It wasn't a question. She was informing herself of her daughter's death. It was as if her own voice was the only one she could believe. 'Who killed her?'

'The same person who murdered the woman I loved.'

'The girl in the photographs,' said Birna.

Callum nodded.

'I knew there was more to that relationship than you were telling me.' Birna was nodding to herself. 'You were too quick to dismiss her.'

'Who killed Ásta?' interrupted Sigriður. She suddenly looked like the old woman that she was.

'I'll tell you,' insisted Callum. 'But first I owe it to Birna to explain the truth.' He took a quick breath and slowly released it. 'You were right about the girl in the photographs . . . Sarah . . . our relationship was more than I let on. We lived together for five years. Before we became business partners, Sarah worked at the main bank in Scotland. Her job was to evaluate applications from people who were seeking new business loans. Way back in 1996 she denied money to this guy, an oddball, a publisher-turned-author who was trying to market some travel guides. He was angry at her decision. He bombarded Sarah with threatening letters over a period of about six months. Pretty soon he was stalking her. I wasn't aware of this at the time. She didn't want to bother me with it.'

Callum looked out the window and addressed the mountain across the bay. 'Sarah had never actually seen this guy, all their exchanges were by mail or phone call. So, the day he joined us on a flight to

Prague, she was not in a position to recognize him. He sat next to us and talked, talked, talked. We felt a little sorry for him. We thought he was one of those sad businessmen who spend their lives away from their families, living out of a suitcase. We thought that this was the reason he was so keen to make conversation with us. He insisted on taking us out for a drink after we'd checked into our hotels. He claimed to have visited the Czech capital many times and, well, we thought he might be able to give us a few tips. But while I pissed my beer into the downstairs toilet of a basement bar in Prague, Iago Kohl killed my girlfriend. And now he has murdered Ásta.'

Birna leaned back on the piano. Had its lid not been down, her elbows would have struck an appropriately dissonant chord.

Sigríður toyed with her necklace, twisting it round her finger until the tip turned angry and red.

Callum shivered a little. A combination of the wet and the cold was bringing on a chill.

'How can you be sure that this person has murdered my daughter?' asked Birna.

Callum reached for the proof in his back pocket, then had a change of heart and quickly retracted his hand. There had to be another way of getting her to believe him without subjecting her to that.

'After Sarah's murder, Kohl sent me an anonymous email,' he said. 'It was written in the style of a travelog, the sort that we used to get all the time at Strawdonkey. Only, in *The Killer's Guide to Prague* as he facetiously titled it, Kohl detailed how he had killed my girlfriend. It wasn't a pleasant read.' Callum reached for the towel again. He folded it over his knees. 'Kohl was released from prison a fortnight ago. The police told me that he was being kept in a safe house, for his own protection, not mine.' Callum allowed himself a rueful grunt. 'But when my office was broken into I had an inkling it was Kohl. And when Ásta's clothes were taken from your washing line, I knew he was taunting me. He was letting me know that I could never be free of him. I contacted the Glasgow police but they are scared to admit that they've lost him. They accused me of being paranoid. For a while I believed them. That's why I didn't say anything. I didn't want to alarm you. I should have told you, Birna. He has taken Ásta and he has murdered her and I am to blame.' Callum was struggling to keep it together. 'I am so sorry.'

'How do I know you are telling the truth?' asked Birna. 'How do I know that you haven't taken her?'

Callum looked directly at her. His eyes were stinging. 'Why would I lie to you about this?'

'Because you have been lying to me ever since we met, ever since I was stupid enough to leave my bag lying open in a Glasgow bookstore and let someone steal my money. For all I know, you could have been the thief.'

'Why would I have done that?' asked Callum. 'That's crazy. Didn't I pay for your lunch that day?'

'Sure. But maybe you paid for it with my money. Maybe you stole from me to engineer the opportunity to chat me up.'

'Has it come to this?' asked Callum. 'That you could accuse me of stealing your money and harming your daughter? Do you know nothing about me?'

'I thought I did,' said Birna. 'But what am I to believe when you keep telling me lies? How do I know that this girlfriend of yours is even dead?'

'Because I have seen her,' said Sigriður.

It took both of them a moment to adjust to her voice, almost as if they had forgotten she was there. True, the room had got very dark as the storm clouds gathered outside. But even though Callum could not discern Sigríður's features, he didn't dare put on a light.

'Callum tells the truth,' she continued. 'I have seen a young woman on his shoulder on more than one occasion. She follows him like a Móri.'

'A Móri?' asked Callum.

'A Móri is a spirit that follows the same family for many generations.'

'Why did you not tell me this?' Birna asked her mother.

'I tried,' said Sigríður. 'I suggested to you that he was hiding something but I could not be specific. It had to come from Callum. I had to see if he was prepared to tell you the truth. But the truth has come too late for all of us.'

'Did you know that his girlfriend had been murdered?' asked Birna.

'No,' said Sigríður. 'If I had known such a thing I would have told you. I only knew Callum had experienced a great loss and that he would not admit it.'

'And am I supposed to feel sorry for him?' asked Birna, raising her voice above a grumble of thunder.

'I don't want you to feel sorry for me,' argued Callum. 'I have never wanted you to feel sorry for me. That's one of the reasons I didn't tell you about Sarah's death.' He scratched the top of his arms. The damp T-shirt was making them itch. 'Let me explain,' he begged. 'When we first met I wasn't sure it could go anywhere. Let's face it: the odds were stacked against us. You lived in Iceland for starters. And although you didn't know it, I was going through hell at the time. I didn't think I could love anyone the way I loved Sarah. But that first weekend we spent in Room 512, our room, I knew then that the feelings I had for you were every bit as strong. I knew we had a chance but I wanted to be sure that you felt the same way about me.'

'I did feel the same way,' said Birna.

'I know you did. And because I hadn't told you about Sarah, I knew that your feelings were genuine. I knew that it wasn't pity masquerading as love. If I had told you about Sarah, I could never have been sure.'

'It would not have made any difference.'

'It might not have made a big difference, but it would have made a difference. You would not have behaved the same way towards me.'

'Of course I would,' insisted Birna.

'You say that. But I had a couple of good friends whose attitude towards me changed after Sarah's death. They were great initially, always phoning, checking up on me, dragging me out to get hammered or making a space for me in their five-a-side football. But pretty soon the phone calls stopped and the drinks dried up and the five-a-sides became "oversubscribed". Nobody wanted to be around me any more. They felt awkward in my company. One of these so-called friends even admitted that he felt he couldn't laugh in front of me. Sarah's death had changed things.'

'But I am not like your friends,' said Birna. 'You should have told me about her. And you should have told me about the man who murdered her. The only difference it would have made is that my daughter might now be alive.' Birna darted her eyes around the room as if she was looking for her cigarettes or trying to remember where she'd set down her whisky. But Birna didn't smoke and she rarely got drunk. She was helpless. She needed a crutch. If he could have gone to her, he would have. But she had put up too big a barrier.

'You need not worry about me ever feeling sorry for you.' Birna was crying now. 'How could I pity the man who has led a killer to my doorstep; the man who has let a murderer take my girl?'

339

The room strobed silently as an electrical storm sparked up.

Birna switched on a light. She examined her face in the glass that covered one of her framed photographs. It was a picture of some mud pools that bubbled blithely like pans of molten chocolate. The central pools had conjoined to form a heart. Birna looked right into it and tugged at the bags under her eyes. She put her hand over her mouth as if the shock of it all had finally hit her and she was about to be sick. She stayed this way for a few seconds. Then she tore the photograph from the wall and threw it with both hands, smashing it on the floor. She ground her bare foot into the cracked glass.

'Birna!' shouted Sigríður.

Her daughter wasn't listening.

'Callum,' pleaded Sigríður. 'I think you should leave.'

He was unable to argue. This was it, he realized. This was the end of the line. Just as their relationship had begun with a petty crime in a Glasgow café, it had now ended with the worst crime of all: the murder of a child. This was more than the breaking up of their relationship. This was the breaking up of a family.

He watched as a young mother screwed her bare heel into fractured glass, juicing her foot like a lemon. He felt like he was about to throw up.

How could he live with this? How was he supposed to go on?

He turned and made for the door.

'Callum, wait,' said Birna. 'You cannot go yet.'

He stopped.

'I want to see the email.'

'Birna I don't think you should—'

'Let me see it!' she screamed. 'I need to know.'

Callum removed the soggy sheets from his back pocket and handed them to her.

'Birna, your foot is bleeding,' said Sigriður. 'Come, let me make a wrap for it.'

'To hell with your wraps!' shouted Birna.

Sigriður patiently persisted. 'You are losing blood. You will get an infection. Come.' She made to grab Birna's arm but her daughter snatched it away.

'Leave me alone! I do not need your medicine. It does not work. It did not work for my father and it will not work for me.' Birna's blood had smushed with the powdered glass to whip up a raspberry sorbet. She ignored the pain and directed her anger at her mother. 'Do you want to know why I never followed you into practising the grass medicine? I will tell you. For years my father grew angelica because you and others like you were convinced it could treat cancer. When he became ill with a chest infection the doctor examined him and found that cancer was eating his lungs. They wanted to take him to the hospital but you insisted on treating him yourself. After a few weeks he started to look better. You thought you had cured him and you sent him back out to work. But I was there when my father collapsed and died. We were standing in a field full of angelica that I had been helping him to pick. What good were you and your stupid plants then?'

Sigriður said nothing as Birna limped out of the room.

'Should I go after her?' asked Callum.

'No. You will only make things worse.' Sigriður knelt down and began picking chips of glass out of the carpet pile. 'You know, Callum, before you came along nothing got broken in this house. We have been visited by earthquakes that have done less damage.'

Callum eyed the dark crack that ran the full length of the ceiling but he said nothing.

'If you had only spoken to me about Sarah, none of this might have happened,' she said. 'I gave you plenty of opportunity to talk about her but each time you dismissed me as a madwoman.'

Callum got on his knees and helped her clear the glass. 'I know ... it's just, all that stuff about auras ... it's not normal, is it? Don't you think it's odd that you can see those things and other people can't?'

'There is nothing odd about it,' said Sigriður. 'It is nature. As humans we exist on different planes. We have our physical body, which is flesh and bone. Everyone can see that. But we also have a spiritual layer, which is perceived as hues or colours by those who are able. It's a beautiful thing, Callum. And it's perfectly normal.'

'That may be so, but what about the paranormal? You said you saw Sarah. You said she was wearing a mask. She died wearing a mask. That's why I freaked with you.'

'I see,' said Sigriður. 'I did not know she had died in this way.'

'Ow!' shouted Callum. His finger was cut. He put it in his mouth.

'Be careful. This glass is sharp.' Sigriður removed two books of sheet music from the piano and used them to shovel up her shards. She emptied the broken glass onto Callum's wet towel.

'What I mean,' said Callum, 'is that you may consider it perfectly normal to see auras, but is it normal to see ghosts?'

'I do not see ghosts,' said Sigriður.

'But you admit that you saw Sarah. And without knowing it, you described how she was dressed when she died.'

'True, I can sometimes see people who have passed on. But I do not think of them as ghosts. A ghost is something cartoonish, something that passes through doors and scares people. A ghost is something transparent that does not possess the inner light of the person. The woman I saw was not a ghost. The woman I saw had that inner light.' Sigriður noticed that Callum had stopped what he was doing and was sitting cross-legged on the floor. He was staring into space. 'You miss her, don't you?'

Callum nodded.

Sigriður sighed. 'It is time to let her go, Callum. Sarah will do fine without you.'

'How do you know?'

'In Iceland we have the word *Afturgöngur* which literally means "those who come back". The *Afturgöngur* are spirits who frequent the places they inhabited when they were living. The only difference with Sarah is that she keeps coming back to you. She thinks you are still grieving for her. She wants to let you know she is OK, so you can stop grieving for her and set her free.'

'This is too weird,' said Callum. He sniffed sharply. 'I don't believe in this shit, so why is it upsetting me?'

'You are upset because you still carry this grief.' Sigriður set her sheet music on the floor and dusted the fine white crystals off her hands. 'Callum, I have a little story for you. Birna was right about her father. But what she does not know is that when I insisted on keeping Svein at home and treating him myself, I did not treat him at all. I knew his illness was too advanced and that nothing could save him. I sent him back out to work because I knew that working was what Svein enjoyed most. I was glad that his last day was spent in a field picking plants with his daughter and that he didn't die in some lonely hospital bed.'

'What's your point?' asked Callum.

'My point is that I knew when to let him go. In my case it was a month before he died. Your situation is different because your girlfriend was stolen away from you, cruelly and unexpectedly. You were not prepared for it as I was. But you must still let her go. Otherwise you are forcing her to stay on your shoulder for ever.'

'And Svein isn't on your shoulder?'

'No,' said Sigriður. 'Though he was on my back for most of his life.' She was smiling. 'When we buried Birna's father I saw a light over the small organ in our church. I knew it was Svein. I could feel his presence wash over the place. He was telling me he was happy. He was letting me know he was on his way somewhere else.' Sigriður shrugged. 'So I let him go.'

Callum removed the photograph of the bubbling mud-heart from its broken frame. It was streaked with Birna's blood.

'And what about Ásta?' he asked. 'Can you see her?'

'No,' said Sigriður, losing her smile. 'Ásta will go to her mother.'

Callum hung his head. 'I can't believe this is happening.'

'It is not your fault.'

'Of course it is. I came to Iceland because I thought I had a chance here. I thought I could do what you said and let Sarah go. And I thought Birna could help me do it.'

'But you would not let her help you. She had no way of knowing that you needed her help.'

'I know that now. I realize that I wasn't thinking about Birna when I kept Sarah a secret. I was thinking about myself. And now Ásta is dead because I was selfish.'

'True, grief can sometimes make people think only about themselves,' said Sigriður. 'But that is not the reason Ásta is dead. Sometimes there are horrible circumstances in life that we can do nothing about. You experienced such a circumstance in Prague. And now we are all experiencing one.' Sigriður wrapped the towel around the broken glass and tied the four corners in a knot.

'I had better go and let you be a mother to your daughter,' said Callum. 'But do me a favour, Sigriður. If Birna shuts herself in her room, keep checking on her, won't you. That email I gave her, I'm worried what it will do to her.'

'She will be fine, Callum. It is good that she is reading it. I think it will help her to know. There is nothing worse than not knowing.'

Sigriður followed Callum to the door. 'Would you like to borrow a coat?' she asked.

'It's OK. I can't get any more wet than I already am.' Callum folded a heart into his pocket and headed into the rain.

But before Sigriður could close the door on him, he turned. 'I've been really horrible to you,' he shouted. 'So why are you being so reasonable?'

'You misjudged me,' said Sigriður. 'I am a reasonable woman.'

24

Back in Room 512, Callum carried the phone over to the sofa. He called John Wedderburn. Either it was the time delay or the DI had a premonition he would call, for the phone was answered before the first ring.

'He's killed her.'

'Whoa there! Jesus, Callum, do I not even get a "hello" or a "how are you"?'

'No time for pleasantries, John. He's killed her. I told you he'd do something like this.'

'Slow down, Cal. One thing at a time. Right . . . let me get my bearings . . . who's killed who?'

'Kohl. He's murdered Birna's girl.'

'Cal . . . I really think you should see someone. And I'm talking as a pal.'

'I'm not your pal, John. And I'm not making any of this up. The bastard has emailed another diary. He has taken Ásta from under my nose and he has thrown her into a river.'

'Kohl has not taken anyone,' said Wedderburn.

'It's all there in the diary,' said Callum. 'I forwarded it to you. Kohl admits to taking Ásta from the swimming pool. This is proof that he's eluded you, John. How could he know that she went missing from a swimming pool, if he was still under your so-called 24 hour protection?' Callum spat the last word.

'Hold on . . . wait just a sec . . . I'm opening up my email.'

Callum could hear the inspector clicking and tapping.

'Got it,' he said.

'Shall I give you a moment to digest it?' asked Callum.

'No need.' Wedderburn's voice had hardened. 'This is bullshit, Cal. Listen to me . . . you're not well.'

'You what?'

'You expect me to believe that this was written by Kohl? Jesus, Cal, I didn't swim down the Clyde in a monkey suit. You've written this yourself.'

'Why the fuck would I do that?'

'To try and get him banged up again.'

'Oh for fuck's sake,' said Callum.

'I'm not stupid Cal, and neither are you. We both know that if Kohl sends you an email it could be viewed as harassment, a breach of his parole. This has obviously been written by someone who wants him back behind bars.'

'But it was sent from Kohl's Hotmail address. He's still calling himself Puppeteer.'

'Anyone could have taken that email address. Hotmail addresses expire after six months if they haven't been in use. Kohl's address would have become available again during the time he was in prison. Anyone, including my own mother, could have registered as Puppeteer. You don't even have to provide your real name or address to do it. That's why it was impossible to trace Kohl during the original investigation.'

'So you're saying that I cooked up this whole thing to make it look like Kohl is harassing me?'

'Look at it from my point of view. I call you to tell you that Kohl has been released and what happens? Straight away you're telling me that girls are getting knocked off horses, offices are getting broken into and clothes are being stolen from washing lines.'

'And geysers are exploding in faces,' added Callum. Though, now that he said it, it did sound faintly ridiculous.

'Even if these things did happen, Cal – and I seriously doubt they did – there is no way Kohl was behind any of it. As I have told you before, we're keeping an eye on him. We know where he lives and we know he has no means of leaving the country.'

'Christ, John, he even mentions the false passport in the first sentence.'

'Then let's suppose he did write that email. We know the guy's a fantasist. Jesus, you only need to read some of the books he used to publish. When I searched his house I found some bizarre stuff. I seem to remember a delightful novella about a zoomorphic necrophiliac, a guy who dressed in a bunny suit and had sex with roadkill. Bunnyman could only pop his cork if he got caught in a car's headlights performing the filthy act. I gave up on it halfway through, but the wife couldn't put it down. Whatever, there's no doubt that Kohl has an overactive imagination.'

'Exactly. And he's using it to taunt me. That's why he sent me the killer's guide to Sarah's murder. He couldn't help himself. He admitted as much in court. And now he's out, he's killed again and he's determined to rub my face in it. So what are you going to do about it?'

'There's very little I can do,' said Wedderburn. 'Not until I can prove that Kohl actually sent the email. And as we know from experience, that could be impossible. He doesn't have access to the Net at his safe house, so it won't come up on his phone bill. In fact, just scrolling through this email, there's nothing in it that can be traced back to him.'

'Rubbish. There are plenty of places out there where he could have accessed the Net. I'll bet if you contact MSN and get them to trace the source you'll get an ISP number of a library or an Internet café. Then you can check their security cameras. There's a time and a date on the email so you'll know what footage you're looking for.'

'And then what?' asked Wedderburn. 'Lots of people use libraries and Internet cafés.'

'They do,' said Callum. 'But if that café or library is in the UK, it would at least disprove your really fucking insulting theory that I concocted the email myself.'

'Who's to say that you didn't get a friend to do it for you?'

'John.'

'Yes, Cal.'

'Go fuck yourself.'

Callum threw himself back on the leather sofa and surfed the satellite news channels. Twenty-two people had died in an earthquake in Turkey. A German passenger train had derailed on the Swiss border, killing five. Raging Californian forest fires had claimed three people and countless homes. And US military had shot down a second British Black Hawk over Basra in another 'friendly fire' incident that had robbed four families of husbands, sons and fathers.

He switched channels. He searched for something to take his mind off death and the rain. He needed something bland and inoffensive. He arrived at an Icelandic natural history programme with English subtitles. He had the beginnings of a headache, so he turned the sound down and read the narration.

One of Iceland's most exceptional diving

mammals, the white beluga whale, can hold
its breath for 17 minutes

. . . and plunge to depths of over half a
mile under the ocean's surface.

The elephant seal is even more impressive.
He can submerge for 2 hours by storing
oxygen in his tissues and blood.

When eider ducks dive, they allow their
brains to cool to low temperatures,
preventing brain damage.

Humans, however, are very different.

As an unfortunate side effect of our
evolution on land, we possess very little
capacity to hold our breath.

The average person can last 2 minutes
before blacking out.

Brain damage occurs after 4 minutes and
chances of brain recovery are virtually
zero after 10 minutes.

This is the reason that so many people die
in the water. Drowning is an amazingly
efficient form of death.

Why did that have to happen? It was the last thing
he had needed to see, yet somehow he had stumbled
upon it. It was like those times when he tried to avoid
the football results until the highlights were screened
on Scotsport, but invariably he would catch a back-

page headline in the *Evening News* or he'd see someone dressed in team colours on the bus home and translate their expression into not only a scoreline, but the names of the scorers and the times that the goals were scored. Why was it that the more Callum tried to avoid something, the more likely he was to encounter it?

He was able to apply the same theory to Kohl. Callum had moved to Iceland to get away from him, yet he now found himself facing up to the killer. What godforsaken corner of the world did he have to go to to avoid him? What actions did he have to take to be free of this sick bastard? Was Callum to be forever imprisoned by grief?

Grief was the reason he had brought so few possessions to Iceland. What are possessions when you have been dispossessed of the only thing that really matters in your life? Grief had taken Callum to a place where he realized that nothing really belonged to him any more.

He hauled himself over to the fridge and removed the bottle of vodka that Birna and he had left on their last night in this apartment. The Germans hadn't touched a drop. He poured himself a mugful. The television may have been off but the subject of the documentary was still dogging him.

As the narrator had pointed out, Kohl had chosen an efficient form of death for Ásta. He had chosen drowning, surely the archetype for all human deaths. Callum realized that, in the end, almost everyone perishes from lack of oxygen: the heart patient, the cancer victim, the elderly and infirm. Sarah had been deprived of oxygen at the hands of her killer. It wasn't lava or fire that had killed Ásta's father; according to Birna, Arnar had died in a haze of poisonous gases and carbon oxides that had replaced the oxygen in his bloodstream. And it wasn't lung cancer that had claimed Birna's father; ultimately, it was the inability of his lungs to draw breath. With his illness, it had taken months to reach that final breath. Drowning, on the other hand, accelerated the process at a horrifying pace.

Was Callum supposed to draw solace from this? Was he supposed to feel grateful that Kohl had at least been expedient in dispatching Birna's girl? Was he supposed to thank God that Ásta hadn't suffered?

Was he fuck.

He undid the belt from his jeans and set it on the worktop. He gulped his vodka and stared a while at the long loop of leather with the heavy buckle at one end. He watched it coil up like a constrictor, its flat head cocked back to expose a silvery barb for a tongue. He wondered what it would feel like to tie it to the door and let it tighten around his neck.

In the end almost everyone perishes from lack of oxygen.

But he was neither brave nor cowardly enough.

He took the vodka bottle to the balcony and looked down at the street below: a street full of happy people undaunted by the weather and cheered by the light. It was nearing 3 a.m. and the kids were still queuing outside Kaffibarinn, hunching up against corrugated walls the colour of frozen blood.

Callum hurled the bottle into the sky and shouted, 'Bastard!'

He came in from the rain.

He switched the television off and sat on the edge of his bed.

He felt himself nodding off, but was roused by a knock on the door.

Callum opened it up and saw Birna standing outside.

'What are you doing?' he asked.

'I was going to ask you the same thing,' she said. She held up a piece of the smashed vodka bottle. 'You nearly killed me with that.'

Callum said nothing.

'Can I come in?' she asked.

'Sure.' He closed the door behind her. 'How are you feeling?'

Birna limped over to the coffee table and threw something onto it: Kohl's email. That steely look was back in her eyes.

'I know where she is, Callum.'

He fed the belt back into his trousers. 'How can you know where she is? Surely only Kohl can know that.'

'He probably thinks that too. He was careful not to name any mountains or roads in his email. He thought he was being clever. But he did not count on his victim having a mother who knows the landscape of this country better than most. He said that he threw Ásta into a glacial river that ran from the south right up to the north coast. I know this river: Jökulsá á Fjöllum, the most powerful river in Iceland, 128 miles of rapids, ravines and waterfalls.'

'128 miles?' asked Callum. 'That hardly narrows it down. He could have thrown her in at any point along it.'

'Já, but I have also worked out the route that he took, so I have a good idea of the place where his car met the river.'

'You think you can find Ásta's body?'

'I think so.'

'But you said it yourself, it's a powerful river with waterfalls and rapids. She could have been swept out to sea by now.'

'If he threw her into a keeper,' said Birna, 'she will be going nowhere.'

353

'Should we not leave this to the police? I mean . . . Kohl could still be out there too.'

'We have been through this. Our police are incompetent. You said the same thing when I drove you back from the station, though you used more colourful language. But you are right, Callum. Ásta's killer could still be out there. That is why you are going to buckle up your trousers and come with me.'

Callum saw little determination in Birna now. He saw only delusion and grief. He knew the feeling. And he knew he had to go softly with her. 'Birna, you're upset, you need to get some slee—'

'Now, Callum!' Her expression was rigid. 'We are going to get my girl back.'

25

She was driving him into Hell.

Rather, she was driving him into Hella. From there they turned inland and followed the course of a river – the Ytri-Ranga – being watched all the while by a dark mountain, just as Kohl had said in his diary.

'Are you sure that's it?' asked Callum.

'I am sure,' she said.

'It doesn't look like a Brazil nut to me.'

Mount Hekla was certainly dominant; not even Callum would deny that. It surfaced in front of them like a killer whale, its broad bulk piebald with snow. Lazy whorls of geothermal steam hinted at life in its belly.

'It looks like it's about to erupt,' said Callum.

'Who knows. Hekla is our most enthusiastic volcano. She last erupted in '80 and '81. You saw both eruptions when I took you to the Volcano Show.'

'Ah,' he said. Callum recalled the film. He remembered watching aerial shots of great smouldering boulders rolling down from Hekla's crest and crashing into a dense blanket of tephra at her feet. This was the 'burnt lasagne' that Kohl had written about and now Birna was driving the road that had been routed around it. Callum could picture the molten lava, glowing red and smoking blackly as it crawled inexorably over the land around him. A petrified forest of stone tree trunks had sprouted from the lava field, formed by gobbets of liquid rock that had at one time belched upwards before solidifying. 'Twisted spires of shiny black obsidian' was how Kohl had described these dead coppices. Callum guessed that they had been formed in the most recent eruption, as time had not yet eroded their sharpness. Everything around them was a field of black cinders, save for the sporadic frills of white and purple flowers that had gained a foothold in the tephra, proclaiming the eternal persistence of life.

'That's the flowers,' said Callum, pointing them out like a kid. 'Kohl mentioned purple flowers.'

'Now do you believe we are on the right track?' asked Birna.

'I never doubted you,' he lied.

'They are lupins,' she said. 'They are part of our anti-erosion programme. Our soils lack clay to bind them, so they are easily eroded. Lupins are planted to stabilize them. The plant is fast spreading and it is an obsessive binder of thin soil. So we attack erosion by dropping tonnes of lupin seed from the air. I knew that this was one of the spots where they grew and it is probably the only spot with spires of lava and a mountain shaped like a Brazil nut.'

'It isn't shaped like a Brazil nut,' insisted Callum. He was glad Birna was talking about the landscape again, just as she used to do. For a short while at least, she had reverted to being Birna the Scientist. This gave him some heart. He knew how much she loved her work. When they had first met, Birna told Callum that she had chosen geology and vulcanology because Iceland was 'the geological candy store of the world'. Callum thought she might now be focusing on her science to block out her grief, as if the land around her was the only thing she trusted. Ironic, he thought, as she was always telling him how volatile and un-dependable it was.

He guessed she needed to find her daughter's body before she could grieve properly.

'I have climbed Hekla,' she said.

'It doesn't surprise me.'

'I saw the most wonderful thing when I was up there . . . a huge block of snow, the only snow on the volcano at the time, all gleaming white and lonely. It stuck out of the rock like the prow of a yacht and it was topped, bizarrely, with a layer of tephra. I worked out that the snow must have fallen in 1980 and then been covered in tephra from the 1981 eruption. The dark ash cooled on contact with the snow, and insulated it for many years. It was really something,' she said. 'I guess I had found proof that there really are snowballs in hell.'

They followed the F26 on Callum's map and dropped into a deep valley, its green and black floor decorated with silver tinsel, rivers that caught the sunlight. They passed the same lake that Kohl had passed, the one that fed a hydroelectric power station.

'We shall follow this road until we get to the Tugnafellsjökull glacier,' said Birna. 'It will take us into some terrible terrain.'

'This bit looks pretty,' said Callum. 'Very colourful.'

'We are in a river valley. Water comes down from the glaciers and makes the ground fertile for plants. I often take a detour here to bring Mother back some white mountain avens or some of those small pink cushions of moss campion . . . look . . . over there . . .' It was Birna's turn to do the pointing thing.

'I thought you didn't believe in Sigriður's medicine,' he said.

Birna went quiet.

Callum regretted opening his mouth. She was clamming up again.

'I was wrong to shout at my mother.' Birna's voice was subdued. 'She means well.'

'She only wanted the best for your father, you do know that.'

Birna nodded.

They drove in silence.

The road, if it deserved that name, was only discernible by the occasional wooden stake and a few tyre tracks that meandered in varying degrees of proximity. It galled Callum to think that the freshest tracks had been made by Kohl. He tried not to think about it as the Suzuki began the slow climb out of the valley. The road quickly degenerated into a sand and gravel dirt track dotted with black cowpats of lava. Callum consulted his map. They were heading into Sprengisandur, the vast desert of grey-black sand that Kohl had complained about.

'That map is no good to us now,' said Birna.

'Sounds ominous,' said Callum. 'Do we have a compass?'

'A compass would also be useless. Volcanic rock is magnetized.'

'Shit.'

'Relax. We will not get lost. For now, there is only one track. So that is the one we shall follow.'

They were barely one mile down this road when Callum sensed the true futility of their search. Birna had driven him into some dark and unfinished corner of the universe: an unending expanse of sand and glaciated rubble where man seemed out of place. It was a scene from pre-history or post-apocalypse, a monochromatic picture beamed back from a Martian probe. Vast boulders had been tossed like dice across this sterile sienna plain by some long-forgotten glacier.

Now and then, a dragon-back of rock would arc out of the sand to break the monotony and remind Callum of their folly in trying to cross this place in a four-wheel drive. A no-frills flight on a pterodactyl would have been more appropriate.

The scale was incomprehensible: what was big was not necessarily close; what was small was not always distant. Get lost in the Scottish Highlands and you miss last orders, thought Callum; get lost out here and the elves will make soup with your bones.

The black dunes rolled on and on like some bloody great slag heap. Pools of muddy grey water filled the hollows in the sand, undrinkably opaque, their surface lashed by the constant wind.

'This is relentless,' said Callum.

'I warned you. God has not finished making this place.'

'Then he should have mentioned that in the scriptures: *And on the seventh day God rested . . . having pencilled in Iceland for some time next millennium.*'

Birna summoned a smile. It was as remarkable an act of creation as anything God could muster, given the circumstances. 'You are nearer the truth than you think. In the geological timescale, Iceland was created this morning.'

Callum looked at his watch. Eleven thirty.

'It still is this morning.'

'That is my point,' she said.

Callum realized they had been travelling for over six hours, having hit the road at around five a.m. They would have got going sooner had Birna not first driven him back to her house. She had needed to tell Sigriður where they were going. Birna claimed this was a sensible precaution when heading into the harsh interior, as there was every chance that they wouldn't get out again. Callum took the extra precaution of texting their bearings to Frikki, on the hour, every hour.

Unsurprisingly, Sigríður had not been keen on them going. She had argued long and hard with Birna. She had used everything she had to get her daughter to see the madness in it. When she finally accepted that nothing would change her mind, she insisted that Birna and Callum sit down to a hot breakfast before they set off. They were about to head into a land where they couldn't buy water, a land so bereft of life that they couldn't even kill for food.

Birna stopped the car, snapping Callum out of his introspection.

'What's the matter?' he asked.

'A river.' She indicated a wide stream that barred their way. 'I will have to get out and look for a safe point to cross.'

'No worries,' said Callum. 'I was about to suggest that we stop and stretch our legs. We've covered a lot of ground.'

They climbed out and walked stiffly to the water's edge. As rivers go, it didn't look particularly threatening. Callum found it quite pleasant in its own way, a rather aimless but jocular babble, but he had heard umpteen stories of large vehicles being swept away by these innocuous-looking tributaries and he was glad that Birna was exercising caution. The tyre tracks at their feet corroborated her concern. Many three-point turns had been executed here, indicating the reluctance of previous drivers to cross.

Birna followed the stream, limping slightly, her foot having been carved up by the glass she had smashed. Every few yards she stepped into the water and jabbed her good foot around, testing the bed.

'This is what you get with global warming,' she said.

'There are many of these glacial streams that used to be no more than a trickle and every year the meltwaters are rising. Up north there are fjörds that are usually covered in ice all year round but now you can swim in them. Things are pretty well twisted.'

The wind was whipping the sand up. It was getting in Callum's eyes and making his teeth uncomfortably gritty.

'You have to respect water,' said Birna. 'It is the antidote to fire but it is also more destructive. Millions of years ago this whole desert was covered in frozen water. The glaciers ground up the underlying basalt and when they retreated they left nothing but this black sand. These days it is *jökulhaups* that do the destruction.'

'Are those the floods that you've been studying?' Callum wanted to keep her talking. More talking, less thinking, that's what Dr Pope had prescribed.

'*Já*,' shouted Birna. She had moved further downstream. She was standing knee-deep in the middle of the water, studying the flow, tamping and prodding with her foot. 'Those glaciers that you see in the distance, they could unleash a *jökulhaup* at any moment. If the volcanic activity beneath them melts the ice cap, the water will reach a critical volume and one or two cubic miles will burst out in seconds as a violent flood. We would be swept away in a rush of water maybe ten times as great as the Amazon.'

'Not good,' yelled Callum, his voice fighting with the wind.

He picked up a fistful of sand: black, damp and cloying, forever devoid of life. He rinsed it away in the stream. He was too lazy to go back to the car for a drink, so he ladled the meltwater into his hand and greedily sucked it up, filtering out the silt with his teeth. He had swallowed several mouthfuls before it occurred to him that Birna had gone quiet. He looked up to see her standing in the water some distance away. From the shape of her shoulders and the roll of her head, he could tell she was crying her heart out.

He ran to her, smashing into the water and grabbing her arms.

'It's OK,' he said. 'It's OK to cry. Believe me.'

'I am sorry. I have been trying not to think about her. I have been trying really hard.'

'I know,' whispered Callum. He steadied her head on his chest.

'She has been taken by a *jökulhaup*,' said Birna. 'That is what it feels like . . . like some sudden, violent force has just wiped her out of my life. What chance did she have?'

'Ásta had no chance. There is nothing you could have done. Nothing.'

Birna nodded.

She removed herself from Callum and backed away a little, like she thought she shouldn't be touching him; like she believed it was inappropriate.

She bent to the water and splashed some onto her face, rinsing away her tears. 'We should get back to the car,' she said. She fixed her hair behind her ears. 'This is a good place to cross.'

After the river, the dirt track circumnavigated the black dunes, disappearing and reappearing, before vanishing on the horizon at a point between two glaciers.

Callum unfolded his map. To their left was Hofsjökull, a peppermint streak that curved evenly across the distant horizon like an upturned dinner plate. To their right, and much closer, stood Tugnafellsjökull: a shimmering ice cap that had been pasted onto dark rock to give it the appearance of a white filling in a blackened tooth.

Callum felt very small beside it, even smaller when he consulted the map and saw that Vatnajökull, a glacier only slightly further to the east, was the size of four hundred Tugnafellsjökulls frozen together. A comparative pipsqueak, Tugnafellsjökull just sat there, funereally silent, as it had done for many millennia. The glacier crept imperceptibly down its flanks, reaching out towards the road before stopping abruptly in a brilliant white snout. Long parallel crevasses gashed the surface of the ice, giving it the appearance of a boiled fish that had flaked into glossy segments.

The Suzuki came to a fork in the track and Birna opted to take the road less travelled, a road that she said was open for only forty-five days in the year. It was impassable in all other weather, she said, and nobody actually lived where it led.

The track undulated wildly and was beset by potholes and pits, its bedrock jiggered by frosts. The unruly corrugations were hard on Callum's bottom and even harder on the hands on the wheel. He offered to relieve Birna of the driving but she rightly pointed out that she was the only one with any experience of negotiating such appalling terrain.

The track pitched madly over slag hillocks, swooping left then ducking right, tyre marks churning in all directions like frenzied python duets. Birna ignored their precedent and seemed intent on carving out her own route. She was determined now, an independent Icelander asserting her free will. Her attitude was fitting.

Callum remembered that this was 17th June, the day when Birna's country celebrated freedom and self-rule, as a Reykjavík concierge had told Iago Kohl.

Would it also be the day that Ásta was liberated from a watery eternity?

But as Callum looked up from his map to see that their vehicle was sliding uncontrollably down a gravel bank towards a deep pit of lava, that day suddenly seemed a long way off.

'Jesus Christ!'

'Try not to panic,' shouted Birna. She was fighting with the wheel, turning it into the slide, but it seemed she was only delaying the inevitable. The Suzuki slid further down the gravel bank, its rear wheels spitting out stones as she tried to employ more traction.

Callum watched the same stones disappearing silently into the deep crevasse beneath them that ran parallel to the road.

'What the . . . shit . . . let her go . . . we should jump out.'

'Abandon the car? That would be suicide.' Birna's foot was flat to the floor. Callum prayed it wasn't her injured one.

'We'll get dragged to our deaths.'

'No, Callum. Nobody is going to die.'

He reached for his door handle but was thrown backwards as, with an unholy screech, the car shunted to a halt.

'We have hit a rock,' said Birna. 'It has broken our slide.'

The car had come to rest about halfway down the slope. The road sat in their windscreen at the top of the incline, some fifteen feet above them. The crevasse remained open-mouthed and expectant in their rear window. They stayed very still, scared to move in case all hell broke loose again.

'Christ, look at me,' said Callum. 'I'm sweating buckets.'

'That is because we have the heating on full.' Birna adjusted the aircon to a blue setting.

'What do we do?' Callum looked into the rear-view mirror and saw mini-avalanches of scree spilling down the slope.

'I think we should get out,' said Birna.

'Are you serious?'

'Callum, one minute ago you were ready to jump. And now you want to stay in the car?'

'I'm worried that if we move, we'll tip the balance. And it won't be in our favour.'

'The car is wedged against a rock. It will not fall. If we can get out and place some bigger rocks under our wheels it should give us enough traction to get back up the slope and onto the road.'

'You're the boss,' said Callum.

They opened their doors and stepped out into a scene of utter chaos. Everywhere Callum looked, colossal black cornflakes of stratified lava were piled on top of each other in a disorganized, patternless mass. It looked like a lava flow had exploded, creating a field of insurmountable jags. Large sections had collapsed to create wide fissures with walls of riven rock. The Suzuki had been prevented from dropping into one of these fissures by a stub of lava no bigger than a traffic cone, the only such outcrop embedded in the loose shale that sloped off the road.

'Fuck me,' said Callum, the reality of it sinking in. 'That was lucky.'

'How can this be lucky?' asked Birna. 'Look at the damage it has done.' She was referring to the large dent in the back of her vehicle.

Callum shook his head. He began hunting for flat rocks of a size that could be wedged under the wheels. The first rock he could manage had a colony of small brown moths hiding underneath it, the first sign of life he had seen in hours. They feathered off into the air, no doubt bemoaning the almost total improbability of having their home disturbed.

Birna suggested laying two lines of flatter stones in front of the Suzuki's wheels to create a ramp back up to the road. Callum agreed, but pointed out the irony of trying to free a hunk of high-tech automobile from a primordial desert using ice age tools.

The look on Birna's face suggested that she did not appreciate it.

When they had all the rocks in position they sat on the road to get their breath back.

'Those are some of the oldest stones in Iceland,' said Birna. 'They were excreted from the earth over sixteen million years ago and shoved outwards by the lava which still erupts from this central area. We are sitting right on top of the mid-Atlantic ridge. Remember how I told you that Iceland is being pulled apart?'

'I recall that you demonstrated it with a dish of butter and a saucer of pickled herring.'

'Well, we are right at the spot,' said Birna. 'For all we know, you could be sitting in European Iceland while I am sitting in American Iceland.'

'You mean you're on the butter while I'm in the herring?' asked Callum.

'Maybe.' Birna wasn't smiling. 'Maybe we too have drifted apart.'

Callum leaned back on his elbows. 'We didn't stand a chance, did we,' he said. 'It feels like we were never meant to be.'

'It seems that way. A Scotsman meets an Icelandic woman. Fire meets ice. It is a dangerous combination. The evidence is all around us. This is the devastation that occurs when fire meets ice. A rift opens up and then all the horrible stuff spills out.'

Birna was sitting on the gravel with her legs tucked into her body and her chin resting on her knees. She surveyed the desolation around them. 'Iceland is a wound in the earth's skin that keeps healing and tearing, healing and tearing, as the planet flexes its muscles,' she said. 'People are lured here by the strange beauty, the silence, the exhilaration. But beneath these reasons there is something else, something they cannot articulate. I think they are drawn to this landscape because it brings us nearer to a sense of our own mortality.'

'I know what you mean,' said Callum. 'I've been thinking a lot about my own mortality.'

'You are worried that I nearly killed you?' she asked.

'No,' he lied.

Splashes of sunlight streamed down through the clouds. They picked out hunched figures in the lava, elemental beings turned to stone when caught outside in the daylight. Perhaps Sigríður isn't so mad after all, thought Callum.

'Birna?' he asked.

'*Já.*'

'Do you fear death?'

'I used to,' she said. 'But then I had Ásta and I started to fear for her well-being more than I feared for my own.' Birna grabbed a sharp stone and drew a circle in the gravel. 'And now Ásta is dead, I do not fear death at all.' She added eyes and a nose to the circle. 'When my father passed on, death was part of everyday life. It was not so long ago that we were accustomed to a relative dying in the household. But today it is different. We rarely get to see death in this everyday way. It is swept away into the sanitized environment of a hospital. Nobody likes to talk about it.'

'Are you referring to me?' asked Callum. 'The fact that I wouldn't talk about Sarah?'

'No,' said Birna. 'Maybe. In a way, yes. What I mean is that people like to deny that death is inevitable. They refuse to speak of it, as if it is obscene.' She scuffed the stone on the gravel, sketching a hairstyle: a girl's hairstyle. 'Do you fear death?' she asked.

'No,' said Callum, without hesitation.

'Then what do you fear?'

'I fear being alone.'

Birna's badly drawn girl only required a mouth. She hovered her stone over the doodle, like she couldn't decide whether to make her a happy girl or a sad girl.

'Come,' she said. 'We need to get back on the road.' She stood up, patted the gravel off her bottom and left the girl incomplete. She tossed her stone into the fissure that had so nearly claimed them.

Clackity-clack . . .

. . . clacka . . .

. . . clock.

26

'This is where NASA trained the Apollo astronauts,' said Birna. 'They believed that this was the nearest thing to lunar conditions that our planet could offer.'

The switchback track weaved through a succession of gorges. Hot sulphur and boiling water vented their gases to the surface to create theatrical bursts of dry ice that hugged the exploding topography.

'If this is what they thought they would find on the moon, it makes you wonder why they bothered going.'

They had been driving for an hour or two along the northern ridge of Vatnajökull, the large glacier that Callum had seen on the map and the one, according to Birna, that had given birth to the 'mother of a river' that Kohl had written about. The huge flat tongue of Vatnajökull's glacial ridge was studded with boulders and patterned with mile-long zebra stripes of rock and ice. The cowering skeletons of dwarf willows were testimony to the harshness of the environment.

'We call this place Ódáðahraun which means the desert of bad deeds,' said Birna. 'This is where our outlaws used to hide. Most of them starved to death on a diet of roots and water, but our most famous outlaw – Fjalla-Eyvindur – survived in a desert like this by eating horsemeat that he boiled in the hot springs. We would be doing the same thing now if I had followed your advice and abandoned the car.'

'Have you ever tasted horsemeat?'

'No. But all this talk about food is making me hungry. Do we have any chocolate?'

Callum retrieved a crumpled wrapper from the glove box. 'Two squares. You can have them.'

'Let's split them. One piece each.'

'No really, you have them. I'm not hungry,' said Callum.

'But you have not eaten anything since this morning. You must be starving.'

'My stomach feels a bit funny.'

'Tell me you are not going to be sick,' said Birna.

'I'm not going to be sick.'

The driving was slow through the fields of block lava. The Suzuki was heading towards an impressive line of tall volcanic mountains. Their throats were choked in swirling mists but their peaks remained proud against the blue sky. Birna caught Callum gazing at them.

'The Dyngjufjöll volcanoes,' she informed him. 'They are dominated by Askja, an active volcano that last erupted in the Sixties.'

'This place never sits still, does it.'

'If you go up there you will see that Askja has collapsed into a giant saucer, many square miles of lava, pumice and snow. This saucer holds a large lake – Öskjuvatn – and the smaller crater of Víti, meaning Hell.'

'Can we stop?' asked Callum, cutting her off.

'Why?'

'It's my stomach,' he complained. 'I think I need to . . . you know . . .'

'You said you would not be sick,' said Birna.

'And I won't be sick,' said Callum. 'The problem's at the other end.'

370

'I see,' said Birna. 'Can you not wait?'

'Wait for what?' Callum was desperate. 'We're in a lava field. We've been in a lava field for, like, weeks. There's not much chance of us finding an executive washroom, is there.'

'You are wrong,' said Birna. 'In about ten minutes we will come to a hut. It will have a toilet.'

'A hut? Why would anyone want to build a hut out here?'

'There are huts dotted all over the remote highlands. They are marked on your map. They provide shelter for walkers.'

'Walkers? Jeez, if you broke an ankle out here it would be a death sentence.' Callum realized what he had said. 'Sorry,' he added.

'Why are you sorry?' I told you that it is OK to talk about death. And you are right. This place has claimed many lives.'

'It's bad enough trying to drive it. Why would any-one in their right mind want to walk it?'

'Maybe these people are not in their right minds,' said Birna.

It was half an hour before Birna parked up outside two huts, one larger than the other. They sat in a rare expanse of coarse but lush grass. Each hut was a basic wooden box with a blue tin roof that sloped sharply to shed snow and rain. Callum didn't pause to debate the architectural aesthetics, however. He ran straight to the smaller hut, guessing that this was the place of ablution. Its door was held closed by a piece of string. He reckoned this was to keep the animals out; not that there were any animals to keep out, and not that any self-respecting animal would have dared to venture in. Callum gagged as soon as he opened the door. The stench was thick and sulphurous. A hole had been cut into a wooden box to create the toilet. He peered into it and was confronted with a scene that could not have been more abhorrent had he gazed into Hekla herself.

His duty done, Callum was glad to step back out into the newly washed afternoon. The rain clouds had moved over Askja, which was now a dark shadow behind a distant shower curtain. The sun shone brightly on the tall wet grasses that surrounded him, tiny droplets clinging like crystals to the blades. The air was clear as a cowbell.

'Feeling better?' asked Birna.

'Not really. I've just shed half my body weight.'

'Did I really need to know that?'

Callum shook his head. He thought that if he opened his mouth to speak, he might throw up.

Birna seemed concerned for him. 'You look like you have been poisoned. I do not understand. We ate the same thing at breakfast and I feel fine.' She placed her hand on his forehead.

'I know. And I haven't eaten anything since then, just a few squares of chocolate and a couple of sips of cold, glacial water.'

'You drank from a stream?' Birna looked alarmed.

'Is that bad?'

'Yes it is bad. How can you know what is in the water?'

'But isn't it the purest, cleanest mineral water on the planet, filtered for millennia through the finest Icelandic basalt?'

'You have been reading too many labels on bottles. You do not know what else it has been filtered through. The water you drank may have passed through the carcass of a dead sheep lying upstream. It could be full of bacteria who now wish to pass through you.'

Callum winced.

'You are lucky that I have a cure,' said Birna.

'You sound like your mother.'

'This is not grass medicine. I am prescribing a dip in a hot pot.'

'Birna, we are hundreds of miles from Reykjavík.'

'No. There is a hot spring behind the huts.' She pointed over his shoulder. 'This area has many springs. That is why we are suddenly seeing this grass.'

Callum followed her over to the hot pot, a steaming pool of orange water fringed by red and yellow rock. It didn't look deep enough to get into, but he guessed it was like one of those deceptive puddles in cartoons that gobble up people on pavements.

'Are you getting in too?' he asked.

'I would not risk it. You might erupt at any time.'

Callum stripped down to his boxers.

'You should take everything off,' said Birna.

'It doesn't feel appropriate. You know . . . now that you and I are no longer—'

'Take your pants off and stop being such a kid,' said Birna.

'OK. But no peeking.' Callum turned his back on her and removed his underwear. He sat on the rocks and eased himself into the spring.

'Good,' said Birna. 'Does that feel better?'

Callum nodded. The water pulsed with every heartbeat of the earth, massaging his legs and glooping over his shoulders and neck.

'This is such a beautiful spot,' said Birna. 'If we came here one month from now, the sun would never set on those mountains. It would just hang above our heads like a big pink disco ball.'

Callum looked up. The sun had caught a few wisps of cloud and turned them gold. They raced across the blue sky like the billowing tails of Icelandic ponies galloping in the surf.

'How far is the river from here?' he asked.

'Shush,' said Birna. 'If you are quiet, you might be able to hear it.'

Callum held his breath and listened.

'I can't hear a thing,' he said.

'You are not trying hard enough. *Hlusta á Þnina*,' urged Birna.

'What?'

'It means, listen to the silence. We do that a lot out here.'

Callum tried again. He closed his eyes and kept himself still in the water. He listened. It was faint but he could just make it out: the whispered roar of distant water, like a conch shell held to the ear.

'Got it,' he said. 'But I couldn't tell you how far away it is. Could be a mile, could be ten.'

'It is close enough,' said Birna. Her hair burned red in the sun and, just for a moment, she reminded Callum of the girl he had first met in that Glasgow bookstore: the girl who had let him pay for her lunch when she discovered her purse had been stolen.

'Are you sure you don't want to get in here with me?' he asked. 'No strings.'

Birna shook her head. 'I think Callum Pope is feeling better already. You have five minutes and then we hit the road. That should be enough time to sweat it all out.' She turned to walk away.

'Where are you going?' asked Callum. He suddenly panicked. 'You're going to drive off without me, aren't you.' He tried to get out of the water but his feet kept faltering in the mud. 'You're going to leave me here without any clothes.'

'Relax. I am just going over to the hut to see if a walker has left us anything. Get back in the water. Enjoy the silence.'

Callum lay back and examined the colourful ring of rock that lined the hot pot. The kaleidoscope of reds, yellows and lime greens was derived from heat-loving organisms that had colonized the fringes to work out their masterpieces of colour and form. They reminded Callum of Birna's photographs, but try as he might, he could not find a heart among them. He closed his eyes again, to listen to the silence, but all he heard was a woman's voice.

'Callum,' she said.

He opened his eyes.

Birna was standing above him. She held a pair of purple trainers in her hand. 'He has been here. Ásta's killer has been here.'

Callum climbed out of the hot pot, his body heat evaporating on contact with the cold air. He covered himself with his denim jacket, tying the arms round his waist and wearing it like a giant sporran. He followed Birna.

The hut had a spartan air about it, and the same damp smell that Callum remembered from the mattresses and sofas that were regularly dumped outside his parents' Glasgow tenement. The smutty little windows buzzed in the breeze.

'I found them sitting on the boot rack,' said Birna, nodding towards the floor and clutching her daughter's shoes to her chest.

Callum paced round the hut looking for more evidence, any clue that might help them locate the exact spot where Kohl had dumped Ásta – a footprint forged from a rare type of mud found on only one particular stretch of the river; a map with an X marked on it – anything at all.

A small visitors' book sat open on a table. Callum flicked through it, but it read like an anthology of German haiku poetry, almost every entry having been penned by a Friedrich, a Franz, or a Jurgen. The landscape had clearly rendered these walkers delusional as their rantings commonly ended in a long line of exclamation marks, like needles in a sewing kit: !!!!!

'It is unlikely that her killer left comments,' said Birna, with more than a touch of sarcasm.

'You don't know Iago Kohl,' said Callum, closing the book. 'It would be just like him.'

Birna wasn't listening. She had set her daughter's trainers on the table and had slipped a hand into each one until they fitted snugly. She leaned on her arms, pressing down hard to gauge the spring in the soles.

'Are you OK?' asked Callum.

Birna walked her hands along the tabletop. 'Over the years, I must have thrown away so many pairs of her shoes. They grow out of them so quickly. I wish I had kept them . . . every pair . . . from her baby shoes right up to these ones. They would help me remember that I reared a growing girl . . . a girl who turned into a lovely young woman.' Birna looked up at Callum. 'I was a good mother . . . *já*? Tell me I was a good mother.'

'Of course you were.' Callum sat on the edge of the table. 'You were more than a mother to Ásta. You were her best friend.' He was shivering now. The cold was getting to him.

Birna removed her hands from the trainers. She lifted one up and toyed with the tongue. 'He has pulled them off her without untying the laces. I always made Ásta untie her laces. He must have been in a hurry to kill her.'

'Don't do this to yourself,' said Callum. 'I can take the shoes and put them in the car if they're upsetting you.'

'No!' Birna whipped them off the table. 'They do not upset me. They make me feel closer to my girl. They give me hope that she is somewhere very near to here. And that makes me happy.'

'You sure?'

'Sure.'

Callum stood up. 'Then let's go and get her.'

According to the map, their route branched onto the F88. It was this road that would take them to the very edge of Jökulsá á Fjöllum, the 'thick blue vein' that Kohl had mentioned in his *Killer's Guide to Reykjavík*. This was the same river that fed Dettifoss, the most powerful waterfall in Europe, or so Birna told Callum. It only added fuel to his increasing belief that they would never find her daughter.

Though he wouldn't admit it, Callum had been sceptical from the moment Birna first suggested the search. He had gone along with it because he knew what it meant to her. But she hadn't thought it through. In the unlikely scenario that Ásta's body was still spinning in some whirlpool like a doll in a washing machine, how were they supposed to pull her out? The river sounded way too treacherous. Callum reckoned they would have to call in a specialist rescue unit and he wasn't sure that these guys bothered with the dead. Not that he imagined it would ever come to that. Ásta's body would have gone over Dettifoss a long time ago.

He jiggled his finger up the map, tracing out the full course of the river. It didn't look good, but Callum refused to let Birna know what was now going through his head: that there was a greater likelihood of her daughter being found over the coming weeks, as, bit by bit, she was washed up on the Öxarfjörður coast. He had terrible visions of Húsavík fishermen dredging up her well-nibbled limbs in their nets.

Birna pulled off the track and killed the engine, but there was no audible drop in sound. The river had replaced it with a rushing, sloshing, white noise of a sound: a sound that made the heart race.

'Right,' said Callum. 'How do you want to do this?'

'We will take sections. We know what we are looking for – a flash of pink – that was how her killer described it.'

They got out of the car and walked to the edge of a canyon that had been carved out by the river. Beneath their feet a violent glacial torrent, creamy brown with rock flour, bullied its way between disjointed banks of basalt and lava. They watched as the swirling, soupy headwaters bounced over boulders and pinballed between rocks. Some stretches seemed relatively shallow while others looked deep and menacing.

'The power is phenomenal,' said Callum.

'That is because it is a floodwater. Vatnajökull is melting. A glacier bigger than all the Alps combined is melting. And now she is releasing the collected rains of ages.'

They walked upstream, their eyes constantly zig-zagging with the flow as they probed the venomous depths. Callum didn't dare admit it but he felt a little ridiculous. This was a pointless exercise. It reminded him of the time he had stolen a jar full of five-pence pieces that his mother had been saving and he had then helped his parents to search for it, even though he knew he had already spent the money on a Talk Talk album.

'How did he kill Sarah?' asked Birna. She kept her eyes on the river. 'Sorry,' she added. 'You do not have to answer that.'

'No . . . no, it's OK,' said Callum. 'He strangled her.'

He left it at that. He thought he should spare her the detail.

'So he followed her to Prague and strangled her, all because she denied him money?'

'It's more complicated than that.' Callum smacked a fly off his jacket. 'Kohl thought that Sarah had stolen his business idea and that she had remodelled it as Strawdonkey. The guy's deluded. He's nuts.' Callum spat a fly out of his mouth. 'It came out that he had a bit of a history. The court case uncovered all sorts of psychiatric problems. Kohl had been raised in Croatia, rather, in the former Yugoslavia. His family sought asylum in the UK when he was a boy, but by that age he'd seen some terrible things.'

'You make it sound like you feel sorry for him.' Birna stopped to look hard at something in the water but quickly moved on.

'I don't feel sorry for him. But there was a while when I thought I should try to understand him. I thought that if I understood him better, it might help me to understand Sarah's death. It had all seemed so meaningless.'

'And do you understand?'

'There is nothing to understand,' said Callum. He flicked at a fly on his sleeve. 'Iago Kohl is a twisted evil murdering fuck-up.'

'I see her!' Birna darted ahead of him. 'Look . . . her jacket!'

Callum chased after her and saw that she was pointing to a large boulder that had crashed, banged and walloped into the most savage part of the river. A maelstrom of greeny-brown froth was churning beneath it. The water bubbled up, then relented, bubbled up again and died down again, each time giving them a teasing glimpse of something dark and pink.

'Look,' said Birna, urging Callum to confirm what she was seeing.

He wasn't convinced. 'It's not Ásta.'

'It is!'

'It's just a jag of red rock,' he said. 'Is it rhyolite?'

'It's not red, it's pink!' insisted Birna.

'That's just the way the sun is hitting it.'

'No.' Confusion was crippling Birna's face. 'No,' she repeated, but the realization was dawning that this wasn't her daughter.

It broke Callum's heart.

And then came the flies. Until that moment they had been nothing more than a mild distraction. But distraction turned to full-blown irritation as the tiny black currants wheeled at Callum's face, careering into his lips and cheeks. They landed in their droves, buzzing in his hair and making loud attempts to set up home in his ear. He spat them out of his mouth. He snorted them out of his nostrils. He coughed one out of his throat. And still they came, they came, they came.

'Fuck off!' shouted Birna. She was slapping her head and dancing a mad dance. 'Leave me alone!'

'Shall we go back to the car?' Callum batted the flies with both hands.

'Fuck this!' screamed Birna. 'Fucking fuck this!' She was spinning and kicking and swiping and flailing. 'Fuck it all!' She ran straight at the river.

'No!' shouted Callum. He dived at her, making a hopeful grab at her waistband. He felt his fingers tightening and the tendons snapping in his wrist. Her body jerked backwards and she fell on top of him, a few feet short of the canyon's edge.

Birna rolled off him and onto the wet rock. The two of them lay on their backs, looking up at a sky full of flies.

'You thought I was going to jump,' she said. 'You thought I wanted to kill myself.'

'And you don't?' asked Callum.

'Why would I want to kill myself?'

'Because you're not afraid of dying?'

'I may not be afraid of death, Callum, but that does

not mean I am willing to embrace it. Jesus, you are so melodramatic.'

'Then what the fuck were you doing?' He was angry now.

'I was running away from the flies.' Birna propped herself on an elbow and looked down at him. 'You really thought I would kill myself?'

'I don't know what to think any more,' said Callum.

'Of course you do. I am not stupid. You think we will not find her.'

Callum didn't deny it.

'Maybe you are right,' she said. 'Maybe this has all been a waste of time.'

'It's not a waste of time, Birna. Not if it's important to you.'

'Is that the only reason you came along . . . because it is important to me?'

Callum nodded.

'So it is not important to *you* that we find my daughter?'

'Of course it is,' he said, acidly. 'But it's unlikely, isn't it.' He rolled onto his front and faced the water in the same position that he remembered Ásta lying in when she had watched the documentary on her father. 'Just look at the water, Birna. Look at the speed of it. Imagine the depth of it. Listen to the noise. And this is only a few hundred yards of the stuff. It goes on for miles. It flows over waterfalls. You really think Ásta has stayed in there for three days?'

The water thrashed between the canyon walls, sounding like a gang of kids charging down an alley while bashing on bin lids.

'No,' Birna conceded. 'I know she has gone.'

It wasn't the answer that Callum had expected.

'If I am honest with myself, I never really believed she would still be here,' admitted Birna. 'But I hoped she would. And I would have continued to hope had I not come out here to see this place for myself.'

She brushed a fly off Callum's leg and sat up to face the water, gazing intently at it.

Callum said nothing.

Birna was mesmerized. The river had a hypnotic hold on her and she remained perfectly still. If the breeze hadn't fiddled with her hair, Callum would have sworn he was looking at a statue. Long, chestnut-coloured strands whipped at her pale cheeks until they stuck to them, heavy from the spray being kicked up around her. Birna jammed her eyes and made fists with her hands, keeping everything tight. After a short moment, she relaxed again. Her eyes opened and her fingers fell loose.

'Now we can go,' she said.

They drove to Herðubreiðarlindir through fields of yellow pumice that had been blown into soft honey-comb dunes, contrasting sharply with the dark lava around them. On the north-west horizon, Mount Herðubreið was a chocolate birthday cake with white icing dribbling down its sides. Birna informed Callum that if he took one of his film crews to the top, they would get a shot of half of Iceland.

Herðubreiðarlindir was a green oasis nestling below the mountain. Sedges and rushes flourished in the springs that welled up from the lava. Birna pointed to some thick beards of vegetation as they drove past. 'Look . . . cotton grass. When I lived on Heimæy we used the cotton grass to make wicks for our fish-oil lamps, in the days before we got electricity.'

'Pre-1990, then,' joked Callum.

Birna stopped the car. Callum thought he was about to be kicked out of it, then he realized she had merely stopped for a few silly-looking sheep that stood in the middle of the track. Birna honked her horn and they skittered away.

'Why did you do that?' asked Callum. 'That was our dinner.'

'You have got your appetite back?' she enquired.

'I could eat. What about you?'

Birna gave a non-committal shrug.

'You don't fancy a big slice of that birthday cake?' Callum indicated the mountain.

'That is not a birthday cake. That is the Queen of Mountains,' said Birna. 'She is perfectly symmetrical. No matter where you stand she is always the same shape.'

Callum squinted at the mountain, then brought his eyes back to Birna. 'Why are you telling me this?' he asked.

'Is there a problem?'

'It's just . . . all this stuff about the mountains and the rivers and the sodding fucking cotton grass . . . why are you telling me? Aren't there bigger things to talk about?'

'I thought I was being helpful.' Birna looked anxious. There was colour in her cheeks. 'You are still getting to know this country.'

'Why would I want to know any more about this country?' asked Callum.

'Because you have chosen to live here.'

'Yes, but for how much longer?'

'For as long as you have a business.'

'Fuck the business! I didn't come here to start a business, Birna. I came here to be with you.'

'Wrong, Callum,' said Birna, in a voice that could spook sheep. 'You did not come here to be with me. You came here because you were running away from . . . him. Or maybe it was Sarah?'

'That's not true.' Callum sighed a resigned sigh. 'That's not *entirely* true.'

'I do not care what you do,' said Birna. 'But you have a business here. You have a responsibility to the people you employ. You can either stay or run away again.'

'And what if I stay? What about us?'

'How can you ask me that?' she shouted, smacking both hands on the steering wheel. 'How can you ask such a thing when I have just said goodbye to my daughter?'

Birna slowed the car. She had pulled into a camping ground. Callum spotted half a dozen brightly coloured tents pegged into a healthy expanse of grassland. There were other signs of civilization: a large hut, a small car park and a flat scuff of land that Callum took to be an airstrip as a windsock was staked beside it (either that, or a camper was drying his smalls). An Icelandic flag waved enthusiastically at them from atop a tall pole.

'We can stop here for the night,' said Birna. 'I keep a tent in the trunk.'

'And where do I sleep?'

'Stop it, Callum.' Birna crunched the car over gravel and parked it beside the hut. 'I will phone Mother and tell her we will be driving back to Reykjavík in the morning. But first we must get something into your stomach.'

Birna climbed out and removed an icebox from under the rear seat.

'What's that?' asked Callum.

'My mother packed us some dinner.'

Normally those words would have been enough to strike mortal terror into Callum's very soul. But right then he was so hungry he could have eaten a horse. Or a gannet. Whatever Sigriður had rustled up.

'We shall sit inside and eat,' said Birna.

The hut they went into reminded Callum of one of his old prefab classrooms at school. Several large maps were pinned to the walls and he was disappointed not to see a blackboard with all the letters of the alphabet chalked along the top of it. A sullen-looking guy, probably French, was sitting at one of the two small tables. He didn't look up at the couple. He squeezed something from a toothpaste tube onto a cork beer mat and popped the lot in his mouth.

That's what this landscape does to you, thought Callum, though he still envied the guy his cheese spread and crackers.

They took their icebox over to the free table. Callum sat in the window and faced in so that Birna would have the view of Mount Herðubreið behind him. They tucked into a picnic of sliced smoked lamb, rye bread, milk, apples and biscuits. Callum opened a carton of milk and brought it to his lips. Thick, cold liquid spilled down his throat and sang throughout his ravaged insides, icy tributaries reaching into every empty crevice.

'So you think it looks like a birthday cake?' asked Birna. She took a slice of the pink lamb and rolled it into a cigar, drawing envious glances from the Frenchman.

'Herðubreið?' Callum turned to look out the window. He studied the mountain. 'I suppose it's more of a Christmas cake.'

'Not a Brazil nut?'

Callum turned back to face her, spilling milk down his chin. 'God, was it only this morning that we passed Hekla? It feels like a week ago.' He brought his sleeve to his mouth, but before he could mop himself up Birna grabbed on to his arm.

'It's him!' She was staring at something behind

Callum, something on the other side of the window. Her grip was firm but her hand was shaking. She looked terrified. She looked like her mother had looked when she had seen the ghost on Callum's shoulder.

'What do you mean, *it's him*?' asked Callum. He didn't know why he was whispering.

'My God! It is.' Birna's eyes were jerking around in their sockets, following something. 'It's really him.'

'Kohl?' asked Callum, too scared to turn round.

'Arnar.'

Callum adjusted his position slightly so he could steal a look out the window.

They watched a tall guy with thick black hair fixing a tent to the roof of a green Cherokee. The Jeep had a large Hertz logo on the side, together with the words *Flugvöllur Keflavík*. A woman with red hair was sitting in the passenger seat with her window rolled down. The guy with the thick black hair got in beside her. The redhead offered him a piece of chocolate but he declined it. She snapped off a square, but didn't eat it herself. Instead, she handed it to the girl in the back seat: the girl in the puffy pink jacket.

27

'Ásta!' screamed Birna as she ran to the Jeep.

The redhead looked up at her, then turned to the man with the thick black hair and shook his shoulder.

'Arnar!' cried Birna.

The Jeep's engine roared into life and the rear wheels spat gravel at her legs. It pulled away from her.

The girl in the pink jacket turned to look out of the rear window.

She disappeared in a dark cloud of volcanic ash.

'Get in the car,' yelled Callum.

Birna tried to retrieve her keys from the pocket of her jeans, but they snagged in the lining. She fought with them but couldn't pull them free. 'Tell me this isn't happening.'

'Slow down.' Callum tried to help her with the keys but she slapped his hand away.

'You are making it worse.' Birna wrestled with her pocket. She was frantic. 'They are getting away!'

'They can't get away,' said Callum. 'Where can they run to?'

'Tell me this isn't happening,' repeated Birna, and Callum wasn't sure if she was referring to the keys or to the fact that both Ásta and Arnar had come back from the grave.

Callum's only concern was for Ásta. She remained

in some evident danger, but she was alive and Callum could at least thank God that he was no longer dealing with a monster like Kohl. This knowledge induced a strange kind of euphoria that washed through him like hot blood flooding giddily back into a dead limb. Kohl hadn't laid a finger on Ásta. Callum had been hasty in thinking it. Sarah's murderer hadn't set foot in Iceland. He had probably been sitting in a safe house all this time, scratching his balls or fiddling with the tag on his ankle. Wedderburn had told Callum the truth. So why had he been so quick to dismiss him?

Paranoia, he guessed. All this time in Iceland Callum had believed he was running away from a flesh-and-blood enemy, a convicted killer who would one day be free to get back at him. That day had come sooner than Callum imagined. But he now realized that his real enemy had been something scarier, something intangible and amorphous. His real enemy was his own paranoia, that dark conspiracy between his inner demons and a world he no longer trusted. He had been too ready to believe that Kohl was the bogeyman come back to haunt him. His faith in the police had been so diminished that he had convinced himself Kohl had escaped. And his overbearing sense that there was no justice in the world had left him feeling vulnerable.

Somehow, Birna's ex had risen from the dead to exploit this.

'Got them!' said Birna. She threw Callum the keys.

As he fired up the engine, Callum experienced another surge of energy fuelled by his urgent desire to get Ásta back. Fate had conspired to give him one chance to be the very hero that Ásta believed her natural father to be, and for her sake, and Birna's, he just couldn't fuck it up.

'Don't panic, Birna. We're gonna catch them.' Callum

clattered the Suzuki through a series of potholes and jumped it over a hump. The Jeep was some distance ahead of them but it remained in their sights. 'There's no way they can lose us. This place is too barren. There's nowhere for them to hide.'

'But this is impossible,' said Birna. 'How could he have survived?'

'The bottom line is that Ásta has survived.'

'I will celebrate that when she is back in my arms.' Birna's head dropped onto her chest. 'This is so confusing.'

'I'm sure Arnar will explain himself when we get hold of him.' Callum checked the petrol gauge: less than a quarter of a tank. *Fuck*, he thought, but he didn't let Birna see his concern.

'It does not make sense,' she said. 'Arnar died on Heimæy. He was seen breaking into the pharmacy. As we sailed away from the island, we could see that the lava had taken it. The roof of the pharmacy moved up and down and at first we thought it was the boat. But then the whole building just popped into flame like a moth on a hotplate.'

'Like I said, all that matters is that Ásta is alive and we're going to get her back.' Callum placed a placatory hand on her knee, but Birna was somewhere else.

'I remember the night before the eruption,' she said. 'We felt vibrations in the house and Mother thought it was a problem with the new central heating system that my father had installed. That night I counted half a dozen small earthquakes; just tiny little shivers. I turned off my light and went to sleep. Growing up in Iceland you get used to the earth making these adjustments.'

'I think my stomach is making adjustments.' Callum removed his hand from her knee and burped into it. 'Sorry. I must have eaten too quickly.'

'That is what it was like,' said Birna. 'For the night preceding the eruption, Heimæy was a big rumbling stomach. The next morning I walked into the town and noticed that lots of little birds were sitting on the ground. Once a year we get baby puffins doing this, but these birds were not a kind that I had ever seen on the island. They were frightened little brown things with forked tails. When I approached them they did not fly off, they just hopped out of my way. I knew that something strange was happening and sure enough, the ground began to shake again. I heard a bang and a plume of fire shot up from behind the houses. I could see from the looks on the faces of the older people that they thought this was a repeat of '73, when our island was almost destroyed.'

Sunlight glinted off the green Jeep on the distant horizon: a tiny emerald set into a ring of fire. Callum couldn't be sure he was gaining on it, as it was impossible to gauge distance or speed.

'Nobody panicked,' continued Birna. 'I guess the islanders knew that this sort of thing could happen again and we were prepared for it. Most people returned to their houses to pack suitcases before walking to the harbour. I remember my mother and I looking round our house and not knowing what we should take. She grabbed a parcel of frozen whalemeat because she believed that food would be more useful than anything.'

'That's Sigriður,' conceded Callum.

Birna wasn't smiling. 'The police drove through the streets with their sirens blaring. This was confirmation that we had to leave. We joined the crowds and made our way to the fishing boats. They were our only escape from the island and Mother was worried that the lava would finish the job it had started in '73 and seal in the harbour for good. She was convinced we were going to be stuck. As we ran through the streets we could smell the gases from the eruption. Our throats were on fire. Mother and I dipped our sleeves into a puddle and used them to cover our mouths. The ground was so hot that people were emptying water bottles over their shoes. And then the ash started to fall, like black snow, hot flakes the size of duck feathers that stuck to your skin and burned.'

'Weren't you pregnant with Ásta?' asked Callum.

'Eight months . . . but I had no time to worry about that. As we queued for the boat we could see that a crack had opened up in the volcano that sits close to the town. A stream of bright orange lava was pouring from the wound. We all knew the damage that lava could do. We could see evidence of it as our boat passed the field of black lava that had solidified into the sea twenty years before. Large boulders that had been caught in that lava flow had just melted like ice cream. We knew the same thing could happen to our town. We did not imagine that this eruption would fizzle out the same day. We thought we were saying goodbye to Heimæy for good. But nobody cried as we sailed away. Everybody was calm.' Birna's eyes were rigid. She was back on that boat.

'We thought that the evacuation had been a total success, that all six thousand residents had got off the island. Then one of the men on the boat said that he had seen Arnar breaking into the pharmacy. He said he was looting for drugs and money. In front of everyone, he told me that I should be ashamed that I was having a junkie's baby. He said that if I had been his daughter, he would have forced me to get an abortion.'

'Jesus. How did Sigriður react to that?'

'She knocked him unconscious,' said Birna. 'With a parcel of frozen whalemeat.'

Callum fought with the gears as the Suzuki hit

another incline. This was nothing like the car chases on the Seventies cop shows that he used to watch as a kid. There were no lights to jump, no side alleys to cut into, no pyramids of cardboard boxes to obliterate and certainly no dead ends. The road stretched on for ever. He was chasing the Jeep into infinity, to the end of eternity, through a landscape mangled by fire and split by ice. Callum could not see this as a place of rebirth and renewal, where the earth was still being created. He could only see it as the scene of some apocalyptic ending.

'Arnar broke into my office,' said Callum. 'I recognize him now. He passed me on the stairs just before I discovered the break-in. He must have been making his exit.'

'You had a break-in? I thought you said that you forced the door yourself when you lost your keys.'

'I know and I'm sorry. I have told you too many lies, Birna. I thought I was protecting you.'

'I can protect myself, Callum. But not when you are dishonest. All I ever wanted from you was honesty. If we could not be truthful with each other, then how did we ever hope to survive?'

Her words turned his heart to stone. She had described their relationship in the unequivocal past tense. Callum realized that he had been thinking about himself in all this and he felt guilty for being so selfish. There was a young girl who needed rescuing and all he could do was imagine his future without Birna. There would be no future for either of them if they didn't get Ásta back.

He kept one eye on the petrol gauge and one eye on the Jeep.

'I cannot believe that Arnar wrote that *Killer's Guide to Reykjavík*,' said Birna.

'He knew what he was doing,' said Callum. 'Nothing

was stolen in the break-in. Arnar was after information and he found it on my laptop. He would have read Kohl's account of Sarah's murder. And if he'd trawled the Net and searched on my name, he would have found links to articles detailing Kohl's release. It must have been then that he had the idea to seize Ásta and make us believe that it was Kohl by concocting his killer's guide.'

'But how did he find us in the first place?'

'Come on Birna, he would have found us easily enough. Reykjavík isn't exactly Beijing. We're not talking needles in haystacks, are we? There can't be too many Birna Sveinsdóttirs in the phone book.'

'I still find it hard to believe that he wrote it. Arnar was never so good with his English.'

'It's been eleven years. You don't know where he's been or what he's done with himself.'

'No, but I can guess. If he got off our island in '92 – and it is clear that he did – he would have done it in a boat full of money and drugs. That pharmacy did good business.'

'Where do you think he went to after Heimæy?'

'He could have sailed to Greenland . . . the Faroes . . . who knows. But one way or another he will have made sure that he had money, enough to set himself up.'

'What doing?'

'Arnar only knew two skills: catching puffin and using drugs. There is not such a big demand for puffin meat outside Iceland. If he has survived this long, he will have done it on drug money.' Birna leaned across Callum and looked at the speedometer. 'Can you not drive any faster?' she urged.

Callum reckoned this was no time to tell her that he was conserving fuel. The needle was hopping in and out of the red. They were heading back towards the black sand desert and Callum knew they would not make it to the other side. Something had to give.

'Maybe Arnar didn't write the email,' said Callum. 'That woman he's with, maybe she wrote the diary for him.'

'Maybe.'

Callum noticed that Birna was pressing her foot to the floor.

'Why would they do this?' he asked. 'If they intended to abduct Ásta, why didn't they just take her? Why go to the trouble of writing the *Killer's Guide*?'

'Like you just said, he did it to make us believe that someone else had taken her,' said Birna.

'I know, but it seems so unnecessary. Arnar may be Ásta's estranged father but he is the last person you would ever have suspected of kidnapping her. He didn't need to make it look like someone else had done it. As far as everyone on this island was concerned, Arnar was dead. The dead don't need to cover their tracks.'

'But that is just it, Callum. We did not think that Ásta had been kidnapped. We thought she had been murdered. Arnar wanted us to think she was dead so we would give up all hope of ever seeing her again. That way we would never come looking for her. He made us believe this by sending you the email. He knew about you and Sarah, and he used that knowledge to convince you that Ásta's killer was very real.' It all seemed to be making sense to Birna. 'He did a pretty good job of it. We had already given up on h . . . on her.' Birna's lip trembled, like a nerve had gone. She steadied it with her fingers. 'I feel so bad, Callum. I gave up on my daughter before I had even seen her body.'

'Don't. You've been given a second chance. Ásta is safe and well. She is sitting in the car in front of us.

394

We're not giving up on her now.' Callum eyed the petrol gauge and said a little prayer. They were running on fumes now. The needle pointed directly at the letter E and it didn't mean East, as they were driving into a setting sun. How Callum wished he was reading a compass sent daft by the magnetized rock. But he wasn't and he knew that, one way or another, this chase was about to end.

'Did Sarah want children?' asked Birna.

'Is this really the time to be talking about Sarah?'

'You have to talk about her some time.'

Callum was sweating now. The steering wheel slipped in his palms. His eyes stayed fixed on the Jeep and he fine-tuned his ears to the engine, listening out for the first jar or cough.

'We talked about having children,' he said. 'But I think Sarah was only flirting with the idea. She thought she ought to have a kid simply because it was expected of her. But deep down, she just didn't have it in her . . . the maternal instinct, that is. She wouldn't admit it though, probably scared that people would think she was less of a woman.' Callum bit on his lip, using one pain to suppress another. 'She bought all the books, though . . . guides to every part of the process, from the baby's conception right up to their first tattoo. What Sarah didn't know about pessaries and prolapses wasn't worth knowing. But that was Sarah all over. She wasn't an instinctive person. She was the practical one in our relationship. Whether we were starting a family or starting a business, Sarah would investigate all the ins and outs before committing herself. I'm more gut-feel than that. I act first and ask questions later.'

'Is that how you decided to come and live with me?' asked Birna. 'You just jumped into it without thinking?'

'You shouldn't have to think about falling in love with someone,' asserted Callum. 'You just go with your gut-feel.'

'What is he doing?' shouted Birna. 'He is driving like a madman.'

Some distance ahead of them, the Jeep was swinging wildly from one side of the track to the other.

'He will crash! He will kill my girl!'

'Wait . . . he's stopping,' said Callum.

They watched the Jeep turning off the track and slowing to a halt. A pinprick figure jumped out of the driver's side. He pulled another figure out of the car. Their bodies merged momentarily, then one dropped to the ground. The taller figure got back in the Jeep and drove off again.

'He has dumped Ásta!' said Birna. 'Quick, we must get to her.'

'I'm going as fast as I can.'

'If he has hurt her I will kill him.'

'Let's just get her first.'

But as they drew nearer, it became clear that the abandoned figure was not Birna's daughter. It was the woman with the red hair. She was standing in the middle of the dirt track, gesturing for Callum to stop.

'Should I go round her?' he asked.

'Go through her if you have to,' said Birna. 'We need to get Ásta.'

Callum slowed the car.

'What are you doing?'

'I can't just leave her.' Callum put his foot full on the brake and stopped the bonnet of the Suzuki inches from the woman's chest. She looked wild, like something feral. Her clothes were covered in ash and her lip was bleeding. She ran to the side of the car and slapped her palms on Callum's window.

He wound it down.

'Please . . . we've got to catch him . . . he's going to kill her . . . I tried to stop him . . . I didn't want this . . . you've got to believe me . . . I didn't want any of this . . .'

'Get in,' said Callum. He thought that she sounded American.

'Leave her!' shouted Birna. 'He's going to kill Ásta!' She pushed Callum's knee, trying to force his foot down on the accelerator.

The redhead opened the rear door and scrambled across the back seat. 'I am so sorry . . . I never wanted this . . . please believe me . . . it was Arnie's idea . . . we thought it was the only way we could have a child . . .'

'Arnie?' asked Callum. 'He calls himself Arnie?'

'It does not matter what he calls himself,' said Birna. 'She said he's going to kill her.'

'OK, OK. We're going . . .' Callum depressed his foot on the pedal and the Suzuki sputtered. 'No . . . don't do this to me.' He turned the key.

'What is it?' asked Birna.

The engine cut out.

Everything went very quiet: as quiet as a barren and unending wilderness can be.

'Fuck,' said Callum. He turned to Birna. 'We're out of gas.'

She looked at him like he had just murdered her daughter.

28

'It was Arnie's idea . . . he was pissed at me . . . he didn't know that I couldn't have kids . . . I didn't tell him . . . I thought he would call off our wedding . . . we've been trying ever since . . . it's been two years now . . . at first I pretended I was OK . . . I didn't want him to know about my infertility . . . I suggested it was his fault . . . I even asked him to take a sperm test . . . but then he tells me that he's already fathered a kid and . . .'

'Enough!' screamed Birna. She looked daggers at the redhead.

The three of them sat on the road, right in front of the Suzuki, like they were protesters barring its way.

The redhead was porcelain pale. Her bones showed through her skin. Callum had thought that all Americans possessed two rows of perfectly aligned, pearly-white teeth, but hers were small and discoloured. She was exhibiting the classic signs of anorexia.

'It was his idea to take her . . . so I went along with it . . . I didn't want to let him down again . . . I thought we could be a family . . .'

'Why would he want to kill her?' asked Birna. She sat with her elbow on her knee and her hand rammed into her fringe. She used the ball of her thumb to crush the few tears that escaped from her eyes.

'If we can't be a family, then why should you guys get to be a family . . . that's what Arnie said . . . I think he's serious . . . I've never seen him like this . . . I tried to stop him but he hit me . . . he told me to get ewt of the car.'

'Ewt?' asked Callum.

'Yes . . . he threw me ewt because I grabbed the wheel . . . I was worried abewt the girl . . .'

'Abewt?'

'What is your problem, Callum?' asked Birna.

'She's not American,' he said.

'Does it matter what she is?' asked Birna. 'She took my child.'

'I'm Canadian,' said the redhead. 'Arnie and I live in Vancouver.'

'Why would he do this?' asked Birna. 'Why would he disappear all those years ago and then decide to come back for his daughter now?'

'Like I said, it was the only way we could have a family,' said Redhead.

'But if he cares about Ásta so much, then how could he write those terrible things and make me believe she was dead?'

'It was Arnie's idea,' the redhead protested. 'He forced me to write the email. I'm good with words. I'm an interpreter at the airport. We both work for Air Canada. That's how we met.'

'Arnar's a pilot?' asked Birna.

'No,' said Redhead. 'But they do call him the Bird Man. Vancouver gets a lot of illegal traffic in rare birds from India, Thailand, Japan. It's Arnie's job to spot them in transit and look after them until they can be rehomed.'

'So Arnar is still catching birds,' said Callum.

Birna laughed a pained laugh.

'Birds, snakes, lizards . . .' said Redhead. 'Arnie has to check all the airfreight for anything illegal. He's the best we've got. He's even made a few drug busts in his time. Arnie knows everything that comes in and goes ewt of that airport.'

'Yeah, I bet he does,' said Birna. 'And I bet that some of the stuff that goes out of that airport goes out of it in his pockets.' She was staring into space now. The Jeep was conspicuously absent from the horizon.

'Why did he try to kill me?' Callum had remembered the sabotaged geyser test.

'He tried to kill you?' The redhead sounded genuinely concerned, which threw him a little.

Birna, on the other hand, seemed nonplussed by this revelation. Callum guessed that she had already given up on him.

'Arnar tampered with a special effects test that I was conducting down at the dockside. He rigged an oil drum so it would explode in my face. I got out of the way but another guy was hospitalized.' Callum would have said he was lucky to be alive, but, looking at Birna, he wasn't sure that he believed it.

'Arnie did not do that,' said Redhead. 'I would have known. We've been in Iceland for over a month and he has barely left my side.'

'Except to break into my office.'

Redhead bowed her head.

'You mean you were part of that too?'

'I drove the getaway,' she admitted.

Birna perked up, like something had just occurred to her. 'You drove the Jeep at Ásta's pony,' she said. 'You tried to kill my daughter.' The anger that she had been struggling to repress now seized her. She made a grab for the woman's red hair but Callum got between them.

'She tried to kill my baby!' screamed Birna.

400

'This won't bring her back,' shouted Callum, gripping Birna's arms. Her legs thrashed in the ash.

'I was not driving that day,' protested Redhead. She extracted herself from the melee and got to her feet. 'Arnie was behind the wheel. But he was not trying to harm his daughter. He just wanted to get her back.'

'Ásta is not his daughter,' spat Birna. 'She is my daughter and you had no right to take her.'

'I know.' Redhead perched herself on the front bumper of the Suzuki. 'I know. And if I am honest, I have always known that what we were doing was wrong.'

'Then why do it?' asked Callum.

Birna had composed herself enough for him to let go of her arms. She stood up and spanked the dust from her jeans. She walked to the side of the Suzuki and checked her face in the wing mirror. She didn't like what she saw.

'When Arnie first told me that he had a daughter in Iceland, I suggested that we make contact with her,' said Redhead. 'It was only then that he told me that he could not return to his homeland . . . because of Birna.'

'What did he say about me?' Birna was pacing about like a dog in a cage.

'He said you were a bad mother. He said that you stabbed him.'

'He what?' shouted Birna. The anger was resurfacing.

'That's what he told me,' said Redhead. She looked a little wary. 'He said that this was why he left Iceland in the first place. And he didn't want to make contact with Ásta because that would mean making contact with you and he was worried that you might get violent.'

Birna laughed loudly but there was nothing in even

the distant vicinity to lend it an echo. For Callum, this only reinforced the hopelessness of their situation. He had already consigned his mobile phone to the glove-box, having established that there was no signal out here to carry a cry for help.

'Arnie convinced me that we should just take Ásta,' Redhead continued. 'He said that it was in the girl's interests to go back to Canada with us because you weren't fit to look after her. So that's when we decided to come and get her.'

Birna turned on the woman. 'Do you want to know the real reason your husband left Iceland all those years ago?'

The redhead nodded. Like Birna had given her a choice.

'I will tell you. He ran away because he was a coward. A junkie coward. He could not deal with life, so he removed himself from it by filling his veins with filth. He could not deal with his pregnant girlfriend or the baby that she was carrying, so he opted out. So do not tell me that after all this time he suddenly wants to become a father to his daughter. For eleven years he made his daughter think he was dead. Have you any idea what that has done to her?'

'Arnie told me that you had filled your daughter's head with horrible stories,' said Redhead. 'He said it was you who made her believe he was dead.'

'Everyone thought he was dead!' screamed Birna. 'The reason he was wary of coming back to Iceland was because he knew that someone might recognize him. He was frightened that if he revealed himself, then he would be arrested for a robbery on our home island eleven years ago. His reluctance to contact me had nothing to do with me stabbing him.'

'So Arnar wasn't lying?' asked Callum. 'You really stabbed him?' He had been quiet for some time and

402

Birna now looked at him like she was trying to remember who he was.

'Arnie showed me his scar,' confirmed Redhead.

'So I'm not the only one who's been keeping secrets,' said Callum. Pointedly.

Birna returned herself to the dusty ground, folding her legs beneath her. She wiped her wet cheeks and they immediately filled up with blood, like she'd just applied a little rouge.

'Arnar would hit me sometimes,' said Birna. 'There was an afternoon, a shitty afternoon when he was very high and I was very low, when he punched me in the belly. So I stuck him with a gutting knife. I was pregnant with his daughter, though he did not know it. Arnar turned his body in time and the knife scored his hip like chicken skin. I thought he might kill me. But he didn't even turn to look at me. He just walked to the front door of the house, banging off the walls and clutching his wound and looking so desperate, like a landed cod that flaps and thrashes and tries to throw itself back into the sea.' Birna clawed her fingers through the grey ash, ploughing it into wavy furrows. 'I have only spoken to Arnar once since that day and that was to tell him that I was having his baby and that he would be having nothing to do with it.'

'Why didn't you tell me?' asked Callum.

'And have you believe I was capable of stabbing someone?'

'I would have understood. I mean, I *do* understand,' he said, suddenly aware that he too had condemned their relationship to the past tense. 'I know that feeling.'

'So you know what it is like to want to remove another human being from your life, to want it so badly that you are prepared to end theirs?'

'I've been there,' said Callum. 'Part of me is still there.' He thought again about Kohl.

Birna nodded. She stared at the ground.

A breeze had picked up, unsettling the ash around them. It powdered their faces and filled in the furrows that Birna had scraped out of the grey earth. They were replaced by dark craters as her tears started to fall. She looked up at Callum. 'If he touches my daughter I will kill him. I will do it properly this time. Arnar will not be coming back from the dead.'

'Then please . . . we can't just sit here,' implored the redhead. 'We've got to stop him before he does anything crazy.'

'And how do you suggest we do that?' asked Callum. 'It may have escaped your attention but we're in the middle of fucking nowhere with no means of getting anywhere other than our legs and, quite frankly, yours look like they can barely support your body. I don't rate our chances against a Jeep.' The wind was starting to sound in Callum's ears.

'Maybe he will not kill her,' said Birna, the colour returning to her voice. 'Maybe he will try and take her back with him, to Canada.'

'Unlikely,' said Redhead. 'You didn't see him. I've never seen Arnie this mad. And believe me, I've seen him pretty pissed. You're not the only woman he's raised a hand to.'

'But Arnar stole her clothes,' said Birna, refusing to empathize. 'Did he not steal her clothes from my washing line?'

'He took some things,' conceded Redhead. 'We needed a few things for the girl to wear while we lay low. That was the plan.'

'And that might still be his plan, once he realizes that we are not following him,' said Birna. 'He has his daughter and he has her clothes. He might try to get her out of the country.'

Callum looked at the redhead. He judged her

expression – part pained, part pitiful – and he knew that Birna's renewed optimism was grossly misplaced. But he didn't have it in him to caution her.

Redhead had no such discretion. 'I hope he takes your kid out of the country. Because if he doesn't, he will not let her return to you alive.'

'What makes you so sure?' asked Birna.

'Him,' said Redhead, turning to look at Callum.

'Me?' asked Callum. 'What have I got to do with it?'

'Arnie hates you.'

'He hates me? Why would he hate me?'

'He hates the idea that you are playing father to his daughter. And he won't let that happen. That's why he got so mad when I asked him to stop the Jeep.' Redhead stood up. She paraded herself in front of them as she talked. 'Arnie tracked Birna down easily enough, by contacting her publisher. He didn't anticipate that she would now have a partner, or that the three of you would be playing happy families, like the time you went riding together. We followed you to the lake that day. We had been waiting for an opportunity to take Ásta, but as time went on, Arnie became less concerned with his daughter and more obsessed with you, Callum.'

'How did you know my name?'

Redhead shrugged. 'Arnie wouldn't stop talking abewt you. It made him angry to see you with his child. He was jealous. He was determined to discover everything he could abewt you. And that's when he broke into your office and got more than your name.' She caught Callum's eye. 'You were pretty high profile, weren't you. A little trawl on the Net brought up your business in Britain, the murder of your girlfriend, her killer's trial.'

This was the very thing that had worried Callum about the journalists in Iceland. If they had wanted a story on him, they would not have had far to dig. He shook his head. What had seemed like an elaborate and calculated plan – to abduct Ásta and make them believe that she had been murdered – had actually been a walk in the park. Once Arnar and this woman had his name, they had everything on him: Sarah's death, Kohl's diary, his release, Callum's departure from Strawdonkey, his setting up of Fire and Ice, his email address – everything.

He had been stupid to try and keep things from Birna. He had been foolish to think he could ever make a clean break from his past. But as he sat in the ash and inhaled the swirling dirt, he realized that it was a figure from Birna's past and not his own that would now determine their present and future.

He could do nothing to stop Arnar. He had no power to dictate Ásta's fate. One bad decision, a dose of paranoia and a dash of bad luck had got him to this place; and it was a place that had rendered him impotent.

Callum Pope would not be the life-saving hero. Callum Pope was a spent man.

The breeze picked up a handful of ash and threw it into his face in a scenario that would have been black but comic had it followed a cremation. The wind had been getting stronger in steady increments. A succession of short, staccato blasts was soon superseded by an almighty gust that rocked Callum so hard he had to splay his hands on the earth, one on either side of him, to avoid falling over. Powder and grit found a way into his mouth and eyes, despite his keeping them closed as the wind boomed and whined.

It was this sound that finally compelled Callum to open his eyes. He needed proof that he wasn't imagining it. For he was sure that this sound was an unnatural sound, a mechanical sound, and a quick look confirmed that the wind was actually the down-draught from a helicopter.

The three of them got to their feet and danced and waved and jumped and shouted. Not that they needed to work hard to make themselves seen in an environment such as this. Callum guessed that the Suzuki would be the only drop of colour discernible from the air in a radius of about a dozen miles. Despite this, the chopper wheeled over their heads and thrummed off into the distance.

'Where is he going?' shouted Birna. 'He must have seen us.'

Callum kicked a small, sponge-like rock into a crack in the broken dirt track. 'We're in the middle of a lava field,' he said. 'Where can he land?'

'The track is wide enough,' said Birna.

'If he tries to touch down here, he'll spray us with rock,' said Callum.

'Maybe he intends to land further uptrack. Perhaps we should start walking.'

But the chopper was an ever-decreasing dot in an ever-expanding sky.

'He might be coming back for us,' said Redhead. 'My guess is that he's already carrying passengers and he needs to drop them off first. Then he'll have enough room to take all three of us.'

'Fuck!' shouted Birna. She slammed both her fists on the bonnet of the 4x4.

'Birna,' pleaded Callum. 'That isn't going to help.'

'And what is going to help? Tell me what I can do to help my daughter.'

If he'd had an answer for her, then maybe Callum could have turned things around. She was giving him one last chance to redeem himself, but, true to form, he passed up on it. He had run out of words and ideas.

'Isn't that a car?' asked Redhead. She was looking

south, in the direction of Vatnajökull, her hand shielding her eyes from the sinking sun.

Callum could see a stirring on the horizon, a smudge of dust that broke the dark, clean lines of the lava plain. As this mini cyclone grew bigger, a red blob popped out of it like a cherry stone. If he wasn't mistaken, the blob was pearlescent salsa red.

'It's the Tundra,' he said. 'Birna . . . it's Frikki!'

29

'How did you find us?' asked Callum.

'Daddi,' said Frikki. 'My DJ friend. He radioed us from his helicopter. I asked him to track you while Anna Björk and I followed by road.'

Anna Björk corroborated with a nod.

'Are you still in contact with him?' asked Birna.

'*Já.*'

'Then you must tell Daddi to track a green Jeep,' she pleaded.

Frikki looked unsure. He turned to Callum, as though he needed his boss to give the order.

'Ásta is alive,' explained Callum. 'But she's in trouble. She's been abducted.'

'*Nei!*' Anna Björk's mouth fell into an elongated O.

'I'm onto it.' Frikki unclipped a handset from a black box on the dash. 'Daddi . . . *í dag*, Daddi . . .'

The five of them were belting along a dirt track that cut through an otherwise featureless void. Callum sat up front with Frikki while the three women filled the rear of the passenger cab. Anna Björk had been instructed by Callum to sit between Birna and the redhead, to prevent a catfight. Not that Birna looked like she was up for a scrap. The life had gone from her eyes, just as it had been drained from the dead fields that sped across her dark irises as she stared blankly out the window.

'. . . *jeppavegur. Tíu fjórir.*' The voice on the radio sounded calm.

'*Takk*, Daddi.' Frikki dropped the handset between his legs. 'He says he is following some tracks. He will radio back when he IDs the vehicle.'

'Nice one.' Callum turned to Birna. 'We'll get her back. She's going to be fine.'

Birna's eyes stayed fixed on the unforgiving world outside her window. Anna Björk took one of her arms and fed it around her own.

The radio crackled into life again. '*Gott kvöld*, Frikki. I have the results of the Reykjavík jury. The twelve points go to . . . a green Jeep.'

'You can see it?'

'I can see it,' said Daddi. 'And he can see me. He has just turned off the main track. He is driving straight into Askja.'

Birna sat upright and leaned in between Frikki and Callum. 'That is madness!'

'Askja . . . would that be the big saucery thing with the lake inside it?' asked Callum.

'So I did teach you something.' Birna removed a tissue from her sleeve and blew her nose.

'*Takk fyrir*, Daddi. Stay with him.'

'*Tíu fjórir.*'

'I do not understand,' said Birna. 'This is crazy. Why would he drive to Askja? The road is a dead end.'

'I thought there were no dead ends out here,' said Callum.

'There is one,' said Frikki. 'It ends at the Víti crater.'

'He has taken the road to Hell,' said Birna.

'To the Devil's cauldron, where horses quake with mortal fear and can hardly stand when taken to the brink,' said Frikki, in that deep voice he only used when he was quoting from some long mothballed text.

Anna Björk kicked the back of his seat and scowled at him.

'At least,' he continued, 'that is how it was described to me in my mother's bedtime stories.'

'Christ, could she not have read you something less ominous,' said Callum. 'Something cheerful, like Chicken Licken?'

'What is Chicken Licken?' asked Anna Björk.

'It's a story about a baby chicken who thinks that the sky is about to fall on top of him.'

'And that is less ominous?'

'Fair point,' Callum conceded.

Frikki slowed the Tundra and broached a right turning, the first time the gravel track had given them any option other than 'straight on' in half an hour of driving. They had gone a few miles down this track when the sun was thrown into transient eclipse by the passing of the helicopter above their speeding vehicle. Frikki conducted another conversation with its pilot, this time in Icelandic.

Birna listened, then put her hands to her face, panicking Callum.

'What did he say?'

'Daddi says that the Jeep has stopped at the entrance to Askja,' translated Frikki. 'A man is walking into the crater. He is carrying a body.'

'I will kill him,' spat Birna. 'If he has touched her, I will—'

'Shush, now,' urged Anna Björk. She threaded her fingers into Birna's.

'We are nearly there,' said Frikki. 'We have made up some time.'

It was another few minutes before Frikki pulled into a small parking area that contained only one vehicle: an empty Jeep. Arnar and Ásta had vanished.

'Which way would they go?' asked Callum.

'There is a track on that ridge.' Birna pointed to a path in the blackish-red slag that led up to a rocky plateau. 'He has taken her into the saucer.'

'The saucer?' asked the redhead.

Birna ignored her. 'The only way up is on foot. We must be quick.' She opened her door and jumped out.

'Shall we bring . . .' Callum turned to the redhead. 'I'm sorry, we never asked you your name.'

'Kathleen,' she said.

'Birna, shall we bring Kathleen?'

'Kathleen can go to hell.'

'Is that a yes or a no?'

'No, Callum! There is no time for this.'

'But she's his wife. She might be able to reason with him.'

'If that bitch had been able to reason with him, we would not be in this situation. Now hurry!'

'I will come too,' said Frikki.

'No,' said Callum. 'You and Anna Björk can watch Kathleen.'

'Does it take two of us?' asked Anna Björk.

'I need Frikki to stay by the radio,' said Callum. 'And anyway, I know how you love spending time with him.'

Anna Björk gave Callum the finger.

'Callum!' shouted Birna.

They hit the path.

Their progress was initially slow. They trudged up a steady incline that took them over a saddle of lava slashed by streaks of yellow sulphur and powderblasts of red iron oxide. Small cones of grey-white sinter hissed and spat and vented out foul-smelling fumes. The steam followed them like a wraith. They were cutting through a boiling, fermenting landscape, with loose lumps of cinder shifting constantly under their weight.

When they reached the top of the plateau, Callum stopped. Spread out before them was Birna's saucer, 360 degrees of snow-speckled lava and incredible, endless rawness. Callum's emotions churned together in an inseparable melee: awe, shock, elation, fear. He imagined that from the air Askja would resemble a giant eye, with a vast blue lake for an iris and a ring of volcanoes for lashes.

'*Komdu!*' commanded Birna, as though Callum were her pony. 'He's taking her over to the crater. He will throw her into Víti.'

Arnar was only a few hundred yards ahead of them now. Ásta had been slowing him down. He set her on her feet and tried to pull her along by her hood but her legs kept faltering on the broken ground. When he saw that Callum and Birna were gaining, he picked Ásta up again and carried her towards the brim of a great hole in the earth – the Víti crater – a deep crucible that held a pool of milky green liquid.

'Arnar! Stop!' cried Birna, now that they were within earshot of him.

But Arnar seemed intent on carrying Ásta to the far side of the crater, onto a tall crest of rock that separated Víti from its neighbouring lake.

'Please Arnar!' shouted Birna. 'We can talk about this.'

'No talking!' he shouted back.

Callum and Birna kicked their way up the ridge after him. Their progress slowed again as the ground became more brittle. The crust of compacted cinders cracked under their feet, suckering their ankles into the boggy putty beneath. Callum became wary of each step, not knowing where to put his feet down, like a cat on virgin snow. And his caution was not misplaced. The rim of the crater was precarious and it was a long drop down blood-red slopes into the pool of steaming green.

Arnar set Ásta on her feet again at the highest point on the ridge. Even her slight weight was enough to dislodge a few rocks and send them clattering into the black murk. The sun had dropped low, casting part of the crater's great bowl into almost total darkness.

Callum and Birna got to the top of the ridge and stopped.

Arnar had his arm round Ásta's neck and he held her with her feet hanging over the edge. Below them, the slope fell sharply into shadow, disappearing from sight altogether before re-emerging at the edge of the milky water. Callum didn't know how deep Víti was, but it was easy to imagine that this great hole was a gateway to the earth's core.

'Arnar, please!' begged Birna. 'Why are you doing this?'

'She is my daughter,' he said. 'She should be with me.'

'She does not want to be with you . . . do you Ásta?'

Ásta didn't respond. She was unable to open her mouth or move her head, as Arnar held it in a tight lock. If she wanted to talk, she had to do it with her eyes. But her eyes weren't talking. They were screaming.

'Ásta wants to be with me,' insisted Arnar. 'She was happy to come with me when I picked her up at the pool.'

'She wasn't feeling well,' shouted Callum. 'And she thinks you're a hero. Is it any wonder she went with you? The poor girl was feeling sick and vulnerable, and then her hero of a father shows up. Of course she was happy to go with you. What did you do, Arnar . . . did you offer to take her home with you? Did you promise to stick around and be her daddy again? Did you tell her that her mother was a bad person for making her believe you were dead?'

'No!' yelled Arnar. His eyes had been cast into shadow, like two bottomless craters under a prominent but anxious brow. 'You talk shit! Ásta wanted to go camping with us.' He turned to his daughter again. 'We have have had some fun, haven't we?'

Ásta nodded but only when Arnar moved her head.

'What did you plan to do?' asked Birna. 'Where did you hope to go?' Kathleen had already told her in part, but she needed to hear it from the horse's mouth. She also figured that the more she kept Arnar talking, the less likely he was to do anything rash.

'We thought we would stay in the interior for a few days,' said Arnar, 'just until the fuss died down or until we read about Ásta's death. Then we would take her back to Canada.'

'And Ásta knew you were planning to do this?' asked Birna.

Arnar looked irritated by the question. 'We were working up to that.'

Callum saw that Arnar's grip on Ásta was loosening. He guessed that his arm was getting tired.

'But you would need her passport to get her out of the country,' said Birna.

'Not if we took her by boat,' Arnar replied.

'Was that how you escaped from Heimæy?' asked Birna. 'How could you do that, Arnar? How could you let me believe you were dead?'

'You did not care about me!' he shouted. 'You ended our relationship and told me that I would never see my child. There was nothing left for me in Heimæy. I saw my opportunity to leave the island for good and I took it.'

With glacial stealth, Callum started to inch himself towards the dark-haired Icelander. He shifted his feet forward in short, imperceptible increments.

'You were seen breaking into a pharmacy,' said

Birna. 'I watched it burn, thinking you were inside it. There was no way you could have got out of that inferno.'

'You are forgetting that it was part of my job to get myself into tight spots and then get out of them,' said Arnar.

'That was more than a tight spot. That was certain death.'

'Not so. Not when I had been collecting eggs on the cliff face that morning,' explained Arnar. 'I was walking back into town when the eruption happened. When I broke into the pharmacy I still had my ropes with me. I got the money but realized that the building was surrounded by lava. I ran upstairs and attached a rope to a medicine chest. I climbed out a window and abseiled halfway down the outside wall. By running across the wall from side to side, I was able to swing like a pendulum and jump clear of the lava flow.'

More rocks spilled from the brim of the crater as Ásta fought to get purchase with her feet. Birna had noticed that her daughter was wearing a pair of white patent sandals.

'I see you have bought Ásta some new shoes,' she said. 'I found her old ones in a hut not far from here.'

'I thought that was a nice touch,' said Arnar.

Callum was getting close to him, sifting his feet carefully over the crumbling cake mix of powdered cinders and sulphurous pumice that threatened to give way beneath him.

'So why come back now?' Birna was aware of what Callum was doing and she was trying to hold Arnar's attention.

'Kathleen, my wife, she can't have children,' said Arnar. 'She has an illness . . . an eating disorder. But I told her it did not matter. I told her I already had a daughter. I promised her we could be a family.' Arnar let out a grunt. Ásta had started to fight him again.

'You did not need to kidnap her, Arnar. You could have knocked on our door.'

'No!' he shouted. 'You said that I would never see her again.'

'I did not mean it. I would have let you see her. How could I not let you see her? She is your daughter.'

'You lie! You had already found a new father for Ásta. You have no idea how angry that made me, to see another man raising my girl.'

'Callum is not her new father.' Birna too had started walking towards her ex. She was smiling at him. 'Nobody could replace you, Arnar.'

'Get back or we will jump!' he shouted. 'Yes, that is right . . . I will go with her. If I cannot be with my girl in life, I will be with her in death.'

'Arnar, listen to me. I have thought a lot about you over the years.' Birna's words were crisp; her tone was cool. 'I have made a mistake with you, the biggest mistake of my life. I see you now and it is obvious just how much you love our daughter. I see that she needs you. And I need you too. I really think we can make a go of it, Arnar. We have been given another chance to be a family . . . just you, me and Ásta.'

Callum and Birna were close enough to touch him but they kept very still. The only sound in the miles of emptiness was the soft breeze underscored by the low whistle of super-heated steam from the slopes beneath them.

'What do you say, Arnar?' Birna placed a hand on his free arm.

Ásta had stopped fighting him now. Her legs hung limply over the drop, like her brain no longer governed them. Her face was as purple as her tights. Callum saw that the hood of her jacket had tightened round her neck. She was passing out.

Callum couldn't take it any more. 'You're choking her!'

'Shut it, Callum!' shouted Birna. 'I asked Arnar a question.'

Arnar looked intently at Birna, deeply, like she was drawing his entire consciousness into her. 'You think this is possible?' he asked. 'That we could be a family?'

'Anything is possible,' said Birna. 'But only if we all come away from the edge.'

Arnar looked into the crater. He looked at his daughter. Her mouth was all twisted. It bubbled and drooled. He looked back at Birna. 'I guess we could try,' he said. Slowly, he relaxed his grip on the girl. He took one step towards Birna and the ground exploded beneath him.

'*Nei!*' she screamed as Arnar pulled her daughter over the drop.

Callum made a grab for Ásta. He caught her legs and the force of it slammed him to the ground. He wedged her shins under his armpits and pressed the full weight of his chest onto her knees. She was bent over backwards with Arnar dangling below her, hanging onto her jacket, his legs kicking and scrabbling to find the crater wall.

'Let go of her Arnar!' shouted Birna. 'You are taking her down with you.'

'We will be OK,' he shouted. 'I have got out of worse situations on the puffin cliffs.' There was nothing beneath him but fresh air and a distant milky green.

Ásta was squealing. Her body was being pulled in opposite directions.

'It's OK, Ásta,' shouted Callum. 'I won't let you fall. I promise.'

'Arnar, let go of her jacket!' screamed Birna.

Callum could feel Ásta slipping. A shuffle of scree skittered down the slope and her legs shunted back so that only her feet were hooked under his armpits.

'*Mamma!*' she screamed.

'You're going to be fine,' shouted Callum. 'I won't let you go.' He turned to Birna. 'You've got to do something. This whole ridge could give way.'

'Let go of her, Arnar! You will kill us all.' Birna picked up a handful of stones and began throwing them at him.

'Bitch!' yelled Arnar as a rock split his ear.

'Let go!'

'*Hjálpa!*' Ásta was flailing her free arm, trying to beat Arnar away as he tightened his grip on her jacket.

'She's slipping, Birna. Everything's slipping.' Callum was desperate now. He could only hope that Arnar's arms would give before his own, and that the brittle ridge would outlast them all.

'Look . . . Callum, look!' said Birna. 'Ásta needs help with her jacket.'

Callum peered over the edge and saw that Ásta was now using her free hand to tug at the zip on her jacket. She wasn't having much joy, however, as she needed her other hand to grab the bottom of the zipper and offer some resistance. Callum reached across her exposed belly and tugged on the hem of her jacket, straightening it out.

'Ásta,' he shouted. 'Push the zip towards me.'

She did as he said and the jacket opened. It fell back over her face but she wasn't free of it. Her arms were still caught in the sleeves. Ásta waggled her free arm – the arm that Arnar wasn't holding onto – but she couldn't release it from the jacket.

Callum could see that she had started to tire. 'Keep it up, Ásta,' he urged. 'You've got to keep trying.'

Birna had stopped throwing rocks. She had stopped shouting too. She looked on silently: helpless and hoping.

Arnar managed to get one foot on the crater wall but it fell away again, dislodging an anvil of rock.

'Do that again, Arnar, and you'll bring us all down on top of you,' shouted Callum.

'You confuse me with someone who gives a shit,' shouted Arnar. He tightened his grip on Ásta's arm. There was an audible crack as it came free of its socket.

Ásta screamed.

Birna looked away. She was crying now.

Callum felt Ásta's body relaxing. He was scared she was passing out with the pain. 'Ásta!' he persisted. 'Ásta you've got to keep trying. You've got to free your arms.'

She didn't respond.

Callum peered down and saw that Ásta's free hand was covering her mouth. He thought she was about to be sick but instead, she placed her pink cuff between her teeth and bit down on it. She jerked her head back and her arm came free of its sleeve.

Arnar was left holding onto the one remaining sleeve. It offered little resistance and slipped down her dislocated arm, whipping itself inside out as it was pulled free of her limp hand.

Arnar brought his daughter's pink jacket up to his face and inhaled deeply as he disappeared into the earth.

30

'Callum?'

'Neil! How the hell are you? Jesus, you're elusive.'

'Sorry, Cal. I should have got back to you sooner but fuck it . . . I've just been having too much fun. Happy birthday, pal.'

'Oh. Right. Cheers.'

'Are you OK, Cal? You sound a bit . . . shite, what's the time your end? I'm always doing this, aren't I? Last week I called Becca at three in the morning Glasgow time and the ringtone woke her bairn. She was up with him for the rest of the night.'

'It's just after three, Reykjavík time.'

'Is that a.m. or p.m.?'

'Hard to tell,' said Callum. 'Where are you?'

'Other side of the planet,' said Neil. 'Malaysia.'

'It's a hard life. I take it you're not thinking of quitting the Donkey, then.'

'Are you mad? Not while Backpackers are flying me around as their international ambassador. I've got enough air miles saved up for a trip to the moon.'

'I've just come back from there,' said Callum. 'It's not all it's cracked up to be.'

'How is Birn—' A gunshot.

Then another.

'Neil? Jesus . . . are you there Neil?'

'I'm fine. It's just the hotel staff shooting monkeys again.'

'Christ, what sort of a hotel are you staying in?'

More gunshots.

'It's not really a hotel. It bills itself as a wildlife refuge, but since I arrived they've all but eradicated the world population of crab-eating macaques. All day you can hear this lovely hooting and gibbering from the trees that surround my room and then the rifles crack off and the hotel staff blast the monkeys to bits to re-establish the pecking order.'

'I can hear screaming,' said Callum. 'This is surreal.'

'You think that's surreal! You should see what the staff do when they get bored shooting the monkeys. They like to catch a large alpha male and spray it with Krazy Kolor hairspray, the sort you and I used to wear when we thought we were punks. Their favourite colours are bright red and Day-Glo green, depending on their mood. And guess what they do to the monkey after that?'

'They shave off one of its eyebrows.'

'No.'

'Give up.'

'They set him free.'

'Do they now,' said Callum. 'Fascinating.'

'But it *is* fascinating,' said Neil. 'You sit and watch him for a bit, this rather dejected and bizarrely coiffured macaque, as he skulks around in the undergrowth not quite knowing what to do with himself. But he doesn't last long. Soon the rest of the monkeys in the troupe spot him and, because they don't recognize his unfamiliar colour, they band together and rip him apart.'

'I know how he feels,' said Callum.

'Things not going well?'

'Understatement.'

'Ah.'

'Ah, indeed.'

'Cal, this isn't anything to do with Sarah, is it?'

'No. Yes. In a way.'

'Birna knows, doesn't she. I always said you should tell her. What was the problem with telling her?'

'I needed a clean break, Neil. It was the only way I could make a proper go of it.'

'Aye, but by the sound of your voice I'm guessing you've made a proper mess of it.'

'A right royal fuck-up, is the phrase you're looking for.'

'It'll be OK,' said Neil. 'She'll be upset for a while and then she'll forgive you. They always do.'

'Do they?' asked Callum, wondering when Neil had become the authority on the fairer sex.

'If she loves you, it's a given.'

'That's a big *if*,' said Callum. 'To be honest, Neil, it's over. I'm coming back.'

'To the Donkey?'

'To Glasgow. Just for a bit, though. I couldn't live in Glasgow again. Too much history.'

'What about your production company?'

'I'm putting it on ice for a few months. No pun intended. I'll make a decision then, but at the moment I just can't imagine coming back to Iceland, not to an interminable winter. October to February is the suicide season over here. Way too dark and dangerous when you're in my state. For now, I'm paying my staff to take extended holidays. One of them's already off to London to shack up with a director we had over, so some good may yet come of this mess. I may have to buy a hat.'

'I'm sorry it hasn't worked out for you,' said Neil. 'I'll be home myself in a couple weeks. Just got to do Oz and New York and that's me. I'll see you in King

Tut's for a few pints of T. We'll set the world to rights.
I owe you one . . . you know . . . for that business at
your leaving do . . .'

'All forgotten,' said Callum.

Another gunshot. Another scream.

'Better go, Cal. The monkeys are shooting back.'

Callum rested his forehead on the office window. The
rain that lashed against it became amplified in his
skull. As he often did, he watched the birds on the
Tjörn. A flock of black geese skimmed across the water
in a wide V, like a stealth bomber engaged in a sortie
under enemy radar. They crash-landed on the lake in
frenetic and feathery unison, but quickly settled, sailing along with their necks proudly raised like they'd
popped out for a Sunday paddle and hadn't just flown
halfway round the globe. Callum wondered where
they had come from and where they were ultimately
going.

He needed to ask himself the same questions.

Birna hadn't said anything to Callum as they flew
back to Reykjavík in the rescue helicopter. She had
been too concerned for her daughter. A paramedic
had popped Ásta's arm back into its socket and the
painkillers had knocked her out for the journey. Birna
had slept too. As soon as they were safely airborne, her
head dropped onto her shoulder. She had been awake
for the three days that Ásta was missing and Callum
guessed that she had a lot of catching up to do.

He, on the other hand, thought he might never sleep
again. He had looked down at Iceland from above and
followed the shadow of the chopper as it wobbled over
the cracked lava fields, the rolling black desert and the
glaciers that rose up into cratered peaks like giant
barnacles. The landscape was far from threatening. It
was beautiful. The inhospitable terrain that had taken

424

them a day and a bit to cross was rendered benign from the air. However Callum was still glad when the pixilated colours of the Reykjavík rooftops came into sharper resolution and the helicopter buzzed over Hallgrímskirkja. The church was an inverted tintack piercing the city skyline and pricking his conscience. He knew then that he had no future in Reykjavík. Birna only wanted to be with her daughter. He knew he had to get out of the picture entirely and return to Glasgow. It would only destroy him to stay in Iceland and not be with the woman – the women – he loved.

Callum stared out of the office window. He watched Frikki parking the Toyota in the rain. The big man crossed the road with an unboxed Mac in his arms. Callum walked to the door and held it open for his assistant.

'The police station was busy.' Frikki lugged the Mac into the room like he'd just stolen it. 'They had arrested two teenagers who robbed a gas station in Kópavogur. The kids only got caught when they returned to the shop to swap the cigarettes they had stolen for a different brand.' He set the Mac on Callum's empty desk. 'You will have to let this dry out before you switch it on. I will get a box from the kitchen and bring up the other two machines in that.'

'Did they find any photographs of naked children on it?' asked Callum. He couldn't disguise his bitterness.

'No, but the officer who arrested you says he may have accidentally wiped some of Birna's pictures when he tried to print them off. He said he had wanted to turn them into a calendar for his interview room.' Frikki removed his new beanie and used it to mop the rain from his face. 'And you are in the paper again,' he added. He unzipped his jacket and removed a pulpy tube from his inside pocket. He unrolled the newspaper on the table, smoothing it out with his hand and smudging the ink in the process.

'What are they saying now?' asked Callum.

'They are calling you a hero. They say that you saved the girl's life.'

Callum was unmoved. Hadn't he heard that somewhere before.

'They say that the guy who tried to kill her was off his face at the time,' said Frikki. 'The medics who pulled him out of Víti found all sorts of shit in his blood. No wonder he was happy to jump in with her. And it says here that he and his wife were both wanted by Canadian police in connection with drug offences. Kathleen Van der Vlugt was the international liaison officer for Air Canada and this Arnar guy used her as an interpreter when he was conducting drug deals in Asia.' Frikki stared hard at the picture of the redhead being escorted through Reykjavík domestic airport. 'I guess he had to see something in her. She is a skeleton in a wig.'

'Frikki, I don't mean to be rude but can you read me something else?' said Callum. 'Call it my birthday treat.'

'Today is your birthday?' asked Frikki. 'Why didn't you tell me?'

'I forgot.'

'You forgot your own birthday?'

'I know. A friend just called to remind me.'

'I would have got you a humorous card,' said Frikki.

'You can cheer me up, as you usually do, by reading me the other pressing news in Iceland.'

Frikki lifted the paper and shuffled the pages. '*A humpback whale was inadvertently caught off the east coast of Iceland yesterday. A farmer and his son were having an unfruitful day fishing for cod on their small trawler when the giant of the sea was accidentally caught in their nets.*'

'Aye, right,' said Callum.

'*Weighing in at over six tonnes and measuring over nine metres, the whale was actually larger than the trawler itself,*' continued Frikki. '*According to the farmer, the humpback could not be freed at sea and had to be dragged to land where it died. Hlynur Guðbrandsson intends to sell the whalemeat in Iceland.*'

'He will then use the profits to buy a large Sunseeker and emigrate to Tahiti where he will live out his days surrounded by beautiful, empty-headed concubines,' added Callum.

Frikki wasn't listening. Another story had caught his eye. 'This is great news!' he said. '*Iceland has risen from seventh position to second in the United Nation's list of high-quality living, pushing Norway back to fifth.*' Frikki punched a fist in the air. 'They can shove their free Christmas tree up their asses!'

'I bet that Norway is still a few hundred places above Scotland,' said Callum.

'Then why are you going back there? You should stay here, in the best place in the world.'

'The second best place,' corrected Callum, pointing at the league table in the paper. 'Behind Sweden.'

'Any country that has produced Roxette cannot be considered the best in the world.'

'True,' laughed Callum.

'So this news does not tempt you to stay in Reykjavík?'

'Not just now.' Callum saw some despondency in Frikki's face. 'What are you planning to do with your three-month career break?' he asked.

'Get drunk,' answered Frikki. 'I am going on tour with The 101 Dalmatians. We have been booked for the Sveitaballs. The money isn't as good as I hoped for, but hey, the women are free.'

Callum felt guilty now. He had given Frikki three

months' wages but he realized that if he decided not to return to Iceland, he was almost certainly condemning the big man to another season on the shrimp boat.

'Listen,' he said, 'it's still fifty-fifty but if I do close the business, I want you to handle the sale of the office equipment. You can keep what you get for it.'

'You will come back,' said Frikki. 'You love this place, despite everything that has happened. Iceland is in your blood now. You can never get rid of it once it is in your blood.'

'The same can be said about malaria,' said Callum.

Before Frikki could respond, a female voice cut into their conversation. 'Hello?'

The two men turned to see Birna standing at the office door.

'It was open,' she explained.

'Já . . . OK,' said Frikki. He looked suddenly uncomfortable. 'Callum . . . I must go down and get the other Macs from the car.'

'You do not have to leave on my account,' said Birna, but Frikki shuffled past her.

Birna looked up at Callum like she was about to deliver some dreadful news but couldn't find the words. It was just the two of them now. It hadn't been just the two of them since they were sitting in a hut in Herðubreiðarlindir, drinking milk and eating smoked lamb. A lot had happened since then. Two people had risen from the grave, only for one of them to fall back into it. Birna had lost Arnar and gained a daughter for the second time in her life. The experience had aged her. The soft light of a rainy day found the creases in the corners of her eyes.

'How are you?' asked Callum.

'I feel better now that I have clawed back some sleep.' Birna sat on Callum's desk and lifted up the airline ticket that was sitting on his passport. 'So this is it. You have decided to go back to Glasgow.'

'I know what you're going to say,' said Callum. 'I'm running away again.'

'I was not going to say that.'

'But you're thinking it.'

Birna said nothing. She thumbed through his passport, pausing on a pink page with a burgundy stamp inked onto it. The stamp featured a small biplane with the word 'Praha' bleeding heavily above it. She flicked to the back of the passport and turned it sideways to examine Callum's photograph.

'When was this picture taken?'

'1996,' said Callum.

'You look good.'

'I used to look after myself back then. Things went a bit pear-shaped after '96 and I'm not just talking about my figure.'

'You still look good,' insisted Birna. 'And your hair is definitely better now.'

'What's left of it.'

'I've never seen your passport before. It says a lot about you.'

'Not so long ago, British passports were big, dark blue cardboard jobs,' said Callum. 'But I suppose you couldn't confuse them with anything else. Not like these new flimsy ones. I once tried to get into Egypt with my post office savings book.'

'Egypt, Indonesia, Cuba, Prague . . .' said Birna, fanning the pages in her fingers and reading the stamps. 'Did Sarah go with you to all these places?'

'She went with me to most of them,' said Callum. 'And she came back with me from all but one of them.'

Birna set the passport back on the table. She looked at him and sighed. 'Call—'

'Birn—'

'You go first,' she said.

'I just wanted to say sorry.'

'Why are you saying sorry?' asked Birna. 'I should be saying sorry to you. I suggested that you had done horrible things to my daughter.'

'You didn't trust me.' Callum shrugged. 'I don't blame you. I lied to you, Birna. I kept secrets from you. Why should I have expected you to trust me? You didn't know me.'

'You did not lie to me, Callum. You thought you were protecting me from the truth. There is a difference.' Birna ran her nail along a groove in the table's grain. 'And perhaps you did not know me either. You did not trust me enough to tell me about Sarah. And at the end of the day it was Arnar, and not Sarah's killer, who took Ásta.'

'Don't go down that road, Birna. Don't beat yourself up about it. Neither of us could have done anything to stop him. Perhaps if I'd kept a better watch over Ásta then maybe she wouldn't have been taken. But Arnar would only have got to her at another time. The only people to blame for Ásta's abduction are Arnar and that wife of his.'

'I spoke with her,' said Birna. 'At the police station.'

'Have you given your statement?' asked Callum.

Birna nodded.

'Me too.'

'They're deporting her this evening,' said Birna. 'She did not look well.'

'My heart bleeds,' said Callum.

'You should not be so hard on Kathleen.'

Callum was surprised. 'So you're on first-name terms now? It wasn't so long ago that you were calling her a bitch.'

'She has just lost her husband,' Birna scolded him.

'And she has an illness. Her anorexia has left her unable to have kids. It must be terrible knowing that you cannot have children. She told me that every day she worked at the airport, children would get separated from their parents. Kathleen would offer to mind them while the airline paged their mothers and fathers. She said that a part of her always hoped that the parents would never show up and that she would get to take the children home and look after them. Just like Arnar got to take his birds home and care for them. Finders Keepers, she called it.'

'So she's as mad as her husband.'

'She's an intelligent woman!' argued Birna. 'She told me that she had been lined up for a top job in Asia when she met Arnar. It seems it all went wrong for her from there, though she will not admit it. Despite Arnar's faults, she loved the bastard.'

'There you go,' said Callum. 'How intelligent can she be, falling for a junkie?'

Birna looked bitterly at him. 'You are forgetting that I fell for the same junkie.'

'Yes, but you had the intelligence to leave him. You would have thought that a supposedly bright woman like Kathleen would have spotted that Arnar was a no-mark when he got her involved in his drug trafficking.'

'She loved him, Callum. Intelligence and good sense had nothing to do with it. Arnar came along at a time in her life when she was most vulnerable. Kathleen has had an eating disorder since her teens. Arnar gave her the love that she could not give to herself. She would have done anything for him.'

'It doesn't make it right,' said Callum.

'I'm not saying that it is right. But just like you needed to understand Sarah's killer, I must try to understand the people who took my daughter. I think I understand Arnar and I am trying really hard to understand his widow. She says that a couple of years back she started using. Arnar started her on a little coke and he quickly got her to heroin via amphetamines. She says it made her feel special . . . *he* made her feel special. Her body was already ravaged by anorexia. Her ovaries had dried out to nothing. Scrambled eggs, was how she described them. What harm was a little shot of heroin now and again?'

'For a couple who spent a lot of their time fucked out of their skulls, they were very lucid in their plan to take Ásta. You shouldn't be feeling sorry for her.'

'I am not feeling sorry for her,' said Birna. 'I am understanding her.'

'Then you must understand that there was nothing either of us could have done to stop Ásta being taken. The only people to blame in all this are Arnar and Kathleen.'

'But we cannot blame them for destroying our relationship,' said Birna. 'We are both at fault for that.'

Callum looked out of the window and saw that Frikki had driven off in the Toyota. He joined Birna, sitting on the table. He put his feet on his chair and swivelled it as he spoke. 'It's hard to know where we went wrong. Maybe you were right when you said that our relationship was like a rollercoaster that had shot off before all the nuts and bolts were in place. I guess we just rushed into things withou—'

'Stay,' said Birna. She looked at Callum like she had just placed all her chips on the zero and she was waiting for the roulette wheel to settle.

Callum took her hand in his. Her fingers were painfully cold. They were still covered in tiny abrasions from the rocks she had hurled at Arnar.

'Birna, you don't mean it. You're still feeling a bit shell-shocked.'

'Bullshit!' Birna leaned her face into his. 'I mean it,

Callum. I want you to stay. Maybe you should not stay at the house just yet, but I want you to stay in Reykjavík. I want us to get to know each other again. It can be like the old days, only this time it will be better. Our relationship will be built on trust because now we know the truth about each other.'

'I thought that you believed a relationship was more exciting when two people didn't know everything about each other, when they still had lots of beautiful revelations to share. You said that a good relationship was like a good story. You cannot know everything by only page four. Your words.'

'But we are not on page four of our story. And there is much that we have yet to discover about each other.' Birna pulled Callum's hand onto her knee. An impish grin appeared. 'For example, you do not know that I had my first orgasm when I was thirteen.'

'Thirteen?'

'I was riding a pony . . . before you get other ideas.' Birna chewed her lip and narrowed her eyes in thought. 'And you do not know that I once had lunch with Eric Clapton.'

'Explain?'

'He is a keen angler and he comes to Iceland for the freshwater fishing. I met him a few years ago when I happened to be analysing the mineral content of the same river that he was fishing. He had not caught anything for many hours and he said that I was scaring the fish away. He was just joking with me. He had boiled up a trout on his gas burner and he offered to share it with me.' Birna was swinging her legs under the table. 'Let me see . . . what else do you not know about me . . .'

'Whoa, stop right there,' said Callum. 'If you run out of stories now, you'll remove all the mystique from our relationship.'

'So we have a relationship?' asked Birna.

'I guess so.' Callum slid his arm round her waist. 'But there are some things that you will never know about me, like the time I burned down a wing of my school.'

'You have just told me,' said Birna, with a smile that could light up a science block.

Callum leaned across to kiss her but she pushed him away.

'What?' he protested. 'Jesus, it happened ages ago. It was an accident. I left a lit Bunsen burner beside a tub of photocopy fluid during our lunch break. It exploded before we got back to the room. Nobody knew it was my fault.'

'I am not concerned about that. Before I kiss you, there is something I need to do.' Birna stood up and pulled her mobile phone out of her pocket. She keyed in a text message.

'Who are you contacting?' asked Callum.

'Your old headmaster.' She returned the phone to her pocket and hopped back onto the table. 'Now, where were we?' She pulled Callum towards her and kissed him.

It couldn't have been more different from their last kiss, the peck she had given him on the morning she got him out of the police station. This kiss was long and purposeful and there was nothing sisterly about it.

Birna broke away again. She placed a hand on his chest. 'Anyway, you should not worry about preserving the mystique in our relationship. The longer we stay together, the more you will discover that I am a woman of many stories.'

There was a cough at the door. Callum looked up to see Ásta standing there: black hair, black dress, purple trainers and a white sling cradling a hand that held a mobile phone. Her other arm was behind her back. She didn't look like a little girl any more. She looked like a young woman.

'Hi,' she said.

'Hi,' said Callum. 'Did your mother finally buy you a phone?'

Ásta nodded and smiled.

'I took your advice,' said Birna.

Ásta gave her mother a hopeful look and received a nod in response. She walked over to Callum and removed her uninjured arm from behind her back. She presented him with a brightly wrapped gift.

Callum didn't rip it open. He carefully unpicked the wrapping. The glossy paper crinkled as he peeled it away, impersonating the rain on the windows, but he managed to remove it in one piece without tearing it. He handed the paper to Birna and examined his present: a jam jar containing about one centimetre of fresh rainwater. A label had been stuck on the jar and Ásta had decorated it with hearts and stars in purple felt-tip pen. In the centre of the label she had written: *Callum – 20 Júní, 2003*.

'Happy birthday,' she said.

From: callum@fail.is
To: travelogs@strawdonkey.com
Date: Wed, 06 Aug 2003, 14:49:20 +0000
Subject: MAKE HEIMÆY WHILE THE SUN SHINES

Heimæy is the largest of the Westmann Islands (known to locals as Vestmannaeyjar) and can be reached from mainland Iceland by plane or boat. I decided to accompany my partner Birna, her mother Sigriður and our daughter Ásta, on the Herjólfur ferry from Þorlákshöfn, a three-and-a-quarter-hour trip across a restless, metallic blue sea that continually bounced the sun into our eyes.

The boat journey brought back vivid memories for Sigriður who had been ferried off Heimæy in 1973 as part of a total evacuation. She had escaped a volcanic eruption that threatened to destroy the island. Over five months of that year, 33 million tonnes of lava spilled out of a fissure on the eastern side of the town. The lava flow consumed large parts of Heimæy and seemed destined to seal in the small harbour, cutting off the lifeline of this remote community. Were it not for the combined efforts of local dredgers who used water cannons to continuously pump seawater onto the encroaching lava, our family would not have been making this boat trip.

'If the fissure had opened up half a mile west of where it did, it would have swallowed the town whole,' said Sigriður, as we sailed between rugged brown bluffs dotted with seabirds – Heimæy's famous puffin pantries. Our boat was approaching the ominous field of dark lava that had rolled into the sea in '73. Ironically, it now offered the town added protection from the elements, creating a windbreak for one of the best natural harbours in the world.

'At the time, the lava seemed unstoppable,' said Sigriður. 'The surface was like thick elephant hide that was always ripping open to release fresh bursts of molten rock. When they began pumping the seawater onto it, people thought it was madness. They called it *pissa a hraunid* which means "pissing on the lava". It was a pointless action, just as it was pointless when people boarded up their windows to prevent bombs of lava from landing in their houses. The volcano spat these great balls of fire into the air and because they were full of gases, they exploded like bombs on impact and red-hot liquid lashed out.' Sigriður gesticulated wildly with her hands to mimic the violent outbursts.

'The lava bombs rained down with many tonnes of rock,' she continued, 'and those houses that didn't burst into flame or get crushed like eggs were buried in dark dunes of ash. The entombed houses would fill with hot steam and cook slowly until their frames came loose and popped free like the bones of a stewing bird. Other houses were torn off their foundations and the lava dragged them through the streets until they broke into pieces and were gobbled up.'

Our boat rollicked into the narrow channel created by the lava and the harbour revealed itself as a long, wedge-like cove presided over by two volcanic stacks: Hegafell and Eldfell. The latter did not exist before the eruption and Sigriður delighted her granddaughter by recounting the story of an elderly local who sat up in his hospital bed and demanded to know where he was. He had been bedridden since 1972, airlifted to Reykjavík during the '73 eruption, and flown back to Heimæy a year later. The nurses tried desperately to calm him down. They explained to him that he was still in Heimæy, where he had lived all his life. But the man pointed to the new volcano that was framed in his hospital window and said, 'I cannot be in Heimæy. If I am in Heimæy, then who put that mountain there?'

As we sailed into the town, Sigriður said she was proud of

the new Heimæy that had risen from the ashes. 'They thought we had no future here. There was concern about gas emissions and some people feared the whole island would explode. I remember that the gas was visible as a blue haze because the humidity was so high. It suffocated birds and it was dangerous to light a cigarette or start a car. The clouds were filled with sulphur and when the rain fell, farmers feared that it would rot their sheep alive. A farmer in Kirkjubær shot his cows on the night of the eruption. He sailed to the mainland, or *fastalandið* as we call it – meaning "steady land" – and he never came back. I remember his farm was a beautiful green pasture covered in clover and now it is buried for ever under thick rock.'

Sigriður leaned over the side of our boat and looked into the water. 'When I last sailed past here, the ocean was boiling. You could see the lava glowing in the depths as we crossed the fissure. I remember the sea exploding and salt water raining down on our heads with fragments of molten glass mixed into it. It didn't burn me but it stuck in my hair and it was impossible to comb out. When I got to Reykjavík I had to get my head shaved. I looked like a convict.'

Unlike many of the islanders, Sigriður had flown back to Heimæy when it was declared safe. 'It wasn't easy moving back. There was a lot of mess to clear up and Birna's father had to build us a new house. When the wind was fierce – and it is always fierce in the Westmanns – the flying ash and pumice broke our windows. But we survived the worst of it and made a life here for ourselves.'

It was clear as we disembarked that the islanders had done more than survive. Heimæy is now a thriving community of 6,000 people. The town itself is a paradox of cheery-coloured buildings built on a reef of black lava. I imagined the Legoland version: lots of pristine, primary-coloured bricks clipped onto a base of melted black bricks that had been left too close to a fire.

As we walked through the town, the evidence of natural catastrophe was never far away. I saw one street that dead-ended in lava and another that was nothing more than a black slope with a chimney stack protruding from it. Birna told me that after the '73 eruption, the ever-resourceful islanders had sold some of the lava to Sweden for the construction of airport runways. I liked their style.

We had come to the Westmann Islands on *Verslunarmannahelgi* – the August shopkeepers' holiday – a three-day weekend when thousands of Icelanders head out of town to their summer houses or camp in the wilds and party en masse. The handful of killjoys who decide to stay in the deserted capital are affectionately dubbed the Reykjavík Rats. A small indoor music festival called *Innipúkinn* (an *innipúki* being a creature who stays indoors) has been created to satisfy those who choose not to embrace the twin pleasures of sleeping on jagged lava and shitting in paperless fields.

Not wishing to be branded rats, Birna and Sigríður had decided to take Ásta and me back to their home on the Westmanns where we would take part in the annual *Þjódhátið* festival that coincides with the *Verslunarmannahelgi* weekend. This festival commemorates the day in 1874 when Iceland got its constitution. Back then, bad weather had prevented the islanders from reaching the mainland so they celebrated independently and have done so ever since.

This independence seemed to be a bit of a misnomer, however, as it was clear from the numbers arriving in Heimæy that a fair proportion of mainland Iceland had decided to join in their fun. Some 10,000 campers were expected to pitch up in Heimæy's lush Herjólfsðalur valley, a natural amphitheatre where it is customary to drink yourself silly, dance badly, eat puffin straight off the bone and then vomit into someone else's tent. That's if you don't incinerate yourself when trying to light your fag on the giant bonfire that rages for the whole three days.

Most of the accommodation in the town had been booked months in advance of our arrival. Thankfully an old neighbour of Sigriður's had donated his house to us while he eschewed the annual lunacy to play golf in the Florida Keys.

It was late on the Friday evening when we dumped our bags on his beds and, as none of us had eaten, Sigriður set about preparing a feast. Her old neighbour had 'kindly' left two skinned sheep heads in his fridge for our consumption. They looked grisly but comical, all pink and raw but with bulbous cartoon eyes that I imagined were spinning in their glossy sockets. Sigriður planned to boil them first and then singe them over an open fire till the cheeks were nice and crispy. 'We eat everything of the sheep,' she boasted. 'And from those bits of the skull that we scrape off, we make *sviðasulta*, or head cheese.'

Sigriður shooed the three of us out of the house while she did the cooking, not that I needed much shooing. I suggested to Birna that we find a Burger King or get the next plane back to Reykjavík, but she was adamant that we take a stroll round the harbour.

Our route took us past the Heimæy aquarium. Though it was closed, Birna assured Ásta and me that it was worth a visit. 'They keep a really bad-tempered catfish,' she said. 'When the second eruption threatened this island in 1992, one of the scientists at the aquarium reported that the catfish swam up to the glass and opened its mouth in a "silent scream of terror".'

We found a seat on the south side of the harbour, a brightly painted bench that had been screwed incongruously into the black lava. We sat down and watched the boats bobbing in the harbour and the gulls suspending themselves on the freshening breeze.

Birna instructed Ásta and me to reach down and place our palms on the dark ash. It was cool to the touch, but when we rubbed away a few centimetres, the ground became so hot that we had to pull our hands back. Birna said that many people still like to bake bread in these ashes. She was demonstrating that the interior of the 1973 lava flow was still molten and that the cool skin of rock we were sitting on was no more substantial than ice on a frozen lake. Apparently the firemen treating the original blaze thought they could stand on this cool crust and it would insulate them from the heat. But quite often their boots would burst into flame, forcing them to jump into the sea.

We sat for a long while until the sun fell down behind the puffin cliffs, robbing us of its warm orange glow. The breeze whistled loudly through the cavitated lava and the sea began to swell and explode, crashing and reverberating around us. It felt like a good moment to ask Birna if she would consider returning to Heimæy and setting up home.

'For sure. When the baby arrives.' She gently patted her tummy, mindful of the new life inside it.

As the light faded and we headed back into the town, three excited-looking children ran up to us, each one clutching a cardboard box. They were shouting, '*Lundi pysja! Lundi pysja!*'

'Pufflings!' said Ásta. One of the children let her open his box and there, sitting dopily inside it, was a baby puffin. Ásta lifted it out and cradled it to her chest. The bird looked up at her

441

with a face still grey and undeveloped, like a clown without his make-up. As Ásta tickled its beak, another puffling waddled across the road and pecked at her shoes.

'What's going on?' I asked.

'The pufflings are coming to town,' said Birna. 'It happens every year. Their parents have stopped feeding them and now it is time for them to leave the nests and fend for themselves. Their first flight should be a short one from the top of the cliffs to the sea below, but every year they are lured into the town by the bright lights.'

'You make it sound like Vegas,' I said.

'To a baby puffin, Heimæy is just as seductive. When I was young, the children would collect up to a thousand puffin chicks in a day, and maybe sixteen thousand in the two-week season. If we did not collect them, they would get eaten by cats or crushed by cars.'

Ásta's adopted baby was nipping at her finger with its beak. She returned it to the cardboard box. All around us, the streets had filled up with young children dressed in traditional woolly jumpers, running around, shouting, and generally behaving like their older counterparts on a Friday night in Reykjavík. But while the Reykjavík rats would be carrying beer bottles, the children carried torches. One hundred mini searchlights patrolled the ground around us. I saw one young girl standing perfectly still with her torch beam fixed on a dark and shuffling ball. She knelt down and scooped up the disoriented puffin chick, placing it in the basket on her bicycle.

'The children will take the chicks home for the night,' Birna explained. 'Tomorrow morning, they will carry the birds to a high point on the shore and release them. This was the best fun when I was a girl. I used to hold the birds with both hands, swing my arms between my legs three times, and then launch the pufflings into the air. At first they look like they are going to fall on the rocks, but then their wings get going and they fly stupidly across the water before splashing down. It is a very special sight, hundreds of children raising their arms and thousands of baby puffins hitting the water like raindrops.'

'It does sound special,' I agreed, 'until you realize that the birds will end up in the net of a puffin catcher and, not long after, in the mouth of a drunken teenager celebrating his bank holiday weekend.'

'The pufflings do not end up on our dinner tables,' said Birna. 'Not until they reach adulthood. We let them have a good life and wait for them to mature. Wine, women and puffins: the older they get, the better they taste. If you remember that, Callum, you and I will never go wrong.'

ENDIR

LONDON IRISH
Zane Radcliffe

'VERY FRESH, VERY FUNNY. I LAUGHED UNTIL I
STOPPED'
Colin Bateman

There are 750,000 Irish living in London. One of them has
to get out. For good.

Summer 1999. Only 157 shopping days until the new
millennium and for Bic (half-Irish, half-Scots, and half-
cut), who ekes out a living selling crêpes to the hordes
descending on Greenwich market, the year 2000 can't come
quick enough. One severed ear, two bizarre deaths, and the
arrest of his dog for civil disobedience – so far Bic's *annus*
has been pretty *horribilis*.

But a silver, or rather, a raven-haired lining appears in the
guise of Roisin. She's from Home, she's heart-stoppingly
beautiful, and she's taken the stall opposite Bic's.
Despite her over-protective brothers, things are definitely
looking up.

At least they were until Bic wakes up the-morning-after-
the-night-before, in his clothes, in Edinburgh, to find he's
the UK's Most Wanted Man. On the run with fourteen
murders to his name . . .

A glorious comic thriller bursting with outrageous
shenanigans, shot-to-pieces with black humour, while
retaining a heart of gold, *London Irish* introduces a singular
and entertaining new literary voice.

'OUTSTANDING . . . DEFINITELY THE BEST NEW TITLE
OF THE YEAR. IT ROCKS!'
Daily Record

0 552 77095 7

BLACK SWAN

BIG JESSIE
Zane Radcliffe

'She emerged from a flurry of windblown rose petals, her pale skin interrupted at regular intervals by bands of red – scarlet bob, scarlet lips, cropped scarlet top, scarlet mini, scarlet knee socks, scarlet boots. She looked like a barber's pole, or a lolly that *had* to be licked.'

Scarlet plucks her twelve-string guitar with nails the colour of glazed cherries and Belfast music hack, Jessie Black, is smitten.

He charms his way on to her tour bus as her band head for Dublin. But the second they cross the border Jessie feels the heat of a sniper's bullet . . .

Who wants him dead? Rather, who *doesn't* want 'Jay' Black dead? Any number of people might justifiably have pulled the trigger.

There's Scarlet's stalker, a gun-toting shoe fetishist. And the still-grieving widow of Northern Ireland's international goalkeeper, Miles Huggins, who Jay inadvertently killed. Not to mention the property magnate who was blackmailed into handing Jay Belfast's first-ever million-pound flat. Or the RUC Chief Constable who has given Jay an ultimatum. Or, now you come to mention it, Sinn Fein *numero uno* Martin O'Hanlon, who Jay has to expose.

It's when Scarlet goes missing that things start getting serious, and Jay has to go it alone.

A story of blackmail, corruption and exploding peacocks, *Big Jessie* is the new firecracker thriller from the author of the WH Smith Award-winning *London Irish*.

'FUNNY, ABSURD AND MEMORABLE. RECOMMENDED'
FHM

0 552 77096 5

BLACK SWAN

WIDE EYED
Ruaridh Nicoll

'A QUIETLY SPOOKY TALE . . . BOTH UNSETTLING AND ODDLY EXHILARATING' *Sunday Telegraph*

A remote fishing village in Scotland seems the perfect place for Betsy Gillander to abscond for a few days with her fiancé. There, in a landscape marred only by a vast MoD range away to the west, the pale winter sun lights up this next step in her happy and structured life.

But then a violent storm wraps itself around the village and for three days the couple are trapped in their hotel. The enforced intimacy opens Betsy's eyes to the indolent cruelty of the man she's agreed to marry, while in the hotel bar the locals gather, increasingly anxious for news of a boat still out at sea.

By the time the sun reappears, Betsy's fiancé has left her and she is adrift in a community shattered by the loss of the boat and seven of its sons. The pain of her break-up in the face of such tragedy produces in her a terrible guilt and Betsy finds herself drawn into a cloistered, close-knit community with a morality far beyond her understanding . . .

'AN ABSORBING YARN . . . WHILE THE NARRATIVE IS WELL-CRAFTED AND BUILDS TO A BRAVURA CLIMAX, IT IS IN THE EVOCATION OF ATMOSPHERE, THAT ELUSIVE ART, THAT NICOLL REALLY EARNS HIS SPURS' *Sunday Telegraph*

'LYRICAL AND COMPELLING . . . NICOLL'S PORTRAYAL OF GRIEF, AND THE NEED TO MAKE SENSE OF CALAMITY IS NEVER LESS THAN CONVINCING. ANOTHER TRIUMPH' *The List*

'NICOLL WRITES INTRICATE, ACCURATE PROSE AND OFFERS ALLURING DESCRIPTIONS OF THE SCOTTISH LANDSCAPE . . . THE LANDSCAPE OF *WIDE EYED* IS BEAUTIFUL AND THE SITUATION IS FASCINATING' *Guardian*

'EMOTIONALLY-WROUGHT . . . IN TURN LYRICAL AND VIOLENT, FABLE-LIKE AND GUTSY' *Sunday Herald*

0 552 99904 0

BLACK SWAN

WHAT WE DID ON OUR HOLIDAY
John Harding

'A WONDERFUL NOVEL . . . WRITTEN WITH GREAT HUMOUR AND RARE GENEROSITY OF SPIRIT. TRULY ORIGINAL'   Deborah Moggach

How old do you have to be before you stop going on holiday with your parents? Nick's 36 and married and he hasn't cracked it yet . . .

Nick could have a great time on Malta if it weren't for one thing. His family. His wife Laura, biological alarm clock ringing, is desperate for children which means a nightly test of Nick's ingenuity to resist her amorous advances. There's Dad, afflicted with Parkinson's Disease, scarcely able to walk or talk, unsure which country or decade he's in and obsessed by sex and lavatories. And there's Mum, weighing in at a formidable 18 stone (although she's convinced she's a size 10) with a personality to match. Then there's the ghost from Dad's wartime past, come back to haunt them all . . .

Tackling a taboo subject with sensitivity, compassion and a total lack of sentimentality, *What We Did On Our Holiday* recalls that time in your life when roles are reversed and you find yourself looking after the very people you'd always assumed would be there to look after you. And it is also almost certainly the first novel in English literature to begin with the word 'toilet'.

'A WONDERFULLY FUNNY, ORIGINAL AND MOVING NOVEL . . . HARDING HAS A KNIFE-SHARP OBSERVATION, IMMACULATE TIMING, AND THE GUTS TO TAKE HIS STORY AS FAR AS IT WILL GO'   Helen Dunmore

'POIGNANT, HILARIOUS AND ULTIMATELY DEEPLY MOVING . . . A REAL PAGE TURNER . . . A WONDERFUL NOVEL'   Marika Cobbold

'A BEAUTIFULLY CRAFTED NOVEL: THE PERFECT MARRIAGE OF HUMOUR AND HEART'   Glenn Patterson

0 552 99847 8

BLACK SWAN

A SELECTED LIST OF FINE WRITING
AVAILABLE FROM BLACK SWAN

77084 1	COOL FOR CATS	*Jessica Adams*	£6.99
77105 8	NOT THE END OF THE WORLD	*Kate Atkinson*	£6.99
99979 2	GATES OF EDEN	*Ethan Coen*	£7.99
77119 8	EDUCATING PETER	*Tom Cox*	£6.99
99985 7	DANCING WITH MINNIE THE TWIG	*Mogue Doyle*	£6.99
77142 2	CRADLE SONG	*Robert Edric*	£6.99
99995 4	HIGH SOCIETY	*Ben Elton*	£6.99
77078 7	THE VILLAGE OF WIDOWS	*Ravi Shankar Etteth*	£6.99
99656 4	THE TEN O'CLOCK HORSES	*Laurie Graham*	£5.99
77080 9	FINDING HELEN	*Colin Greenland*	£6.99
99609 2	FORREST GUMP	*Winston Groom*	£6.99
99847 8	WHAT WE DID ON OUR HOLIDAY	*John Harding*	£6.99
77178 3	SLEEP, PALE SISTER	*Joanne Harris*	£6.99
77082 5	THE WISDOM OF CROCODILES	*Paul Hoffman*	£7.99
99796 X	A WIDOW FOR ONE YEAR	*John Irving*	£7.99
77110 4	CAN YOU KEEP A SECRET?	*Sophie Kinsella*	£6.99
99859 1	EDDIE'S BASTARD	*William Kowalski*	£6.99
77104 X	BY BREAD ALONE	*Sarah-Kate Lynch*	£6.99
77216 X	EAT, DRINK AND BE MARRIED	*Eve Makis*	£6.99
14240 9	THE NIGHT LISTENER	*Armistead Maupin*	£6.99
77090 6	HERDING CATS	*John McCabe*	£6.99
99904 0	WIDE EYED	*Ruaridh Nicoll*	£6.99
99905 9	AUTOMATED ALICE	*Jeff Noon*	£7.99
99849 4	THIS IS YOUR LIFE	*John O'Farrell*	£6.99
77095 7	LONDON IRISH	*Zane Radcliffe*	£6.99
77096 5	BIG JESSIE	*Zane Radcliffe*	£6.99
99645 9	THE WRONG BOY	*Willy Russell*	£6.99